GIRLS

IN

WHITE

DRESSES

By: Alexandra Gates

Girls in White Dresses

Copyright © 2017 by Alexandra Gates

Cover Design: Pink Ink Designs

ISBN-13: **9781520976358**

To My Husband

Chapter One

Don't you love beginnings, London?
The first touch. The first bite. The first taste...
-Him

The roses wilted, and the champagne went flat.

Romance wasn't dead, but this couple sure was.

A puddle of blood pooled from the lifeless bodies and trickled to the door. One unceremonious boot print later, and I accidentally autographed the Air B&B's spotless white entry rug with my boot's heel.

"Damn..." I stepped out of the blood, cursing the unnecessary blemish to the crime scene. I doubted the couple cared. Calling to the bodies was probably idiotic. I did it anyway. "Hello? Cora? Anyone hurt?"

Yeah, *hurt*. Ever the optimist.

I surveyed the blood, bodies, and gun. The couple had planned quite the romantic night before the murder. Warm fireplace. Fur rugs. Wine glasses. They'd even scattered rose petals over the box of unopened condoms. At least the carnage had been ribbed for her pleasure.

Blood and leather didn't mix well, and neither did uncompromised crime scenes. I kicked off my boots, but the blood had already soaked into the material. At least it cleaned off the trail of crusted salt. Unfortunately, my knee-highs didn't match. One black stocking peeked from under my slacks, contrasting the other—charcoal grey and in desperate need of a mate before laundry day. Classy. Not that my missing person would care.

Even if Cora had been dressed to kill.

Usually, people didn't mean it literally.

I skirted the blood and tip-toed a path through the tiny cottage, checking the secondary rooms for any other crimes, witnesses, or a reason for the date-night slaying. But Cora and her mystery man had planned to be alone. Figured.

Soft music still hummed from a Bluetooth speaker. Sexy songs—the Celine Dion, Michael Bolton. The soundtracks of movies from the nineties used to set the mood. I paused the weepy ballad before the romantic instrumental became a dirge.

Homicides.

Some of the guys said they were *easier* than Missing Persons or Family Crisis/Sexual Assault cases.

This didn't look *easy*.

This was a goddamned tragedy.

And such a *waste*.

They'd obviously intended last night to be a hot date. Cora was nothing but frigid now, courtesy of an opened window in the corner. No sign of forced entry—the night had just become a little too steamy for the couple. January's chilly wind sliced through the room. It'd make the time of deaths harder to determine.

But time wasn't as hard as answering *why*.

I wasn't a medical examiner, but, if I had to guess? The date ended somewhere after the kiss at the door but before the first bite of dinner. Red, flaking wax slipped over the silver candleholders and onto the otherwise pristine tablecloth. The Cornish game hens remained untouched. I hoped the cauliflower rice smelled better freshly prepared.

Someone had put a hell of a lot of effort into impressing their partner, but the evening had tipped from *bad* to *criminal* before they'd toasted their champagne.

I'd my share of terrible dates before, hitting thirty meant my date nights consisted of Netflix marathons and avoiding lactose after nine. Not exactly puppy-love or cinnamon spice, but James never complained.

Even if I avoided most romantic movies, music, and declarations, I respected Cora's efforts. Dying scattered in rose petals. It'd be poetic if it wasn't so regretfully pointless.

No. Cruel.

It was cruel.

I carried my boots, picking a path over a once immaculate hardwood floor. The couple had collapsed in an undignified heap before the fireplace. Not even touching in their final moments.

From the shoulders down, the man had a decent body. Lean and fit, he filled out his clothes with a subtle muscle—the kind that bulked in everyday use, not the occasional lift at the gym. Blood soaked through his outfit, but at least the caked crimson enhanced his tan. His collar had opened. A peek of pale skin contrasted his bronzed neck. Maybe he worked outside?

The bullet to his jaw marred his silhouette. Bits of bone and tissue disfigured what I assumed was a once-handsome face. Brown hair?

Potentially. Sun-bleached at the very least. I doubted it could handle any gel or product, but the matted blood and other tissues wasn't great for his style either.

Cora crumpled near him, her body blown backward, crashing near a decorative wicker chair in the corner. The bastard shot her in the chest. Did her heart break before he obliterated it?

Those were the sort of questions I couldn't ask myself. It was hard enough staying detached from my cases when the *missings* showed up alive. I'd lost a couple victims to drug overdoses. More than a few were still missing with no leads.

But murder?

Rare.

Heartbreaking, but rare.

I radioed in the discovery and petitioned for a tech team to hurry to the scene. The promised backup had an ETA of thirty minutes. Not bad for a Tuesday morning. Enough time for me to scope out the Air B&B. An opportunity to figure out what had gone so terribly wrong.

A murder-suicide? Nothing in Cora's past had indicated she'd been in any sort of trouble. Hell. No one even mentioned a *relationship*, let alone something as intricate as…this.

The candlelight and soft music surrendered to police lights and sirens. Dinner sat untouched on the table. Even the bathtub, surrounded by more melted candles, was now cold and bubbleless.

The only evidence of fun was the nibbled down bar of chocolate tucked into Cora's purse. Only one square missing. She hadn't wanted to ruin her appetite.

At least she died with some chocolate in her stomach. If she had drowned in a vat of coffee, it'd have been the perfect way to go.

Forensics arrived after twenty long minutes, pulling along the cottage's quiet street only to blast it with slamming doors, flashing lights, and the stomp of cold feet trying to warm up in the cold morning. Homicide joined minutes later, taking their time to investigate the *perimeter*. Funny how the cigarette smoke cordoned off the area better than police tape. But I couldn't blame them. Eight AM was too early to uncover a murder scene.

Especially when it never should have happened in the first place.

Not that there was ever a good murder to discover.

I should have chased her credit card report instead of her ex-boyfriend. I thought I was saving time—that I'd find her in a moment of weakness with an old flame. Damn. I'd thought that low-life drunk would be this case's only dead end.

And *that* was the sort of guilt the veterans on the force warned me to ignore. Unfortunately, I hadn't accepted the complimentary pack of cigarettes or binge night at the bar just yet. I'd find another coping mechanism. Grinding my teeth had worked well so far. And who could resist the allure of the vending machine on the second floor? Twix was my preferred stress reliever—one candy bar for each thigh.

"Nice place." One of the techs admired the kitschy cottage. "Looks nice."

"A cute place to visit," I agreed.

But not to die.

The cottage breathed clutter. Quilts and cuckoo clocks and vases of pussy willow were smooshed into five hundred square feet of whimsical charm. For a quiet retreat, the Air B&B was nice, nestled in the prosperous neighborhood of Highland Park. Which, until today, had been the scene of only one crime—vacationing during January in the heart of Pittsburgh.

And now their rented cottage had become their tomb.

The home was quiet, private, and isolated from the street. If the lovebirds had met in a hotel, someone might have heard a disturbance. Fighting or gunshots. Suspicious activity. But here?

Cora Abbott and her mystery suitor took their secrets to their graves, and who knew what sort of ugly, dirty truth I'd dig up.

The cavalry descended on the scene with the usual bluster of flashing cameras and early morning smoker's cough. Within minutes, the solemn misery of death shattered with the frenzy of squawking radios, the crunching of equipment, and impractical demands.

"Who's the responding officer?" Detective Lucas Riley assumed command of a situation that required tact and a delicate touch—traits as foreign to the veteran detective as leaving an aluminum beer can uncrunched on his forehead. "Who found the stiffs?"

His younger partner, Joey Falconi, tossed a digital camera to a patrolman and pointed in my direction. "This is McKenna's mess."

"*London?*" Riley scanned the room, found me, and gave an amused nod. He directed me to his side with a snap of his fingers.

That had never worked before, not sure why he kept trying it.

Riley's smirk lacked charm, but it never stopped him from opening his mouth before. The tug of his beard was meant to darken his expression. It didn't really work. The scruff was hardly more than a three o'clock shadow. Fortunately, the peach fuzz wasn't what intimidated his perps. On his thirty-fifth birthday, he gave a gift to himself—bench pressing his own weight. The washboard abs came courtesy of a messy divorce. She got the kids, he got the gym membership, and the station was plastered with his flyers for an after-hours weight-lifting club.

"I thought you were working Missing Persons?" Riley asked.

I stole a latex glove from a passing tech and blew into it before snapping it over my hand. I pointed to the dead woman. "I am. I just found her."

"Easier to find when they're lying still, huh?"

Not entirely untrue. "Yeah, but I wish I'd found her breathing. Definitely worth the extra paperwork."

"Way of the world. Some live. Some kill. Everyone dies. Least they can do for us is die in new and interesting ways." He picked a path through the blood just to shame the dead man. "Couldn't even do that, could ya, buddy?"

"I'm sure he sends his regrets," I said.

Riley glanced at the boots in my hand. "Why don't you make yourself at home, London? Get some champagne. We'll make it a real party."

His grin was crooked, but so where his teeth. It balanced out.

I held up my boots and took an evidence bag. "Stepped in the blood."

"Rookie mistake."

I wasn't a rookie. Far from it, but hell if I could convince veteran homicide detectives that working for two years in Missing Persons and the Sexual Assault/Family Crisis unit had opened my eyes to more horrors than stepping in a pool of blood.

Falconi leaned in beside me, his voice low enough to seem sensitive but still loud enough for Riley and the rest of the techs to hear. "This scene's pretty damn gory. You doing okay in here, McKenna? Wanna step out?"

Yes. And no. But I didn't need protecting from a little blood. "I'm fine. I just want to figure out what happened."

But Falconi had donned the white knight armor, and it was too damn heavy to drop as easily as the subject. "But if this makes you uncomfortable…because of what happened…you know…"

Jesus. I'd worked hard for ten years so people wouldn't have the opportunity to pity me. I tapped the badge hooked to my belt. "Blood doesn't bother me anymore."

Riley snorted. "Yeah, it's what people do *with* the blood that's the problem."

I focused on the crime scene before the two newbie techs asked any intrusive, clarifying questions about my past. "This is Cora Abbott. She's twenty-seven years old, lives in Lawrenceville with her toy poodle and half a dozen potted plants. No drugs. Drinking only on the weekends. Her mother reported her missing yesterday morning. Cora took her mom to her chemo appointment every Monday. She's never missed an appointment since her mom was diagnosed—breast cancer, stage three."

"She might be missing a couple more appointments…" Falconi ducked into the bedroom and returned. "The bed's untouched. Only fireworks these lovebirds saw shot out of the gun."

"Of course, you'd notice that," I said.

Falconi sipped from his travel mug like he choked down gold. His uncanny ability to conjure coffee out of mid-air was legendary. He claimed he hated the stuff, but two sets of twins under the age of four fostered the man's caffeine addiction. "I'm just sayin'. All this effort?

Dinner and dancing? Half a rose garden chopped into potpourri on the bed? A man would expect more than a mint on his pillow."

"I'm sure he didn't expect a gun in his face."

"Maybe he did." Falconi winked. "Did it himself. Check the gun."

Riley edged around a tech, nearly knocking over a little yellow card marking the location of a bullet shell. "So, hubby and wife share their glass of champagne..." He walked himself through the night. "Pay attention, McKenna. You might learn something."

"I'll bask in your wisdom."

Riley winked. "So hubby dearest agrees to this fabulous night out with his sweet little wife. Brings home a bouquet of roses. She gushes about dinner. Everything is going to plan."

Falconi took his cue. "But the gloves came off before the panties."

Riley agreed. "The little missus pissed him off. Said too much."

"Or not enough."

"Tempers flare. They start to fight."

Falconi licked his finger and smoothed his unruly eyebrow, but the bushy cowlick popped back immediately. "It's not your typical fight though. He was upset. Shot her point-blank. She saw it coming." He gave the brutal play-by-play like he discussed last's night final score at the buzzer. "Seen it before. Maybe the wife's getting a little on the side. Hubby learns about it. This is their last attempt to reconcile the marriage—a romantic getaway to cure all ails. Celebration of their love..."

"*Till death do they part*," Riley said. "But something happens. She says the wrong thing. He refuses to listen. They start to fight. She can't calm him down. And then...*pop!*"

His clap echoed in the room. Everyone flinched.

"She goes down…" Riley shakes his head. "And not in the good way. Might have avoided this if only she had."

Falconi was a bit more sensitive. "But the husband comes to his senses. Once he realizes what he's done, he's insane with grief and regret." He tapped his chin with his fingers poised like the barrel of a gun. "One shot, and that's the end of the happy couple. It'd be tragic if we didn't find one of these every six months."

"Bleak," I said.

Falconi always was a bastion of half-assed insight. "The way to a man's heart is through is stomach…but the way to his grave is paved with the shells of a .45."

"Get that written on a fortune cookie."

The detectives gestured for the techs to take their spot and begin their forensics investigation. I stopped them with a raised hand. Cora deserved better than a crackpot theory as a eulogy over her body.

"It's an interesting story…" And the academy was waiting in the wings to give them an award. "But that's not what happened here."

Riley straightened, but his words were a little too gentle to not be patronizing. "London, honey, I think it's too late for you to start your investigation."

I let the *honey* slide. Everyone got one, and I wasn't picking fights before my second cup of coffee. But their theory was wrong, and the wedding ring on the man's finger proved it.

"They're not married," I said. "At least, not to each other. Cora Abbott is single."

This revelation intrigued them. Riley circled the bodies, even bending closer to get a look at what remained of the man.

"Sneaky bastard," he chuckled. "Know who he is?"

I didn't examine the body, but I also made sure they didn't catch me *not* looking at him.

I'd worked my share of dead bodies before. And most of the homicide unit would admit that working the *live* cases—the rapes and child abuses—were oftentimes harder than dealing with death.

But this scene was bad. Ugly. Suicide always was. For as badly as the victim wished to leave the world, the mess they left behind wasn't any way for a family to remember their loved one.

If they wanted to remember a murderer at all.

But theirs was a good question, one I had wrestled with since nearly slipping in a puddle of evidence. "I don't know who he is. Cora wasn't currently dating. Her mother only spoke of one ex-boyfriend, and he was dumped a year ago."

Falconi's eyebrows quirked. "She's not gonna tell her cancer-ridden momma about banging a married man."

And, unfortunately, she hadn't told anyone else.

Riley harassed the lead forensic tech. "Anything on him?"

The tech was no rookie. The grizzled boomer, Eddie Mayview, was one cigarette short of a good morning on his best days. He barked for the detective to give him space, and Riley heeded the warning. Carefully, Eddie scanned the body, patting pockets and the dead man's coat.

"Got something." Eddie grunted. "Looks like a book."

The leather-bound book was nestled in the man's pocket, and it took a bit of wiggling to wedge it free. He handed the worn, tenderly read bundle to Riley. The edges curled, and the buff leather had faded in spots over the face. The grooves matched a hand, carried and held so often the dead man was lucky his fingers hadn't eroded through the cover.

We all shared Falconi's question. "Is that a Bible?"

If nothing else, Riley and I had one thing in common—we practiced our Catholicism religiously…every Christmas and Easter Sunday. He crossed himself.

"Doubt the Lord blessed this scene," Riley said. "Anything else on him?"

"Not ready to roll him yet," Eddie said. "Busy yourself with the good book. Might save your ass one day, Riley."

"Hasn't yet." He tossed the book to Falconi. "You hold it. I don't want to burst into flames."

Falconi flipped through the pages, his jaw tightening. "There's a couple verses highlighted."

"Doubt it was *Thou Shalt Not Kill*," I said.

"*Children are a heritage from the Lord, offspring a reward from him. Like arrows in the hands of a warrior are children born in one's youth. Blessed is the man whose quiver is full of them. They will not be put to shame when they contend with their opponents in court.*" Falconi closed the book. "Psalms 127: 3-5."

A good reminder for me to take my pill as soon as I returned to the station. "Are you serious?"

"What?" Riley asked. "What's it mean?"

"It's the quiver-full passage," I said. "My college roommate wanted to join the movement until she got her first stretch mark."

"Those religious jagoffs?" Falconi groaned. "The ones who have babies by the bucketload and get a TV show for it? Hell. I knock my wife up with twins *twice*, and I'm still waiting for a producer or Jesus to hand me a contract."

"Yeah," Riley laughed. "That busted condom sure is doing the Lord's work."

I stared at the mess. Blood? Suicides? Clandestine affairs?

How the hell did a guy like this get involved with Cora Abbott?

Riley surveyed the cottage with new inspiration. "Okay. Maybe our preacher friend had plans for Miss Abbott. A little soft music. Some champagne. Maybe he propositioned her."

"*Hey baby, your uterus is looking mighty empty.*" Falconi laughed.

"Is this his house?"

"No," I said. "I tracked Cora's credit card. She rented this place— it's an Air B&B. Scheduled to stay for a couple days...but they didn't make it through the first night."

"Where's the owner?"

"He lives in the house next door. Just rents this space to anyone who wants it, like an extended-stay hotel."

"I'll want to talk to him. See if he heard anything."

"Me too."

Riley frowned. "You too?"

"This murder-suicide doesn't make sense." I took the bible from Falconi. Nothing else inside except for more highlighted passages. "This man is obviously religious. Why is he having an affair?"

Riley edged his elbow into my ribs. "You're young, London, but you aren't *that* naïve."

No, I wasn't. Not anymore. "He's religious. She didn't tell anyone she was dating him. They obviously have some history. This isn't a first date. They're celebrating something. Why would he suddenly...snap? What triggered it?"

Falconi wasn't as intrigued. "A bad hair day. She mouthed off. The tin-foil hat fell off. God told him to do it. Take your pick."

"And some people are evil." Riley didn't look at me. "You'd know that best of all."

They quieted. Damn. I'd finally clawed my way into the department, worked my ass off on patrol to get my shield, and earned the title *Detective* instead of *the girl who got away*. My only goal should have been solving crimes. Instead, I spent too many hours trying to make people forget the ones that happened to me.

I hadn't broken yet. Wasn't planning on it anytime soon.

I spoke out loud, walking myself through my own scenario. "So a young woman in her twenties with a limited romantic history gets involved with a highly religious man. Can you tell how old he is?"

"Shame you can't just count the rings," Falconi said.

"I can count one—that wedding ring." And it still didn't make sense. "They've come here for an affair. Cora rented the house, made a fancy dinner. Hell, she even drew a *bubble bath*. And then…"

Eddie groaned as he stood, his knees popping as loud as a gun. "He shot her, then turned the gun on himself. Self-inflicted." He pointed to the crimson splatter on the wall, abstract but revealing one harrowing story. "Both bodies dropped around the same time, a couple minutes apart."

"Not exactly Romeo and Juliet," Falconi said.

"Still a tragedy." I took too deep of a breath. Twelve hours was enough time for the crime scene to stick to my clothes, hair. I didn't want it in my lungs too. "Why didn't she tell anyone about this affair?"

Riley shrugged. "Everyone has secrets, London."

Secrets, yes. Murder-suicides? No.

In Missing Persons, not all stories had happy endings, and most never made it past my desk. People didn't just vanish, and the ones who had reason to leave didn't slip quietly into the night. They left trails. More secrets. Lies. A clear path, like a wounded animal. Some didn't drip blood, but they'd still be messy when I found them.

But this?

I never blindly trusted my gut—it had let me down once before, and those scars didn't heal easily. But some instincts were worth a listen. The nagging grumble twisting my stomach told me to look closer at the scene.

"Cora's iPhone is charging on the table beside the sofa." I tip-toed my way around a splatter, handing my bloody shoes to a confused tech. I moved a ruffled throw pillow off the couch. "Her laptop is here too, set up in the kitchen. Her bags are in the bedroom."

Riley nodded. "*And?*"

"Where's *his* stuff?" I tightened my gloves and turned on her phone. The recent calls blurred as I scrolled.

Mom. Mom. Office. Cindy. Mom.

Her texts were the same, only she had a new entry. *Clark*—also known as Dad. Estranged, but supposedly reconciling enough that she took a job working in the family furniture store once again.

"No calls to any likely boyfriend."

Falconi whistled. "He's so slick he even has his mistress covering for him."

"Anything else in his pockets?" I asked Eddie. He gave the body a gentle frisk and shook his head. "What about a phone?"

"Nope," he said. "Not on him."

Riley gave a sharp whistle, startling the four techs combing the cottage. "We're missing Casanova's cell. Someone find it."

"You won't to find it," I said. "He doesn't have one."

"Doesn't have a cell phone?" Falconi seemed more horrified by the lack of technology than the overabundance of bullet holes.

"No credit cards either." Eddie fished a blood-soaked money clip from the man's pocket and handed it to Riley. "No ID. Just cash."

"He's paranoid," I said.

"No, he's careful." Riley turned the money over in his hand before bagging it with the rest of the evidence. "He probably left his cell at home so his wife couldn't find him via GPS. Also carries cash, so she doesn't check the bank account to see where he went while he was away. Cora's been sleeping with a regular Jason Bourne."

"How can you be so sure?" I asked.

Riley darkened. "Takes a bastard to know one. Sounds like he read through my divorce transcript."

Falconi agreed. "And he had it all planned out...until he killed his mistress. Good thing the wife doesn't know where he is. I'd rather my wife find me in bed with the babysitter than collapsed in a pool of my own blood."

It made sense—and ensured the sales of hundreds of gallons of chocolate ice cream every day to broken hearted women—but something didn't fit. "What if he doesn't have a cell phone? Or a driver's license or credit cards?"

Riley shook his head. "Don't over think it. Ockham's razor. Simplest solution is usually the right one. He didn't want to get caught sleeping around."

"*Or*...he's a highly religious man, marking Quiverfull passages in his Bible, who doesn't believe in technology and stays off the grid." I knelt, teasing the end of his pantleg with a pen. The wool soaked through with blood, stained and ruined, but the mystery remained. "These are hand-sewn pants."

"What?"

"*Hand-stitched.* Like…with a needle and thread. Someone *made* these clothes."

"Detective or fashionista?" Riley laughed.

"He's got homemade clothes. No cell phone. No ID. And he's hauling around a Bible?" I waved over his body. "This guy probably lives off the grid with his church somewhere. So why is he in *this* cottage with Cora? And why kill her?"

"So? He's a prepper loon." Falconi shrugged. "He's still a cheating husband who doesn't want to get caught. Doesn't matter if you think the Wifi is gonna fry your brain or Big Brother is in your iPhone. This is an affair gone bad."

Riley agreed. "Who knows? Maybe she planned to tell his wife. Pissed him off?"

"Then why the ceremony?" I lamented the good bottle of champagne gone to waste. "This wasn't a confrontation. This was a *seduction.*"

"And the romance ended at the door." Riley frowned. "London, you better get in contact with her family and friends. See if anyone knows who this guy is or why this happened."

And I'd get nowhere with them. I'd already spoken with her closest contacts. A frightened mother searching for her dutiful daughter. A panicked father who feared he'd upset the daughter he'd finally reconnected with. The best friend who'd laughed hysterically at the possibility of her being with a man. Even her Facebook page was devoid of updates. No new posts. No pictures. No secret lover in her private chats. No romantic ties.

And yet Cora Abbott had snuck away to a rented home for a week to spend her last moments with a man who presumably wined, dined, and danced with her before pulling the gun.

This didn't feel right. Worse than finding a missing person dead. Those were never good, but they happened. None had ever left such a knot in my stomach before.

We were missing something. Something big.

An answer to a question we had yet to ask.

Problem was, the only one who might have helped was a John Doe who spoke his last words with a gun barrel in his mouth.

I headed outside. Two officers searched the interior of Cora's SUV. Every door and the trunk were open. I peeled off my gloves and approached a patrolman. The curious neighbors poked their heads out their doors. Enough dog walkers and early morning joggers passed the house that the patrol set up a quick barricade by the walkway to the porch.

"Did you find a cell phone?" I asked the officer.

He shook his head, his breath a puff of fog. "No. But there's something else. The SUV is clean. *Really* clean."

"How so?"

"There's not even a crumb on the inside."

Fantastic. "What about prints?"

"Only on the steering wheel. But the rest of the interior was recently cleaned. Found Clorox wipes in the glove box."

Champagne. Roses. Bubble bath.

And a meticulously scrubbed car.

Not exactly my perfect romantic night.

"Shout at me if you find anything of his," I said.

A man yelled, jerking his dog's leash hard, hauling the black lab out of the road. He swore at a fire-engine red pickup as it peeled out a little too quick for a residential street. Clumps of frozen mud fell from the wheel well. The truck turned a hard right and sped off through the neighborhood.

Strange. People in the city had pickups. A lot of them. But not many had mud caked over the frame. The potholes were bad, but times weren't that tough yet.

"McKenna!" Riley called from the doorway. "Need a statement. Get in here."

I hesitated, still searching the street. The truck had peeled out in a hurry. I checked my watch. Eight-thirty. Probably just trying to make it to work on time, but a night of running after a case and a morning soaked in blood didn't make me the most trusting soul.

I wished I'd grabbed his plate.

I wished I'd made it to Cora in time.

I wished I had a reason, an explanation, to why this had happened.

But I couldn't invent more trouble to answer *why*.

Mysteries like that often resulted in more than *trouble*.

They'd put me in more danger.

Chapter Two

Go ahead. Struggle.

I'd never deny a woman a chance to squirm.

-Him

Blood and coffee fueled the homicide department.

Detective Riley hollered for me just as I sat at my desk. "London! Meeting in five about the Abbott case. Bring coffee!"

Coffee politics were the only thing more dangerous than the criminals we hauled into the station. Most of the guys in homicide had ten or fifteen years on me. It was hard enough earning their respect as a second-year detective without amending the demand with *cream or sugar?*

I checked the time, but I'd stopped seeing numbers halfway through the night. The intervals now marked in fading opportunities in which I could become human once again. A block for writing my report to avoid the inevitable call from my sergeant. A chunk for a shower so I could at least pretend to be awake. A few minutes to readjust my hair and lip gloss.

Vanity thy name was job security, even if I had to play games to fit in with the others at the station—women and men.

A ponytail outed me as too informal—playful and young. But a bun looked severe—intentionally stoic, like I dared people to question my past. I could have had it styled and highlighted the dirty blonde, but would it look professional, or like I tried too hard to hide who I was?

Appearances weren't everything, but I needed every edge in my career. Not only for the families I helped and criminals I chased, but so I could instill *some* trust in my colleagues. Just to get on the force required more psych evals and probational periods than my union rep liked, but it had worked.

My past was off-limits except for the usual water-cooler gossip, and I'd swapped the patrol uniform for a pair of pantyhose and shield.

It was worth the struggle.

The folder for the investigation held only a couple pages of notes. Enough to get us started, but not enough to make sense of the murder. And while Mom said I could crack a conspiracy in a game of Boggle, John Doe had more secrets than blood to spill. I could feel it.

"*Bingo!*" Falconi's excited declaration echoed as I entered Homicide.

A chorus of groans heralded his victory lap around the unit, and a few detectives tossed wads of paper in his general direction.

Homicide's offices often juggled morbid sincerity with callous amusement. While the computers and desks, sprawling layers of paperwork and constant squeal of opening and closing doors shared similarities with the Missing Persons Unit, we had yet to invent our own clandestine BINGO game. Sample boards passed through the station with players winning based on weapons, locations, and types of murders.

"That'll be an Andrew Jackson, lads." Falconi showed his board to a grumbling detective. "You know who he is—the one from the musical."

"That's Alexander Hamilton," I said.

"Hamilton. Jackson. Doesn't matter which white boy is on the back of the money as long as it adds up." He demonstrated his win. "Diagonally. *Vehicular homicide, South Side, a drug-related incident, plea deal,* and a liberal use of the *free space.*"

Riley forked over a twenty from his wallet, but waved me towards his cubicle. I handed him the folder. He expected the coffee.

"*Caffeine,* London. Come on."

"Your prayers are answered. Linda made a new batch an hour ago." I pointed to the pot in the corner. "Bet it tastes even better when you serve it yourself."

The lines in Riley's face actually deepened as he shuffled his butt to the machine, grumbling under his breath. Falconi, fresh from his victory lap, returned to his desk a richer man. His smile faded as I dropped the folder into his hands.

"Any news on our John Doe?" I asked.

Falconi took the coffee cup from Riley, accepted the obligatory profanity, and sent his partner for another cup. "Coroner's got the body now."

"Anything on his prints?"

"Nothing in the system."

"DNA?"

He snickered. "You want the results in this lifetime or the next? Get in line, darling."

Riley returned, jealously guarding his coffee. He read my notes and nodded. "Did good today, McKenna. Hand this off to my sergeant and go home. You look like shit."

Felt like it now too. "What do you mean...*hand it off?*"

"Give him whatever you have from the scene and the file on Cora Abbott."

Oh, hell no. "I have work to do on the case yet. A couple more leads. Her family. A couple friends."

Falconi waved a hand. "Don't worry about it. We can take it from here."

"Can...or *will*?"

"You did more than enough. Thanks for the help."

Riley took his chair and promptly spilled most of his coffee. His curse echoed. Mine would too.

"I can still work this case," I said. "Just because she's dead doesn't mean I can't investigate—"

"Investigate *what*?" Falconi shrugged. "There's not a case to solve here. John Doe killed his mistress, turned the gun on himself."

"But *why*?" I flipped through the folder, tapping Cora's schedule, credit card invoices, and the few cryptic messages I'd found on her phone. Without dumping the logs to see who exactly she'd called, I had nothing, save for the slew of friends who spent more time rescheduling plans with her than actually hitting the bar. "She was hiding this affair for a reason. And this man, whoever he is, is more covert than an undercover agent."

"Great. He's CIA now." Riley didn't buy it, no matter how hard I sold it. "London, come on. He was banging her. They had to keep it on the DL. She wanted to avoid the gossip. Maybe he was getting a divorce and any time spent with Cora would line his ex's pockets. They met up. He lost his cool. Now they're dead."

Falconi shook his head. "Didn't even get some before he died. If he did, you might have had a cause to investigate."

"I can handle more than sexual assault cases."

"Then we'll call you when we get one." Riley tapped his watch. "Go home, London. We'll find our John Doe's name, notify the family, and close the case. You did your part."

"You can't take my case from me."

"*Your* case?" He laughed. "Cora Abbott stopped being your problem the moment she became our victim."

"She's *my* missing person."

"And now she's *our* corpse. Talk to your sergeant. He made the call. Homicide is taking lead from here."

Getting pissed off would only reveal that I had a bad temper.

But I wasn't rolling over because someone commanded it.

Cora Abbott was *my* case. My responsibility.

My failure.

It was only right that I try to figure out what the hell had gone so wrong, so quickly.

"The case is strange," I said. "The John Doe. The Bible. No cellphone."

Falconi chuckled as he tossed a worn stress-ball from hand to hand.

"*Serial adulterer.*" His diagnosis would certainly save the station overtime hours. "Case closed. Enjoy the rest of your night, Detective."

I didn't run my mouth, but nothing stopped me from exacting an imaginary revenge involving my two favorite homicide detectives and a trusted nightstick.

I'd already let Cora down once. I wasn't going to disappoint her again.

And my sergeant knew exactly what I was going to say before I spoke—or, at least, a Rated-G version of the events. I slammed the door to his office behind me.

Bruce Adamski glanced up from his paperwork. "It's been a good week since you're feathers got ruffled."

"Yeah, and somehow, I always get plucked."

"I know what you're thinking."

"That you're going to buy me my choice of lunch every day this week and next?"

Adamski had just turned fifty-seven. He was twenty years past his prime, fifteen from the station's good ol' boys club, and ten from retirement. Only repetition moved his chair-flattened butt out of bed at six every morning, served him lunch at noon, and gave him a second wind at five-thirty, every day, come rain, sleet, flu, or hellish efficiency meetings.

"We're backlogged," Adamski said. "I need you working Missing Persons, not investigating homicides. We're supposed to find our victims *before* this happens."

Not fair. "This wasn't my fault."

"No one said it was." Bruce hiked his pants, but he'd hit that age where he gained a gut and lost his hips. The belt had to sit at either his navel or knees. "Relax. It's too early in your career for that chip on your shoulder."

"It's not a chip." It was Cora Abbott's body. It wasn't the first I couldn't find—most of our cases were unsolvable. But this one hurt. "We're missing something about these deaths."

"Then Detectives Riley and Falconi will figure it out."

Because Frick and Frack had been so thorough before. Bruce read my mind. He pointed a prematurely arthritic finger at me, the rheumatoid swelling the knuckles badly today. "You're gonna see enough trouble in your career. Don't go poking around for more."

"But—"

A woman's shrill scream echoed through the office. I flinched, my coffee spilling over the floor. Bruce didn't have the reflexes to leap to his feet anymore, but he grabbed for both his gun and the nearest blunt object. His potted cactus would not serve him well in emergency situations.

"Help me!"

The frantic woman's wails were haunted with agony. She raced past our receptionist and collapsed in the middle of the unit.

"My sister's been kidnapped."

Chapter Three

I selected you specifically. I wanted you more than I've ever wanted anyone else. Don't cry. You should be flattered.
-Him

Terror did terrible things to victims, families, and the responding officers futilely balancing impartiality with the cold spike of helplessness driving into their spine.

It was even worse when thrust into the middle of the station with no warning.

"I'm sorry!" Linda, our twenty-year veteran receptionist, swaddled herself in a knit cardigan and rushed to contain the sobbing woman. "She wasn't supposed to come back here."

Linda juggled both her coffee and an iPhone still connected to her current call. I'd take a wild guess how the frantic woman had bypassed our crack security.

"It's okay." My heart minced against my ribs, but at least my words steadied. "I'll talk with her. Follow me, ma'am."

"London." Linda tapped her temple, pressing hard against curls dyed an unnatural shade of melted-popsicle red. "She's...having a hard time."

Crazy then. That I could handle.

I'd dealt with my share of hysterical woman. Crying. Screaming. Collapsing at my feet and begging any god above to help find their missing loved one. They'd be pale and frenzied, frazzled and stumbling over their memories repeated so many times even they jumbled details.

But this woman...

She wasn't hysterical. Or terrified. Or even insane.

A pure determination strengthened her with grim purpose and desperate intentions.

"Please, listen to me." She clutched my arm with nails chewed to the quick with worry. "You're my last hope, Detective McKenna."

Was I already working her case? "Have we met before?"

"No." She straightened, her voice rock solid even if her hands quaked. "But I know you. And I know you're the only one who can help me now."

No pressure.

Adamski gestured from his office, silently asking if I needed assistance. But if I couldn't handle this, I didn't deserve the damn badge. The lady was wound up, but she wasn't a danger. The true crimes were the dark circles under her eyes. She looked exhausted. Judging by the wrinkled blouse under her grey peacoat, the messy ponytail losing a ridge of looped hair by her ear, and the Kleenex and papers spilling from her purse, she probably slept the last time I did—and I doubted either of us could remember when that was.

"Let's...take a seat." I showed her to my desk. "Can I get you—"

"I only want *answers*. It's been so damn long since…" She shivered in the chair, rubbing away the winter's redness prickling at her nose and cheeks. "I need to know where she is. I can't stand not knowing."

Panic had aged her. At first I thought the woman was older—late forties maybe. But as she scattered the stray pencils, pens, and papers off my desk to make way for her purse and photographs of her sister, her hands betrayed her true age. Smooth, taut skin—the same as her face if only she had reason to smile for once. She must have been my age, but thirty had hit her harder than me.

"I have information…" She rummaged through her bag, abandoning recipes and tiny notepads to dig under her cell phone. When that didn't work, she dumped the contents on my desk and handed me her prize. A photo album. The organized collection of sorted photos featured the same smiling girl, a pretty thing no older than fifteen.

The album was labeled *Anna*, and the woman protected the book with her life, cautiously placing an arm between the pages and my lidless coffee cup.

"It's up to you, Detective," she whispered. "No one else can find her."

"Okay…" The authority in my voice was masked as a soothing whisper. "Let's start at the beginning. Take a deep breath for me, and we'll talk—"

The woman shook her hair. Even the cocoa curls bounced with a forlorn futility. "I have pictures. Dates. Times. Everything. Just tell me what I can give you that will help."

Easy enough. I grabbed a pen and scribbled a blot of ink in the corner of the page. "Let's start with your name."

"Louisa Prescott."

Good. Her wild-eyes began to soften, losing the feral hardness.

"Okay, Louisa. You said your sister has gone missing…"

"No! Not *missing*. She's been *kidnapped*!"

"What makes you think she was kidnapped?"

"I don't think it, Detective. I *know*."

It was hard to fake that sort of sincerity, but grief made fools of us all. At least Louisa's words were no longer a tumble of panic. We'd come back to the kidnapping angle. First, I needed a missing person.

"What is your sister's name?" I asked.

"Anna. Anna Prescott."

"And how old is she?"

"Thirty." Louisa didn't wait for my next question. "She's about five eight, was around one hundred and thirty five pounds. Chestnut hair, lighter than mine. Freckles. Pale complexion. She has a birthmark on her neck—a port wine stain, the red blotchy type. There's one on her shoulder too. She has no illnesses or allergies and was not mentally ill. She had every reason to come home and no reason to run away or leave her family."

Louisa wasn't crazy, but it was rare for anyone to come to the station prepared with anything but the usual lies, deceit, and stubborn refusal to admit anything to us which might have gotten the missing person in trouble. Saving lives was secondary to sparing reputations, despite my best efforts.

But with Louisa? Hell, I might have learned Anna's preferred drugs and sexual positions if I'd promised it'd help find the girl. Fortunately, I didn't need all her secrets yet. Just the basics.

"Where did she go missing?"

"Outside our house. In Braddock. We were walking together. Talking. Not paying attention. I didn't see the man behind us. He knocked me to the ground, and my head hit the concrete. It all happened so quickly. I couldn't stop him from taking her."

Oh, *Christ*.

I leapt up, but my stomach dropped to my feet. I dove for my radio. "You were attacked?"

"Yes. And I know what the man looks like, but I blacked out when he hit me. I was unconscious long enough for him to take my sister and drive away."

"You hurt your head?"

She tapped her perfectly smooth, unblemished, and uninjured forehead. "Yes. Right here. I went out *cold*."

She didn't have a mark on her. No bruising. Certainly nothing like a scrape of concrete or a bump from a swinging fist.

I lowered the radio, giving her a second, more cautious glance. "You don't look hurt, Louisa."

"I was."

Was? "Why don't you tell me what really happened?"

Wrong phrasing. Her voice shrilled, slicing over the precinct. "*I told you*! My sister was kidnapped!"

"Near your home in Braddock?"

"Yes!"

"By a man who attacked you, threw you to the sidewalk, and grabbed your sister?"

"Yes!"

"Even though you have no visible scrape, cut, or bruise from where you were assaulted?"

Louisa puffed an insulted breath. "It *healed.*"

My pen dropped. I frowned. "When did this all happen?"

"July 5th, 2002."

Now I really needed another cup of coffee.

I'd had enough crackpots, conspiracy theorists, schizophrenics, and alien enthusiasts wander into the station with irrefutable proof of their particular oddity, deity, and abnormality. Louisa's declaration didn't surprise me.

The only thing stronger than the constant, forward march of time? Denial.

I tossed the pen down. "Louisa, that was...*fifteen years ago.*"

She didn't blink. "And?"

Scratch the coffee. I needed a shot of whiskey.

Fifteen years ago I was some twerp in the marching band. I had the Rachael from Friends haircut, plastic bracelets on my wrists, and planned to graduate high school and study psychology. That was the year I started dating my first real boyfriend. Ricky Palmer, the only kid from Seneca Valley High School to get trapped on a sinking canoe during a thunderstorm as he attempted to retrieve a "left-handed smoke shifter" for his fellow boy scouts.

It had been a good time in my life, but any time before my kidnapping had been good years.

Louisa looked down, ringing her hands in her lap. The frantic tension melted from her with a long, weary sigh. "I know how crazy I sound. But I'm only asking for you to hear me out, to know the story. You can find her. I know you can."

She squeezed my arm. I didn't shake her off, but I abandoned my notes in favor of the computer. The database for Missing and Exploited Children should have had all the information we needed.

Sure enough, Anna Prescott was still listed, even age-progressed to look approximately twenty-five years old.

"This is her?" I angled the monitor so she could see.

She hesitated. "Yes."

I hated this part. "I don't know what else I can do. The police took your report. She's entered into the database. If anyone found her or her remains—"

"She's not dead!" Just the possibility cracked her voice and glistened her eyes with tears. "Why won't you listen to me?"

Damn it. I hauled her back into the chair before she stormed off. "Sit. I didn't say she was dead. But if we had any indication that she was, we'd have received notification. She might still be alive."

"She *is*."

"So what can I do? How can I help you?"

"You can find her."

"Nothing would make me happier," I said. "Honestly. But…" The stack of folders piled high on my desk. I pointed to each. "This case is a missing five-year-old girl, presumably abducted by a biological father who has skipped his last three meetings with his parole officer." I tapped another. "This is an elderly, eighty-year-old man with advanced Alzheimer's. He's been missing since last month. His son *forgot* to tell us he had wandered off—but he made sure to cash his social security check at the beginning of January."

"I understand," Louisa said. "I really do."

33

Maybe the workload, but not the pressure. Those two cases had the department running ragged every day, trying to investigate any missing angle while sacrificing sleep to follow up every lead we could concoct.

"And this is the weirdest one." The last folder plagued me more than the others. "This girl ran away from home at age twelve. She was lost for two years before randomly appearing back at home. She wouldn't say where she had been or who she had lived with. Then, after two weeks…she vanishes again. The family is worried sick, and we have no idea where she's gone."

That was the case that didn't let me sleep soundly at night.

The mystery was like a popcorn kernel wedged in my teeth. It dug into me. Twisted me up. Whoever had taken her before had stolen her again.

God only knew if they'd punish the poor girl for daring to escape them. I didn't have high hopes for finding her alive.

Louisa took a breath. "I know my sister was kidnapped long ago…"

I interrupted her before she even thought it. "No case is unimportant. Believe me."

"But?"

"Some cases are more inherently dangerous than others. What happened to your sister is heart-breaking, but…" I ran my hand through my hair. "I'll pull the old case files. I'll talk to the officers who took the initial reports and run through the scene again. But the likelihood of solving a cold case—"

"Detective, it's not cold. I saw the man who took her."

The terror in her words rose the hair on my neck. "You saw him? When?"

"Today."

I sucked in a breath. It lodged in my chest. "Where?"

"In the Strip District. He was getting into a white Dodge Grand Caravan, but I only caught two of the digits on the plate. *GP.*"

It was useful information, but it'd have been better if they'd found that van a week after the abduction—or even fifteen days. But after fifteen years…

No one would ever blame Louisa if her memory of that day was a bit hazy.

"I know you're trying to help your sister," I said. "But are you *sure* you found the right man?"

Louisa's voice lowered—deep and graveled by whatever shards of her childhood she'd swallowed over the years. "I will *always* remember that man. Until the day I die, every time I close my eyes, every time I sleep at night, I'll see his face. He took something from me. *Someone.* I love my sister so much. I don't know what he did with her, but I know he's still out there. Waiting. He knows where she is, and I won't rest until I find her."

"And I'll help you, but people change—faces change."

"You wouldn't forget a face like his."

"Why?"

"Have you ever seen pure evil, Detective?"

The question pitted in my stomach.

And then I was there again. With him. A monster. A demon.

A man whose face I could never, would never, and refused to forget. I didn't want to answer Louisa or to remember that cold, ruthless stare.

Evil didn't believe in mercy. And now, neither did I.

My voice didn't weaken, only flattened, hollow and guarded. "I've experienced things you couldn't imagine."

Louisa shared the same pained shadow in her words. "Then you *know*. I can't forget him. He's out there, Detective. Help me find Anna. You have to stop him before he takes another innocent girl."

Chapter Four

Trust your instincts, London.
They're never wrong...
-Him

The alarm went off, but James and I weren't sleeping.

The wake-up call was *premature*, and we both groaned. A few moments of rushed, unceremonious enjoyment later, and we resigned ourselves to face the morning.

He rolled away, his bare chest gleaming with sweat. He took a satisfied puff of air, rubbed his chin, and once more morphed into the calm and composed Doctor James Novak—handsome, attentive, and every girl's dream boyfriend.

Or psychologist.

Not mine, but close enough.

The alarm buzzed again. James smacked it. His badge fell off the nightstand into his overnight bag. The gold shield glittered in the low light cast from the crack in my white curtains. Since the kidnapping, I didn't like complete darkness. The white muted the brightness instead of suffocating in the dark, and that was better.

Just enough darkness to sleep even if I could still read the insignia on his badge.

FBI

Ten years ago, the bureau had completely invaded my home and privacy. Every secret, every friend, every place I'd ever gone was categorized, scrutinized, and weighed for *patterns*. They'd found nothing, no reason for me to be targeted.

Once I came back, once I was *safe*, they left.

James stayed, but it still took five years before I accepted his offer to buy me a cup of coffee.

It's personal, he'd said. *Not professional. We won't talk about it ever again. Not unless you want to.*

I hadn't believed him then, but, to this day, he'd stuck to his word. Just as I did mine. I'd never forgive what happened to me, but I could sure as hell forget it. Every day I focused only on helping others, doing everything I could to ensure no one ever endured that sort of hell again.

The awkward quiet settled—a comfortable moment after the rush of adrenaline that should have been caressed with sweet words and other such declarations. I gave the silence ten seconds before it prickled at me.

"When are you leaving?"

James had caramel eyes, a mocha voice, and enough sweetness in him to give me cavities. He tucked his arms behind his head, and I pretended I wasn't impressed with the strength that bulged the defined muscles. He stayed in shape, even if he couldn't do the field work anymore. Despite the tinge of grey against his temples—well-earned for a man of forty—he looked good.

He claimed he didn't have a sly smile. I knew better. "Are you that eager to get rid of me?"

"Just planning my day."

It had taken two years of dating the man, but I could finally roll out of bed naked and walk around the room without worrying about grabbing a robe or shirt to cover my scars. It'd probably take another two years before I'd let him see me with my wet hair in a towel and conditioning mask on my face. Had to save some mystery.

"I've got a couple cases to check on today." I sipped from a bottle of water I'd left on my vanity yesterday. Or was it the day before? "I don't know if I should be back for dinner."

"If I said I'd be here, would you make me something?"

Silly man. "I'd definitely *order* you something."

"With meat this time?"

My vegetarianism wasn't a choice. I hadn't touched meat in ten years, not since the knife had aimed for me. James could do what he wanted though—even if his cholesterol had gotten better since sharing my meals.

"You can have extra pepperoni on your pizza."

"That's my happy homemaker."

He checked his watch instead of the clock radio on the nightstand. He still squinted while reading the numbers. His vision was poor in the mornings. And in low light. He didn't say it, but I knew it was bad at dusk now.

It was one of the reasons he was pulled from the field and strapped behind a desk. At least, until his sight got too bad for that too. But the doctors said he still had time before considering those possibilities. We didn't talk about it much. Neither of us wanted to worry. There'd be enough time for that.

"I'm flying to DC this afternoon," he said. "Don't expect me before Saturday—and that's if we're lucky."

"That's okay. I might have to pull some overtime."

"Has anyone ever told you that you work too much, Detective McKenna?"

"Projecting, Dr. Novak?"

He smirked. "You know, we could make this easier on ourselves."

"How so?"

"Move in with me."

And those were the words that'd haunt me more than Louisa's ominous *have you ever seen true evil* question.

I'd take law, justice, and a good mystery over the roast in the oven, white picket fence, and weekends with the in-laws. Maybe one day. Maybe some time.

But not now. Not yet.

I arched an eyebrow. "Move in with *you*? Your house is closer to the FBI offices. It'll add fifteen minutes to my commute."

"Then I'll come here."

My handsome Victorian home was far too big for a single occupant who spent most of her time passed out in the bed or rummaging in the fridge before heading to work. And James already had a toothbrush in the bathroom, DVD in the player, and his very own spice rack in the pantry.

I led him with a question he'd answer too honestly. "Are you that eager to spend your life with me?"

James lowered his voice, his words a hushed promise of time and commitment and *space*. All the damned things I wished a man as good as him wouldn't offer. "I'm waiting for you to start yours."

"I've told you before. I don't think I'll ever be right. I put as many pieces of me back together that I could find, but not all of them fit. I'm still missing most of them."

"Then I'll fill in the gaps."

"Is that fair to you?"

He let it drop, checking the messages on his phone. "Nothing has to happen before you're ready, London."

"What if I'm not?"

"We do what we've done for the past ten years. Take it day-by-day."

"Like it's that easy."

"Watch." He smiled. "I'll go to DC. You go to work. And we'll see how we feel at the end of the day."

I hated to tell him, but he already knew. I always felt the same at the end of every day.

Empty. Angry.

And in absolutely no place where I could give my heart to a man as good as James Novak.

"Call me when you land?" I asked.

"Always." He called to me before I ducked into the bathroom. "Love you."

I tapped the door frame, averting my gaze.

"You would, wouldn't you?"

***

Seven AM was a hell of a time for a summon to Homicide.

Ten years ago, I'd made a deal with the devil not to die before lunch. It was such an odd plea for mercy, he'd agreed. His bargain had lasted from the moment I finally escaped that blood-stained cellar to the present day. Unfortunately, a greater evil existed in the world. Working before the sun rose? Worse than a lake of fire.

Riley ate only apples for breakfast. Falconi had snatched one of his kids' Lunchables. He carefully layered the fake pepperoni on the cardboard crust and gave me a wink.

"Got a job for you, McKenna."

I needed another roll in the sheets before I'd be able to fake a pleasant smile.

"Thought you guys were taking the lead on the Abbott murder?" The question was probably too hostile. They didn't notice.

"Your sergeant told us we could grab you for any odd task that might help the investigation," Falconi said.

"And now Adamski owes me another lunch."

"What?"

"Nothing."

Riley handed me a folder. "Feel like playing with the big boys today?"

"And here I thought I'd have to amuse myself with paperwork all morning," I said. "What's so tough you two strapping men can't handle it?"

Falconi took the bait with a chuckle. "We found our John Doe. His name is Alan Henry. Twenty-five years old. No priors. Squeaky clean."

"How's a guy like that just suddenly snap?"

Riley shook his head. "Got a more important question—*where's his wife?*"

"You lost Mrs. Henry?"

Falconi inhaled his fake pizza, nearly dripping the sauce over his papers. "This is a good job for you. Find his wife. Someone's gotta notify her."

"Oh." I bit my lip before saying something distinctly unprofessional. "So, you want me to spend *my* morning tracking a woman you can't find so *I* can be the one to give her the news that her husband wasn't just an adulterer but also a homicidal maniac?"

"That's the plan." Riley rocked his chair and pushed a photograph towards me. "We found this in his Bible. It's a picture of his wife, apparently. Old picture, I'd guess. Maybe from when they were younger. Says Rachel Goodman on the back."

The scribble did read as *Rachel Goodman*, but it was wrong.

That gnawing twist in my gut returned. I stared at the photograph, studying her hair, her eyes, the little scar that sliced through her left eyebrow.

"This isn't his wife," I said.

"Don't tell me he has *another* mistress." Falconi swore. "This guy thumps more than his Bible."

"Good reason to head back to church," Riley said.

"Bless me Father, for I have sinned."

I lunged over Riley, stealing his keyboard to bring up our database. He grumbled, but he entered his login so I could scan the files for a face so familiar it curdled my breakfast.

"This isn't his wife." I scrolled through the listings. "I know this girl."

"How?" Riley batted my arm away and tried to take control of his mouse.

"She's one of my runaways."

Falconi sat on the edge of the desk. "What the hell is a runaway doing married to this creep?"

The information flashed on the screen. Her picture followed. The same brown eyes, harshly angled eyebrows, and slightly gap-toothed smile. Alan Henry's photo was definitely her, but it was older than anything her parents had. Someone had taken it *after* she ran away.

"This is Nina Martin. She went missing in 2014 at the age of twelve, was gone for two years, and just came home."

"Jesus, she's *fourteen*?" Riley grabbed the picture. "Looks older."

"Looks tired," Falconi said. "Do you know where to find her? Is she with her family?"

"No. That's the problem. Nina went missing again *three days ago*. I've got Amber Alerts issued. Damn it! I *knew* there was a reason she ran! He must have taken her."

"Has anything come in on the alert?" Riley asked.

"No." I tucked her picture into my pocket. "It doesn't matter. I'll find her."

"How?" Falconi shrugged. "You've been looking for her for two years. If she's gone—"

"They're never *gone*. A person is easy to find—but the reason they run? That's the challenge." I stared at the entry in the database, a new fire burning deep in me. "Why did Alan Henry have a picture of a *fourteen-year-old girl* in his wallet?"

Falconi's voice darkened. "You know the answer to that. The question is…where do you find her?"

Two years working with sexual assaults left little to my imagination anymore. I hated the thought.

"If Nina Martin was involved with Alan Henry…he's the reason she's disappeared."

Chapter Five

You know what curiosity did to the cat.
Still want to know why I've chosen you?
-Him

"This can't be happening again."

Nina Martin's distraught mother tore her Kleenex to shreds. None of them were tear-stained. After so many years, so many unanswered questions, so many heartaches, I had no idea how she kept breathing, let alone weeping.

What should have been a gentle thirty-five years of life had instead greyed her hair and skin. Her eyes puffed, perpetually swollen. She tugged at dulled, untreated brunette hair with chubby fingers. Nina had been my first Missing Persons case two years ago. I remembered a different Emily. One thinner. Prettier. More stable.

"She just came *home*." Emily lowered her head into her hands. "Why? Why would she leave? Where would she go? This is her *home*."

Nina's father, Ryan Martin, sat silently in his Lazy Boy. The beige chair was broken, stained with a discolored ring from where a beer can usually set on the arm. Ten in the morning wasn't a good time to be drinking around the police, but no one faulted him. Two years ago, he'd been the first suspect in Nina's disappearance. The suspicion and investigation wore him out. He lost most of hair after Nina left. Nearly lost the marriage too. Counseling helped, but no one had answers to this.

Usually, teenage runaways split because of abuse or mistreatment. Often an untreated mental health condition explained reckless decisions. Not in this case. Plus, Nina was a good student, had dozens of friends, a solid church community, and a good relationship with both parents.

Two years ago, Nina had simply vanished. And now? She'd done it again.

"She wasn't the same." Ryan forced his words through a clenching throat.

"Don't." Emily snapped. "Don't say it."

"Jesus woman, you know it. I know it." He pointed at me. "Even Detective McKenna knew something was wrong with that girl."

"She's not *that girl!*" Emily stood. Half a dozen tissues tumbled from her lap. She wound herself in a faded blue robe, twisting her hands in the belt. "She is our daughter!"

"She wasn't the same." Ryan sipped his beer. "Right, Detective?"

I hedged. "You knew her best."

"Yeah. I thought I did."

"Was she traumatized?" I'd kept my notes from the interview with the girl after she'd returned. I'd underlined, circled, and drew arrows to the word in my notes. Whatever had happened, wherever she had gone, the experience had silenced her. "The psychologist told you to expect it."

"It didn't get better." Emily groped behind her, feeling her way to the couch without looking. "We thought...we'd give her time. Maybe she'd talk to the pastor or...or the therapist. But the more we pushed..."

"She ran," Ryan said. "Shouldn't have tried so damned hard."

And I was just as guilty. Too many calls. Too many questions.

I should have known better. No person—abducted or coerced—was *right* after returning home. Even once they could fake it, even when they had everyone convinced and answered the right questions, every memory hurt. A slice of the past cut even deeper than the hell they'd lived through. Remembering was a self-inflicted abuse. Nina couldn't face it. So she ran.

"She was so scared," Emily murmured. "She'd jump when the phone rang. Flinch at loud noises."

Ryan's sigh bit the air as the breath passed through reluctant lungs. I had him pegged as an old-school quiet type. The steel mill guy who worked long hours, came home, and did his damnedest to find a moment's peace before crashing at night to start the dirty monotony all over again.

"People came to visit," he said. "Family. Friends. She knew them. Should have remembered them."

"But?" I prompted.

Emily answered while he took another swig of his beer. "The doorbell...stressed her. She was so afraid of people coming to the house that...we told the family to stop coming after she kept getting sick. It just wore her out."

I remembered those symptoms. PSTD was an unforgiving bitch. It wasn't the diagnosis any parent wanted for their child either, especially a girl who refused to talk about what had happened to her. And the parade of well-wishers nebbing in her life? It didn't help her heal. Probably only made her more overwhelmed, more ashamed.

The job didn't make me an optimist. I thought the worst. Heroin, prostitution, rape were only my first assumptions.

But at least now I had a new angle.

Alan Henry.

And I'd find out why the murdering bastard kept a picture of a fourteen-year-old girl.

I opened my laptop—impersonal, but I typed faster than I could write. "I'll be asking you a lot of questions you've already answered. Be patient and give me as much detail as you can. I have a new lead, but I need your help."

Emily leaned forward, gripping a fresh tissue. "Anything, Detective. Just bring her home again."

No family wanted to relive the worst day of their life, but neither of them had ever mentioned Alan Henry to me. Either they had no idea about their daughter's relationships, or they had lied.

I hated ignorance, but I preferred it to deception.

"What happened the day Nina disappeared?" I asked.

"Which time?" Emily swallowed. "The first time she ran…or after she was kidnapped?"

The word was a sucker punch. "*Kidnapped?* Did something happen? Did someone call? You didn't say anything about a kidnapping—"

"What other explanation is there?" Emily spat. "She came *home.* She was here, with us. We fed her. Clothed her. She was warm and safe and she knew she didn't have to tell us a thing. We *loved* her! We just wanted to *love* her." Emily rubbed her eyes, smearing more mascara than tears that couldn't fall. "And now she's gone again. No note. Not even a goodbye. Something must have happened to her..."

Or someone scared her enough to run again.

No one knew where Nina had been, and that made coming home that much harder for her. If she was scared for herself or her parents' lives she might have done anything to escape.

"Walk me through the night of her disappearance," I said.

Emily bit her lip. "I...I don't know what time it was. I was asleep. I checked on her before bed, but I didn't think to look in on her when I got up to use the bathroom. I didn't want to disturb her..."

Ryan nodded. "She kicked out the screen in her room. Your team said so. It was pushed out, not pulled."

"That doesn't mean anything." Emily hissed. "Maybe someone was in the house—maybe they threatened her!"

I'd taken the initial report when Nina went missing again. Nina's own shoe made the imprint on the screen we found in the bushes outside the house. With no other forced entry into the home, and no calls made to the house that night, I'd believed Nina left under her own power. Whether she was in her right mind or not was a question only she could answer.

"What time did you notice she had gone?"

"Around ten the next morning," Emily said. "I wanted to make her pancakes. Pancakes are her favorite. With chocolate chips. I make strawberry syrup from scratch. She'd eat it up with a spoon."

I hated the pain in her voice, but I couldn't get distracted or sentimental. "Did you notice any changes in her behavior?"

Ryan scoffed. Emily shushed him again, but he didn't listen.

"She was *completely* changed," he said. "That girl...she wasn't ours anymore."

Emily gave a soft sob. "She was still our little girl!"

I interrupted the fight as gently as I could. "What exactly was different with her?"

"*Everything.*" It was a mother's betrayal, but even Emily couldn't deny it. "She spoke differently—more formal. Pleases and thank-yous, sirs and ma'ams. Almost..."

He snorted. "Submissive."

"*Ryan!*"

"That's what she was! Not speaking unless spoken to. Not looking you in the eye. She was like a beaten dog begging for scraps."

"I thought she was just polite," Emily said. "Like she was scared. She didn't want to make any fuss. But it was more than that. She...she used to love all those pre-teen bands. Taylor Swift and One Direction and whatever jelly belly music was on the radio. Once she got back, she pulled the posters down. And then she only listened to hymns."

Not too many children found God on the streets.

Most times, the Devil got them first.

"She wasn't a bad kid before," Ryan said. "But when she came back, it was like someone had taken our daughter and scrubbed her brain with soap. She wasn't just wholesome or polite. She was..."

"Vacant," Emily whispered. "What's the opposite of *corrupted*? I've heard so many stories from other parents of missing kids—they said their girls would act out, would be promiscuous, would be *troubled*."

Ryan frowned. "Nina came home out of the *blue*. Knocked on the door. Called me *sir*. Asked to come inside like this wasn't the same

51

house she'd run in and out her entire life. She wouldn't eat junk food. Refused to watch TV. She never listened to her music."

He abruptly stopped. I gave him a moment to piece together what he wanted to say.

He apologized. "She had a Bible."

Emily breathed her husband's name. "Detective, you know us. We're good people. We're just not…active. You understand?"

The Catholic guilt took root in me, and I figured one day I'd turn into a pillar of salt. Despite what the priests would say—what my priest said—not everyone would find *answers* in the church. But to go from non-practicing to devout? One hell of a change.

"I asked her where she learned these things," Emily said. "I thought she'd found a church group or someone to take her in while she was away. But she never said."

"Do you have her Bible?"

Emily shook her head. "No. She took it. The only thing she had with her when she left. She didn't even pack her clothes this time. It was like…"

"She had somewhere she could go," Ryan said.

And I knew just where she'd end up. I broached the subject gently. "Did she ever talk to you about a Rachel Goodman?"

Emily glanced at her husband. "No. Was that one of her friends?"

"It was an alias she used while she was away from home. Has anyone attempted to call or contact you about a Rachel Goodman?"

Her shoulders slumped. "No. I've never heard that name. But she didn't tell me anything…her own *mother*."

And she had reason for that. Nina wouldn't have hid anything from her mother out of spite or hatred. It was because she loved her that she'd stayed quiet. Emily wouldn't understand it.

My mother never understood it.

Twelve-year-old Nina's picture was centered over the mantel. It wasn't recent—but they had nothing recent from her. For some reason, Alan Henry was the only one with a photograph of Nina at fourteen years old. The implications sickened me.

"Did your daughter ever mention a man named Alan Henry?"

Emily rapidly slapped her husband's arm. "*Yes!* That's the man Nina talked about. The one who helped her!"

Ross straightened. "Yeah. Alan Henry. I asked if he was a cop or something. She said he…watched over her."

The words hung in silence. I wished they hadn't curdled my stomach.

"Were they friends?" I asked.

Emily shrugged. "She wouldn't say, but she spoke his name *fondly*."

I hated what I had to ask. "Were they romantically involved?"

"Romantically?" Emily gave a weepy laugh. "She's fourteen."

"Did she ever say anything about Alan Henry being her husband?"

"Her…her *husband?*" Ryan's beer tipped, spilling on the carpet. "She's a child! She's not *married*."

"Ryan…" Emily's whisper was a crush of pain. "*Ryan…*"

"She's a child. She's not *involved* with anyone. If anything ,she got taken advantage of on the streets. Christ only knows what she went through, but you're asking if she *willingly* gave herself to someone?"

"Ryan!" Emily's voice rose, a heretical screech to a woman who hardly had the courage to get out of bed every morning. "The ring on her finger…"

We quieted. Ryan shook his head. "No. No, don't even think that."

"She wore a ring when she came home!" Emily pointed to her left ring finger. "A plain band. She wouldn't take it off. I asked her, but she just said that it was *hers*. Oh, my God. It's not possible. How could she get married if she was that young?"

"You'd have to consent," I said. "Legally, she couldn't marry without your approval."

"But this Alan Henry? He sounded…older?"

"He's in his mid-twenties."

"Oh God. Oh, no." Emily shook her head. "She left us to go to a pedophile?"

Ryan pointed a shaking finger at me. "Tell me you know where this son of a bitch is. Tell me, or so help me God—"

"We know," I said. Not that it would help anyone. "We found Alan Henry dead yesterday morning. He committed suicide after murdering a woman we assume was his lover."

Emily nearly fell from the couch. "Oh God. *Nina?*"

The only good news I could offer. "It wasn't Nina. She was a twenty-eight-year old woman from Lawrenceville. Cora Abbott. Do you know the name?"

Emily couldn't speak. Her cries muffled into the knitted afghan she'd dragged off the couch.

Ryan answered for her. "No. We don't know her."

"Was it…was that the woman who helped her?" Emily sniffled. "The one…"

"No." Ryan helped her to the couch. "That was…Ellen? No. Eve."

I jotted the name down. "Who was Eve?"

Emily shook her head again. "You don't understand, Detective. We only got bits and pieces of information out of her. She only mentioned names when she…when she wasn't paying attention. She'd say something about Alan in passing. Or about Eve…she liked Eve. I thought it sounded like…"

"Like what?"

"Like Eve was a mother figure. Someone who'd cared about her."

"This is good," I reassured her. "All these names. I can use them."

"What about Alan Henry?"

"Homicide is investigating him now," I said. "They're looking for his family and friends. The name Eve might help us locate someone who knows what happened to Nina or where she might have gone. We'll find her, or she'll find us. She's come home before."

Emily sunk deeper into the couch. "It wasn't by choice. She wasn't happy to be here. I think…"

She was looking for a chance to leave?

I changed the subject. "Can you think of anything else unusual that's happened? Strangers lurking around the home? Threats or times you felt uneasy?"

"No," Ryan said. "Nothing like that. Just the usual bad luck."

"What sort of bad luck?"

"My credit card got stolen, but we didn't think anything of it."

I frowned. "When did this happen?"

"A couple days ago. The day after Nina left. With all the fuss, we didn't notice anything was wrong until I got an email about the purchases."

"What did they buy?"

"Nothing to do with Nina."

Desperate times called for desperate leads. "Anything can help."

Emily shrugged. "It's not like they bought anything extravagant. I told Ryan not to report it."

"*Why?*"

"Everything was purchased from a Babies R Us," she said. "And that's all they used it for. It was a lot of money, five hundred dollars, but the person hasn't used it since. Seemed cruel to report it."

"*Cruel?*" I blinked. "Why?"

"It was all *baby* stuff, Detective. We thought…I thought it was a first-time mother who got ahold of his card. If the thief bought all electronics or something, we'd have stopped it. But whoever stole the card obviously needed help." Her voice weakened. "And I know what it's like for a mother to be scared and worried for her child."

I slammed the lid shut on my laptop, pitching it into the bag. Emily and Ryan stood with me, confused. I hated what I thought—and I hated even more than I knew I was right.

The poor family didn't understand—either willfully ignorant or completely naïve.

I almost envied that obliviousness, but then no one would be able to bring their daughter home.

"I need to contact that Babies R Us," I said. "And I need to do it now."

"Why?" Emily demanded. "What about Nina?"

"Nina's the one who stole your card."

"Why would she take our credit card?"

Fourteen was too young for this.

Too young to run. Too young to hide.

And too goddamned young to handle it on her own.

"Nina is pregnant."

Chapter Six

You wish you didn't know the truth.
But where's the fun in that?
-Him

But where's the fun in that? -Him

The clerk at Babies R Us didn't remember Nina Martin, but I hadn't expected miracles. Dozens of pregnant women waddled the aisles every day. The ones ready to pop might have attracted attention, but Nina was young. I doubted she was even showing. She'd have passed unnoticed.

Especially since she didn't give her real name.

Nina Martin hadn't made any purchases, but Rachel Goodman cleared out the store.

The delivery was made last week, but, like everything else with this case, it didn't make sense.

Nina had chosen to nest in a city well outside of Pittsburgh. The community of New Castle wasn't a fantastic neighborhood to raise a family, but it did a damn good job of hiding people who didn't want to be found.

The steel crash in the eighties devastated most towns surrounding the knot of the three rivers. Like a lot of the littler towns, New Castle never forgot. The town stayed in a stasis of times past. The only revitalization came from a new Giant Eagle grocery store, a Sheetz gas station, and all the soup and salad anyone would want from the local Eat N Park. The homes were old, the people tired, and, according to the FBI, the area had the distinction of being the second most dangerous city in Pennsylvania.

Not a place for Nina.

I parked outside a tiny house—more collection of timbers than anything resembling the sweet family home with picket fence and pretty garden Nina had left. I took careful steps over the half-rotten porch and knocked on the door.

Nothing.

If she had run, I didn't expect her to welcome me with opened arms.

"Nina! It's Detective McKenna from the Pittsburgh police." I pounded again. "Remember me? We talked two weeks ago with your mom and dad."

Silence. And not the good kind where you could hear someone listening back.

"Nina!" I pounded harder. The wood rattled against the frame. "Open the door!"

"*Lady!*" An irritated man hollered at me. "You break that door, and I'm suing!"

I turned, greeting a huffing, puffing man as his robe began to fail. He mercifully restrung the belt before I had to arrest him for indecent exposure—though, judging by the quick flash he awarded me, it'd be the proudest moment in his little life.

He hauled his pot belly between me and the door and pointed a sausage finger in my face.

"What the hell do you think you're doing? This is my property. You can't just bash your way into it."

My turn to flash him, but the badge carried a bit more heft. Sufficiently cowed, he apologized with a quick wave.

"Sorry. Just protecting my rental."

"And the tenants?"

"Yeah. Sure."

Right. "Are you renting this home to a girl by the name of Nina Martin?"

"Who?"

"Nina." I pulled her picture from my coat and handed it to him. "Recognize her?"

"Yeah, but that ain't Nina. That's Rachel."

"Rachel Goodman?"

"Yeah."

"How long has she lived here?"

"About…three months? Maybe?" He fidgeted on the porch, stomping his slippered feet against the cold. "She okay? I didn't get this month's rent yet. Figured I'd cut her a break since she was so young—"

I frowned. "More than *young*. She's *fourteen*."

A dozen guilty realizations flooded his expression, and he tightened his robe a bit more. "*Fourteen*? Nah. You got it wrong."

"Listen…" I prompted him with a wiggle of my eyebrows.

"Frank. Frank Delain."

"Look, Frank. The kid's fourteen. A minor can't legally sign a rental agreement, and I got a feeling you didn't ask for ID when you let her move in. So, let's do it the easy way. Let me in the apartment."

"Why?" He bristled. "I know my rights. You got a warrant?"

"This girl has been reported missing by the Pittsburgh Police Department. There's an Amber Alert out for her return."

"Shit."

"And a man she's associated with just murdered a woman in the city before taking his own life." I frowned. "There's reason to believe they're married."

"Wait, wait, wait." Frank rubbed his face, his hand not stopping until it brushed into the receding gray around his temples. "Alan? You tellin' me *Alan* murdered a woman?" His voice lowered to a hiss. "*You tellin' me they're married?*"

"Do you know Alan?"

"Know him? Christ. He paid me the first two month's rent! I had no idea they were married!"

They weren't. Not legally. "They're involved. Now he's dead, and you haven't seen or heard from Nina…Rachel? She hasn't contacted her family in two weeks, but I know furniture for the nursery was delivered here last Friday."

"Holy Christ—she's *pregnant?*"

I didn't have the patience for this. "Let me save you the hundred bucks. Unlock the door before I put my boot through it."

"You wouldn't…"

I sniffed the air. "Smells like smoke to me."

"Fine. Just wait." His face shaded a shamed red as he hunted through his pockets for the key. "Can't believe she's pregnant."

"Really?" I hardened my voice. "Got a reason to be worried?"

"I never touched her. Never did anything wrong. Honest. Couldn't have." He fiddled with the key, his hands shaking too hard to get it in the lock. "She was…*weird*."

"How so?"

Wrong key. He fumbled with the ring and it clattered to the porch. I resisted the urge to bust the damn thing in.

"Quiet. Too quiet. She wouldn't look anyone in the eye. Hell, she wouldn't talk to me unless Alan was here. It was like…" He shrugged at me. "She was afraid of men."

My heart twisted, but I'd expected that. Two years was a long time to be away from home and more than enough opportunity to find trouble. But she could still change it. She could go home. Face what happened. And her family would help her—and her baby.

The lock clicked open. Frank gestured for me to head inside.

I gave it one final knock. "Nina?"

Nothing.

Fine. We'd play it her way.

"Rachel? It's the police." I pushed open the door. "You're not in trouble. I just want to talk—"

That stench.

I gagged. So did Frank.

The reeking secret of death lingered the house.

I tasted it in my throat, but death had a funny way of tasting a lot like my own horrified bile.

Frank retched in the doorway. "Oh, God. What the hell is that?"

Nothing that should have ever happened to this girl. Not now. Not once she found her way home and had been *safe*.

My hand poised over my gun, but it was too late for any heroics. I knew what happened before I peeked into the kitchen to see for myself how many lives Alan Henry had ruined.

Nina Martin stared lifelessly at the floor, a bullet hole through her back.

And like that, I'd lost another chance to save a missing person.

Her blonde hair was matted with the pooling blood, surrounding her body in a halo of crimson. She'd been dead for nearly two days, left to die alone, cold and scared. She'd been running before she died. An overturned chair lay near her body, and her dinner spilled from the crash.

SpeghettiO's.

Because it wasn't enough of a crime that someone had stolen her childhood. He had to take that last bit of innocence.

Why had she run away from home for this place? Her parents' house was warm and clean. White carpets and pictures on the fridge. Schedules posted over the alcove, right where they kicked off their shoes, so everyone knew their loved ones appointments for the day.

Nina died in a kitchen with a stove that only had one functional burner. The cabinets sat off-kilter on their frames, and the limestone encrusted faucet dripped a coppery tinted water.

The appliances rusted. The curtains faded. The heat wasn't on, and the single pane windows let the cold slip under the sills.

Nina was murdered in a slum. Killed by a man who had lured her away from a perfect home to inflict whatever hell he could on an innocent girl. It wasn't enough to kill himself, and Cora Abbott didn't sate his lust for blood. The monster had to kill a *child* before ridding the world of his filth.

I surveyed the room, mourning how the blood had dried through the kitchen, spilling into a heat register before pooling under the fridge and trailing beneath a highchair—brand new, the tray still wrapped in plastic.

Oh no.

In the sink, three sippy cups, pink and purple, sat out to dry.

Next to it was a handful of plastic toys, rattles and noisemakers, sitting on a towel. Clean. Ready to be used.

My pulse surged.

I didn't want to think it. Didn't want to even consider it.

But the truth terrified me more than discovering Nina's corpse.

I sprinted from the kitchen. The living room was still pristine, untouched. And in the corner…a bouncy chair perfect for a *toddler.*

Nina hadn't bought furniture for a newborn. She hadn't run because she was pregnant.

She'd already had the baby.

I raced to the stairs, tripping over the first as I launched up the steps. Old wood creaked under my feet, squealing as I burst down the hall, checking the first door. Just a bedroom, bare save for a few of the Babies R Us boxes waiting to be broken down. I turned, rushing to the hall. The bathroom door slammed against the wall too hard, rattling her razor and toothpaste off the sink. The drinking glass toppled too, shattered on the tile floor.

The crash echoed.

But no baby cried.

I race to the last door, but I nearly retched before knocking it open. Adults were one thing. Kids another.

But a *baby*?

I didn't know anyone on the force who'd have the courage to walk into that room unless they hoped beyond hope to save someone.

The door creaked open. I held my breath as I crossed inside.

The nursery was untouched. Pretty, despite the curling wall paper and thread-bare carpeting. Nina had tried to make it look like a home. A changing table was pushed against the wall. A white crib nestled cozy in the corner, next to a picturesque rocking chair.

That must have been where she held the baby.

I bit my lip. No father could do this to their child. Only a monster could murder so many, so close to him, without *reason*.

I forced the step towards the crib.

But inside was just as horrifying.

I found *nothing*.

No blood. No body.

No baby.

The bedding wasn't even wrinkled. In fact, it looked...freshly made.

I spun around. The changing table had an unused trash can next to it. Empty. No diapers. The baby's supplies—diapers, creams, lotions, baby wash—all untouched.

Unopened.

It didn't look like a child had ever been in this house.

What the hell was going on?

I rushed back to Frank, wheezing in panic on the stairs.

"Any other rooms?" I asked.

"No. Well, the basement, but it's full of boxes. Is that a..." He stared into the pink-tinted room. "A nursery?"

I gritted my teeth, facing him with a frantic growl as I grabbed my cell to call in the murder. "Didn't you know Nina had a baby?"

"A *baby*?" Frank shook his head so hard I could hear his teeth chatter. "She didn't have a baby!"

"What do you call that?" I pointed to the nursery.

"She didn't say she had a kid with her! It's not on the lease!"

"Don't lie to me, Frank."

"I swear! She never mentioned a kid! I even had to fix a busted shower head for her. I never saw a baby. No crying. No nothing!"

This didn't make sense. "You had to see *something*."

"I'm telling you! Nina lived here *alone*. There wasn't a baby!"

I ran a hand through my hair, staring at the nursery, the crib, the toys. Someone had bought toys and supplies for an older baby. Not a newborn. Six months? Twelve?

So where was the child?

Nina's bedroom was the only messy room in the house. The bed hadn't been made before she died. I didn't touch it. I'd order forensics to check it—to make sure the son of a bitch hadn't raped her before murdering her in cold blood.

But nothing in the room said *fourteen-year-old girl.* No pictures hung on the walls. No knick-knacks or anything personal decorated the top of her dresser. The closet was only filled with dresses. I passed through them, one by one. Nothing stylish, that was certain. Paisley print. Long sleeves. Almost like they were...

Hand-stitched?

But weirdest of all was Nina's newest hobby. I crossed to her nightstand, picking up the needle, thread, and embroidery hoop. The project wasn't finished, but her needlepoint seemed perfect, not a stitch out of place.

She'd used dark brown thread to craft the trunk of a tree and decorated the inside with lighter thread, forming two hearts within the wood. Inside, she'd written names.

Rachel. Jonah.

And in the green leaves of the tree, sprouting from the apparent love of the parents, a little girl's name scrawled in pin-point needlework.

Rebecca.

The baby's name was Rebecca.

But who the hell was Jonah?

And what had he done with the baby?

Chapter Seven

Maybe this is hell. Or maybe the pain has driven you insane.
Maybe it's a little of both?
-Him

"Jonah Goodman." Falconi slapped a folder on my desk. "Mother-fucking-Alan-Henry's real name is Jonah-*fucking*-Goodman."

This perked me up more than my half-drunk coffee and untouched Chipotle bean burrito.

Finally, something I could work with!

"Does everyone in this case have a fake name?" I asked. "Nina Martin apparently thinks she's *Rachel Goodman*. Jonah Goodman uses the assumed name of *Alan Henry*."

"Gonna find out." Falconi twirled his car keys. "Riley and I are notifying the family."

"All of them?"

"I guess his *wife* already knows he's human slime."

My stomach pitted. I didn't let it show. "Oh, she knew. That man took advantage of her long before he ever killed her. And the baby—"

"*Is* there a baby?"

I groaned. "Not you too."

"Just saying, McKenna. No one ever saw a kid. And if she was only *now* buying supplies for it...?"

I gritted my teeth. "Leave the missing persons to me?"

Falconi winked. "Promise to find them alive this time?"

Not funny. I didn't have enough patience or coffee for any of them today. "Go bother the family. Let me find this baby."

My middle finger mercifully recoiled to my fist before it caused any incidents or revealed me to be too unladylike. He knocked twice on my desk before leaving, calling to Riley in the hall with the address.

Forest County?

Goddamn. Jonah and his *wife* died a long way from home.

I returned to my computer, guzzling the coffee, staring at a screen that refused to give me the answers I needed.

But I'd stay here all night if that's what it took.

Someone knew where that baby was.

And whoever did could tell us why Jonah Goodman AKA Alan Henry murdered two innocent women before taking his own life.

But three hours and no leads later, my cell vibrated next to my ear.

I jerked awake, wiping my chin before the report on Nina Martin/Rachel Goodman got covered in drool. Not the DNA anyone wanted to find.

James's name flashed on the phone. Two years ago, he'd promised he wouldn't be the type to constantly check up on me. And he wasn't, though on the days he was out of town, he always had something important to tell me every night around eight.

I didn't need protecting from the shadows anymore. But I also didn't mind hearing his voice. And, as FBI consultant to the department, he had a hell of a lot of insight to our cases. I'm sure the call was purely professional.

"Hey." A single word from him was soothing, like a mug of hot cocoa. No wonder people so easily spilled their hearts and sins to him. "Any luck?"

"If by *luck* you mean *headaches*, then yes."

"That bad?"

The click of laptop keys chattered over the connection. He needed a quieter computer, but he liked his. The screen was big, and the resolution sharp. He could still see the letters in the document crisp and clear, without fiddling too much with the font size or brightness settings. The doctors warned that'd come in time. Sooner, if he didn't stop straining his eyes by working so late.

The computer was supposed to be off by eight. The TV by ten. Despite being a psychologist and attending medical school, James still thought he knew better than the doctors.

...Or he wanted to do all he could for the bureau and his cases before his vision forced him out.

I tucked the reports and papers away, staring at the picture I'd taken of Nina's nursery. "I've never had a case this weird before."

"No one has any information?"

"I talked to the Martins. Nina didn't mention having a boyfriend, let alone a *baby* with this man. The landlord never saw a child in the house. I've searched public records under the name Rebecca Martin and Rebecca Goodman—there's nothing about this baby. No medical records. No social security information. It's like the child doesn't exist."

Only James could pose a question so gently, so innocently, it was as if the question came from inside my own head, my own conscience. I hated it, but it was a damn good talent for a criminal profiler.

"Are you sure there is a child?"

"She had a nursery. Crib and changing tables and diapers. Clothes in the closet, and bottles washed and ready to go. But…"

"But?"

My pen blotted a dark stain in the corner of my notepad. I gave it a good push before answering. "I had the forensics team comb the place, hoping to find some of the baby's DNA just in case there's a hit somewhere."

"And?"

He made me say it. I sighed. "The only prints and hair in that house belong to Nina. There's not even one slobber covered teething ring to help ID the baby."

"So, what do you think?"

I'd lost count of how many times James had ever asked me that question. He'd always said people revealed more to themselves than to others. But the day had tapped me out. I had no idea.

"You tell me. Expert opinion."

"You know the answer, London." He paused, giving me time to answer. But no sense saying what he wanted to hear—not when I knew it wasn't true. "Nina Martin ran away from home just after her twelfth birthday. She was lost for two years. You don't know where she went, who she was with, or what happened to her. Suddenly, she reappears with an entirely new personality. Her parents hardly recognize her, and, after two weeks of abnormal behavior, she runs again—even though they had provided her with a home, safety, food, everything."

And there *had* to be an explanation. The most obvious one.

"She had to get the baby," I said. "She left to find the baby."

"*Or...*" James let the word hang. "She'd experienced such a traumatic event with this Alan Henry—"

"Jonah Goodman."

"...He has another identity?"

"Told you it was strange."

"Well, her time with Jonah Goodman was frightening enough, traumatic enough, and painful enough, that she invented a world in which she would be safe."

"I don't believe it."

His voice warmed. Damn me for trusting his instincts. How often could one man be right?

"The child might be a delusion invented by Nina to shield her from the intense trauma inflicted on her within Goodman's care. Maybe something originally manifested in her mind at twelve, and that's what caused her to run away. Without proper treatment and care, the symptoms became more severe. Goodman prayed on a weak, mentally ill girl, and she reacted to the abuse by fabricating a more perfect life for herself—one in which she had this child."

But the statistics didn't lie. "Childhood schizophrenia is rare."

"It still happens."

"You didn't see the nursery, James. This girl put so much work into it. She had everything—things I didn't even know a kid would need. She must have had experience with a kid. She bought what was necessary."

"That type of delusion might harbor obsessive tendencies—say studying childcare and self-help parenting books."

"Didn't find any in the house."

"You didn't find a baby either."

I rubbed my temples. The station went quiet after eight o'clock, and most had gone home, crossing by my desk on the way out. Great. How many people had caught me sleeping on my files? I'd either look dedicated to the job or obsessed with the case. Dedicated was good…unless it antagonized the other officers for not working as hard. But obsessed pinned me as unreliable and untrustworthy. Just another scale on the balance of life that tipped the wrong way.

"You sound tired," James said. "You should head home."

"What about you?"

"What about me?"

"When are you coming home?"

He paused. "Depends. Which home do you mean? Mine or yours?"

Up to his old tricks. "I meant *Pittsburgh.*"

He hummed. "I could make it back quicker if I knew I had someone waiting for me."

He was the only one I'd ever waited for—and I still wasn't sure what that meant. "Then I guess I'll see you soon."

He didn't say those three words, but I felt them. "Try to stay out of trouble."

"I don't find it. It finds me."

"That's what I worry about." He murmured my name. More words unsaid. "I'll see you soon. Go home. Get some sleep."

I promised him I would, though, for some reason, I never slept as well without him in the bed next to me.

Strange how I could go from wanting nobody to needing a certain somebody. He'd love that I was getting soft.

Maybe I did need sleep. Fair enough. It'd been days since I had a full-night's sleep, and the fatigue burning my eyes started to seem familiar. I gave them a rub before pushing away from the desk and grabbing my things.

My desk line rang before I made it to the door. I hesitated, hand on the knob.

Fine. So I was obsessed.

But I wasn't about to leave the station if someone needed me.

I dropped my stuff in the hall and raced back to the phone, catching it on the seventh ring.

"*Detective McKenna!*" The panicked voice screamed over the connection. "Please help me!"

I stiffened. The fear leeched through the call, chilling me from the hand holding the receiver to my frantically thudding heart. I pressed the receiver hard against my ear, straining to hear.

I recognized that voice.

That desperation.

"*Louisa?*" I asked. "Is that you?"

"You have to help! He found me!"

"Who? Who found you?"

"He's here! Please! You have to help! I don't know what he's going to do! He knows I'm looking for Anna!"

My stomach rolled. "Where are you?"

"At home! He's outside now! He has a gun—"

A shot fired.

And the line went dead.

Chapter Eight

There's a subtle difference between charred and well-done.
You'll know it when you feel it.
-Him

Fifteen seconds could mean life or death during a gunfight.

Fifteen *minutes* passed before my Crown Vic skidded into Louisa's driveway.

I radioed to dispatch that I'd arrived, but my backup had an ETA of five minutes.

We didn't have that time. From the road, a telltale orange glow flickered from inside. The flames had already spread inside her home.

Christ, what had he done? Was I too late?

Had he already killed her and set the fire to cover the crime?

I parked, throwing open the car's door for cover.

No shots fired. No movement shifted from the exterior of the house.

I kept low, darting over the loose gravel on the secondary street. This area of Braddock was old, and the brick houses practically leaned on each other against the slope of the front yards. The old company homes had been here since the twenties, long enough for the orange brick to fade to brown, the chain link fences to rust, and the darkness to hide any number of men waiting for a kill.

Louisa's gate swung wide and got stuck in the mud. I darted up the crumbling steps. The front door popped open, trapped in a tug-of-war between the cold January air and the swirling heat erupting from inside the house.

The front window's glass had shattered, shot out in a violent explosion of gunfire. The shards spilled over the porch letting the pouring smoke snake out of the house.

The gunshot was warning enough. But the fire?

Whoever did this desired more than a quick scare. He wanted her dead.

These old houses were built out of matchsticks and stuffed with asbestos. It wouldn't go up immediately, but it sure as hell would smolder.

I rushed to the door, coughing in the foul smoke creeping onto the porch.

Louisa screamed from inside.

Trapped.

"Fire on the scene!" I radioed to dispatch. "Single victim trapped inside. Officer responding, attempting rescue. Notify the fire department that I'm entering the structure."

This was a terrible, dangerous idea.

I sucked in a mouthful of the night's cold air before plunging into hell.

"*Louisa!*"

The fire raged, but it hadn't spread through the entire house. Black ravenous smoke churned in every corner, devouring the old wood. The spray of orange embers crashed through each room, leading the flames ever forward. The home wasn't safe. I shouldn't have gone inside.

"Louisa! Answer me!" The smoke suffocated my words. "Where are you?"

"*Help!*" Her scream came from the upstairs. "*London!*"

The fire clawed through the basement, but it hadn't burst to the upstairs yet. The toxic, agonizing smoke consumed what the flames did not. It coiled behind me, above me, *through me*, layering my body in soot, grime, and greasy regret for being so damn stupid.

I crawled to the stairs, coughing the grit from my mouth. Louisa wasn't in her bedroom. Or maybe she was. The smoke burned my eyes, and I squinted through the disaster that was her ransacked room. Bedding tossed off. Drawers ripped from the dresser. Clothing and paperwork littered the floor.

A crash echoed from the next room.

Running would save her. I only inhaled more acrid smoke. I fumbled into the bathroom, retched in the sink with a harsh cough, and grappled for any washcloth I could find in the dizzying mess of black-and-white tiles and too many hair care supplies plugged into the lone outlet above the pedestal vanity.

The wet cloth helped me to breathe, but we'd be dead in minutes if we didn't get out of the house and into fresh air. I crawled along the floor, diving inside the secondary bedroom.

Louisa had trashed it. She stumbled, hacking and crying, into an overturned box of old papers. She dove at the box and slashed it open with bleeding fingers. Her frantic cry no longer begged for help.

"I'm not going! I have to find it!" Her scream crackled like the roar of the fire downstairs. "Don't make me leave! I have to find it!"

And I wasn't above dragging her ass out. "Let's go!"

Louisa shrugged me away, pirouetting off balance and crashing into a twin bed loaded with more boxes and old clothing. She lunged for another banker's box, shrieking in joy as she grabbed a thick, leather-bound photo album. She pitched it into an open duffle bag and frantically crashed into another box.

"I can't go! I can't leave!" She fell to the floor, gasping for polluted air between sobs. "This is all I have left of her!"

"Of who?"

"*Anna!*" Louisa rushed for another picture—a framed image of two teenaged girls sitting on the curb of a brick road. "He took her from me once. Now he wants to destroy everything else!"

It must have been shock. She couldn't see the danger. "Your house is burning down! We have to get out *now!*"

"*But my pictures!*"

What about her *life?*

Her bag filled with bobbles and trinkets, framed photos and pictures. Nothing of her own. No purse. No cell.

No more time.

I zipped the duffle and tossed it over my shoulder. Louisa struggled, but a quick flick of my fingers to the pressure point on her wrist drove her to her knees.

"We're leaving! Stay close, and I'll keep you safe!"

"I can't believe he found me..." Tears streamed over her face, staining her smudged, soot covered cheeks in a river of revealed, creamy skin. "He's going to kill me."

And me too, if we were both tremendously unlucky.

The lights cut, the lines melted by the fire. It didn't matter. The hallway bled darkness from the thick smoke. Louisa gripped my hand, but I had her cling to my shirt instead. We'd lose each other in six inches of smoke.

If we didn't die first.

The barber carpets frayed under my hand. It'd torch like a tinderbox the instant the flames leapt from the stairs to the hall. I scurried along the wall, passing the damp cloth to Louisa as her coughing slowed her crawling and racked her with a consuming shudder.

A curtain of unrelenting smoke billowed up the stairs. Behind it, the flames surged along the banister. Heat blistered the paint on the walls. I leapt back, dodging a rush of superheated air.

And all I felt was my cold, shivering sweat.

We were too late.

The fire trapped us in the narrow hallway, wedged between two bedrooms and a bathroom. The attic wouldn't offer any refuge. And the creaking staircase was gone.

We didn't have much time. The house shuttered and groaned, threatening to combat the heat and fire the only way it knew how—collapsing down to smother the flames with hundred-year-old timbers and dust.

If we lived to see that.

Every breath laced with bitter ash. It'd only take one wrong gasp to split our lungs.

I pushed Louisa towards the side room. This was a different neighborhood, but the floor plan matched that of my childhood home. Mom hated the weather-worn windows and the tin porch roof—worried someone would scale the gutter, cross over the awning, and break in through the bedroom windows.

Just her luck—he'd grabbed me off the street.

The double-paned windows had clouded with the white film of age and decades of condensation. The smoke followed. Louisa shut the door. I shouted for her to block the bottom crack with whatever fabric she could find. The coughing ripped through my lungs, hurting just as much as breathing, as not breathing, as moving.

But I wasn't done fighting yet.

I fought against a window lock that hadn't been opened since the seventies. My fingers grasped for it, lost their grip, and slammed into the window frame. A nail splintered up the middle, but Louisa's frantic gasps hurt more. Hopefully my tears would wash away the burning soot before the smoky debris scratched my eyes as blind as James.

"It's stuck!" Louisa's screaming only hyperventilated her. "Oh, God. We're going to die!"

I shouldered the window. The glass didn't budge. Damn it. I grappled for my flashlight instead, smashing the base against the window's lock.

The hinge busted.

The window didn't move.

Screw it. My heart already thudded too hard, too fast, and too terrified to stay in the house any longer. I pushed Louisa away and grabbed the heaviest object I could find—an antique iron lamp with a decorative glass shade. I pitched the shade, yanked the cord from the wall, and crashed the base into the window.

The window shattered, but our fresh air didn't last. The smoke dragged outside, sucked up by the clean night's chill. The iron base made quick work of the remaining shards of glass still imbedded in the sill.

Louisa wasn't wearing shoes. It'd hurt, but at least she'd live. Coughing and gagging, I yanked a comforter off the bed and laid it over the glass. She bolted for the window.

The ominous orange glow consumed the stairs. The house groaned, and a new roar of heat and destruction sucked away my last bit of strength. I shoved her through the sill and dove outside, catching my slacks on a jagged piece of glass. The material tore over my thigh, but it hadn't cut me too deeply. I could still run.

We had no other choice.

Louisa clutched her bag and scampered over an unsteady awning, pieced together with more pine needles, leaves, and muck than solid aluminum. Our steps rattled the thin metal.

A surge of heat and burst of unrepentant flame launched out of the window. We dove over the awning, flailing backwards as the uneven, hail-dented rooftop offered no traction. Louisa tumbled. I leapt for her, grabbing her arm before she dropped ten feet onto the cement retaining wall.

A couple gulps of air, my strength returned. The flashing lights of my responding backup shaded the yard in reds and blues, just in time for the wail of the firetrucks to squeal from the station only a mile away. Louisa's bag fell first. I guided her to the edge, holding her arms as she shimmied off the gutter and lowered her down. She collapsed in a wailing heap entirely too close to the house.

I followed, grimacing as the roof's grime smeared over my legs, the cut, and the rest of my clothes. But I'd rather clean a wound than patch a burn.

I hung over the edge of the roof, took a breath, and hopped to the cement. Louisa reached for me, and I dragged her away from the house as she sputtered and threw up in the grass.

"He found us!" She repeated the terror-stricken cry over and over. "He found us!"

I held her close and radioed to the responding officers. Three squad cars pulled alongside the road, making way for the first of the fire trucks on scene. The firefighters burst into action, and I led Louisa to a nearby patrol car. They didn't have oxygen, but they tossed a blanket over her shivering frame.

"No one can get you now," I said. "You're safe."

"You don't understand!" Her eyes widened, the whites wide and frightened against the dark stain of soot on her face. "Detective, *this isn't my house!*"

My stomach clenched. "Who's is it?"

"This is my *parents'* house! They died six months ago. I've been trying to clean it out!" She grabbed my hand. "He's come back here!"

"Why?"

"Because of *Anna!*" Louisa stared at her family's burning home and clutched the bag of photographs to her chest. "He wants to destroy everything about her. He'd make us forget she ever existed! If no one remembers her, he can keep her *forever.*"

I tasted the smoke, the ash, and now a profoundly bitter truth.

The man who had taken Louisa's sister was remorseless, methodical, and homicidal. He'd stop at nothing to protect what he thought was his.

Even if that meant murder.

But Louisa's voice hushed with a new excitement, bumbling with chills as the night plunged us from the hellish inferno into the frostbitten January air.

"That means she's still alive. My sister is *still alive*. He hasn't killed her. She's been alive all this time. *Fifteen years*." She actually smiled. "There's still hope."

No. There wasn't.

I wished the fire had taken Louisa's every memory. Destroyed every picture. Burnt every memento. Reduced the home to ash.

Anna might have been alive—but she'd lived with a psychopathic bastard for fifteen years.

Fifteen years of captivity.

Of abuse.

Of worse.

Anna died long ago. What remained was just a shell of survival. A body tested, bent, and broken.

Louisa might have hoped her sister had lived all this time, but I knew truth.

Just as I had done so long ago, Anna would have prayed for death.

Chapter Nine

I hate silence. There's enough silence in death. So talk to me, London.
Talk to me, or I'll make you scream.
-Him

A funeral made for a lousy interrogation.

Not that I expected any answers out of Nina Martin now. The body wasn't talking. The family had nothing left to give.

For two years, the girl had lived a double life. No law enforcement agency had located her. No media outlet reported on her. No compassionate passerby ever recognized her.

And maybe she hadn't wanted to be found?

Or maybe Jonah Goodman decided that for her...

And their baby.

I attended the services much as I hated funerals. I'd had enough grieving in my life—mostly for people who thought me dead. Nina's friends and family left before I dared to confront my grief, selfish as it was.

My tears weren't mourning the girl who died...I cried for the runaway I hadn't found.

I sat on a bench near the grave site. Cold and concrete and exposed to every chilly gust of air that covered Jefferson Cemetery. The groundskeepers waited until the afternoon to ride in on their backhoe, preparing to cover the frostbitten ground with the displaced frozen dirt.

This was the part of the burial no one saw. The moment no one should have seen. It wasn't a final rest. The earth opened up and *swallowed*.

Lost to the uncaring earth and buried forever.

Not a way I wanted to go.

The backhoe's tracks mixed mud into the pristine snow and trampled a path between other silent graves. The machine roared with that diesel rumble of hard work. The first bucket of dirt covered the grave. I looked away, but it hadn't been sunshine and rainbows discovering her body either.

If I had been at the station or sitting in the funeral pews, I might have blamed the stinging of my eyes and nose on the cold air. But alone, why hide the misery? No one could see me. No one would know how badly this missing had affected me.

For once, I didn't have to hide behind dark humor or pretend she was *just another stiff.*

I could be *me.*

And I could be sad.

And I wouldn't have to worry about how my fellow officers would judge me.

It wasn't because I was a woman. Enough of us had entered the force. Hell, women commanded two of the city's enforcement districts. The reason I faked stoicism and ignored that past damage because I was *London McKenna.* The girl who escaped. And if I ever wanted to graduate from *victim* to *partner*, I had to prove I could handle these types of situations. The familiar ones—kidnappings, abductions, abuse.

I'd been luckier than Nina Martin. Rachel Goodman. Whoever she decided that she was.

My hand's dressing caught on the bench—a quick wrap over an inconvenient cut on my palm caused from the frantic escape of Louisa Prescott's home. The wound was a hell of a lot better than a burn. I picked at the binding. A fresh line of crimson looked black in the brightness of the afternoon. I squinted against the sun as it beat against the fresh snow. The cut would need to be rebandaged. Last thing I wanted was an infection on my dominant gun hand.

It wasn't fair. Nina had lost a hell of a lot more blood than me. Runaway cases weren't supposed to end like this. Sometimes the kids needed a break from home. Other times they snuck out with friends. Met a boyfriend. Find a biological parent. Usually, the kids got in more trouble than they deserved, but *most times*, they came back.

Those other times? I redressed my wounds at their funerals.

I pushed from the bench to retrieve the first-aid kit I kept in my car. The supplies were usually low—the Neosporin and band-aids always running out on me. I called it clumsiness. James preferred *death wish*. Never said if it was a joke or diagnosis. I never asked.

I wrapped fresh gauze and a bandage over the cut and snapped the kit shut. I had nowhere else to be—crawling through a fire had earned me a personal day. Not something I'd recommend to the other officers. Louisa had gone to the hospital overnight. No better time than the present to get her detailed statement.

My keys scraped the ignition when a white van rumbled down the narrow path, parking off the side of the road near the grave site.

I checked the time. Three o'clock? The funeral home had no other services scheduled today, and the gravesite was deserted long before the groundskeepers began to tuck Nina's final blanket over the coffin.

Who was coming to pay their respects now?

Jefferson Cemetery had buried half of Pittsburgh and the surrounding South Hills for nearly one hundred years. The van might have parked close by to visit any number of family members buried over the property. But it'd take one hell of a dedicated family to visit a grave in single digit weather. Christ, I ached to be one of the damned dead burning in hell just to warm up my toes.

The van opened, and swirls of black emerged from the seats.

Dresses. Mourning wear.

Donned by six different women.

No...*girls*. Teenagers, if they were lucky.

The girls had cloaked themselves in black—boots, skirts and dresses. Even black shawls wrapped over their hair. They huddled together in the cold of the parking lot, stomping their shoes against the salt-stained pavement. They stared only at the ground.

Waiting?

For who?

I squinted. The black made some of the girls indistinguishable from the others, but a few stood out.

How could they not?

Two of the six were pregnant.

Heavily pregnant.

Their bellies tugged at the dresses, but their draped shawls failed to cover the bumps. Nothing was hiding those babies except a doctor and a pair of forceps.

The girls kept their heads down as the wind kicked up, but even once the icy pain died down, they averted their eyes. And then I saw why.

A single man led the girls. Tall. Broad shouldered. Wearing a heavy work coat, coveralls, and boots. His knit hat and scarf bundled over his face. He didn't need to speak. The women just *followed*. He pointed. They walked. He tensed. They quieted.

What the hell was this?

The man gathered them behind the van and gestured, marching them off of the road and into the graveyard. The women obediently followed, except for the smallest in the group.

She turned and looked at me.

For some reason…my heart sank.

The little girl was a doll. Blonde hair. Blue eyes. Pink cheeks. She couldn't have been older than ten. She followed, surrounded by the pregnant women. They held her shoulders. Offered everyone tissues.

And, above all else, stayed silent as they walked through the cemetery—

Directly towards Nina Martin's grave.

Maybe they had the answers I needed.

Or maybe they'd answer some new ones.

I tugged a pair of leather gloves over my hand, grimacing as it squeezed the cut. The zipper on my jacket pinched into my neck, but at least it kept the wind at bay as I burst into the cold after the girls.

The skirts marched in obedient strides after the man, pausing only to help the pregnant ones over an icy patch between the path and grass. They diverted towards the fresh grave, held hands as they approached, and stood in silence, waiting as the groundskeepers backed away to give them a moment of peace.

I wasn't as courteous.

They huddled closer together, watching my every step while pretending to bow their heads in honor of the grave. Good thing God didn't mind people peeking during their prayers. At least, I assumed he didn't. Wouldn't have set well with these girls. They seemed…religious.

Their clothes gave them away. All handmade, every last piece. Skirts. Jackets. Hats. The clothing was either wool and stitched or knitted and woven. Even their shoes appeared to be hand-crafted— leather heeled boots. Practical for the winter and almost fashionable in a chic-retro way.

If any of them knew what retro *was*. These girls were so damn *young*, especially the pregnant ones. The oldest looked to be about sixteen. The youngest? Ten? Maybe?

I had no idea what was happening here, but I didn't like the way their *driver* loomed over them. He raised a hand to the girls. None of them flinched, but that didn't mean they weren't terrified.

"Say your prayers." The man told them. He stepped between me and the group, letting the full foot of height he had on me speak louder than his words. "Now."

I tucked my hands in my pockets to reach for my badge. Hopefully, I wouldn't need its persuasion. "Hello, there. The funeral is over. You're late."

"Never too late to pay respects." He said the words, but I didn't know if he meant them. Not with a face like his—weather-worn and stark. Like he worked outside and stared for far too long into the sun, deadening his gaze.

He was too old to be with these girls, but I didn't feel like he was a father to them. Grey hairs sprinkled through his eyebrows and beard. Had he removed his knit hat, I doubted much of that hair would have been immune to the aging silver. The deep lines in his face matched a solid build. He seemed to be a man who worked with his hands, outdoors. Probably harder than he should have worked as he seemed to favor his right knee.

He wasn't handsome. Wasn't ugly. But something twisted in my gut. That hardness in his jaw. The bushy furrow of his brow. He studied me as intensely as I studied him.

Except he angled himself between me and the girls.

Like he was protecting them.

Or *hiding* them.

"What's your name?" I asked.

His voice sounded sun-burnt. Raspy, as if perpetually clogged with dust. "If you don't mind, we're here to mourn."

He didn't realize how helpful that was. "Oh. Did you know Nina?"

He offered me nothing else.

I sidestepped him, addressing the girls. "Did any of you know Nina?"

Their prayers stopped, and the youngest grabbed the hand of a pregnant brunette. The tension thickened, and these girls—all around the same age as Nina—went eerily still for a group of teenagers.

I didn't like being ignored.

"Leave us," the man said. "Have you no decency?"

"Ask the one who put her in the ground." I flashed my badge. "I'm the detective in charge of her missing person's case." Now a homicide, but I wouldn't tell them I'd surrendered my files to Falconi and Riley. "I'd like to ask you a couple questions."

My challenge must have irritated him. His eye twitched, and I got the distinct impression he was used to talking to the little ones cowering behind him.

"We need to pray now," he said.

"This won't take long. Did you know Nina well?"

"*Ma'am*." The respect seemed foreign to him. "I want a moment with the grave. Leave us."

Absolutely not. "Did you have any contact with Nina in the past three weeks?"

"I won't ask again."

"Funny. I will." I smiled, slicing through his dismissal. "Best to answer my questions now. Easier for everyone...unless you'd like to speak at the station?"

The man didn't have to turn to gain the girls' attention. "Go back to the van. God will hear our prayers just as loudly at our chapel as he will here."

Oh, hell no.

I stepped between them and the path, blocking the girl who appeared to be the oldest in the group. She waddled, her belly ready to pop any minute. Poor kid. I hated seeing girls in trouble like this.

"When was the last time you saw Nina?" I asked her. "Any information can help us in the investigation."

She stilled, absolutely rigid, so panicked I feared her water had broken. Her eyes widened—tired, but sharp enough to look past me to the man commanding the others.

I *hated* that. Always had. Working patrol for five years and dealing with the family crisis and sexual assault cases had hardened me to domestic violence issues. It was never their fault, but even broken, bleeding, and terrified, most women couldn't meet my gaze. They looked only to the person who had hurt them, as if asking permission to speak the truth.

The brunette clutched at her belly. Protecting the baby?

I called to her, my voice gentle. "You might have known her as Rachel."

Her breath caught in a choked acknowledgement, but she slammed her mouth shut before speaking. Her eyes diverted to the ground.

Damn it.

"I need information on Rachel Goodman." I turned, waiting to see if the name struck anyone else as profoundly. Every girl flinched. "You know she's dead. You know she was murdered. I need to know about the man who was with her." My eyes narrowed on their self-appointed chaperone. "You'd know him as Jonah Goodman. He's dead too."

The youngest girl began to sob. The others rushed to her aid—brushing at her hair, rubbing her shoulders, comforting her in every way save for actually speaking.

Nothing about the display reassured me. Something was wrong here.

I knelt before the young one, looking up into a face bright with youth, hope, and innocence. Eyes so blue a jeweler would have tried to set them in a white gold band. She was a beautiful girl.

The man guarded her most of all.

"Did you know Rachel, sweetheart?" I gave her a smile. "Were you friends?"

The man barged between us, his scowl darker than mourning. "We're here to pay our respects. Don't interrogate us at the edge of a grave. Especially since they're in delicate conditions."

Delicate. Yeah. I lowered my voice, letting the accusation hang. "They're a little young to be pregnant."

"The Lord works in mysterious ways."

"And a condom works ninety-nine percent of the time."

That thought seemed to disgust him more than standing over the grave of a child. "You would insult God's will?"

"With all apologies to God, he's not giving me answers about the deceased. These girls can."

"They're not answering your questions."

"You don't speak for them."

His hiss warned, the moment before a strike. The air puffed from his mouth like he'd spit fire.

"Forget you ever saw them, Detective." He waved a hand. "Girls. Van. Now."

The group hurried away, even the pregnant ones shuffling too quickly for their condition. The man prevented me from following too closely.

That was fine. I'd yell.

"Where's the baby?"

The words hung in lifeless silence. The eavesdropping dead, buried in the graves, listened hard enough to crackle the frost.

"Rachel was preparing her apartment for a baby. An older one. Maybe six months to a year old. The baby wasn't with her when she died. In fact, she had never been in the apartment. So, I'm asking all of you—*where is the baby?*"

The oldest girl broke the quiet, but she didn't offer me any answers. She prayed for them.

"Our Father, who art in Heaven..."

Goddamn it. "I need to find the baby. I can't save Rachel now, but I can help Rebecca."

"—Your will be done, on Earth as it is in Heaven."

A second girl chanted with her. She encouraged the youngest to join. Cold and terrified, her lips moved, but no sound emerged.

I showed them the badge again. "I'm a detective. I'm only trying to help."

"Lead us not into temptation..."

The man knew better than to lay a hand on me, but he pressed his luck right up to my face. Only a night in a lonely cell might have wiped that sneer away, and I begged him to give me a reason.

"We're not answering any questions, *Detective*. And if you continue to harass us, I'll take your badge number and lodge a complaint with your commanding officer."

He wouldn't be the first.

And it wouldn't stop me.

Everything about this man set me on edge. His gaze was a creeping prickle, his voice a self-righteous commandment that'd sooner create cement shoes than chisel stone tablets for those who doubted his authority. The girls' prayers, their clothes, their crying...

The pregnancies.

I'd unwittingly stumbled into something far bigger than Nina Martin and Jonah Goodman, and the implications soured my stomach. I *felt* their fear. A consuming, *familiar* memory.

They weren't afraid of disappointing the man.

They dreaded what might happen if they disobeyed him.

"Fine." I held my hands up, edging away from the man and towards the littlest girl

Her coat had fallen open, and the scarf fluttered in the wind. I gave her a smile before tightening her buttons and rewrapping the material over her shoulders.

And, with an imperceptible flick of my wrist, I tucked my business card inside her pocket.

The girl had to keep it safe. She did well, not looking into the jacket where it sat.

Good. I didn't trust the man to act rationally if he found my phone number.

I stood again as the girls clustered around her and led her away. My attention refocused on the man. I straightened. It didn't impress him. Something told me he only respected a woman when she laid flat on her back, and even then, it was a passing amusement, not genuine admiration.

"What's your name?" I asked. "I'd like to contact you once your...*family* is out of mourning."

He shook his head. "That won't be necessary."

"Let me see your ID."

"You have no cause or suspicion to see it, Detective."

He knew his rights. I couldn't fault that, even if it made my job harder. But it did nothing to sate my curiosity. His refusal baited me to pounce. If he was lucky, I'd sheath my claws.

"A girl is dead. Her child is missing. I'm going to find out why."

"May God have mercy on her..." His words lowered. "And may he protect you, Detective."

I tilted my head. "Do I have cause to worry?"

He smiled.

Then turned and followed his brood of little women.

Frustration tasted like copper, or maybe that was from me biting my cheek to silence myself. I couldn't stop them from leaving, but nothing precluded me from following as they returned to their vehicle.

A white Dodge Caravan.

...With a license plate beginning with *GP*.

Maybe Nina couldn't help me now, but that van would.

I scribbled the rest of the plate down and rushed to my car.

Was this the same van Louisa saw?

I didn't want to roll on the the chances of that...

But those girls knew Rachel Goodman. They knew why she'd died. They knew where the baby was.

I threw myself into my car, diving for the laptop on the passenger seat. The scribble of paper crunched in my hand as I ripped off my gloves with my teeth and logged into the database. My fingers hadn't warmed yet, so I slammed each key into place as I typed in the plate.

The results appeared instantly.

"Son of a bitch."

The van belonged to *Jacob Goodman*.

Chapter Ten

What will you tell them about me, London?
You know they'll never believe you.
-Him

Anna Prescott's kidnapping was a fifteen-year-old cold case.

How the hell did she wind up in the middle of a double murder-suicide investigation?

I had no idea what Anna Prescott, Nina Martin, and the Goodmans had in common, but I'd demand answers from God himself if it helped solve this mystery.

Fortunately, I had the opportunity.

The Goodmans had their own personal connection to the Lord. And their charity pledged to do His good works across the state.

Harvest Dominion Farm tucked itself within the National Forest of the Alleghenies, shadowed by mountains, hidden behind pristine streams, and practically inaccessible by any vehicle not equipped with four-wheel drive.

Legally, they owned two hundred acres. Some of the land had been cleared and tilled for modest fields, livestock pens, and greenhouses, it retained many of the original trees. The forest protected it from the few roads passing through the county.

The handful of reports I could pull on the charity mentioned that it catered to *troubled, Christian youths.* Lots of children. No CPS calls. No police reports.

Trouble always seemed to find me, but what sort of insanity lived on this farm?

Harvest Dominion wasn't just a shelter. The Goodmans had built a miniature compound on their property. My Crown Vic bounced along a packed dirt road towards the impromptu town square. A gazebo marked the center of the residential area, with a multi-colored playground hidden behind a little parkette. Enough for a handful of kids to play between bushes and fruit trees.

A dozen or more cottages, almost Mennonite in structure, nestled within the acres of cleared pastures. The small, wood framed homes were painted bright and pastel, neatly finished with vibrantly white trim. They might have been only two or three bedrooms, but the footprint stayed tiny, as if it were expected that most of the residents' time would be spent outdoors on the farm.

The sheltered community seemed picturesque. Covered porches welcomed visitors from off the "road," though I doubted anyone not-related to the family or charity had ever visited. Puffs of pleasant smoke coiled from chimneys, and the sharp peaked roofs dazzled with hanging icicles. Each home had a different colored door—charmingly quaint and yet...

It was a shell of normalcy. A shadow of something sweet and wholesome, hidden from the world miles off the main road and surrounded by a row of trees that penned everything—and everyone—inside.

I parked next to a fire-engine red pick-up truck, caked in mud.

Looked *just* like the one I'd observed outside of the cottage where we'd discovered Cora and Jonah's bodies. Hardly felt like a coincidence now.

Despite the fresh snow, someone had cleared the sidewalks leading to and from the homes. A bare path stretched from the houses, around the larger buildings, and towards the fields, pastures, chicken coops, and oversized barn.

Solar panels attached to every home and structure and lined the entire roof of their barn. In the distance, a row of wind turbines patrolled the far field. I didn't have to guess—in this area, the farm must have used well-water and septic for their needs.

Either the Goodmans were some of the most environmentally conscious farmers in the region...

Or they found a perfect opportunity to stay off the grid.

While twelve smaller homes were built around the path—a thirteenth and fourteenth's foundations already poured—the largest and grandest structure occupied the center of the town. The steeple pointed high into the air, visible from every inch of the farm courtesy of an ivory-tinted cross. The gardens sparkled under a layer of snow, and the patterned, stone steps welcomed all into the only mason-brick building on the farm.

Some questions might have been answered inside, but not the ones I needed. I'd bestow that honor on the grand house seated in a position of power next to the church. Larger than the others. Ornate even in its simplicity. The porch wrapped around plantation style, but I doubted I'd be welcomed inside.

Nothing in this place felt *right*.

Curtains moved in the cottage windows. Children peeked from behind glass that immediately fogged with their breath.

So. Many. Kids.

Little girls and boys darted window to window until abruptly pulled away by what I assumed were a mother's cautious hands. Older children, upwards of eight or nine, tended to their chores across the fields with cautious glances towards me and my car. The boys shoveled snow. The girls abandoned the chickens and ran home.

Five older girls—possibly old enough to be women—carried crafting supplies from a cottage to the chapel. Rolls of toile, candles, table cloths, material. A handful of younger kids followed, hauling white chairs decorated with tissue paper.

Not the black I expected for a mourning ceremony.

More like…a party?

A wedding?

It was all very Little House on the Prairie, but I prepared for anything—a snowball to the face or a bullet to the back of my head.

I knocked three times before cursing myself for not immediately identifying as a detective. A place like this undoubtedly stored guns in every nook and cranny. Hell, they probably sprouted in the fields.

The door opened with an antique squeal.

And a rosy-cheeked teenage girl with a bundle of red curls and storybook blue eyes peeked at me from the crack between the door and frame. One of the girls from the cemetery, though her mourning blacks exchanged for a sweet homemade dress of pinks and whites. I twitched, glancing over her.

She'd let out the hand-stitched dress, but the bulky material couldn't hide the truth.

This girl—no more than thirteen years old—was pregnant.

What the hell was happening here?

"Hi." I forced a cheer into my voice. "My name is London. We met the other day."

She said nothing. Not sure what I was expecting.

"Is your mom or dad home?" I asked.

The girl froze. My pulse quickened.

She didn't seem to be hurt. Wasn't malnourished or too skinny. Her hair was done properly—cleaned, washed, and styled into a pretty, albeit modest, look. She had no visible bruising or injuries, but that bump in her belly was no new miracle.

Someone did that to her.

And every instinct in my body screamed at me. It had happened *here*.

"May I come in?" I smiled. She didn't. "I was hoping someone could help me. I'm looking for anyone who might have known Rachel—"

A grunt interrupted us. A burly hand covered in thick, black hair gripped the girl's wrist. He didn't yank, but she couldn't have resisted him as he hauled her inside. His shadow fell over her, and she slunk into the darkness.

"Go tend to the young ones, Abigail." The man barged between her and the door. "I'll handle this."

So we met again.

My weatherworn buddy from the cemetery was careful to step onto the porch and close the door behind him.

I held my hand out. "Detective London McKenna, Pittsburgh Police. Remember me?"

He didn't shake my hand. "This is private property."

"I wanted to apologize for intruding on your family's moment at the cemetery. You were all in mourning and had come to pay your respects. I should have waited to speak with you."

"I told you then, and I'll tell you now. We have nothing to say to you."

He stepped towards the door. I edged forward.

"This is an important case. I only need a few questions answered. I hope you don't mind me paying a visit to your home."

His eyebrow arched. "I didn't give you this address."

"I have my ways, Mr. Goodman." I gave a quick hum. "Now...which Goodman are you?"

He drew the silence out like taffy—sticky and long. "Simon."

A brother then. I mentally ticked the check mark next to the family tree I'd drawn up with the help of Riley and Falconi's meeting with Jacob Goodman. Jacob owned the farm, but his brothers—Simon, Mark, and Matthew—helped to manage it.

Whatever *it* was.

"Nice to meet you, Simon." I gestured over the land. "Beautiful place."

"Why are you here?"

"Just wanted to check on a few things. It was surprising finding you all at the gravesite. At least, until I realized who you were."

Simon laced his question with ice. "And who *exactly* are we?"

Persons of interest. "No wonder you missed Nina's....I mean, Rachel's funeral. It's quite a trip from here. You're so far from the city, and all those pregnant girls..." I frowned. He didn't react. "They must have needed bathroom breaks all the way down."

"We prayed over the grave. We did our mourning."

"And then?"

"We held a private ceremony here."

"Right. For Rachel and Jonah?" I tilted my head. "Jonah would have been your...nephew?"

"You know the answer."

I did, because I had already pulled as much information about the family as I could find. Surprisingly, for a religiously affiliated charity, there wasn't much to go on.

"Jonah murdered two women," I said. "His girlfriend, Cora Abbott, died only hours after he killed Rachel. Then he took his own life."

"Those sins are his own."

"You know what else is a sin?" I leaned close. "Marrying an underage girl."

"My nephew wasn't married."

Bullshit. "He was in a relationship with a minor."

"Was he?"

"That's what I'd like to find out."

"Who knows why kids do what they do."

"Their parents should. Or uncles, maybe."

Simon's lips tightened into a thin line. "All a family can do is help one and another. *Fathers, do not provoke your children to anger, but bring them up in the discipline and instruction of the Lord.* Ephesians 6:4."

I couldn't tell biblical scripture from the nutrition facts on a box of Frosted Flakes, but I knew the law. Unfortunately, so did Simon.

"So, you *helped* Jonah?" I asked. "Like you've helped the pregnant girls that were at the cemetery yesterday?"

"Is there a problem, Detective?"

I sure as hell hoped not, but I wasn't so naïve anymore. "There's an awful lot of pregnant girls on this farm. I've counted at least three so far. And, if Rachel had been here…that's probably four."

"Harvest Dominion Farm is a religiously affiliated outreach program. A shelter for children in need—those who have no other place to go."

"And?"

Simon smiled, as if that cracked grin could ease anyone's concerns. "We tend to our flock. Our home is meant as a haven for troubled Christian youths. A place where they can be safe, learn the scripture, and live their lives according to God's will and discipline."

"And the pregnancies?"

"Those girls need the most protection of all."

Of that, I was absolutely certain. I leaned against a column supporting the porch roof. Quite a cozy little alcove Jacob had here, but it wasn't comfortable. For all the talk of God and scripture, Simon hadn't invited me inside and out of the cold.

This good Samaritan only stopped for search warrants.

"Where are the boys?" I asked.

"Excuse me?"

I gestured over the farm. "You didn't have boys at the cemetery yesterday. I see more girls than anything. Aren't you taking in boys too?"

"We take in whomever has the greatest need."

"And then what?"

Simon extended his hands. "We do good works. This home is a happy one, Detective."

"The girls didn't look happy yesterday."

"They weren't. They attended a *funeral.*" His steps forward were meant to corral me off the porch. I planted my feet. "Fortunately, we see very little sadness here. Our lives are improved by the will of the Lord. Our days are spent in worship, and we are rewarded for our faith."

"Sounds lovely," I said. "What a noble charity you're running. I should probably offer my compliments to the man in charge."

"You can speak with God at any time—in prayer."

Cute. "I'll wait to get his email address. Until then, I'll talk with his second command. I want to meet with Jacob Goodman, Jonah's father."

Simon dropped what little cordiality he'd offered. "No."

"No?"

"Jacob is terribly busy."

"Doing what?"

Simon nodded towards a pack of women, hauling supplies, boxes, and fabric in and out of the cottages and to a secondary building behind a chapel. A fellowship hall?

"We're preparing for a wedding," he said.

The word crept over my skin like a cobweb in the dark. "A *wedding?*"

"Some joy can be found in all this sorrow. It requires a tremendous amount of work, and, as you can see, we're all very busy—"

"Right. A wedding is a huge endeavor. You must be *ridiculously* busy. In fact, you were probably busy five nights ago?" I gave him a moment to think. "Around eight o'clock?"

He didn't hesitate. "Everyone was at the farm."

"Are you certain? Shouldn't you ask around, make sure everyone was snug as a bug in those..." I glanced at the cottages. "Bunk houses?"

"Everyone was at home, Detective. We have very little reason to leave the farm. We're completely self-sufficient. The Lord has provided for us."

"Is that so?"

"You can see our bounty, Detective."

"Does that bounty include a white Grand Caravan?" I hummed. "Someone spotted it in Pittsburgh last week."

"Did they?"

"And they also saw the driver of that van."

"Interesting."

"Does the name *Anna Prescott* mean anything to you?"

"No."

Punctuated and confident.

A lie if ever I heard one.

"Take your time," I said. "It's been fifteen years since she's used that name."

Simon's shrug tensed his shoulders. He leaned a little closer, breathed a little harder, and spoke just a little harsher. "What's this about? Why are you here?"

"Where is Rachel Goodman's baby?"

"I don't know what you're talking about."

"Before she died, Rachel was preparing her home for a daughter. I want to know if she is here."

"She's not."

"Go ahead and check for me. There's so many kids around here. Maybe you've overlooked one."

Simon silenced as a pair of boots crunched hard on snow. His gaze shifted from me to the man taking the porch steps two at a time. He appeared to be about Simon's age if not a little older. He retained less of his hair, but the sun hadn't roughened him as much. In fact, everything about him seemed far cleaner than Simon. More suit and jacket than shovel and hoe.

The man pointed a single finger at the living room window to shoo whoever had been peeking from behind a curtain. Then he faced me with the damned swagger of a cat carrying a freshly pounced canary.

All lawyers were the same.

I didn't let him speak. "You must be Mark...no. Matthew Goodman. Am I right?"

Matthew wasted no time. His voice rang with a courtroom authority, bristling with all the confidence a purchased law degree could offer.

"We're not answering any more questions, Detective."

"They're easy questions."

"You've overstayed your welcome."

Because it had been such a pleasant chat freezing on the porch. Simon didn't hide behind his brother, but Matthew sure as hell would use his rights to tighten the noose around my neck. I didn't have time to waste.

I raised my chin. "Jonah killed Rachel. Did he kill the baby too?"

"I would advise you to cease your harassment of my family," Matthew said.

"I'm trying to help your family."

"We don't need your help. We have the Lord."

"And you also have my card." I handed it to him. "I would like to talk to Jacob. Please have him call me at his earliest convenience."

Matthew tore the paper in two and let it flutter into the wind.

"You are not welcomed on our property," he said. "Leave now, or this situation will become decidedly…unpleasant."

Two things got me through most days. One was the potential to snag a batch of freshly baked chocolate chip cookies delivered for the station by the local bakery. The second was arresting someone stupid enough to issue a threat against my life. I grinned.

"I think I can handle a little unpleasantness," I said. "But why risk it? I'd like you both to accompany me to the station. Answer my questions back in the city. Let me give you a ride."

"Force us from our property, and I'll serve you with a half-dozen lawsuits, from harassment to police badgering." Matthew reserved a spot of condescension for me, just enough to sweeten his voice and offer me that chance to be a *good girl* and escape. "London McKenna, I think you should do as you're told."

"I've never followed orders well."

"It's a wonder you've survived this long." Matthew bared his teeth in a forced smile. "I've heard being a detective is a very dangerous job."

"I can take care of myself."

"See that you do. Accidents happen all the time. No need for anyone to get hurt."

Of course not.

Simon crossed his arms, the muscles bulging. His threat was nothing compared to the blitz of bureaucracy Matthew would reign against the station. If my suspicions were right, and something criminal was happening on this farm, I couldn't risk any active litigation threatening my case.

Not with the lives of other girls at stake.

This wasn't over, but at least now I knew who I was dealing with. I backed off the porch.

"Have a good day, gentlemen."

They didn't respond, slamming the door behind them. Good riddance.

But I'd be back.

I planned to return to my car, but a quick detour never hurt anyone. I slipped past the main house to scope out the chapel and communal building where most of the women headed.

Most.

"Aaron, let that rooster be!"

One woman shouted over the stillness of the farm as if the winter's anxious silence and the men's unchallenged authority hadn't bothered her. She hauled a box in two arms, but stopped to balance it on her hip. She whipped her finger towards the boy, chastising him with a calm, but determined, poise.

The most confident woman I'd seen on the farm. I didn't think they had that sort of strength left in them.

"You're scaring that bird half to death!" She tisked her tongue. "You pluck a single feather, and I'll pluck out your hair one strand at a time, just try me."

The boy slowed his chase with a groan. The woman pointed.

"You get that rooster back to the coop. It's freezing out here."

He nodded, though his desperate attempts to trap the rooster ended with him nearly toppling into a snow-drift. The rooster hobbled over the snow, jumped a bumpy path, and flapped unsuccessfully until landing on the porch railing nearest me.

The boy stopped suddenly, but I gave him a smile as I pulled my cell from my pocket. With a goofy grin, I posed in front of the rooster, aiming the camera between our heads. A quick flash, and I had what I needed.

The boy—blonde with two missing front teeth—frowned at me. "Who are you? What are you doing here?"

"Haven't seen a rooster that close before," I said. "Better catch him now before his tenders freeze."

"His what?"

"Never mind."

"Aaron!" The woman called. Her pale face, reddish curls, and delicate cheekbones didn't belong on a farm. Yet as soon as she whistled, the child and bird instantly obeyed, bolting to her side. "Bring him to the coop and get inside for your lessons. Algebra is easier to learn without pneumonia—you hear me, Mister?"

"Yes, Eve."

The boy grabbed the rooster and rushed back to the woman. Eve guided the child away, watching carefully to ensure I walked only to my car.

I gave her the benefit of the doubt—starting the engine and traveling down the path. But I stopped before the road—far from the farm with the kids, animals, and the men who had so ungraciously banished me from the property.

No wonder they wanted me gone.

They hid one hell of a secret.

I stared at the picture on my phone. It blurred over the woman in the background, but the image was still clear enough to reveal every terrifying implication.

That woman's name wasn't Eve.

Fifteen years had passed, but I knew it was her.

She wasn't dead. She hadn't run away.

She'd been kidnapped.

The woman trapped on the Goodman's farm was *Anna Prescott.*

Chapter Eleven

You think you can outsmart me?
Maybe. But I can overpower you.
-Him

I slapped a print out of my farm selfie on the department's white board and drew a circle over the fuzzy image of Anna Prescott.

Homicide was more impressed by the rooster.

"Nice cock, McKenna," Falconi said.

Riley hid his chuckle by taking a swig of his Pepsi.

I might have cracked a smile if I'd gotten more than two hours of sleep. Still, I pretended to be good-natured about it. Who knows if they bought it?

For once, I wasn't trying to convince them I was stable, healthy, and otherwise fit for duty. This time, I had to convince them that I'd uncovered the craziest case of our lives.

"I didn't call you guys here because of the rooster." Some things were better left unsaid, but I couldn't trust Falconi and Riley to pay attention before their customary breakfast at Pamela's Diner. God help the waitresses who'd overhear their bloody talk over a cup of coffee and plate of pancakes every Monday, Wednesday, and Friday. "I'm onto something. Something big."

"Old MacDonald had a Missing Persons case?" Falconi whistled. "With a gunshot here."

Riley joined. "And a runaway there."

"Here a lead."

"There a lead."

I talked over them. "I went to Harvest Dominion Farm yesterday."

They didn't like that. Riley sighed. "Raking in the gas expenditures."

"I'm looking for Nina Martin's baby."

"Jesus, McKenna. Didn't you start out in psychology? Nina Martin didn't have a baby—she had one hell of a mental illness. That's why she ran away from home. Twice. That's why she ended up dead. She fell in with Jonah Goodman, he took advantage of her, and he went nuts and killed her."

I wasn't arguing that. "But the baby is *real.*"

Riley ran out of patience. He leaned over his desk, head in his hand. A lazy blink revealed all he thought of my theory.

"Then where is it?" he asked.

"She."

"Then where is *she?*"

I pointed to the photo taped to the whiteboard. "The same place a lot of missing persons are ending up. At Harvest Dominion farm."

Falconi pitched his paper coffee cup and miraculously sipped from a new full one. "Wait. That church has the baby?"

"And this girl." I tapped the picture. "This is Anna Prescott. She's been missing for fifteen years—a presumed runaway from Braddock. Last seen on July 5th, 2002."

"Holy shit…" Falconi squinted at the white board. "Are you serious?"

"Absolutely."

Riley knew my game. "Wait, wait wait. Not the right question. Are you *sure?*"

I hesitated. "It's…complicated."

"No. It really isn't."

"I didn't pull out her hair for a DNA sample."

"Then what did you do?" he asked.

"A visual assessment."

"You took her *picture,*" Riley said. "You need more than that."

"I've got a witness who says she could identify Anna's kidnapper. She's the one who spotted the vehicle. She's the one who gave me a partial on the license plate. It led me to this charity or church or whatever the hell they're calling themselves. And I saw her myself."

"Anna Prescott."

"Yes."

Falconi nodded. "Did she identify herself?"

"…No."

"Did she try to come to you? Make a scene? Ask to be rescued?"

"No. But she was…" I pointed to the rooster. "She was watching the little boy who was chasing the bird."

"And this particular barnyard animal was more important to her than the opportunity to escape her kidnapper after fifteen years of captivity?"

They didn't have any idea what fifteen *minutes* of captivity could do to an innocent girl.

"She might have been scared." I said. "Coerced. Under threat to not speak a word. Hell, there were so many kids around. Maybe she was worried about them."

"Maybe it wasn't Anna Prescott?" Falconi said. "You don't have a recent picture of her. How can you be sure?"

"Because her sister came in a few days ago and told me about the kidnapping. Then some lunatic shoots a bullet through her living room window and burns her damned house down."

Falconi whistled. "That'll do it."

"Louisa Prescott gave me the leads that implicated the Goodman's farm with the murder-suicide we were working." I took a breath. "That's why I need your help."

Falconi and Riley had worked together long enough to finish each other's sentences. Fortunately, I spoke before either of them said something the other would regret.

"Something shady is happening at that farm," I said. "I saw it."

"Then why do you need our help?" Falconi asked.

I didn't answer. Not directly. "They say they're a religious charity— a women and children's shelter for homeless and runaway kids. But there's a *lot* of kids there, all working the farm."

Falconi sipped his coffee. "Are they in school?"

"I was there mid-day on a Monday. Didn't see any school buses."

Riley shrugged. "Homeschooling's not a crime."

"No, but sexual abuse is. A lot of the girls there were pregnant. I'm talking under sixteen, most under *fourteen*."

"That shit happens, McKenna. Don't tell me you haven't run into those sorts of cases in your workload."

"There's too many of them."

Falconi scratched his beard. "But they're *runaways*. They probably got into trouble on the street or with whoever took them in. What if they went to the charity shelter for help?"

Any other charity, any other place, and I'd have sided with a devil's advocate.

But this farm had too much of the devil in it already.

"Where did you talk to Jacob Goodman?" I asked. "To tell him about Jonah?"

Riley jerked a thumb over his shoulder. "He came here. Talked to us in the station, viewed the body in the morgue to ID what was left of it."

"Then you didn't see this place…or the girls and women on it."

Falconi laughed. "London, you see zombie hillbillies in Point State Park. Lump three trees together, and you think it's Deliverance."

"Not this time. This farm is old-school—stone-age. They take some hardcore positions from the Bible. Like the passages that say women and children should be seen and not heard? They don't talk. They don't meet your gaze. They obey the men—go here, head back inside, get into the van. They make no decisions for themselves."

Falconi sighed. "Again. Not a crime."

Riley elbowed his partner. "Might be a blessing."

"Like any woman is gonna put up with your bullshit," Falconi said. "You'd tell her to get in the kitchen, she'd head straight to the knife block to chop off your—"

"They're a cult," I said.

They collectively groaned before attempting to escape my department. I blocked their path with outstretched arms and a raised eyebrow.

"They're isolated on a private plot of land. Multiple families live on the single compound. They're completely self-sufficient, living off the land with their own sources of power and water and the farm for food. They're religiously motivated and extraordinarily fundamentalist in their views."

"Enough screwing around," Falconi said. "What *exactly* do you think is happening there?"

Voicing it would make it true. I hesitated only a moment.

"I think the Goodmans are holding the girls captive on the farm."

"Abusing them?"

I swallowed, but poison would have tasted better than this filth. "Raping them."

"Did you see it happening?"

"No."

"Anna looks pretty happy in this picture."

"Simon Goodman said they were planning a wedding," I said. "Nina Martin was *married* to Jonah Goodman."

Riley frowned. "What do you think?"

"I think you need to ask your commanding officer what *he* thinks." Sergeant Adamski's voice boomed over the unit. "And I think we've already got a harassment call on this."

I turned to face my superior, but he took one look at the picture on the whiteboard, grimaced, and shimmied his pants up past comfortable to where he felt it made an effective statement against my investigation.

"London, what the hell are you doing? I just got off the phone with Lieutenant Clark. Apparently, *he's* been on the phone with a Matthew Goodman this morning."

That rat bastard went through on his threat? "He wouldn't dare."

"I walked into a goddamned mine field this morning, taking it on the chin for you. The lieutenant wants to fry your ass for harassing the *lawyer* you attempted to intimidate yesterday—without a warrant, probable cause, or even any reasonable suspicion."

My jaw clenched so hard it popped. "I didn't *intimidate* anyone. I needed them to answer questions for a case."

"Did they invite you to the farm?"

"I found their address."

Adamski snorted. "You followed them into a *funeral*, verbally insulted the *children* attending the services, and tracked their address via plates you ran in the parking lot—"

"Which matched the partial plate Louisa Prescott gave me."

"A *partial*. That's not enough for a DA, and you know it. What are you trying to do?"

"I'm finding Nina Martin's baby."

"And harassing a grieving family, reeling from their death of their *murderer* son, was the way you decided to find her?"

Oh, this was ridiculous. I faced my sergeant with as much professionalism and confidence as I could offer without appearing to be whiny, petulant, or—a death knell to my career—a complete bitch.

I was right.

I knew it.

I *felt* it.

And if I had to convince everyone in the damn station, I'd pull up the chairs, pop the popcorn, and preach the sermon until my lungs gave out.

"I didn't harass anyone," I said. "I asked if they knew the deceased. Six girls attended their little service, but the only time they opened their mouths was to recite the Lord's Prayer."

"Because you terrified them." Adamski groaned.

"No." My voice sharpened. "Because *Simon Goodman* scared them. He intimidated them into silence. But they knew what happened to Nina and Jonah, and they know where that baby is."

The department wasn't big enough for a disagreement to go unnoticed. The Missing Persons Unit turned into a slick sideshow punctuated with a blurry picture of a rooster. My fellow officers dropped their calls and put off their investigations for another few minutes, hunched over their desks, ears strained in our direction.

Didn't matter to me. The more people aware of the problem, the more opportunity we had to save those girls from the Goodman's perversions.

Adamski sighed. "Why didn't they give any information about the child?"

"I'm not sure. I want to talk to them again."

"Why?"

It sounded less insane in my head. "I think they're hiding the baby."

"Did you see a child there?"

My laugh turned cold. "I saw a lot of children there. Too many, and every one of them in trouble. Know what else I saw? A red pick-up truck, stained with mud, that looked *identical* to a truck I watched pull away from Jonah and Cora's murder scene. There's coincidences, and then there's *reasonable* suspicion. Let me investigate this. Something isn't right."

Adamski huffed, shoving his hands in his pockets. He jingled his keys so hard he must have bent them over his fingers. He nodded to Riley.

"You talked with the Goodmans?" he asked.

Riley nodded. "Yes, sir. I spoke with Jacob Goodman a few days ago. Informed him of what had happened with his son."

"Did you get a read on him?"

Falconi was more of a people-person. He fielded the question. "Cold. Thought it was strange because it was his youngest son, but he said Jonah was estranged from the family. Had been for months. It seemed like...they expected something like this. But he seemed to be a decent man. Religious, but that's never hurt anyone."

"Except Anna Prescott," I said. Adamski arched his eyebrows at me. I didn't let him interrupt. "Don't tell me that's not her. I know it. Hell, her sister, Louisa knows it. And now they're doing everything they can to silence her."

"Can you prove that Goodmans set fire to her house?" Adamski asked.

"*Someone* tried to scare her, and they did a damn good job of it." I held my hand up, still wrapped in an awkward bandage. "If I hadn't gotten there when I did, she'd have died."

"That doesn't mean it was the Goodmans. What other leads do you have on the fire?"

I hated my answer. "Forensics is still investigating the shell casings they found at the scene. The fire marshal hasn't made his report yet."

"Prescott lives in Braddock, right?"

"Yes."

"Not a great neighborhood."

"Oh, come on." I tapped the whiteboard with my bad hand. "This wasn't some teenaged prank. This was *retaliation*. They're trying to scare Louisa. And she *should* be scared. We all should be scared. Those girls were kidnapped, and they're being kept on that farm."

They stilled. Glanced at each other. Looked to the board.

Then their gazes focused on me.

And I *knew* what they were going to say before the words passed over their lips.

It was the same excuse, the same *worry*, the same damn condescending accusation they'd tossed around in whispers in the hall, when checking my case load, and any time I faced a dangerous perp.

"This isn't the same." They didn't believe me. "It's not the same!"

Adamski gentled his voice. "London, you have great instincts—"

"You should listen to them."

"And you should take a step back from this. Get some objectivity."

"Why?"

"I think you're…" he paused. "What's that shrink word for it?"

I answered for him. "Projecting."

"That's it."

"I'm *not*."

Adamski groaned. "You found yourself in an isolated location where you thought young girls were being held in captivity. London, any person who has been through what you've been through will assume the worst in any given situation—"

"Go to the farm. See the girls there. Tell me I'm wrong."

"You're sensitive to these sorts of cases," he said. I didn't need that superficial kindness. I'd heard that tone for years. It never made what I went through any easier. "You are the epitome of a victim's advocate,

London. You have a unique perspective on these sorts of things, and you've worked tirelessly to protect women and children and families from dangerous situations, but—"

"This has nothing to do with my past, Sergeant." My skin prickled, marching over the scars left by *his* knife. "I get it. It changed me. But my kidnapping is irrelevant here. That family is capturing young children to rape them. They're not..."

Disfiguring them.

Torturing them.

Slicing them apart bite-by-bite for his own perverted and cannibalistic ritual.

"I'm talking child abuse, not a serial killer," I said.

They didn't meet my gaze. This was the conversation no one wanted to have. No one knew what to say, what to ask, or how to face the one woman who managed to escape one of the deadliest serial killers in the country.

One still at large.

Hiding.

Waiting.

"We need to help those children," I said.

Adamski frowned until his lips thinned and disappeared into his prickling chin. He nodded one too many times at the ground before speaking.

This conversation wouldn't go in my favor.

"London, we've been down this path before."

Son of a... "Oh, come on."

"Last year, you had the *same* gut feeling."

"Bruce—"

"Accused that man of raping his daughter and her friends."

Yeah, but that particular runaway had the bruises, petty criminal history, and attitude to match a proper victim. "She exhibited the signs. There was evidence—"

"He was innocent. You were the one who pushed. You had a *hunch*. You were convinced—"

How many times did I have to say it? *"This isn't the same."*

"It better not be, London. You nearly lost your badge. This department is still wrapped up in the lawsuit. Nothing you found then supported your *hunch*."

I couldn't let them walk away. I had to make them see. Not for me. Not to make sure I was right. I had to protect *them*. "The girls are in trouble. They need help."

He paused, long and deliberate. His profanity broke first. I suppressed a grin.

"Then you bring me *proof*," he said. "And do it without harassing that family. If you can't find me anything in two days, this is over. Got it? There's enough crime and misfortune in this city. Don't go chasing after imaginary evils."

"This evil isn't imagined," I said. "But I guarantee. In two days? You'll wish it was."

I didn't care what it took. I was going to rescue those girls.

Before any more innocence was lost.

Chapter Twelve

You can't stop me with brute force.
Think, London. It's the only way you'll survive.
-Him

Crime didn't pay, but it put a hell of a markup on the goods it produced.

The Abbott's Antiques storefront was a Pittsburgh staple, proudly owned and operated in the Strip District for the past fifty years. The store served the city and its residents with antiques, new pieces, and, famously, hand-crafted artisan furniture.

Most of which came from the Goodman farm.

I poked through the cluttered aisles, studying the furniture. It was an artist's work. He'd taken the time to craft the chairs to rock without creaking. The dining room tables were decorated with an elegant flower pattern inlay. The dressers were heavy, but sturdy. The chairs balanced and simple. Even the bed frames claimed an antique look ornamented with modern carvings. Perfect craftsmanship. Infinite care.

The Goodmans had talent, but they also kept secrets. And I'd learn them all.

Starting with Jonah.

"Detective."

Clark Abbott silenced the tinkling bell on his old-fashioned register. It was for show. He rang up all his purchases on an iPad with a credit card swiper, but that didn't suit the store's aesthetics. The merchandise wasn't outdated—it was *antique*. The scuffed floors weren't dirty, but *rustic*. And the cramped aisles? Just bursting with new wares. Expensive wares. Crowded, dusty, and haphazardly tossed onto a shelf.

Apparently, Clark hadn't found anyone to help him manage the store since Cora's death.

"I take it you're not here as a customer?" In a slow, tired motion, he swept his glasses off his face, rubbed his dark-circled eyes, and sighed.

"If I was, would you recommend anything for me?"

His eyebrows rose, thick and dark. He pointed over an aisle of glass vases and stacked picture frames. The wooden box looked as if it had gone untouched for years, though someone had lovingly etched the carvings into the front.

"A hope chest." He gave me a once over and noted my bare ring finger. "Getting to be that age, Detective."

"Looks like a fancy cat bed to me."

"I have some knit socks in the back for those cold feet of yours."

James had been rubbing them for a year with no luck of warming them up. "I have a little time left before I need to worry about that."

"Cora thought so too..." Clark choked on the words and turned away. He busied himself with an antique scale and rod-iron sculpture in desperate need of a dusting. "Detective, I can't talk about her—*it*—anymore. I'm sorry."

"I know it's painful. I can't imagine how it feels."

"And to be *grilled* by those other detectives about her...like she was just part of an investigation...like she hadn't been *alive* just a few hours before..."

Homicide had the tact of a schoolyard bully with Turrets. Cora had been my case. It should have been my responsibility to return to Clark, even if it had been his ex-wife who'd reported Cora missing.

"I'm sorry," I said. "I know she meant so much to you."

"Shouldn't have happened." He leaned against his counter, arms crossed. "I gave her those days off, Detective."

"Don't blame yourself."

"I do. I..." He wove his fingers over his head, a father helpless to save his little girl. "I needed her here, at the store. But things had been so rough between us for *years*. My divorce was...challenging. And her mother wasn't always kind. I was trying my damnedest to *keep* Cora close. I wanted her to be happy, so I let her take the time off. If I had acted like a parent instead of a friend—"

"You had no idea what Jonah Goodman planned to do."

Just his name twisted Clark's expression into a sneer. "That boy. That damn...I can't even get rid of this damned furniture now. Cost me too much to buy it. Now I gotta stare at in my store, thinking about what he did to my baby girl." He rubbed his face. "I should turn it all to kindling. Should have never taken his pieces in. Should have..."

"It isn't your fault."

"Maybe."

I kept the implication gentle. "You hadn't told me that they were involved."

"What?"

"When Cora was reported missing, and I came to speak with you...you didn't mention him as a friend or boyfriend."

His hands knotted into fists. "I didn't know."

"Didn't you see Jonah often?"

His swore. "I got enough guilt weighing me down here, Detective."

"I'm sorry. I'm just trying to understand what happened. And I think you are too."

"I had *no* idea. Christ, I hardly knew anything about Cora. And I was trying to fix that. By God...I hadn't really had a conversation with her after she was twelve years old and her mom got full custody. And when she came back, it was tense, but we worked it out. I gave her the job. Bought her a car." He rubbed his face so hard his nails left red streaks. "But I didn't know she was missing until my ex called."

"It was a difficult arrangement. These types of relationships always are."

"Doesn't mean I shouldn't have...tried to get closer to her. Now I'll never have the chance."

The store wasn't busy, and weekday afternoons didn't see much foot traffic. He pulled a stool from one of the table sets and sat with a heavy sigh as if hearing the news for the first time. The weight nearly sunk him into the floor.

"She lived with her mom growing up. Blamed me for the divorce. Once Shelly got cancer...Cora wanted to reconnect with family before she lost the most important person in her life. But she kept me at arm's length. I respected that. Didn't talk about anything personal."

"You never had an inkling about Jonah?"

"Never would have thought twice about him. He wasn't her type."

"How do you know her type?"

He chuckled. "Jonah wasn't *anyone's* type. Nice looking kid, but…very conservative. No, that's not the right word. Traditional?"

I sat in the seat next to him, leaning close. "Like, how he dressed?"

"Everything. For a while, I figured his family was Amish or Mennonite. But they shaved, drove cars, had electricity. And I had to call them occasionally for their custom orders. I sold all their wares here."

"Which were?"

He gestured over the tables, chairs, dressers. "Furniture. Jonah's actually. His grandfather, Adam, was a master carpenter. Jonah took after him. Made me a lot of good pieces. High-quality for a kid so young. But I guess that's what the family did."

"What do you mean?"

"I've been working here a long time, Detective. I remember Jonah when he was little. Family would bring him by when he was six, seven maybe." He rapped on the table. Apparently, this piece was Jonah's as well. "He knew then he was going to be a carpenter."

And I wanted to be a crab fisherwoman at that age. "Isn't that a little young for a life plan?"

Clark winked. "I thought so too, but the Goodmans had it worked out. Jonah wasn't as bright as his older brothers or cousins. They said *God willed him* to work with his hands. The other son, Luke, was going to be a lawyer, taking after his Uncle Matthew. I'm not sure about the eldest, John. Probably taking over the farm once Jacob dies."

"What about the women?"

Clark tilted his head. "Women?"

"Did the Goodmans ever bring any women or girls to the store?"

"No. No, not that I remember."

That didn't surprise me. As far as I could tell, the Goodmans kept their women on the farm—isolated and alone. At least they didn't throw them in the barn.

"Did you think it was strange you never met the women?" I asked.

"We didn't have a real personal relationship. Talked with them only when they came by—weather and such. It was business."

"How often did you see them?"

He heaved a breath. "Jonah would bring the furniture up once a month or so. I'd pay him. That was it. I guess…" Clark smacked his lips. "I left Cora to manage the account. She's the one who had more contact with him. I didn't realize how much. I should have paid attention. Know what she told me one day? Weeks ago? She said…" He scoffed. "That we needed to *help* Jonah."

I tensed. "Help him? How?"

"I told her the only thing that would help that boy would be a stiff drink and some time off the farm. Too much church in him. Made him a little crazy."

"Was he always strange?"

"No." Clark waved a hand. "Though…yes. The last couple times he came here."

"Was he acting aggressively?"

"No. The opposite. That's the weirdest thing." Clark ran his tongue over his teeth. He pointed to a few knick-knacks positioned on shelves and by the register. "Jonah started selling things himself. Little things. Coming in between scheduled drop-offs to give me additional merchandise. Nothing big. But trinkets. Bobbles. Nice carvings, but people generally want furniture, not art."

That was a new development, and one that didn't make much sense. "Did he say why he was selling more things?"

"No, but now I get it. All the money from the furniture went right to the family. Lined Jacob's pockets to keep the farm running. Jonah was probably saving for his own nest egg. Might have wanted..." He swallowed. "Some money to take Cora out."

"How much did you give him?"

"Quite a bit, actually. Some of the pieces he made were just extraordinary." His eyebrow rose. "Especially the doll furniture."

"Like...for a dollhouse?"

"Oh. You've never seen a dollhouse like his. I almost felt bad taking it. He spent a lot of time on it, but he said he needed to sell. Insisted on it. I gave him a good price, but I think he would have gotten more enjoyment out of giving it to that little girl."

"What little girl?"

"The one he made it for."

I stood, nearly knocking the stool over. "Did it sell yet?"

"Not yet. It's a steep price, but a collector will want it, make no mistake. Got a guy coming in from Cleveland next week—"

The aisles crowded with everything and anything just to block my path. I darted between a rocking chair and display of handmade quilts.

And stopped in a dumbfounded silence.

This wasn't a doll house. It was a *mansion*.

A beautiful, scaled version of a Victorian masterpiece. Jonah had created intricate carvings and real furniture, windows with honest-to-God glass. He'd painted wallpaper, sculpted flowers, and carved everything from a clock with moveable parts to an entire tea-set, painted a paisley blue. I half-expected a butler to pop out of a closet and a fire to spring in one of the two fireplaces.

"Jonah put a lot of work into this," Clark said. "And he looked absolutely sick to sell it. That's why I held onto it. I hoped he'd change his mind, want it back."

I examined one of the beds, tugging on the little blankets strapped to the real mattress. Curtains hung in the windows, and tiny stitched rugs patrolled the house's entryways.

"Look at the detail here. The stitching on the cloth. It's...*embroidery*." My chest tightened. "Someone helped him make this."

"Oh. Probably Rebecca."

I spun to face him, accidentally dropping the furniture to the floor. The *baby*? "*What did you say?*"

"Maybe Rebecca helped him."

"How do you know Rebecca?"

"I don't." He reached inside of the home, pulling out a tiny toy chest buried in the detail of a little nursery. He handed me the miniature, and I stared at the name carved into the wood.

Rebecca.

Chapter Thirteen

"You'll have to sleep sometime."

-Him

"What do you know about cults?"

It wasn't exactly a proper *hello*, but James was used to our conversations, especially the strange ones at five in the morning.

For some reason, a simple *hello* felt too…personal? No. *Comforting*. At some point, I'd have to admit to him that I just liked hearing his voice. After a sleepless night of staring at the ceiling, I'd finally rolled over and cuddled the pillow on his side of the bed.

Since when did he have a side of the bed?

"Cults don't wake up before dawn." His voice thickened with sleep. He jostled the phone, and his voice muffled against a pillow. "What are you doing, London?"

"You've learned more about cults than me."

"Thinking of joining one?"

I smirked, running my hand through my hair. I hadn't slept much, but somehow the braid had come undone during the night. Should have just knotted the damn mess and been done with it.

"Maybe if the price was right," I said.

"Still looking for some meaning in your life?"

"No." The early morning made me too honest. "Pretty sure I found it."

"Your job?"

No.

It was *him*.

He'd saved me long ago, but why I didn't—*couldn't*—tell him was a mystery for another psychologist to decipher.

"You sound tired." I stated the obvious.

"It's the middle of the night."

"You always wake up at five."

He hesitated. "It's not five here."

"Aren't you in DC?"

Another pause. "I went there. Yes."

"Where are you now?"

"Somewhere else."

I sighed. "And here you thought you'd never get to play Secret Agent Man again."

"Secret Agent Shrink."

"Must be an interesting case if you're traveling to consult on it."

"Wish I could tell you about it." For a psychologist, James didn't fluidly switch topics of conversation, but that was probably on purpose. "You aren't sleeping well."

"Got a lot on my mind," I said.

"Cults?"

"Nothing's adding up. Something's wrong."

"Tell me."

And that was James. Honest. Helpful.

Hopelessly in love with me.

I studied my ceiling, tracing the same plaster swirls that had helped me solve cases before. This time, the ridges and missing chunks of white offered nothing.

Because I was looking in the wrong place.

"Jonah Goodman sold furniture—hand-crafted—to help support his family." If you could call it a family. "But recently, he started selling things on the side."

"Pocketing the rest?"

"Yes."

"Why?"

"That's what's strange." I flung the blankets off me. The room's chill shocked some energy into my joints. "Jonah sold a dollhouse—this incredibly beautiful and detailed piece of *art*. He had made it for his daughter."

"How do you know?"

"He carved her name into it."

"But you can't find this baby?"

"I could…if I was given the chance."

"Where would you search for her?"

My braid was unsalvageable, and now the curls kinked into uneven waves. I bundled it into a bun and spoke with the hair-tie clutched between my teeth. "The Goodman farm."

"Why wouldn't the family say they took her?"

"Because Nina Martin, aka Rachel Goodman, was in a relationship with Jonah. Underage. Significantly underage."

"And they're still protecting Jonah?"

"You'd think…but they never protected him. He was off the farm. In a relationship with Cora Abbott. It doesn't make sense."

The echo of running water splashed over the phone. "But you have a theory."

"You won't think I'm crazy?"

"No more than I already do."

Then I had some wiggle room. "Jonah and Nina were trying to escape the Goodmans."

"Then why did he kill everyone and commit suicide?"

"What if he didn't?" I asked. "What if he was murdered too?"

Saying it out loud did sound insane. I exhaled, but in my gut, a churning and chilled realization flooded through my veins.

I was right. I had to be.

"Jonah was part of the family," I said. "Born into it. Raised in an extremely fundamentalist environment with traditional values. Men are the heads of the household. Women the baby makers. And the family lived alone, far from the rest of the world so they could live by those principles." I shook my head. "Isolated so they could take in young, impressionable girls."

"For what reason?"

"To increase their little church's ranks the best way they know how."

"You're certain they're raping the girls?"

"Yeah. They must have done it already. Many times. James, I was at that farm. There were too many pregnant girls there." I tugged on my clothes, pacing the room. "I have no doubt that the girls are there against their will."

"What about their charity?"

"Are we still speculating?"

"Unless you have any proof to back it up…"

"If I had to guess…" I didn't. I *knew*. "The women's shelter is a cover so no one asks questions. They kidnap those girls and rape them. If anyone gets suspicious, they cite the charity and say the girls were already pregnant when they took them in."

"And Jonah had enough of it?"

"Yes. He escaped with Rachel, took her back to her family. Then he tried to hide out with the woman he really loved—Cora."

"And the baby? Could a mother leave her child?"

And there was the thorn in my side. "Maybe they didn't have a choice? The farm wouldn't hurt the baby, and if they had to get out, they'd know she'd be safe with them. At least until they could raise enough money to get her back."

James's voice stayed low. "So the Goodmans killed Cora and Rachel?"

"Yes."

"But I thought Jonah's wound was self-inflicted." He paused when I didn't speak. "London?"

"…It was."

"Are you sure he didn't kill the women too?"

"What if he was coerced?"

"*How?*"

The obvious answer. "*They had his child.* Maybe they threatened him with the baby. They had to keep the family's secret. If Rachel revealed what she lived through, or Jonah went to the police, their little commune would crumble."

James said nothing. Bad news. If James was unreceptive to the idea, then I couldn't imagine Falconi or Riley giving a damn about reopening their cleared case.

But I wasn't wrong.

"Louisa Prescott came to me about her sister's kidnapping," I said. "She ID'd the van and the kidnapper. Then she's suddenly attacked in her home?"

"Are they responsible?"

"If Jonah was trying to escape, they'd do what they could to stop him. If Louisa was attempting to find her sister, they'd scare her away. Jacob Goodman will stop at nothing to protect his farm and family."

"How are you going to prove it?

A simple question with no good answer. "The women won't speak to anyone. The men threaten anyone who gets close. I can't snoop around on the farm anymore, not without a warrant...but I can check the town."

"Are you sure you want to do this?" he asked. "You might be kicking a hornet's nest."

"I've been stung before."

"And you haven't learned your lesson yet."

"I've learned plenty."

"But not *objectivity*."

I gritted my jaw. "Not you too."

"Oh." James hummed a knowing sound. "So someone else called you on it?"

"On *what*?"

"London, you have a great deal of empathy for victims of crime. Even better, you know how to put yourself in their situations—"

"That's not what I'm doing."

"That's what you *always* do. That's what makes you good at your job. That's what saves the lives of the people you want to help. It doesn't matter if it's a missing person or abused child, you know the risks better than any, and you'll stop at nothing to prevent something similar from happening to others."

"This isn't about my kidnapping."

"It will *always* be about your kidnapping."

This was not what I needed to hear at the crack of dawn.

Or ever again.

"London, the more you hide what happened to you, the more you pretend like it doesn't impact you, the worse it will be."

"I'm over what happened to me."

"No. You're not. He held you captive for three weeks—"

"And I'm home now."

"He tried to kill you—"

"And I escaped."

"He tortured you. Peeled off your skin. Started to eat you *alive*—"

"And I *survived!*" The declaration didn't seem as forceful when my pajama tank top couldn't hide the slices, patches, and jagged scars on my arms. Fortunately, it hid the worst ones—the long slices of skin he'd ripped from my belly. "Look, James. No one is *eating* those girls on the farm. But they are getting raped and assaulted and held against their will."

"And you're sure of it?"

"Do you think I'm just paranoid?"

"If I were you, I'd never trust another soul."

Yeah, well, I trusted him. Wasn't sure if that was a good idea yet or not.

Nothing like sleeping with the FBI profiler of my murderous captor.

And falling in love with the only man who had ever gotten into a serial killer's head.

I said nothing, letting only my ragged breath speak for me.

The quiet abruptly shattered.

And the crashing of glass echoed from outside.

I shushed James with a harsh word and dove for the window.

The pre-dawn dark swallowed the street outside, but a figure loomed near my Jeep. A silhouette in the streetlight crept towards my car door. Another crash, and his arm was inside my car. Within seconds, he took off running.

"Son of a bitch!" I slammed a hand against the windowsill. "James, I gotta go."

"London?"

"Hold on!"

I leapt over my bed, grabbing the first pair of footwear I could find. Fuzzy bunny slippers. Fantastic. A present from my mother who thought all ails could be cured with a soft and pink fuzzy lining. I cobbled together a robe and jacket to cover some of my shame and ran for the door.

Never in my life did I think grabbing a gun would feel *routine*—like tossing a scarf over my coat or hat over my head.

But, Christ, was I glad I had it. I didn't need to be a cop to trust these instincts.

The asshole breaking into my car wasn't some punk teenage reject.

He had found Louisa. And now he was coming for me.

Last mistake he'd ever make.

I bounded outside, flashlight searching in one hand, gun poised in the other.

Silence.

No firing of a car engine. No crunch of gravel under boots. Just…nothing.

I scanned with the flashlight, but I couldn't pierce the entire darkness even with the high-intensity LED. Turning my back to the alley behind my house didn't leave me with the warm and fuzzies, but I scanned my porch. No one lurked in the shadows, but this wasn't the neighborhood for vandalism or worse. My Victorian centered itself in a nicer part of town, a wholesome street in Shadyside bordered by trees. They now offered too much privacy, as did the empty homes to my left and right, thanks to industrious house flippers who'd gone overbudget on renovations and couldn't swindle grad students with the exorbitant rent.

A chill crept over my spine. Whoever had trashed my Jeep hadn't stuck around.

I snuck forward, approaching my vehicle with a mounting paranoia—bad for a trigger finger. The bastard had slashed my tires. Whether that came before or after the rock through my windshield didn't matter much now. Glass exploded over the gravel, and I doubted the pink slippers would protect me from a wayward shard.

The perp must have darted down the alley. Hell, he probably made it two blocks before I even raced from the house.

Damn it.

"London!"

James's muffled voice called from my robe pocket. I lowered the gun, but I didn't put it away. Not yet.

Not while the hair on my neck still prickled, and the air stilled, waiting for the flash of a bullet. I didn't like being watched.

Would they wait for a reaction?

Or did they seek an opportunity?

I pulled my phone as I opened my Jeep. "I'm fine."

"What the hell is happening?"

"Someone took out their frustrations on my car."

"Are you okay?"

"Tires slashed. Window busted. Whoever did it came and left..."

My slippers *squished* against the floormat. I twisted, but the seats felt just as...

Slimy.

I reached over my head, retching against the coppery tang in the air. The scent stuck in my throat. I smacked the dome light and rolled out of the vehicle.

Blood.

Everywhere.

The crimson stained my seats, my dash, my floors. Thick, blotted puddles dripped over the interior, as if my seats had transformed into a slaughterhouse. I checked the back, but the vandal hadn't stashed anything on the seats.

Was that a good thing? Had I expected a *body?*

Who the hell drenched the inside of my car with *blood?*

The calmness of my voice was all that prevented James from fulfilling his threat to leave then and fly home.

"There's blood in my car," I said. "Someone broke the window and pitched a bucket of it inside. I gotta call this in. Patrol might be able to find the idiot who did this."

"Go back inside, London." James often tried to order me around. It never took. "I don't want you out there with a loaded gun."

I grimaced, wriggling out of the blood-soaked robe. "You worried about me?"

"Worried about whoever pulled this practical joke."

"Do you think it's a practical joke? Just some vandalism?"

"I'm hoping that's all it is."

I edged towards the house, but my steps slowed as the blood wasn't just splashed over my car. A message was scrawled across my door, staining the white with blotches of dripping scarlet.

"*Deut 32:35,*" I said.

"Deut?"

It took me a minute too. My poor mother never forgave herself while her oldest daughter slept through most of Bible study. Hated it even more when I threw the priest out of my hospital room during my *recovery*.

Forgiveness, he had said. *It would help me to heal.*

Funny. The skin grafts were more helpful.

"Look up a Bible verse for me..." My voice strained as I stared at the dripping words. "Deuteronomy 32:35."

"Why?"

"The *pranksters* left me a note."

James did as I asked, his voice low and grave as he quoted. "*Vengeance is Mine, and retribution, in due time their foot will slip; For the day of their calamity is near, And the impending things are hastening upon them.*"

"You're the psychologist," I said. "Still think this is a *joke?*"

"No. This is a threat. London, get inside the house. You're in danger."

Chapter Fourteen

Tell me what you think.

I'm very curious.

-Him

Pig's blood.

The asshole had soaked my Jeep in pig's blood.

I slapped the forensics' report onto Adamski's desk. He nursed two tabs of alka-seltzer and his bruised ego as I waited in quiet vindication. He plopped a third tablet into his glass before acknowledging the folder.

With a sigh, he read the findings, his eyebrows popping up. "Not very original, are they?"

"Message received though." I tapped my foot—the bunny slippers exchanged for my boots once the patrol made it to my house and stole my clothes as evidence. "Not the best wake-up call."

He knew me too well. "Were you really sleeping, McKenna?"

"I was awake enough to hear someone try to break into my Jeep."

"I should send you home. You need *sleep*. You're wired."

"You should send me to Forest County."

Bruce guzzled the water, snorting over the bubbles. "Why in God's name would I do that?"

"Who else has access to *pig's blood*?"

"Any person who goes to the grocery store and asks the butcher."

"Great." I followed him from his office to the coffee machine. The pot was empty, and the grounds leftover from last night. He refilled the water anyway. I pushed him away, slamming the filter with the caked-on grounds against the garbage. "Here's an idea then. Start calling butchers in the area. You speak with the Shop N Saves. I'll call the Giant Eagles and Aldis. Someone should check Whole Foods, and then we'll get the rest of the department on the local shops…"

The fresh coffee was bribe enough. He waved me away. "Okay, McKenna. What do *you* suggest we do about this?"

"We ask Harvest Dominion Farm. Jacob Goodman is already suspected of harassing other people close to this investigation."

"*You. You* suspect Goodman. I'm not kicking your ass, London. I'm saving your badge. You need more proof than a *gut instinct* to go snooping. I can't get you a warrant without proof."

"These people targeted my *home*."

"Was Agent Novak there?"

I stiffened. "Why would that matter?"

"Isn't he staying with you?"

"That really doesn't matter."

"That's a shame. I'd like to hear what Novak thinks of all this."

"My instincts aren't good enough?" I threatened him with the freshly brewed coffee, my fingers curling over the handle. "I swear to God, I'll dump it out."

Bruce surrendered. "Look. *If* what you're saying is true, we've got something a lot more complicated than a murder-suicide on our hands."

My eyebrows rose. "I just want to take a ride up to Forest County. Get a little information about the farm and charity."

"And what do you hope to find?"

I hated to say it.

"I was wrong before."

Adamski nearly toppled over. "Jesus, Mary, and Joseph, what did you say?"

"Don't get smart."

"I've never heard you say the *W* word before."

"Well, this one is on me. I've been looking at the case wrong. You were right—"

"I don't think my wife has ever pleasured me as good as I feel at this moment."

I ignored him. "I thought the Goodmans were kidnapping young girls just to rape them."

"And they're not?"

"No. When I visited the farm…they were planning a wedding."

"Whose?"

The thought sickened me. "They didn't say, but I suspect the wedding is for one of the little girls."

"But *why?*"

"Because it's not about the rape. It's not about sex. Jonah Goodman *married* Nina Martin—even if it wasn't in the legal sense. To the Goodmans, they were man and wife. Why would they do that if it was just for rape…unless they planned for something to come of it."

"Like…?"

A reason for Jonah to highlight his Bible verse. "The Goodmans aren't kidnapping children for pleasure. They want to fill their quivers. Every girl on that farm was kidnapped for a specific purpose." My voice cracked. "The Goodmans want them to bear children, to give them sons so they can fulfill God's plan."

"Are you sure?"

I hoped to God I was wrong.

"The Goodmans kidnapped those girls so they could be bred."

Chapter Fifteen

Why am I doing this?
I thought you had me all figured out...
-Him

Conventional thought said that small towns originally sprung up near rivers and streams. That was wrong. Most towns popped into existence around beer distributors.

Tionesta had two distributors for a population of six hundred. No one would have faulted a rural Pennsylvanian town for developing a crippling addiction to alcohol, but Tionesta had more charm than trouble.

For such a tiny town, it had a thriving market district—though the definition of *district* could be loosely interpreted. Without formal development from big-name corporations, the town had created their own homegrown outlet mall. Vendors of all sorts, jewelry to cupcakes, staked a claim in one of the dozen miniature storefronts poised along the main street. The vendors operated from little more than sheds, but they'd decorated the fronts in vibrant colors, planted shrubs out front, and adorned their stalls with cheesy chalkboards, signs, and decals.

Somewhere *someone* in the market knew the Goodman's secrets, and I'd buy all the muffins and cupcakes the village could bake to make them spill.

January tourism was gawker-slow, the kind that welcomed strangers to the town with stares, whispers, and a healthy dose of curiosity bordering on suspicion. Only four of the town's twelve stalls were open, and I doubted many were doing any business.

Gossip, on the other hand, thrived.

I could weasel CIs into my pocket all I wanted, but the best way to get information was to target the little old women in hats. Back in Pittsburgh, babushkas meant a code of silence. In the sticks? Old hats meant old news, stories they couldn't wait to share with people who had heard them a dozen times before.

And judging by the size of the town, there weren't many new stories.

The baker seemed the best bet for any gossip. Not hard to find either. Her booth—princess cream sprinkled with a pink framing—housed a plump older woman, wrapped in a pastry pink shirt slathered with screen printed cupcakes. She wore scrub pants dotted with wrapped-candy decals, Keds painted to look like a cake, and four cupcake shaped barrettes buried in her cocoa hair.

Oddly enough, her apron was covered in cartoon cats.

"Well, now...*you're* not from around here." The baker leaned over her counter though the shed was so small I doubted she ever stood up straight. "And who might you be?"

"London McKenna," I said. "I'm just passing through."

"Nice to meet you, doll. I'm Debbie Riker." She rapped on her wall, shouting to the next-door booth. "Hey, Doris. Come here. We got a visitor!"

"A customer too." I pointed to the deepest darkest most chocolatey cupcake she had on display. "I'll take that one. Two if you got 'em."

Game point.

Tionesta's Little Debbie got to work, and I smiled at her busybody friend, craning her neck out of her stall to peek at the stranger in the town. The would-be barista shared her friend entrepreneurial spirit...but not her fashion sense. This lady served her homebrewed coffees and teas bundled in jeans and a parka, completely mummified in scarves, mittens, and hats.

"I'll take some coffee," I said. "It's cold out here!"

And the sense of commodity struck. Both women set to their tasks with a newfound glee. Debbie, however, boxed only one of the cupcakes. She instructed me to take a bite of the other before I paid.

"Go on, London." She waited while I took a bite of the moistest cupcake I'd ever tasted. "Everyone says it."

I accidentally smeared most of the icing over my lip. She handed me a napkin in exchange for the compliment.

"Very good!" I spoke with a mouthful of chocolate. "Delicious."

"Best in state, four years running." She knocked on the ribbon nailed to her stand. "Would have won it last year, but the judges chose some no dairy, no gluten, no taste excuse for a dessert. Looked pretty, but if I wanted no processed sugars, I'd eat a salad, thank you very much."

I nodded. "Well, this is blue-ribbon in my book."

"Locally sourced too. Eggs and milk right here from the middle of nowhere." She shared a chuckle with her friend. "Can't get good produce anywhere else. When those big corporations came knocking on Bill Maxton's door, offering him those special, name brand chickens and zombie seeds—well…" Debbie winked at me. "We showed him some good old-fashioned hospitality with our boot up his you-know-what."

"Do you get many business propositions like that?"

"Oh heavens, no," Debbie laughed. "We're just a small community, but we watch over our own."

"Have you lived here for a long time?"

"All my life." Debbie boasted of the fact. Her friend, Doris, offered me coffee and confirmed the same. "We're born and bred here."

"Well, good. Maybe you can help me." I sipped the tea, grateful for the paper cup's warmth spreading through my gloves and into my fingers. "I'm a little lost right now."

"Oh, Sugar. There's not many places to go from here. Take 62 to the East, follow the river, and it'll put you back in Oil City in no time."

"Actually, I was looking for people who live here." I gave an apologetic shrug as I showed her my badge. "I'm a detective with Pittsburgh Police."

Debbie cackled. "You *are* lost."

"I'm part of the family crisis division," I said. Not a lie. "And I work with a lot of troubled teenagers." Also not a lie. "A couple of my girls were out this way recently." Nina had *technically* lived here. "I had a break in a case, but it felt better to talk with them in person."

Debbie clapped her hands. "Which girls are you looking for? I know everyone in this town—going back two or three generations. But no one from the city ever came here…"

151

"They might be staying on a nearby farm."

"Oh, Lord!" Doris snuggled deeper in her parka as she waddled from her booth to the bakery. "Debbie, she's talking about Harvest Farm. We know the girls you mean."

Debbie accepted a cup of coffee from her friend. "Yep, that's right. You want the Harvest Dominion Farm. The Goodman's place. They're up the road a ways yet. Ten miles, I'd guess. Across Route 666."

My eyebrow rose. "Route *what?*"

"Don't fret. That road is a beauty. Rides straight through the game lands. Just gotta keep an eye out for deer and elk. Their farm is tucked away nice and cozy in the forest. Has to be, for what they do."

And that's what worried me. I took a bite of the cupcake, endearing me to the women. But I needed more information. I pointed to her display.

"Could you pack me up another dozen?" I asked. "I'll put them in the squad room."

"Bless your heart." Debbie grinned. "Best sales day I've had in weeks."

She busied herself in the store, and Doris settled in close, nursing her own cup of tea.

"So…do you know the Goodmans?" I asked.

"I knew the dead one."

I bit back my surprise. "Jonah?"

"Oh, Lord no." Doris huffed an uncomfortable breath. "Poor thing. I've never heard anything so terrible before. To think what that boy did…but no. I knew Jonah's *grandfather*. Adam. He's the one who made the bulk of their money. Had a whole slew of kids, they had their own broods, and that farm took off. Richest in the county. Probably the center of the state."

Yeah, that'd eventually cause its own problems in lawyers and trial delays, but I had to prove the truth first. "Did Adam start the runaway shelter?"

"Officially, I think. But that farm's always been a safe haven. Adam's sons—Jacob, Simon, Matthew, and…" She snapped her fingers at Debbie. "Who's the last boy?"

"Mark."

"Mark. That's right. When they were boys, they helped their father run that farm. Adam always had people coming to stay. Friends and family. Mostly from out of state. They opened it up to the public about twenty years ago. Said the Lord had a plan for them."

A plan, divine retribution. Who was I to argue with the Goodman's delusions? "So they've helped a lot of people?"

Debbie clucked from behind the counter. "Oh, it's a wonderful charity. Taking in all those troubled girls."

Doris agreed, sipping her coffee. "Not a lot of places would waste their money on trouble goods like them."

"Oh, Doris, for Heaven's sake." Debbie wrapped the cupcakes in a pretty box, binding it with a glittery ribbon. "They're hardly damaged if they *repent*."

"And they repent at the farm?" I asked.

"Well, sure. Children like that need *structure*. Discipline. They certainly didn't receive it before, or they wouldn't have been in their…way."

"Pregnant, you mean?"

Debbie busied herself with the box. "It's a cryin' shame that those girls ended up that way, but the farm is a haven for them. No one judges them, no one harasses them. And they learn the value of clean, wholesome living in the name of the Lord out there. Straightens them right out."

"And those boys of theirs?" Doris gestured with her coffee. "Just pure gentlemen. Never saw a harder worker in my life. When they come into town, they'll drop everything they have to help a woman carry groceries or cross a street, bless them."

"How many boys?" I asked.

"*That* family? Who knows! The new generation seems to spring up right out of the ground."

Nothing that innocent. I pulled Anna's photo from my jacket and showed the women. "I'm looking for a woman. She's older now, about thirty. Maybe you know her?"

Debbie shook her head. "I doubt that. They're usually kept on the farm."

My stomach tightened. "*Kept?*"

"Well, there's so much to do." Doris raised an eyebrow. "Ever milked a cow? Collected chicken eggs? Worked in a greenhouse?"

"No...I bounced from college right into the police academy. Can't say I know much about farm life."

"Well, the Goodmans keep it...*traditional* up there," Debbie said.

"How so?"

Doris studied the photo. "The women are doing the household chores and taking care of the babies. That's part of the shelter. Someone's gotta teach those young ones how to raise their babies so they don't end up in the same way."

"Oh, hush, Doris," Debbie rolled her eyes at me. "The way she talks, you'd think she kept an aspirin between her knees until she was twenty-five and married. Well, I got two words for you, Doris—*Fred Mueller.*"

"Lord as my witness, I'll pack my things up right now, Debbie, so help me." She wagged a finger at her friend. "I'm just saying, at the Goodman farm, the men and boys work in the fields, and the women and girls tend to the children. It's worked for thousands of years everywhere on this green earth, and it's keeping those girls out of trouble now." She handed the picture to Debbie. "My goodness. Do you know who this is?"

Debbie glanced at the picture and tutted. "Oh, that poor thing."

The cupcake threatened to rise back up. "What? What's wrong?"

"Oh, this one…that's Eve Goodman."

Goodman? I didn't like them sharing a last name. "She's not one of their daughters?"

Debbie gave a shrug. "No. It's a little unorthodox, but they just got along so well."

"Who?"

"Why, Eve and Jacob."

Oh, God.

No…

"This girl is married to *Jacob?*"

"Well, yes, honey. Been married for…oh, twelve or thirteen years now."

Just enough time for her to hit eighteen before Jacob took his kidnapped bride and made it official.

"She's so much younger than him," I said.

"Jacob was married before. His first wife died…" Doris counted on her fingers before giving up. "Oh, years and years ago. Cancer. Very sad. When he married again, it was no surprise. Even the devout like them young and pretty."

"It was noble, what he did." Debbie interrupted her with a wave of her hand. "Especially after what happened."

"Did something bad happen to Eve?"

"Ages ago. When she first came to the farm. She was this little thing. Pregnant. Big as a house." Debbie lowered her voice, checking the corners to contain the gossip. "She had some complications."

"She was just too young to have a baby," Doris said. "Plain as day. Whoever did that to her nearly took her life. Her body couldn't handle a pregnancy, and that's the God's honest truth. Look at what happened."

Debbie shook her head. "It's not really polite to talk about."

I feigned general curiosity instead of back-biting panic. "I had no idea what became of the girls after they were sent to the farm. I thought they were safe."

"Oh, safe as can be, but every pregnancy is different." Debbie sighed. "That girl nearly bled to death right here in the middle of the street. Jacob had rushed her down to the doctor, but our little medical clinic isn't prepared for things like…that. The nearest hospital is almost twenty miles away. She was lucky she made it."

Doris frowned. "I wouldn't say that."

"She lived."

"But the baby…"

I swallowed. "She lost the baby?"

This particular gossip was too heavy to speak in more than a whisper. Debbie leaned close. "Yes. Lost the baby. Nearly lost her life, and those complications…Eve can't have other children."

"How do you know?"

"Word spreads," Doris said. "Especially with something that…terrible. Jacob married her so young, but nothing has come from it."

Debbie agreed. "And not for lack of trying. Jacob had seven children with his first wife—that poor woman probably died of exhaustion. Eve and Jacob ordered fertility drug after fertility drug to the local pharmacy—Dr. Caldwell had all sorts of crazy stories. But nothing took. But Jacob kept his vows to Eve, just the same, even knowing she couldn't give him any more children. That takes a good man."

Or an evil one.

He wasn't some heroic man saving troubled girls. He was a rapist. A child abuser.

A man who had impregnated a girl too young and small to have a baby. His lust nearly murdered Anna Prescott.

"I'm surprised you know this much about the Goodmans…" I arched my eyebrows. "I thought they were more private."

"It's a small community," Debbie said. "Word passes easier than a cold around here."

"And the Goodmans used to come down every Sunday," Doris explained.

"Church?" I asked.

"The United Methodist right on the main street. They used to attend the services with Pastor Kerst."

That didn't make sense, not when they shielded themselves in scripture. "Why did they stop attending?"

"Well....because of Jacob's oldest son, John."

"Did he convert the family?"

Both women laughed. Debbie shook her head. "Oh no. They've always been...devout. John went to the seminary. Took his vows a few years ago. They have their own services now."

Doris grumbled her relief. "A blessing in disguise with that many kids packed into that church. Didn't matter how many girls they had wrangling them. Now we can have our pews back, and Pastor Kerst can run the church how *he* sees fit."

"Oh, hush. They were harmless."

"The Goodmans didn't agree with the pastor?" I asked.

"Who does anymore?" Doris gave a snort. "In my day, we listened to our reverends. Didn't question them."

"The *Goodmans* questioned the Bible?"

"No. They questioned *Pastor Kerst*. His faith. And no one should stand for that. Not at all."

So the church wasn't orthodox enough for the Goodmans. Made sense. Not many people could find the right passage in the Bible that allowed men to capture children for their pleasure.

A few cars rumbled passed, and Doris called to a parking truck, giving a wave to the occupant. My cue to split before I'd get tangled in invitations to dinner and tales of the more innocent parts of Tionesta. I took my box of pastries and smiled.

"Well, I should get moving. Find my girls and give them the news about their case."

Debbie grinned. "Farm is just up the road. You can't miss it. It's the only thing out there in the forest."

"Thank you." I sipped the rest of the coffee, but Doris hopped up, offering me a second cup for free.

She practically forced the cup into my hands. "It's a cold day."

Not to me. The flames of hell practically licked at my feet.

The Goodmans might have had the town fooled with their piety, but I saw the truth.

They used the gospel to justify abuse, captivity, and rape.

And I bet good old Pastor Kerst would have all the information I needed to put them in jail for the rest of their mortal lives.

And once I had my justice for the girls?

The devil could do as he wished with his prized sinners.

Chapter Sixteen

Never was a good Catholic.

You'd think I'd like the blood and body.

-Him

I'd ordered cupcakes to bribe the women into talking, but I'd never by what the preacher was selling.

Been there. Done that.

I'd lived through hell once, but my tormentor hadn't given me the privilege of dying. If he was what waited at the end of the tunnel, I wanted my money back. That mystery of the afterlife had already been spoiled for me.

The door squealed as it opened. I edged inside, immediately regretting the heavy coat, gloves and hat. Did every Methodist church contain one broken ceiling fan? Too hot in the summer, even hotter in the winter. I stripped off the coat, picking a path along the weather-worn runner protecting the floor from salt-caked shoes.

No one prayed in the sanctuary, but a phone rang somewhere down the hall. It didn't take a parishioner to know their way around. I still had scars on my knees from when I was eleven and fell on the cement path leading down to St. Thomas More's fellowship hall. Most churches were the same.

Same incense smell. Same administrative layout. Same gossip shared more than hymnals.

It still felt dirty to flash a badge to a minister, and even worse to question one. I had a feeling Pastor Kerst had never been asked anything about his congregation before.

"Can I help you...?" He had that thin and lanky demeanor of a man who spent most of his time indoors but still attempted an evening job once the guilt of one-too-many church bake sales tightened his vestments. "Officer..."

"Detective," I corrected. "McKenna. I'm from the Pittsburgh Police Department."

"You're a long way from home."

So were too many of the girls trapped on the Goodman's farm. "I was wondering if I could ask you a few questions."

Pastor Kerst gestured to the seat opposite his desk. Not much of an office. He shared his space with two bookshelves stuffed to the brim with books and a dozen folding chairs precariously stacked against the wall. I edged into a seat, waiting for the office to collapse upon itself. Pastor Kerst didn't share my unease. He pitched an empty Diet Pepsi into a garbage can and shoved a few papers into a briefcase to make room.

"I have to visit an elderly parishioner in a few minutes," he warned.

"This won't take long." I laid the photo of Anna on his desk. "Do you know this woman?"

His glance was quick, but he gave a fond smile. "Yes. That's Eve Goodman."

"What do you know about Eve?"

The smile faded. "Is she in trouble?"

Only for the last fifteen years. "I'm investigating a Missing Persons report. Eve might have some information for me."

"Eve? But she's…" He shrugged, his palms folding. "You'll forgive me, but I doubt she can help with anything from Pittsburgh. The Goodmans rarely leave their farm."

"Do you know them well?"

"I'm not sure anyone knows them well. They're very insulated. Very private."

"Hiding something?"

He stiffened. "I wouldn't say that."

"What would you say?" I kept my voice light. "The only Goodman I know is Jonah."

"Don't judge a family by the one who strayed, Detective. Jonah was a good man. He simply…lost his path."

And made one hell of a detour. "Has anyone else in the family lost their way?"

"No."

"Are you sure?"

Kerst shifted, his words bred of caution, the only way a man of the cloth could hedge. "What exactly are you looking for?"

Nothing worked better than the truth. "What sort of man is Jacob Goodman?"

Apparently, this truth was more difficult to share. Kerst hesitated and gave a bob of his head. This necessitated a second can of pop. He cracked open the Diet Pepsi, offering me a bit. I declined.

"Jacob is a very pious man." He took a big swig. "Serious. Devoted to the Lord and his family."

"And his charity?"

He lowered the Pepsi. "The shelter? Well, of course. He's taken in so many girls."

"How many?"

"Oh…probably a dozen or more."

A *dozen*.

And those were the ones the minister could remember.

God only knew how many others Jacob hid on the farm, and only the devil saw the sins he committed with them.

"Did you see these girls?" I asked.

"Occasionally, if they came to any services."

"Have you ever been to their farm?"

His voice turned somber. "Not as often."

"Why?"

"They weren't happy occasions. I was only called to the farm for funerals. They had a family plot on the land, buried their own."

The chill strummed my spine. "Did you do many funerals?"

"No, thank the Lord for that. Adam Goodman died, but he was old, and it was his time. Jacob Goodman's first wife died of cancer—a blow to the farm. And then…" He looked at the photo. "There was Eve's child."

"The miscarriage?"

"He only lived for a few minutes. They tried to save him, but it wasn't God's will. The miscarriage nearly took Eve too, but, she fought. Hard. She's strong. Very strong."

She'd have to be strong to survive what she'd gone through. "Do you remember when this happened?"

He puffed his breath out. "A couple years now, I'd wager. She was a very young mother."

"Can you give me an approximation?"

"Well…I guess I could check the records."

Hallelujah! Records with no warrant? How lucky could one girl get?

"Did you keep them?" I asked.

"Oh, yes. I keep the programs for my baptisms, and I have the accounting for my funeral services."

"Do you have any for the Goodmans?"

He gave a laugh and gestured over his office. "Well, yes, but see how cluttered this place is? The basement is ten-times worse. I try to stay organized, but once I go to store them…this church is a one-man operation, Detective. I have a part-time volunteer from the parish who helps, but it would take me time to sort through the records."

I leapt at the chance, nearly diving over the desk for the opportunity. "I'll do it. I don't want to take up any more of your time."

"I can't guarantee it'll be easy to find it, but we are a small community. Not many events per year." He tapped a pen against his desk calendar. He wasn't lying. Most of the days were blank. "But, Detective…the information will be old. The Goodmans haven't joined us in worship for a few years now."

"You said they were devout."

"*Very*. But they often had their own interpretations of the Bible. Some which ran counter to current cultural ideals."

The understatement of the year. "Such as?"

"The place of a woman in the home. The importance of child-rearing. How man was destined to seed his world."

"So, they kept their women barefoot and pregnant?"

He chuckled, but his nod was solemn. "They're free to interpret the Bible as they wish."

"Did any of the women complain?"

"The Goodman farm is a sanctuary for runaways—children scared and alone. They were given warm beds and food. There's not much for them to complain about."

Except for the abuse.

I dropped the small-town charm and planted my feet on the floor. The closer I leaned in, the further he pushed away.

I forced him to look me in the eyes, meeting a grey-brown stare that had seen far more than he'd revealed.

"Did they ever come to you, Pastor?"

"What are you asking me?"

"Are these women being abused?"

"*No!* No, nothing like that. The farm is traditional. They follow some very core fundamentals, but they are not a danger to those who seek their help in the shelter. In fact, Jacob's oldest boy is a minister himself. They believe every word of what they preach, Detective. The Lord comes first, and through Him, they care for those in need as much as they protect their own family."

But who knew what the Goodmans demanded in return for their *charity*. The price the girls had to pay was steep.

What if they'd refused? What if they had tried to escape?

My stomach twisted. Something inside me whispered that terrible truth.

Jonah, Nina, and Cora weren't the only people who had been killed to protect the Goodman's *beliefs*.

Kerst stood, guiding me from the office and to a locked door along a side hall. The stairs below coated in dust, and the overhead light flickered, but the bankers' boxes stacked neat and orderly on a sturdy, wire shelving unit. Dozens of them, each organized by audit year.

"I've been here for eighteen years," Kerst said. "My predecessor was originally a CPA. He kept the records in a very specific manner, and I tried to replicate it as best I could. These are organized…meticulously. I'll ask that you keep them that way."

"Of course." I stared at the boxes, already calculating the years I needed in my head. "Thank you, Pastor."

"I'm not sure what you're looking for, or what you think you'll find…"

"Me either. But I'm hoping I'm wrong."

"The Goodmans have never caused this community harm. They do good works and love each other. Jacob might be harder than most, but he's taken over the head of his family and led them into prosperity through charity. His brother, Simon, manages the farm. Matthew is an accomplished lawyer. Mark, a very good doctor. All of their sons have brought honor to the family and this country. Some are veterans. Some farmers. All highly educated."

"And their wives…?"

Kerst breathed deep. "They might not work outside the home, but they help with the charity, the family, and the children."

"And how many children are there, Pastor?"

"We did quite a few baptisms until they began to worship with John."

And the most important question. "How old are the mothers, Pastor?"

"It is not our place to judge what might have happened to those girls before they came to the farm."

"No, but it's important to ask questions about what happens to them once they're there." I hauled a box off the shelf and lowered it onto a table with a grunt. "How many of them married men on the farm?"

Kerst shoved his hands into his pockets. "Some."

"Just *some*?"

"Any marriage is a good marriage, Detective. They're young, but nothing improper happened. The girls were always of age."

"Once you saw them."

"Detective, I assure you, the Harvest Dominion Farm is a *good* place. A loving place. And I can prove it."

"How?"

"Because they've taken in many girls over the years." He smiled at me, completely oblivious to my horror. "And *not one* of those girls have ever left the farm."

Chapter Seventeen

Always look behind you, London.
You never know who's watching.
-Him

My camera's shutter cracked like a shotgun blast in the silent forest.

I flinched with each photo. Listened.

The snow didn't care. It lay heavy over the forest, cocooning me into a private winter sanctuary bundled within the bare trees and scraggily bushes.

Nice and quiet. Good.

I hadn't regretted a single shot yet. Each clear photo offered me a window into the terrifying world that was the Goodman farm.

The digital image appeared on the camera's screen. The girl in the frame had no idea I had taken her picture, courtesy of a Canon four-hundred-millimeter lens. Apart from being heavy and entirely too expensive to screw around with, the camera snapped clear shots from the hill overlooking Harvest Dominion farm.

Technically, I didn't violate Sergeant Adamski's orders if I wasn't technically on the Goodman's land.

But I couldn't collect the evidence I needed while freezing my ass off doing surveillance. The real truth was inside the house. I'd love to get in, but it wasn't happening. Not yet. This investigation was too important to blow on a stupid, reckless mistake.

Not when the girls needed me.

I searched through the camera again. A dozen children padded around the farm, working their chores between snowball fights in the fields. Older girls and women followed, calling to the little ones so they could wipe their noses or bundle their coats a little tighter.

But this wasn't a wholesome little family. The girls tending to the kids were pregnant.

A spindly tree branch obscured my shot. I aimed the camera, held my breath, and tried to steady the image.

The girl in the frame couldn't have been older than fourteen. Already, her belly had swollen. Hard to hide it on her. She'd kept her skinny, rail-thin shape, only now the material on her dress stretched, bulging like she'd swallowed a volleyball.

The poor thing should have been out playing on a JV team somewhere. Instead she patrolled the kids, called to a dog, and tossed him a tennis ball. The collie lurched through the snow, kicking up plumes of white fluff. The children loved it, chasing after the collie and racing to fetch the ball themselves. The dog pranced back and forth, bowed low, and bolted away.

I took another shot as the pregnant girl shouted, yelling at the dog as it abandoned the tennis ball to chase the wily, escaping rooster. The bird squawked. The collie barked. The kids laughed.

And the pregnant girl struggled to distract the dog from the insulted and increasingly featherless rooster.

Abigail?

I checked the copies of the baptism records I'd found in the church.

No. Couldn't be her.

The baptism program had named Abigail as a mother to Benjamin. It hadn't listed a father, but it did highlight a date. *March 4th, 2015.* But the only boy toddler outside scurried after a different girl. Someone older—around sixteen. She nursed another child, juggling the bundle at her breast.

So that sixteen-year-old had two children. She seemed old enough to be the record's *Abigail.*

Which meant the girl in my frame...

I snapped another picture before flipping through the baptism programs. My gut told me she was an unknown, kidnapped after the Goodmans had left the church. The child she carried would be her first, and she looked six months along. Maybe more.

I marked the Jane Doe in my notebook. That made three so far. Two of which were pregnant.

What sort of sick, twisted men did this to young girls? And how was I going to save them?

Legally, I had no grounds to suspect *anything*, but only because my smoking gun wasn't admissible in court.

I stared at the records, my gut churning, absolutely sick with the vile truth.

Anna Prescott was taken on July 5th, 2002. Her son's funeral was held on March 13th, 2003. Less than *ten months* after her kidnapping.

I'd pasted a newspaper clipping next to the few records I had on Anna. The headline, *Local Farm Provides Charity To Those In Need*, only told part of the story. After a series of terrible storms left three Tionesta families homeless, the Goodmans stepped in, providing blankets, supplies, and food. More interesting than their benevolence was the picture of a young Anna Prescott, handing a mourning family blankets and mugs of hot cocoa.

The article originally ran on July 31st, 2002.

Anna had lived with Jacob Goodman since her kidnapping. She'd been held in captivity.

Raped.

The child fifteen-year-old Anna miscarried belonged to a then *thirty-seven-year-old* Jacob Goodman.

But I couldn't charge the bastard with anything.

The rape occurred over fifteen years ago, and the statute of limitations for witness reporting had expired. I needed Anna to collaborate the story now. Only she could reveal to the court that she'd been sexually abused. Without her? We had nothing.

I peered through the camera. Anna must have stayed inside, out of the cold. I didn't see her.

Or the men.

But I had enough pictures of them.

Jacob, the family leader. Simon, his muscle. Matthew, the attorney. And Mark, the family's doctor.

They had been plentiful in sowing their seeds. Little boys stomped through the snow from the houses to the chapel. And Jacob's sons and nephews claimed the little cottages inside the compound for their own families.

But I saw no daughters. No women older than fifteen…unless they were pregnant. They must have been the wives.

So where were the young female children?

My mock family tree looked a little sparse. Jacob's sons were easy—John, Luke, and Jonah. But I knew he had daughters. At least four of them, if I could believe the gossip in town. His daughters would be older now—in their twenties. But none of them lived on the farm.

If I had to guess, the Goodman daughters met the same fate as Anna Prescott.

No doubt the family had similarly-inclined associates. The girls were probably married off, forced into relationships with strangers so they too could be bred like livestock.

Men like this wouldn't stop until their quivers were full and their seed had corrupted the earth they tended.

I'd save them.

I just needed time. Evidence. A valid reason to kick my boot through the door and rescue all those girls from the cold hell trapping them.

I blinked. In that moment, the forest disappeared. The hills and trees, snow and puffed breaths of white fog vanished.

And I was back in my own captivity, bleeding, broken, and bound within the stones and chains once more. The copper scent of blood had gagged me. But the roasting meat?

That had smelled good.

How terrible for the girl he'd butchered and cooked.

My phone vibrated in my pocket. I flinched. The farm returned, but my arms ached.

How long had I been holding the camera?

How many more times could he trap me in that nightmare?

My cell didn't have great service in the middle of the woods, but the text came through. Adamski made short work of my day off.

Break in Frost Custody Kidnapping. When can you come in?

I swallowed a profanity. The cold lodged it in my throat, or maybe the dread choked it out of me.

Damn it.

No matter what pictures I took, or how quickly I could convince my squad of a problem…those girls would spend another night in their rapists' beds.

I texted back. **I can be there in 2 hours. Maybe 3.**

He didn't like that answer. **Where are you?**

Out of the city. Forest County. Got a lead.

The delay wasn't because Adamski didn't have the right words to say. His thumbs were too arthritic to type his frustrations.

I gave you two days. It's done. Get back before Lt. Clark gets involved.

Damn it. This was my day off. My only chance to keep working on the case.

I was onto something. I could *prove* it.

But only if my commanding officers let me do my job. If they got involved, if they decided I was *overreacting*…

There were only so many times a woman could meet with the station's assigned psychologist then go home to her own in the evening. The last thing I needed was anyone to recommend yanking my badge because the case *got to me.* But that's why I had to be here. I knew what sort of terror these girls felt.

Since no one had come to help me, I *owed* it to these innocent girls to do whatever it took to help them.

I texted back. **OMW. I'll be there ASAP.**

I shoved the camera into the bag, but my fingers tangled in the zip as a twig snapped in the shadows behind me. The scrape of branches against slick material echoed the break.

I froze, listening for the telltale drop of boots against frozen ground, crunching snow and ice against the rocks.

I heard three sets of boots.

No.

My heart lurched.

Five.

All pacing. All watching.

All too close.

I dropped the camera bag and spun, pulling the gun from my belt as the five men emerged between the trees. The dark camo cloaked them like the spiny, dead branches and limbs choking the farm from freedom.

Each man carried a hunting rifle, cocked and ready to fire. My gun didn't stand a chance against all five barrels, even if two of the hunters looked young. Early twenties. *Jonah's age.* They must have been his brothers or cousins, the newest generation of Goodman depravity.

This wasn't a fight I'd win.

Or a fight anyone would ever know I'd lost.

The Goodmans had more than enough land to dump a body, and I wouldn't be the first buried in the depths of the forest.

Simon stepped forward, ripping off his ski mask and exposing a lecherous, confident sneer.

"Oh, this isn't good, Detective," he chided. "You're trespassing on our property."

I shook my head. "I checked the county's property map online."

"You checked wrong. We purchased this land last year. Haven't consolidated the lots yet. The map you saw was wrong." He gestured with his rifle. "Drop your gun."

Sweat chilled me. At least they couldn't see it under my heavy layers.

I didn't have a choice. Without a clear shot and path to escape, I had to do as I was told.

It'd be the last time I surrendered to them.

I emptied the clip and dropped the weapon.

Simon nodded, and one of the younger men scooped it up, pocketing my only defense against the monsters.

"Spying on us?" Simon gave me a cruel smile.

"Conducting an investigation," I said.

"You have no proof that we've done anything wrong."

"*Yet.*" I let the word hang. "I'll find it."

"And what *exactly* are you looking for?"

"Evidence of Jacob Goodman's crimes. And he's got a *lot* to answer for."

Simon stepped too close, letting the gun angle just under my chin. "Tell you what, Detective. Why don't we go have a talk with my brother? You're probably dying to meet him."

And, once the introductions were over?

I'd be dead.

Chapter Eighteen

I've kept you longer than anyone.
I might keep you forever.
-Him

They didn't kill me where I stood.

If they'd planned on murder, they'd have shot me in the forest.

Simon ordered the other men to gather my belongings. Nothing like chivalry at gunpoint.

I couldn't let them capture me, but with a thudding heart and freezing feet, I wouldn't make it far if I attempted to escape by tumbling down the icy knoll and trying my luck in the half-frozen stream below.

"You *gentlemen* don't need to escort me to my car," I said. "I can find it myself."

"But can we trust you to *leave?*" Simon asked. "For some reason, you keep finding your way back to our property."

"Can you blame me? This location is perfect. So secluded and private." I flashed a smile that bared more teeth than charm. "I bet you can do anything you want here."

"You have no idea."

"I have plenty of ideas, Mr. Goodman. I know *exactly* what happens out here on your farm...especially when no one is around to stop you."

Simon slowed, his boot crushing the snow, churning the pristine white into mud. "Think carefully about your words, Detective."

"Why?"

"You can't go around accusing men of such crimes."

One of the younger men snorted, his sneer less cordial and more primal. "Shouldn't be accusing men of anything."

"That so?" I asked. "Maybe I should be seen and not heard?"

"Works for our women." He stepped a little too close. I regretted surrendering my gun. "Keeps them out of trouble."

"And what happens when they get in trouble?"

"We punish them."

"Try me."

Simon bumped me, forcing me to walk once more. "Don't give us reason, Detective."

I'd give them *every* reason.

I wasn't one of their kidnapped slaves, and they wouldn't dare touch me. Sergeant Adamski knew exactly where I was. They could threaten and intimidate, but they couldn't keep me hidden from the world inside their fortress of perversion. They had to keep me safe.

Couldn't give the police any more reason to investigate what *really* happened on their farm.

But that didn't mean I liked being led inside their compound like the hunters' freshly gutted kill.

The Goodman farm didn't look like a trap—not with the rows of pretty little cottages, paved walkways, and the laughter of children. It wasn't a water-stained basement with no windows, doors, or hope, but it was just as dangerous.

I followed them through the little town square. The dizzying pounding of my heart blurred my vision and threatened to ice my blood in panic. Once, I had been weak. Helpless and frail. I thought submission would appease a deranged lunatic. But that frailty was just what the Goodmans wanted. They longed to break their prey and force them to surrender their independence and dignity.

I'd never relinquish that again. I'd fight. I'd scream. I'd hurt.

I'd die if I had to.

The men didn't have time to clear the farm. The women and children scattered underfoot. Two little boys tossed feed for the chickens. The other group of three focused on building a teetering snowman. Two older women, maybe in their forties, the oldest I'd seen, carried an ivory painted trellis from the basement of their chapel towards their communal hall.

"Big wedding coming up, right?" I asked.

Simon said nothing. The men didn't react.

"Who is the lucky, *little* lady?" I gestured to the group of pre-teen girls. They didn't look like they'd been pregnant. They must've been next for the slaughter. "Why don't you mail me an invite? My +1 might be the entire SWAT team though. But we'll share the dinner."

Simon took a great pleasure in his words. "Detective, you are not invited."

"I don't need a formal invitation. I'll come as soon as I have probable cause."

Simon stopped me before the largest house in the compound. I steeled my spine, but the courage rusted away as the men encircled me.

"We've been kind so far, Detective," Simon whispered. "Don't make us regret it."

"I love the hospitality."

"You have no idea what you're looking to find here."

"Enlighten me. I'm ready for your confession."

"I confess my sins only to God."

"You think he'd listen to a slime bag like you?"

Simon tensed. His arm raised. I *dared* him, but before he could make that mistake, a voice called to us from the porch.

"*Oh*! Hello, there!" The woman chastised Simon with a voice softer than the click of the screen door. "Shame on you, Simon Goodman. You didn't tell me we had guests."

I turned, but my stomach didn't. It dropped out of me, leaving me stunned and silenced.

Anna Prescott grinned from the porch.

"Really, you should have called to give me some warning." Anna dusted her flour coated fingers on her dress and waved me towards the house. "Come on inside. No sense sitting out in the cold."

It *had* to be her.

She hadn't grown since she'd been kidnapped. I stared at all five-foot-five, one hundred and thirty pounds of Eve Goodman—complete with her chestnut hair, hazel eyes, and the port wine stain birthmark stretching over her neck and dipping beneath the neckline of her powder blue dress. She hadn't worn her hair in a French braid at fifteen, and her last pictures teased her in a mini-skirt, but I knew who she really was.

Anna Prescott.

And the only lingering doubt giving me pause was that she didn't run screaming as soon as she found a police officer.

"It is simply *freezing* out here." She called me up the stairs and shoo'ed Simon and the men with a flick of her hand. "Only half an hour until chapel. Go drop off your gear and change. And don't forget to wash up. I won't have you tracking mud through the church again." She smiled at me—a grin sweet and innocent and completely obvious to the danger. "Last week, we spent two hours chipping mud off the back of the booths. Such a shame too. It took Jonah a year to build those pews for the chapel, and fifteen minutes for the boys to muck it all up. John was livid. No need to start a holy war over muddy boots, right?"

"Uh…" The bubbly enthusiasm blindsided me. "Right."

Who was this woman?

Healthy. Vibrant. Anna acted as if her kidnapper's porch was the most comfortable retreat in the world.

"I'm Eve." She spoke the name naturally. "Come inside. Make yourself at home. I'll put on a fresh pot of coffee."

"No, thank you." I stepped inside, somehow more tense inside a perfectly pleasant home than surrounded by guns in the forest. "I'm Detective London McKenna. I think I should speak with Jacob."

"*If only.*" Anna rolled her eyes. "He's so busy lately. Hardly has time to chat with me. But come in. We'll have a cup of coffee and see if he comes out of his office."

Anna patted her braid, accidentally leaving a handprint of white flour in her chestnut locks. She brushed at her hair, sighed, and ignored the smudge while welcoming me inside.

The house smelled of cinnamon and apples, yeast and bread. Overwhelmingly so. A window opened in the far corner of the living room, but the heat smothered the home. Anna fanned her face.

"The ovens have been on all day. It's like my own little bit of summer in here, don't you think?"

Sure, summer. But *where*?

Anna's home appeared modern enough—white leather couches, hand-crafted tables and chairs, and subdued crimson rugs that popped against the hardwood and cream walls.

No TV. No radio. Anna didn't have a laptop or iPad plugged into an outlet. A lone recipe book sat on the kitchen counter, faded and worn like it had been handed down generation to generation with a detour into a soapy sink. Someone recently rebound the blue spiral binding and attempted to repair the tears and stains. Anna picked it up and carried it close.

"Please excuse the mess." She collapsed in her chair with an *oomph*. "It's my baking day. I've been so busy that this is my first chance to catch my breath. Up and down, rolling and baking, prepping and scrubbing, peeling and stirring, crimping and sugaring. It's exhausting just listing it."

Exhausting hearing it too. But Anna practically vibrated with energy—more than most of the meth head perps dragged through the station house. I'd have demanded a piss test if I wasn't sure I could twist her enthusiasm into information.

If the excitement wasn't a cover for something.

Nerves? Fright?

But Anna prattled over her kitchen, stepping on her tip-toes to reach the coffee mugs and reloading her French press for another brew.

She tutted her tongue at the pile of dishes in the sink. Loaf pans and pie tins, spatulas and cookie sheets. She abandoned a search for a spoon and used a butter knife to stir the milk into her coffee.

What was creepier—a Stepford wife who had everything perfect for her husband…or the little captive woman so unapologetically imperfect that the house looked absolutely *normal?*

But none of this was normal.

Anna was a thirty-year-old woman, forced into a fifteen-year relationship with a man old enough to be her father.

He'd kidnapped her. Impregnated her. Held her at the farm against her will.

And this was my chance to save her.

If she wanted to be saved.

Anna looked perfectly peaceful in her kitchen, doting over her *baking day* and serving a complete stranger a cup of coffee.

"Oh, let me get you a slice of pie!"

Anna nudged a gorgeous apple pie towards the edge of the counter. She'd baked it well, golden crust even dazzled with a sprinkling of coarse sugar. She'd even braided the dough into a perfect ring around the crust. A pie like that belonged in a New York bakery, not hidden in a farm-turned-prison.

"It's a family recipe, so I won't take sole credit for it," she said. "But I can eat it until I burst."

I stared at this woman. Was it an act, or was she really this naïve? "I couldn't, thank you."

"Just a taste?"

"You haven't even cut it. I'd hate to spoil something so pretty."

"What good is an uneaten pie?" Anna winked and gestured to the oven and cooling rack. "Besides, I've baked three more over there. I'm swimming in desserts. You'd be doing Jacob's sugar a favor if you take a piece."

My stomach was empty, and if I ate, she'd warm up to me. Maybe that would make her drop the Martha Stewart act and become Anna Prescott once more.

"*One* piece. Small. A sliver." I gestured with my hands. "Smaller than that!"

"You're a little thing, Detective. I won't tell if you don't." Anna sliced a hulking piece of pie, slamming what had to be two apples worth of gooey filling onto a plate. "You won't regret it."

Light footsteps creaked the hall's wooden floorboards. Anna didn't turn before addressing our interloper.

"Mariam, you have twenty minutes before your behind better be sitting in the chapel's pews..." Anna glanced over her shoulder. "Get cleaned up now. I want you and the baby in fresh dresses for the service."

I turned, my stomach twisting. I recognized the little girl—the ten-year-old pixie from the cemetery. I'd tucked my card into her pocket, but she'd never called.

Christ, I hope I hadn't gotten her into trouble.

Mariam kept her head down, almost like scolded child caught, but she obediently approached under Anna's direction.

"We have a guest," Anna said. "Detective McKenna, this is Mariam. She's one of our new girls here. We're so lucky we've found her."

"We've met…" I arched my eyebrows. "Do you remember me? I'm London. I'm the detective from the cemetery."

Mariam didn't answer. She looked up at Anna.

For instruction.

No. She edged closer to her. Almost like…

She looked to her for protection.

"What's wrong?" Anna asked.

Mariam swallowed, hard, avoiding my gaze. "Should the baby wear a jacket too? Or just the blanket?"

The baby?

Anna teetered on the decision, humming to herself. "Last night, John nearly sweated us out of the chapel. Simon was supposed to fix the heat…just a blanket for now. No sense melting the poor thing if it's still hot as Hades in there."

Mariam nodded and skittered past me as quickly as she could. She bolted from the kitchen before I had a chance to ask her any other questions.

My eyebrow rose. Anna simply chuckled.

"She's shy. You'll have to forgive her."

"She's very young."

At least Anna couldn't deny the obvious. "Poor thing. Thank God we found her when we did. She's blessed all our lives."

She was *ten*. I didn't trust a Goodman's blessing.

"Where are her parents?"

Anna helped herself to a piece of pie as well, taking a tiny bite of hers only once I tried mine. Her fork twirled in the sugary syrup and apples. "Unfortunately, we don't know. Not many of our girls will even admit to *having* parents. They ran, they found us, and we took them in. The farm is the only love they've ever experienced."

"Did the families abandon them?"

"Some." Anna nodded. Was she lying, or did she believe it? "Others hid away from abuses I can't even imagine…but I suspect you can, being a detective. What is your field?"

I spoke slowly, watching for any twitch, any little reaction in her expression. "Missing Persons."

Nothing. Anna didn't miss a beat, though her voice darkened, solemn and fierce. "Then you must see this often. The poor girls—out in the world all alone. It breaks my heart."

"I see too much of it."

"How do you cope?"

I held her gaze. "By rescuing as many endangered children as I can."

Anna smiled. "Then we're very similar."

Not in the least.

The pie was delicious, and I delayed my next question with a large mouthful. Anna approved, sneaking her own nibble.

"Mariam…" I said. "She's living here permanently then?"

"That's right."

"And she's…babysitting?"

"Oh, yes. She's been a godsend with the baby." Anna pointed her fork at me. "I know what you're thinking."

"…I doubt that."

"You don't like a girl her age babysitting. Well, Mariam is young, but she's more than capable of caring for the baby. This is good practice. How else will she learn to care for her own children?"

The pie soured in my stomach. "She's got a lot of time before then."

"Perhaps."

The baby began to cry, echoing from upstairs. A young cry, not newborn, but not toddler. I tensed, but Anna didn't react beyond a curious glance to see if she might be needed.

I played dumb. "Is it your baby?"

"Oh no. She's the daughter of another one of our girls. Poor thing. That ray of sunshine is just a little fussy—growth spurt. She's not sleep-trained yet, and her momma...well, it's hard enough being a teenage mother. She needed a little help, so Mariam volunteered to watch the little princess."

"What's her name?"

"Oh, it seems to change day-to-day. By the time we're satisfied, the baby will have picked it herself."

"How old is she?"

"Eight months."

The perfect age for Jonah and Nina's child. I sucked in a breath, but Anna was too quick.

"Do you have children, Detective?"

"No. I'm a bit more...career focused."

"You're with the Pittsburgh Police?"

Was it hope in her voice, or just curiosity? "Yes. I can show you my badge."

She shook her head. "This is a small community. We trust you."

"Maybe you shouldn't."

"I'll always err on the side of trust, especially in our little family," she said. "Sounds like you need to get out of the city more."

If it meant saving these girls, I'd be here every minute of the day. "Maybe."

"What brings you all the way out here?"

I glanced over my shoulder. Mariam had gone upstairs. Jacob hadn't appeared. For the moment, we were alone.

If only she knew how valuable that privacy was.

"You did," I said.

Anna crinkled her nose. "Me? Have we met before?"

"I'm here to help you."

My promise amused her. "Unless you can cook, clean, sew, and organize an *entire* wedding..." She winked. "Mark's wife, Elizabeth, is pregnant again. Ready to pop. I told her that I already scrubbed the chapel floors once. I won't have her water break and ruin a freshly waxed floor. No thanks. So I put her in bed last week and told her to rest until the baby comes. Been watching her grandkids and helping with the other children in the meantime. Between diapers and the wedding, dinners and cleaning, it's been absolutely insane here."

Insane was one word for it.

I leaned in close. "I'm not talking about helping around the home."

"That's a shame. There's always a diaper to be changed, cow to be milked, or wood to be chopped. Fortunately, the family is big enough that we can all chip in and help." She hummed. "But you're not here to talk chores, are you?"

"No."

"Detective, is there something I can help you with?"

Anna watched me with wide-eyes, a chipmunk's enthusiasm, and all the charm of a school girl. How was this possible? Stockholm syndrome was a powerful and unfortunate consequence of captivity, but this was beyond anything I'd ever studied in my psychology classes.

Anna seemed…*normal.*

Completely unfazed by her kidnapping.

She acted as though the farm's pregnant girls had arrived for the charity and support, not because they served the desires of the men who'd captured them.

Whatever trauma Anna had endured, she preserved. Lived through it. Seemed *happy.*

How?

How could she just…get over it? How could she smile so bright?

I'd lived through three weeks of hell with my captor, and I was ruined.

Anna spent fifteen *years* with her attacker, and she loved her life.

What had happened to her?

No. What had happened to me?

I swallowed, fearing the worst from this conversation—not that I couldn't get her out, but that she wouldn't want to leave.

"Eve…" I surrendered and used her false name. "Your sister sent me."

"Sister? Someone from the farm?"

"No. Your sister, *Louisa.*"

Anna frowned, her entire face scrunching almost into a pout. "I don't know a Louisa. And I don't have a sister. Plenty of in-laws, of course, but no biological family."

I pulled the photo from my bag, showing her the grinning images of teenage Louisa and Anna, sitting on the porch steps of their new home in Braddock. They shared the same smile, freckles, and even ice cream flavors.

"This is you," I said. "*Anna Prescott.*"

Anna glanced at the photo before laughing like I was the delusional one. "Detective, my name is Eve. Eve Goodman."

"And how long have you used that name?"

"I've been Eve my whole life."

"You've been Eve since you were fourteen."

She dug into her pie, heaping a sticky apple onto her fork. She licked the cinnamon juice from her bottom lip. "I don't talk about my past very much, Detective. I prefer not to."

My heart rate jumped. "Why? What happened to you? When you were younger?"

The fork clinked against her plate, and she surveyed her kitchen— bright, comfortable, and obviously well-tended. "My life before Harvest Dominion? It was horrible. I was in a bad place with bad people who didn't care about me, my wellbeing, or my eternal soul. When Jacob found me…it was like a message from Christ himself. I saw that the world could be bright and good. This farm has been my salvation. *Jacob* has been my salvation."

"You married your savior?"

She actually blushed. "We fell for each other. He lost his wife years before we met. I think we just…fit together."

"You were young."

"You know how these things happen."

"You were too young, Eve."

A realization flooded her features, but she merely laughed. "You're worried about *that*? Detective, just say so. You can check the county records. We married *after* I was eighteen."

"And before that?"

"You have nothing to fear. Jacob is the greatest man I know. I fell for him. Couldn't help it. He's so…" She sighed, like a school-girl infatuated with a high school quarterback. "*Magnetic*. He understands this world and the next. He does the Lord's work every day and in every way. *Godly* doesn't begin to describe him."

"He sounds perfect."

"We all have our sins, Detective. Jacob Goodman just has fewer than most."

No wonder Anna acted the way she did. She didn't see the danger.

Hell, she couldn't even comprehend it.

Whatever Jacob had fed her, whatever lies he'd snaked into her brain, worked.

Anna Prescott was completely brainwashed.

And I could only imagine the other girls suffered the same delusions.

This complicated things. Endangered them and me. I had to be careful.

I took another bite of the pie and sipped my coffee, as if I was just a friend, sitting down for a chat with a charming and delightful acquaintance.

"So you're happy then?" I asked.

"Oh, very." Anna eagerly answered. "The farm and this life must seem like a lot of work, and it is. Not only do we tend to the Lord's fields, we're tending souls of children who have only seen darkness in the world so far. But I wouldn't trade it for the world."

"Not even the diapers?"

She groaned, rolling her eyes. "*So* many diapers."

"How many children are here?"

"Well...five in diapers. Three who still have the occasional accident."

"Where are yours?"

That stole her smile, but only for a moment. "Oh. I have...none. I lost my son some time ago."

"I'm sorry." I reached across the table and patted her wrist. She liked the contact.

How damaged was she if she *liked* being touched after what happened to her?

How damaged was I that I *hated* to be touched after what happened to me?

"How long ago?" I asked.

"A while."

I tilted my head. "Fifteen years?"

Anna's gaze snapped to mine, and in that instant I saw something sharper, something far more intelligent than I had given her credit for. "I don't think you can understand this pain, not if you've never had a child. The day is forever seared into my memory, and it kills me every moment of every day that I never got a chance to hold my son. But the Lord needed my boy with him, and so he's now in Heaven. Safe. I regret that I can't give Jacob any more sons, but his first wife had provided him with five beautiful children. He has the large family he's always wanted."

I eased back from the subject. "Everyone here has big families?"

"Yes." She relaxed. "The children complete our lives. It might seem old-fashioned, but we're…devoted to large families."

"Quiverfull?"

She gave a wishy-washy shrug. "If a man and woman are truly husband and wife, then we should welcome every blessing the Lord gives as long as we are…capable."

I softened my voice and lied. "I'm sorry. I didn't realize…"

"The miscarriage had complications. I don't believe I'll ever have another child. But I have many nieces and nephews, grand-nieces and nephews, and of course, my own step-sons and daughters."

"What about Rebecca?"

"Who?"

"Nina Martin's baby."

"Nina? I don't know anyone—"

"Rachel. She went by Rachel while she was here. Jonah's wife."

Anna covered her heart with a hand. "Those two poor souls. Detective, I know what you must think, but Rachel was *so* young. She lived here for over a year, but she wasn't well. She became infatuated with Jonah."

"Did Jonah feel the same way?"

"I can't tell you what Jonah felt or thought…" She seemed to crumble, a deep breath all that kept her from weeping. "If I could, I might have prevented him from…I might've saved us this ugliness."

"You can't blame yourself," I said. "But I need some information."

"I'm not sure how much I can help…didn't the homicide detectives already speak with my husband about all this?"

"They discussed Jonah. But I'm interested in Rachel. Her real name was Nina Martin, and she ran away from home at twelve. I know just before she was murdered, she had prepared a nursery for a baby." I paused, long enough for Anna to look up. "Where's her baby, Eve?"

"There is no baby."

"Why did she have the nursery?"

She shook her head. "Rachel...she was a special girl, but she wasn't well. We did what we could for her, but she endured such trauma from her time homeless and alone—just like most of the girls experience before they find safety here. I don't know exactly what happened to Rachel, but it hurt her—mentally. She was sick, Detective. There's no baby."

The lie came so easily.

Did she believe it, or did the confidence come from spinning the story herself?

But Anna seemed so *honest*. No fidgeting. No hedging. No telltale twitches or shady glances to the side that might have precipitated a lie.

I'd done my share of interrogations. Either Anna was the greatest liar I'd ever met, or...

Even she didn't know the difference between the truth and Jacob's perverted inventions.

"We can't save everyone," Anna said. "That's what Jacob says. Even his own *son* was tempted to an evil we couldn't understand. I wish I had protected them, but Jonah and Rachel knew what would happen if they left. The world isn't safe outside of our farm."

"Why not?"

Anna pushed her plate, stealing only the apples from inside the pie and leaving her crust. "You see it every day, Detective. Violence. Cruelty. Hunger. The farm protects us from all of that unpleasantness."

"Is that why no one leaves?"

"What do you mean?"

"Pastor Kerst mentioned that the girls you take in don't leave the farm."

"Why would they?" Anna asked. "This is their *home*—doesn't matter if they're ten like Mariam or sixty. They can stay for as long as they wish. Pastor Kerst is a lovely man, but he doesn't understand our ways."

"Is that why you don't attend his services anymore?"

"You *have* researched us, haven't you, Detective?"

I shrugged. "And there's still lots I have to learn. I'd rather know the truth than gossip."

Anna nodded. "Wouldn't we all? The truth is, we disagree on a few tenants of Pastor Kerst's flock, and Jacob thought it best to have our own services right here. And with John finally out of seminary, it was time."

"Did you disagree with Pastor Kerst?"

"Oh..." Anna smiled. "I defer to my husband in those matters."

All matters, probably. "Faith?"

"Of course faith. He is the head of this household."

"And you submit to that?"

Anna wagged a finger. "You make it sound so terrible. But you're a detective. Surely you have a commanding officer. A sergeant? And he answers to the captain?"

"A lieutenant."

"It is the same with our family. As a wife, I support my husband. And he acts as the head of our household and church. He defers to God."

"From what I've learned about Jacob…it doesn't sound like he defers to anyone."

It earned a chuckle. "He is a willful and stubborn man, yes."

"I would like to speak with him."

"So would I. But he's been so busy lately with the farm and preparing for the wedding."

"Who's getting married?"

"One of our family."

I nodded. "I'd like to meet them too. You should call her over. There's plenty of pie to share."

"If only…" Anna murmured. "Unfortunately, the girls here don't like the police. They've had bad experiences in their past, and…" She lowered her gaze. "Well, they've been traumatized. In many ways."

"*You're* talking to me," I said. "Are you braver than them?"

"I'm Jacob's wife, Detective. I must be brave. Strong."

"Why?"

"Because this is his farm. His charity. His love. As his wife, I've taken on more responsibility than you realize."

"Like?"

"Someone must care for the children when they come here. Someone has to love them, has to show them that there is nothing left to fear or hate or run from." She hesitated. "I love Jacob, but the marriage means more than my feelings for my husband. It's a *responsibility* to this church and home and farm. I watch over the girls."

But who watches over them once they've been given to the men?

The chiming of bells echoed over the farm. The clanging cadence rang harsh and jarring. Anna stood, quickly, fretting over her hair and dress.

"Oh, I'm just a mess for evening prayers." She patted the flour from her skirts as best she could. "Serves me right for scolding all the others about getting ready. Here I am, going to the chapel with a pocketful of bread." She scooped a handful of flour out of her apron before tossing the whole thing in the sink with a sigh. "A woman's work, right, Detective?"

"You're called to prayers?"

"It's a pre-dinner ritual here. A nice tradition to end the day before we sit down and eat as a family." She grinned, her eyes widening, bright and excited. "You *must* come with us. You can sit in on prayers, and we'll all have dinner together. Won't that be nice? We so seldom have guests..."

A heavy creak from the hall diverted her attention in mid-sentence. She silenced, turning to face the shadow that cloaked the room in a sudden chill.

I rarely had cause to reach for my gun.

Jacob Goodman's presence was all the reasonable suspicion, probable cause, and direct threat I needed.

But his brother had kept my weapon, and I had nothing beyond a badge to defend me from whatever retribution Jacob decided to inflict.

Jacob's shadow filled the parts of the kitchen his huge bulk did not. I hadn't expected the beast of a man. Jacob wasn't the first bull to tower over me, but my every instinct screamed caution. No matter the grey peppered in his hair, the lines in his face, or how affectionately his wife called to him, I recognized the true *danger* in this man.

"Wouldn't that be nice, Jacob?" Anna asked, her suggestion a demure whisper. "The detective could stay for dinner."

His voice didn't rasp. It dragged like sandpaper against the words, grating the sounds with a primitive grunt. His deep, throbbing baritone knew only command and order. I doubted he had ever raised his voice. Probably never needed to.

"Maybe another time." His eyes flattened, a colorless dark. Dead and searching for more misery. "This is a family service tonight."

Louisa was right.

He was evil.

Any doubt, any hesitation I'd felt during my conversation with Anna? Gone.

Jacob Goodman wasn't larger than life. He controlled it.

Every breath taken on the farm, every word spoken, and every baby born was because of his will. He gave the permissions, and he decided the punishments.

My trespass in his home wouldn't be forgotten.

Or forgiven.

The cold fear clutching my heart wasn't worry for myself. I stared at Anna.

How much danger would she be in for talking to me?

Would he know she had remained loyal? She'd lied for him, but would he care?

Or did I endanger her life too?

"I should be going," I said. "My sergeant texted me to report back to the precinct."

"Well...wait." Anna pulled a glass plate from her cupboard and sectioned off a giant segment of pie. She plopped it onto the plate and wrapped it up tight with plastic. "Take some pie home. It's not often I get to entertain guests."

I stared at Jacob. No wonder.

"Detective." He reached for his pocket. I tensed, but he handed me my gun. Nothing was left in the clip, but at least he returned it. "This is the last time you'll visit."

It wasn't a question. More a command.

Not one I was likely to obey.

"I might have cause to return…" Soon. "Thank you for the hospitality."

Anna guided me towards the door. "Let me walk you out, Detective."

Jacob's warning wasn't one she should have ignored. "Eve. You'll be late for prayers."

"I can hurry over in the snow, don't worry. I'll be there."

I prepared for violence, but Jacob said nothing, letting his wife escort me from her home. She delayed only to toss a shawl over her shoulders.

The farm burst to life as the bells tolled, and the family scattered to the chapel. Anna called to a boy sprinting over the frozen dirt.

"No running, Isaac! You'll break your neck on the ice *you* forgot to salt!"

The boy apologized and immediately slowed his steps. She chuckled.

"The kids here get so excited. But it really makes the place…come alive." She extended her hand, but her brow furrowed. "Where's your car, Detective?"

Parked somewhere in the woods where Simon had undoubtedly uncovered it.

I didn't release her hand. "You should come with me."

"Excuse me?"

"I know who you are, Eve. I know what's happened to you."

Her lips twitched into a thin line. "I'm afraid I don't understand—"

"I can help, if you give me the chance."

Her shoulders slumped, but she gave a short sigh. "Detective, there's nothing to help. Don't worry about me. Protect your own soul."

My stomach clenched. I met her gaze, and her eyes—more green than brown—haunted me with an unwavering conviction.

"Why should I protect my soul?"

"Because you've already endured enough hellfire."

Was it a code? Louisa's fire?

Damn it. *Did she know?*

She must have heard, must have realized it was her husband who ordered someone to endanger her sister's life.

No wonder she didn't want to talk.

She was protecting Louisa!

Just as she attempted to protect me.

"Eve, if you're in trouble," I said, "if *anyone* is in trouble, I can get you out."

She took my hand, holding it tight. "The only person who is causing trouble is you. We are safe with Jacob. But you..." She glanced to the chapel, watching as her husband spoke with his three brothers outside of the building. "You shouldn't return."

"I'll save you. I swear it, Anna."

She released my hand, taking a few quiet steps backward, towards her family.

Her captors.

"But, Detective...who is going to save you?"

Chapter Nineteen

Of course, you want to go home. I understand.
You won't ever leave, but I understand.
-Him.

"You went on their *property*?" Adamski slammed the door to his office. "It's like you're gunning for a mistrial!"

Oh Lord. "The Goodmans tattled on me?"

Adamski hiked his pants a little higher. Over his navel meant one hell of a lecture. "Pull this shit, and I won't just kick you off the case. I'll suspend your ass."

"I didn't realize it was their property."

"You entered their *house*."

"That was *after* Simon Goodman and his family convinced me to stay for pie and coffee."

"How?"

"Well, the five rifles aiming at my head were real hospitable."

Adamski's blood pressure could only take so much. "*What the hell happened?*"

I dropped the camera equipment on his desk. "I was doing my surveillance, trying to determine who each woman is. I needed decent photos to scan with the FBI's facial recognition software. I *know* those women are in the Missing Persons database. This could prove it." I arched an eyebrow. "But Simon and his brothers and sons found me first."

"Did they attack you?"

"No. They took me back to their compound." I smirked. "I ate dessert with Anna Prescott."

He plopped into his chair, scanning my expression for any doubts. He wouldn't find them. "Are you sure it's her?"

"Same features. Identical to her pictures. Portwine birthmark on her neck. It's Anna."

"Then why the hell didn't you bring her with you?"

That question had caused a night's worth of insomnia. "It's complicated. Anna acted as if she didn't know who she really was. She called herself *Eve*. Talked about the farm as if she belonged there. She, apparently, *loves* her husband." Not that he understood the meaning of the word. "If she would verify it, I could prove Jacob Goodman raped her when she was underage. But she's…"

"What?"

"Brainwashed."

"London—"

"I'm serious." I paced the office. Most of the guys had gone home, but if I could have had them here, listening, *helping* me to free the girls from the farm, I'd have traded all the favors, coffee, and pastries I could find. "We have to get them out of there. As soon as possible."

"*If* you're right…these things take time. We've gotta get warrants, SWAT teams organized, briefings, maps of the property—"

"They're planning a wedding." The words sickened me. "And the only available girls to wed…they're *kids*. Teenagers if they're lucky, Bruce."

His knuckles rapped the desk—swollen today. He didn't wince, only stared into nothing, thinking.

"Did Anna admit to being raped?" he asked.

"No."

"Did anyone there exhibit any physical, observable signs of abuse?"

"No."

"Did you see *anything* that might have implied any sort of misconduct?"

"Goddamn it, *no*."

"Then what do you want me to do? We can't legally go in without probable cause."

"What about Nina's baby? Can't we use her for a search warrant?"

"You have no proof that they're keeping Nina Martin's baby on that farm."

"I *heard* the baby. She's the right age. She's living in Anna's house. That is Jonah's child—a child he created with an *underage* Nina Martin."

"And the DA will ream your ass from one side of the station to the other if you can't bring her any evidence of her paternity."

I slammed my hands on the desk, spilling his Coke and scattering pens. "They're holding these girls captive! They've brainwashed them! Raped them!"

"And until we see one of them doing it, we have no leverage. The farm is a haven for troubled teens. The paperwork is sound. Taxes are filed. We need probable cause to get onto that farm, and if you can't even get CPS to file a single complaint, we have nothing."

I bit my cheek before I said anything I'd regret.

Didn't bite hard enough.

"Then another little girl is going to have her innocence stolen. And we're going to sit here and do *nothing* while they hurt her."

I'd put my foot through the door, but an officer opened before my wages were garnished for any repairs.

Bruce called after me, shouting as I kicked my chair away from the desk. "I'll talk to my CO. Maybe Lieutenant Clark will have an idea."

Unless it involved a SWAT team and an immediate evacuation of the farm, I didn't want to hear it.

And unless I got out of the station and went home to sleep, I wouldn't have to worry about the girls. An aneurysm would kill me first.

I gathered my purse and checked my phone. I'd missed two calls. James—but I could text him back. The second call worried me.

Mom.

Oh, this was going to be fun.

I loved her, but Mom was often as intense as a hangover without a shot of aspirin to dull it. I skimmed her three-hundred-word text message. She wasn't technologically impaired, just socially bewildered. Because the message was important, she not only sent the text but also called, leaving me a voice mail as she narrated the entirety of the message.

I waited until I was in my rental car before playing the voice mail on speaker phone.

"London, hiya baby girl. I know you're busy, and your father said it could wait until the weekend—I'm telling her, Charlie...no, it's a message, I'm telling her what

you said…yes, I'll mention it…I know, Charlie! Let me finish the message. Go watch your shows, you're driving me nuts! London, honey, I just wanted you to know that someone mailed you a letter, but it came here. Looks important, but I didn't open it. I thought maybe it could be something classified. You have classified material at the station right? Not that I would know, you never talk about your work. Sometimes there's things you can't tell us about your cases, so I'm not mad…No, Charlie. I'm not mad at you. Well, now I am. Will you let me finish…"

It wasn't fair heading to my parents' house without a dose of liquid courage. Hell, even some antifreeze would have made Baldwin more bearable. Nothing like navigating the tangled, miserable failures that were the insane intersections and illogical roadways of Pittsburgh's South Hills during rush hour on a Friday.

My family had never left the South Hills. Generations of McKennas damned themselves to living just outside the city's shadow. Not because they liked it, but because the roads, construction, and general disarray that was Pittsburgh's urban sprawl trapped the residents inside the South Hills, unable to escape a nightmarish MC Escher styled traffic pattern.

In the 1940s, The Van Trapp family escaped Austria by trekking over the Alps. South Park residents couldn't make it across the five-road intersection to get to the freaking McDonalds.

My childhood home on Leona Drive looked the same as it always had since I was twelve—an orange brick split-level with a forty-five degree inclined driveway. The retaining wall crumbled, losing a battle against endless waves of crabgrass. Shrubs planted in the front, Mary garden converted from half a bathtub in the back. Second toilet and shower in the basement. It was the Pittsburgh classic.

During my kidnapping, I'd *longed* to see this place again.

Now?

Like any other adult returning to their childhood home, I wondered how many minutes were appropriate to visit, if I could make it out without staying for dinner, and if we could avoid scheduling any weekend plans.

If that didn't prove that I'd become a normal, well-adjusted person, what else would?

Vienna was here too. I parked behind my sister's Tahoe and hoped to God she'd remembered to put her emergency brake on this time—unlike two Christmases ago when we'd decked the halls with her insurance company.

I hopped the steps to the front door, took a breath, and raised my hand.

Was I supposed to knock at my parent's house? It felt weird if I didn't. I gave a little half-rap and twisted the knob. But the door swung open.

I looked down.

"*Aunt London!*"

A blur of brunette and braids launched at me. I froze as my four-year-old niece wrapped her arms over my legs and squeezed as hard as she could.

This was the part of family that I truly dreaded.

"Clementine, you shouldn't open the door to strangers," I said.

My niece giggled. "But I know you!"

"Did you check to see if it was me before you opened the door?"

She nibbled on her fingers, her cheeks puffing in a pout. "Maybe."

"Don't lie, Clem."

"But—"

"Don't open the door until your mom says it's okay." I waited. She pouted. "Say it back, Clem. Don't *ever* open the door for strangers."

Clementine's eyes welled up with tears. She slipped out of my grip and sprinted to the kitchen with a wail.

Fantastic.

Why could I talk to child victims easier than my own family?

Mom sat at the dining room table, sprawled on the bench with her leg under her. She scanned the newspaper for decent coupons, though she had an uncanny knack for clipping the foods I wouldn't eat. Still, she couldn't resist setting them aside for me.

A cop doesn't make much money, and you need to start taking care of yourself. Charlie, isn't she looking thin? You look thin, London.

"Hey, Mom."

Mom squealed. "Oh, London. There you are!"

She smooshed her cigarette in the ashtray that had ten years' worth of gunk layered in the bottom. Mom had quit smoking when we were little, but, once I'd been kidnapped, the vice resurfaced. She'd gotten me back, but the habit stayed.

"I'm so glad you came over!" She held me at arm's length for the usual inspection. "You look tired. Charlie, does she look tired to you?"

Dad slept in his living room chair. Not surprising. He had the ability to fall asleep anywhere. Holding a purse while Mom shopped. Waiting in the car while Mom shopped. Pushing the cart while Mom shopped. He snorted and woke, giving me a lazy wave.

"Hi, Princess."

"Hi, Dad."

Mom puttered over the house, collecting everything she had set aside from me since I last trekked south of the city to visit—a week and a half ago. During that time, she'd found a Groupon for Omaha Steaks (*You don't have to shop, they ship them to your house!*), a sweater from college (*It was stored with my clothes, can you believe it, I haven't been your size in thirty-five years!*), and a cookie jar she found at Macy's with a little sparrow on it (*I just thought it was cute*).

Mom was sometimes scatterbrained—the type to sign her Secret Santa cards with *Love, Mom*. But no one could say she wasn't thoughtful.

"How's James?" She gave me another hug. "Tell him to come by for dinner."

"He's out of town."

"Doing what?"

Questions neither of us had clearance to answer. "He couldn't say."

"If you two get married—"

"Mom!"

"—They can't keep sending him on all these secret agent missions, can they?"

"We're only dating. And he's not exactly a secret agent. He's helping with a case."

"You're not getting any younger, London." Mom wiped her lipstick smudge off my cheek. "And he's a good man."

"I know."

"After all he did to help find you."

"There's more to it than that—"

"He stayed with you *every day* for a month after that ordeal."

"That was his *job*."

"He did it because it was *you*. That man's been in love with you since forever."

Or ever since I became the only link he had to the case that had mystified him for years.

When all his other victims were only found in freezers or with bones severed and meat butchered, a living victim offered James a treasure trove of gory details and insight into a mind no one should have ever understood.

But James understood him.

And he understood me.

And maybe that was the problem.

"You said you had mail for me?" I switched the subject before Mom grabbed her datebook and started wedding planning once again.

She nodded, brushing a hand through her hair. She'd tried for a pixy cut a year ago, hated it, and had valiantly attempted to grow it out. But the red dye she used to keep it looking *youthful* made it brittle. She'd been struggling with chin length curls since Thanksgiving.

"I'll find it." She began leafing through mail and cupboards. "I just had it here a minute ago…"

"*London!*"

Vienna's screech made the place feel like home. My older sister skipped the last stair like she always did, but instead of flinging a hair tie at my face and stomping on my toes, she opted to scold instead. Developed a good, stern voice for it too. Probably came from the husband and baby.

"*London.*" Vienna crossed her arms and scowled, still looking as vibrant and rosy-cheeked as ever, even at thirty-five. "Can I have a word with you? Please?"

The tension settled square in my neck, but I managed a nod. "Sure."

Vienna had a bad habit of pouting first and apologizing never. She motioned for me to follow with a curled finger—perfectly manicured twice a week thanks to her husband's salary and an all-day pre-school for Clementine. She might have been wearing a ponytail, but the yoga style was only a ruse. The curls were styled, and the ends trimmed. She dressed for success in any occasion, and she aimed for the jugular in every fight.

I followed her into the den, smiling as Clementine cannonballed Dad and woke him with an unceremonious elbow to his groin. Dad's breath *oofed* out, but he didn't swear.

"*Horsefeathers…*" He gasped. A benign word Vienna strictly enforced around her daughter.

She edged me around the corner. "We need to talk about you and Clem."

"What about her?"

"She was in *tears* when you came in. What did you say to her?"

"Never to open the door unless *you* give her permission." I held her stare. "You never know who might be waiting on the other side."

She couldn't argue with me, but she'd try. "Let me discipline my own child."

"I didn't discipline. I told her to be careful."

"You made her cry."

"*How?*"

"Clementine is *sensitive*. Jesus, London. You work with kids. Shouldn't you know how to act around them?"

Yeah. Probably. "I'm sorry."

"This isn't the first time."

"I said I'm sorry."

"You've been acting weird around her all month. What is it?" Vienna held her arms out. "No hugs. No presents. No *nothing*. You're *avoiding* my daughter."

"I am not," I lied.

"She's *four years old*. What the hell is wrong with you?" Vienna slammed a hand across the doorframe, preventing me from leaving. "London. For real. What's going on?"

I gritted my teeth, but against my better judgement and the power of my jaw, the words slipped out.

"I had a case six weeks ago. A girl about Clem's age." I looked up, slow. How much did I want to say? How much would give my sister nightmares? "She was hurt. By a lot of men. Okay? I got her somewhere safe, but she's just like Clem. Same hair. Same eyes. Same smile. I just…I don't want to imagine that happening to her."

Vienna exhaled. "You're supposed to be detached from the *victims*, London. Not your *family*."

"I told you what was wrong. I'll get over it."

"I don't think you'll ever get over anything."

"What?"

"*Everything* gets to you. Every case. Every memory. Everything you see sticks to you like you're covered in superglue. You can't pry it off without peeling your own skin. And God knows how little of it *he* left on you."

"Stop."

My sister shook her head. "Why did you do this to yourself?"

"Do what?"

"Why did you become a *cop*?" Vienna spat the word. "Do you have any idea what it's doing to you?"

"This is my job."

"No. It's your death sentence."

I picked at the wallpaper, a fading cream that had yellowed with age. Without both of us in the house, the den became a catchall for everything Mom didn't want to deal with. Eight packs of paper towels from Costco. Bags of clothes to donate to the family. Amazon boxes piled ten deep.

But the pictures remained. One of me at my high school graduation. Another month after I'd returned from the ordeal. I smiled in both. Only one looked genuine.

"You should have gone back into psychology," Vienna said. "You'd have been happier."

She had no idea. "That wasn't possible."

"You used to want to *help* people. Even when you were little. You planned on becoming a psychologist so you could make people well again." She took my hand. "There's still time. You can get out of this job before it kills you. Go back to school. James will support you."

"No."

"You have a chance to get yourself well again. To keep *recovering*. But the longer you stay in that dark and terrible world, the less chance you have to survive."

"Vienna, you don't understand."

She refused to let me leave. "Then *tell* me. Talk to me. Like how we used to talk."

"Some people can't be fixed."

"I can fix you."

"I'm not talking about *me*." I gritted my teeth. "I'm talking about *psychology*. I'm talking about the evil people that exist in this world.

They're monsters. Vile. Cruel. Those people can't be helped. The only thing that stops them is the law. That's why I became a detective. So I could help the people who deserve to be helped—not the monsters of the world, but their *victims*."

Mom called from the dining room. That was as good excuse as any. Vienna didn't follow, and I could breathe easier once she dropped that soul-wrenching stare.

She never babied me.

Didn't have to. She was always right.

Mom handed me a letter. "A box came with it, but it was addressed to Clementine."

"Really?" I didn't recognize the writing on the envelope. Hand-written. Sloppy. "There's no return address."

"Oh. Huh. Who's it from?"

I exhaled. "I don't know, Mom. There's no return address."

The envelope ripped as I opened it. Glitter poured out.

"Oh, that's probably from your Aunt Eliza." Mom scurried to the cabinet to grab the dust-buster. "She's always stuffing letters with confetti."

I stared at the dust on my hand.

This wasn't confetti. It rubbed into my finger. Stuck.

I flinched as a larger piece of jagged, clear glass imbedded in my skin.

"What the hell..." I held the envelope over the table and unwrapped the letter. More glass dust fell out, coating the table with a glittery shine.

The letter was scrawled in an uneven cursive.

I will execute great vengeance.

Then they will know that I am the LORD, when I lay my vengeance upon them.

Ezekiel 25:17

Mom read the note over my shoulder. "What in the world does that mean? Aunt Eliza isn't religious…"

Oh, *no.*

"Mom, you said there was a box that came with this. Where is it?"

"It was a teddy bear. For Clementine—"

Mom paled as the first screams echoed through the house.

First Clementine's.

Then the agonized terror of her mother.

Chapter Twenty

Are you angry with me?

I love it when you're angry.

-Him

Clementine needed ten stitches in her hand, three in her finger, and a dozen in her wrist.

Mom ordered a sedative.

Vienna nearly got arrested for assaulting the doctor.

Dad parked in the emergency lane and fought with the hospital over the ticket.

And I had nothing to do.

Nothing I could have done.

I collected the evidence. Helped with the report. Simmered with an unconscionable rage too dangerous to wield with a regulation weapon strapped to my hip.

Fortunately, I knew the responding officer. Pete Bradly was a twenty-year veteran on the force, and though he dyed away all the wisdom peppering his hair, he retained some perspective. He bought me a cup of coffee and forced me to drink every drop before I made any mistakes.

"Doesn't matter who you think did it," he said. "Keep a level head."

Pete carefully bagged the offending teddy bear as evidence. Had to be careful. It didn't seem dangerous, not until Clementine had hugged it, it not until the glass the Goodmans had stuffed inside poked out of the thin material.

Clementine was lucky that she hadn't been more badly hurt.

But she was damn unlucky to be my niece, bleeding because of this madness.

Pete kept me away from the family, forcing me to drink my coffee and cool down in the hospital cafeteria. The plastic chair wobbled against an uneven linoleum floor, checkered black and white and stained with old food.

I wasn't doing anyone any good sitting around, waiting to check my *niece out of the hospital.*

Someone had targeted her.

Because of *me.*

Because I was getting too close.

Because they'd do a hell of a lot worse if their secret finally came out.

Adamski called. Probably at Pete's bidding. He spoke quick.

"Want me to come down there?" he asked.

I picked at the loose bit of rubber sealing the end of the table. It ripped clean off. "Get me my search warrant."

"Give the bear and the envelope to forensics. We'll try to find something we can tie to Goodman."

"It was them. It's retaliation."

"You've pissed off a lot of people in your short career," he warned. "The more good work you do, the more enemies you make."

"But only they are evil enough to target my *four-year-old niece.*"

"Go home. Get some rest."

"And do *what?* My car. My family. What's next?"

"They'll make a mistake, London. And you have to be of sound enough mind to find it. Go get some sleep. I'll see you in the morning. Tell Officer Bradly to drop off the evidence. You don't touch it. Got it?"

"This isn't over."

Adamski sighed. "No. I'm afraid it's just getting started."

I hung up. Pete patted my shoulder and took the bear, stuffing the pictures of my niece's cuts into the bag.

And Adamski wanted me to *go home?*

To *sleep?*

No.

That wasn't happening.

Why should my family lie in bed terrorized and confused while the Goodmans slept soundly next to their child wives? The wrong people had been punished today.

And I'd make sure it never happened again.

Clementine fell asleep in her mother's arms. I didn't bother sticking around. I said my goodbyes, fortunate that Vienna didn't want to wake her daughter. She'd scream at me tomorrow. Blame me for it.

I couldn't argue. This was my fault. And I had to fix it.

I only went home to change my clothes and scrub my niece's blood from my hands. If I had no peace tonight, neither would the Goodmans.

I'd go back to the farm and question every last man, woman, and child on the land until they kicked me out.

And, if we were especially lucky, someone would raise another hand to me. Assaulting a police officer was a one-way ticket back to the station.

I checked the time. Quarter after twelve. It'd be a long night, but who needed sleep? I parked my rental in the driveway and left my coat in the car. The cold air would perk me up. Keep me sharp. Help me to think about the best ways to drag a confession out of Jacob without cutting out his damn tongue.

I climbed the steps to the porch, keys in hand, but I didn't need them.

My door was unlocked.

A chill struck me in place, and every nerve ending fried with a sudden burst of adrenaline.

I *never* left my door unlocked. Never. Not after I'd encountered the worst types of people in this world—the ones who'd creep inside a person's life just for the joy of destroying everything inside. I'd never give them a chance to hurt me again. They didn't deserve a second glance, a polite word...

Or an unlocked door.

My gun sat fifteen bullets heavy on my hip. Armed once more and ready for action I hoped I'd never have to take. I'd worked the police force for eight years, and despite the dangerous circumstances, no one had died in my custody.

But luck wasn't on my side tonight, and it sure as hell didn't wait on the other side of *my* unlocked door.

I held my weapon close and checked the surroundings. No lights on in the house, but that meant nothing. A streetlight shone through the kitchen. I'd have a clear view there, but I'd have to cross the hall first.

The entry would offer some visibility, but was it better to flip on the light and come at the intruder head-on…or sneak in and gain the advantage?

I needed the advantage.

Whoever was inside must have heard the car approach and the door slam. They'd be waiting for me.

I backed away from the front door. I'd go in through the back.

But the porch stairs creaked as I pulled away from the door. The crackling pop practically echoed down the street.

Damn it.

I might as well have shouted to the intruder. He'd have heard it, especially if he listened as hard as I did, held his breath like me, waited with sweat prickling his neck.

If he was trying to get the jump on me, he'd be listening, figuring out everything I was doing.

Especially why I wasn't coming inside yet.

I needed a plan. A delay. The cold settled over my arms.

Perfect.

I darted to my car. My coat was a great decoy. If they were watching, it'd buy me time as I grabbed it from the backseat and wrapped it over my arm with my gun.

My breath puffed hard as I hurried through my side yard towards my back door. The round, cement pavement stones didn't muffle my steps, but the garden hid me well enough. The home's previous owners had put a lot of love into the garden—flowers and bushes and even a tiny gazebo in the corner by the fence. A little bit of peace on a busy street. I usually forgot to water the garden in the spring and pull the dead bits out in the winter, so the overgrown foliage gave me cover.

I edged to the backdoor, peeking inside the kitchen.

Quiet and still. That was a good sign. If I were going to attack someone, it'd be by the front door, as soon as I walked in.

Or the bedroom, but it was best not to think like that.

My key slid into the lock one millimeter at a time. It scraped, but I moved it slow, pausing before daring to turn the tumblers.

It didn't click. That was lucky. But the door often stuck, and the rubber on the bottom always clung to the hardwood or the braided rug on the floor. I bit my lip and pushed. Slowly. Cautiously.

Damn squealing.

The door inched open, the *whoosh* of metal frame against the hardwood a literal dead giveaway to my location. The hinges popped. The knob clicked to its original position.

But I had an inch. I waited, listening hard.

The *thunk* came from upstairs.

Son of a bitch. He *was* waiting for me in the bedroom.

And here I thought I was too old for the Goodmans.

I'd have considered their attentions flattery if the disgust hadn't rotted into rage in my gut. I deliberated calling for backup.

They might have helped.

Or they'd get in my way.

If one of the Goodmans broke into my home, the last thing I wanted was Detective Riley or Falconi impeding my own investigation. An interrogation room had *rules*. My house came with the protection of the Castle Doctrine. I had every right to use force against an intruder.

The right…and the *pleasure*.

That didn't make the rush of blood in my ears any softer. Didn't help the swirling pit of nausea that festered in my gut.

I edged into the kitchen, opening the door only as wide as I needed to slip inside. I closed it immediately. Last thing I wanted was an untimely gust of wind ruining my hidden approach. The lights stayed off. Instead, I quickly flashed my cellphone over the hall.

Empty.

The wall provided enough cover. I scanned the living room on my way to the stairs. Clear. The powder room in the hall had a closed door. I yanked it open and checked. Nothing.

I was alone.

The hard stomp of feet echoed from above.

I reached the stairs, but my heart raced my steps. One stair for every hundred frantic beats. Christ, I'd pass out before I climbed to the top.

But panic never helped.

And I'd already survived so much *worse*.

I held the gun steady, crouched and ready. My bedroom light flashed on, a stream of brightness under the door.

Got him.

A shadow moved inside. He wasn't getting away this time.

Three.

Two…

One—

I burst inside with a shout.

"Hands where I can see them! On your knees, *now*—"

James shouted. His arms shot up, but he went down, twisting hard on his knee as a wet towel landed on the floor. He stopped himself before diving for his gun on the nightstand and instead gave me a shit-eating grin while crouching naked on the floor.

"London, if this is your idea of foreplay…" His chuckle launched a brilliant smile. "I'm…okay with it."

The adrenaline crashed. I dropped the gun and rushed to the bathroom to throw up.

Jesus.

Sweat poured off me, just as gross as losing the contents of my stomach in a nervous, terrified frenzy.

It'd been years since I'd felt that terror.

I didn't have my finger on the guard.

I'd half-squeezed the trigger.

I might have killed him. I *almost* killed him.

I almost—

The asshole walked into the bathroom, tugging on his jeans. "London?"

I flung the first thing I could at him, cracking him across the knees with the rat-tail of a wet towel.

"What the hell are you doing here?"

"I texted you." James hissed and avoided the next *whap* of the towel. "I told you I was coming back. Thought you'd like the company."

I slammed the lid of the toilet down and flushed away that weakness. The stress and panic passed.

I couldn't let him see me like this.

I *never* wanted him to see me like that again.

"Jesus, James." I brushed the hair from my face. "You scared the hell out of me."

"Yeah, likewise." He rubbed my shoulder. I tried hard not to flinch away. I liked his touch, even if I hated to feel the warmth of a hand against me. "Since when do you patrol your own house?"

I stood, nearly retching with the foulness in my mouth. The coffee hadn't tasted good going down, but it felt like hell coming up. I pushed him out of the way and grabbed my toothbrush. If I loaded it with enough toothpaste, I wouldn't have to answer the question.

Unfortunately, James had an excess of patience and an indomitable will. He waited while I brushed, spat, and even handed me a warmed washcloth.

He never once broke his gaze. As much as I loved those golden eyes of his, I couldn't have him looking at me now. Guessing at my thoughts.

Understanding me.

"I thought you were someone else," I said.

"*Obviously.* Who? Where have you been all night?"

"The hospital."

I pushed past him. He let the comment slide without raising his voice, but he followed close.

"Are you hurt?"

"Not me. Clementine."

Now he worried. "*Clem?* Is she okay?"

"The Goodmans sent my family a threatening note. They also included a present for Clem. A hand-stitched teddy bear stuffed with broken glass. She cut herself pretty bad." I picked my gun off the floor with only a slight tremble in my hand. It'd pass. It had to. "And now I need some answers."

"From who?"

"Jacob Goodman."

James took my arm before I changed clothes. "You aren't going up there tonight."

"Like hell."

"London, it's after midnight. You can't go busting into their house on a hunch."

"It's not a hunch."

"Did he sign the note *Jacob*?" James asked the frustrating questions. "Did you run the letter and teddy bear past forensics? Get their fingerprints? A stray hair?"

"No."

"Then why jeopardize your case because you're scared?"

"I am *not* scared!" I twisted to face him, my voice venomous. "I am not afraid of them."

"Then what are you afraid of?"

"Nothing."

James let me go, but his voice tangled me more than any hold on my arm. "That's a lie. Go ahead and try to convince me, but I'd expect a bit of respect and courtesy from you—"

I pointed at him. "Don't you dare pull that shrink shit on me. Not tonight. Not ever again."

"This isn't about me being a psychologist. This is me being your *partner*. We work together on these things. Did something change?"

"Don't start, James. How can you say that?"

"You're not talking to me. You're not *trusting* me."

"I gave you a house key, didn't I? That's *trust*."

"Trust would be remembering that I might *come home* at night." He crossed his arms. The bulging muscles shouldn't have belonged to a PhD. "You never *once* thought it might have been me in your house, did you?"

That wasn't fair. "You didn't tell me where you had gone or when you were coming home."

"Home here?" He threw my own line back in my face. "Or home *Pittsburgh*?"

"What do you want from me?" I dropped the attitude. It wasn't a surrender, but I didn't have the energy to play mind games with an FBI trained profiler. "Just say it, James."

"I want the truth."

"What truth?"

"Why you are so *scared*? All the time, London. Everything you do is premeditated based on *fear*."

"That's not true."

"No?" James picked up my slacks from the ground. "How long did it take you to pick out your outfit today?"

I laughed. It was fake, and he knew it. "What's that supposed to mean?"

"How long did you stare at your closet looking for the *perfect* blouse and slacks? The ones that made you look feminine, but not unprofessional? Young, but not inexperienced. Tough, but not unapproachable..."

I ripped the clothes out of his hands. "Not too long."

If only because I had the outfits organized and planned ahead of time.

"You're so afraid of what people think of you," he said.

"Is that such a bad thing?"

"It is when you let it ruin your life."

That was cute. "My life was ruined long ago."

He didn't share my amusement. He'd never laugh about it. Never stop thinking about it. Never stop blaming himself for it. "And you're still letting him do this to you."

"I don't want to carry that with me. It's not a *choice*." I gritted my teeth. "I spend every waking moment trying to forget what's happened to me. I live my life now to help others, to prevent them from getting hurt!"

"Because you're afraid."

I pitched the clothes into the laundry. Missed. They collided with a lamp, knocking it over.

The crash jolted me. My heart fluttered too quick.

He saw me jump.

Was that what he wanted? What good would the truth do?

And why the hell was I hiding it?

"You're goddamned right I'm afraid," I whispered.

"Of what?"

I lowered the gun onto the nightstand, never far from my hand. "I'm afraid of being a victim forever."

James went quiet, straightening the lamp I'd knocked over and tossing the rest of the laundry into the hamper. Like he'd done it a thousand times before. Like he belonged here.

He turned, the thick muscles of his back just as tense as every inch of me.

"No," he said. "That's not it, London."

What more did he want from me? "I told you the truth!"

"No, you didn't." He dropped the soothing, gentle tone. "You're still afraid of *him*."

How dare he.

"I'm not."

"You see him everywhere. In your victims. In your perps. In your nightmares."

"*You* said it was good to be vigilant. I learned how to cope by protecting others."

James faced me, his eyes golden, warm, and absolutely heartbreaking.

"You see him in me."

I wasn't ready for this conversation.

I couldn't handle that mental exhaustion. It was worse than three weeks hidden away in a dirty, blood-stained basement. Worse than the ripping of skin from my stomach, arms, legs. Worse than a bite to my calf, ravenous and enraged, tearing the flesh like a damned animal.

They thought the only scars I bore were from my captor.

They were wrong.

I'd been interrogated harder than any perp that ever crossed our station.

And it had all began with James's simple question ten years ago.

What do you remember?

"You were in his *head*." I kept my voice low. "But I was in his *basement*. Believe me, James. I'll never fear you."

James paused. "But it bothers you—my profiling."

"Of course, it bothers me! You know him better than anyone."

"Not you."

227

"I didn't *want* to understand him. You do." I looked down, almost chuckling at my skinny frame, messy ponytail, and trembling hands. "God. What would he see if he looked at me now?"

"Don't do this."

"You brought him up." I shrugged. "Tell me. Would he look at me and see another potential victim? Someone weak and timid? Or would he see someone trained in self-defense, able to defend herself, ready to protect others?"

James was silent for a long time.

And I hated the heartbeats that passed. Like I asked for his *approval*. His judgement.

"I think you're his prime target, London."

The floor would fall out beneath me and I'd still beat it down to hell.

I stayed standing, but I didn't understand.

Would never understand.

"But I've done *everything*," I whispered. "I've changed. I'm not as weak as I was."

"But you're *his*. His favorite. His failure. It doesn't matter what you do, where you go, or what you make of yourself. You will *always* be his target." He approached, a hand to my cheek. "But you don't have to be his victim. Not anymore."

His touch became a kiss, and his kiss something better. I clung to him, kissing and breathing and aching. James stared at me, his face so gentle and so *patient*.

"Don't go to the farm," he said. "Stay with me tonight."

"And then what?"

"And then you can go back to your job. Back to saving lives and stopping the bastards who would hurt those little girls." His kiss warmed me. Always did, even when I thought I'd forever be trapped in that cold nothingness. "Tonight, stay with me."

And like always, I agreed.

And like always, I never regretted a moment.

And like always, I never told him how much it meant to me.

How much *he* meant to me.

***

And in the morning, before the alarms chimed or dawn got too bright, my phone rang.

I groggily answered, batting at the cell, too exhausted to clearly read the name.

"Get up, McKenna." Falconi never once charmed a girl with that sing-song tone. Hell, it was still surprising that he ever woke up with a woman. "Rise and shine, Detective. You ain't gonna believe this shit."

I groaned, untangling my arms from James. He always was a cuddler.

Could someone learn to cuddle?

Maybe one day.

"What is it?" I asked.

"Forensics reported on a couple backlogged pieces of evidence for us. A murder weapon. Thought you'd be interested in it."

"Why?"

"Because the gun that killed Jonah Goodman, Cora Abbot, and Nina Martin?" Falconi laughed. "That gun is registered to *Louisa Prescott.*."

Chapter Twenty-One

You underestimated me.
Will you make that same mistake twice?
-Him

I did my best work in the interrogation room, but I never thought I'd be interrogating the sole witness to a reprehensible kidnapping.

Falconi and Riley kept Louisa waiting—a kindness and a curse.

At least she'd talk to me, maybe give me an ounce of the truth without making me work too hard. But that meant she had to wait. I stared through the one-way glass. Watching.

Trying to figure out how I got this so *goddamned* wrong.

I didn't look at Falconi or the report. "You're sure it's her gun?"

"The serial number matches the weapon found in Jonah's hand," he said.

"How the hell did the Goodmans get the weapon?"

Falconi gave a smirk, far too amused for how complicated this case had become. "You tell me, McKenna. You're best buds with the Goodmans now. Chit-chatting over coffee. Meeting the family. Making friends."

"Friends who deliberately hurt my niece."

"To be fair, they did hand-stitch a teddy bear." He leaned against the window. "You don't find that sort of craftsmanship in a weapon anymore. Ask them nicely, they might just knit you a confession."

I ripped the file from his hands. "I'll prove it was them."

"How?"

The only way I could.

By using the only other person who had contact with them.

"Last night, my niece slept in a hospital. I'm done screwing around. I'm getting my answers."

Falconi toasted me with an empty coffee mug. I didn't need luck.

Just the truth.

For once.

I pushed the door open. Louisa flinched, the momentary terror in her face fading as she recognized me.

The woman looked awful. Her sable hair dulled to a muddy brown, and the ring of smudged mascara and eyeliner darkened the circles under her eyes. She clutched her purse. The leather strap twisted in her hands—over, under, rubbed, knotted. If I hadn't known better, I'd have thought the fidgeting to be a side effect of some sort of drug.

But guilt was worse than any withdrawal.

"Detective…" She patted the table. Her nails were bitten raw. "What's going on? They won't tell me anything."

I took the seat next to her. My silence only terrified her more.

"Oh, no. It's Anna, isn't it?"

Louisa crumbled, falling to the floor. The sobs crackled through her. Fifteen years of mourning condensed into fifteen seconds of tears.

I hauled her into the chair. She clutched at my arm.

"Anna's dead?" Louisa hiccuped. "He killed her. Oh, God. It's my fault. This is because of *me.*"

Interesting. I'd have pressed her, but no good information was ever born of hysterics. We didn't have any Kleenex in the interrogation room, my usual tactic with female perps. I signaled to Falconi to find a box before Louisa blubbered all over my table. He stuck his head in for only a moment, tossed me the tissues, and the door closed.

I offered her one and kept my voice calm. That wasn't easy after the hellish week I had.

"Anna's fine. Nothing's happened to her."

Another break. Louisa leaned over, face in her hands. But the relief was short-lived. Her fingers curled tight, and she tugged at her hair instead, nearly wrenching a handful from her shaking head.

"Why haven't you helped her yet? I can't do it on my own. I can't...I can't keep *imagining* what's happening to her. We have to *help* her."

Yes. We did.

But not like this.

"I spoke with her," I said.

Louisa's shock silenced her. She stared at me, mid-quivering breath.

"She calls herself *Eve.* And she's well. Not going hungry. No signs of visible abuse. She takes care of the children. And she says she loves her husband." I watched as Louisa murmured a mournful cry. Sounded honest. "But you already knew that, didn't you?"

"Knew what?"

"Everything."

Louisa pretended not to understand, but the uneasy glance wasn't confusion. It wasn't even *remorse.*

233

"I don't know what you mean," she whispered.

I'd make it easy. "You lied to me."

"I…"

"You said you *just* saw your sister's kidnapper. That it was a random occurrence. That you *happened* to find him that day in the Strip District. And when I pressed you, you claimed you'd never forget a face like his, even after fifteen years."

Louisa paled. "But…that's the truth."

"No. It's not. You knew exactly who had Anna. You knew who he was. Where he lived. The cars and vans he owned. His habits. His business partners. You knew it *all*."

She presented her trembling hands, motioning for me to wait so she could collect her thoughts.

Would they be any more truthful jumbled?

"You don't understand," she said.

"Oh, I understand perfectly. All the information you gave me was good because you had already spoken to them."

"Detective—"

"Don't lie to me."

"*I had to lie!*"

My patience and pity ran out long before we dredged up the documents I tossed before her. I opened the folder to the first record.

"I never thought to run your name through our system," I said. "Imagine my surprise."

"I can explain. *Please.*"

"Harassment. Stalking." I met her gaze. Lies made people shake. She shivered half-way off the chair. "The court ordered a PFA against you on behalf of Jacob Goodman. You're not allowed within one hundred yards of the Harvest Dominion Farm."

For the first time, Louisa's voice darkened. She gripped the table.

"Don't tell me you're *defending* that animal."

"I just want to know why you said you had *no idea* who'd kidnapped your sister even though you'd been *stalking* the family responsible for years."

"It's complicated."

"You claimed you saw *two* of the digits on their license plate. Tell me, Louisa, how long have you had the entire plate *memorized?*"

"It's not how it sounds."

"You gave me *nothing* to solve this case even though you knew, the entire time, every last detail."

"I had to, Detective."

I heard enough. "You lied to me."

"Only about this!"

"Bullshit." I flipped to the second page—a copy of her gun registration. "Got another secret to tell me, Louisa? Cause, I'll be the first to admit...I don't have an explanation for this. Your gun was the weapon used in Jonah Goodman's double murder-suicide." I flashed the autopsy photos of Jonah, Cora, and Nina. "Your gun was in Jonah Goodman's possession. Given your *predilection* for his father, our DA will have her choice of charging you with any number of accessory crimes."

It wasn't true, but Louisa burst into tears. "No! *Please!*"

"Tell me *right now* how Jonah Goodman got your gun, or I can't help you anymore."

Louisa cried out, kicking her chair away so she could collapse to the floor. "I'm sorry! But he has *my sister!*"

"And you think stalking the family and lying to the police is going to save her?"

"It was the only thing I could do!" Louisa panicked. "It's a *cult* detective. That farm is a portal to *hell*. Do you know what they do there? What they did to Anna?"

"I have an idea."

"No. You don't have a *clue*. Those men are taking girls. Young girls. They kidnap them off the streets, force them into that church. They're *brainwashed*. Starved and sleep deprived and completely dominated. They break them, Detective, through beatings and terror and all manner of evil. That's the only way to control them. The girls are scared and alone, and they're forced to do these terrible things in the name of *God*."

The cold pricked my skin. Tears streamed over Louisa's face. She gasped. Hiccupped. Turned beat red as she sobbed at the table.

It was either a damned good performance or the truth.

"They did this to Anna?"

"Of course, they did," she sniffled. "The instant they get a new girl, they keep her *isolated*. Left alone in the dark and cold. It's a room under the barn. That's where they *do it*. Where they beat and starve the poor thing and do...other evils. They call it *Repentance*. Once the girl is cleansed of her sins, she can go free to the farm where she's welcomed with warmth and love...and her new husband."

"What are her sins?"

Louisa tore the Kleenex in her hand. "Their former life."

"They punish her for her *life*?"

"She's a sinner, no matter what. She's listened to the wrong music. Spoken the wrong words. She may not have worshiped in *their* way. But her greatest sin is not devoting her soul to God and body to her *family*.

They punish them for not doing as God intended—providing children to a man as soon as their body is physically capable." Louisa looked away. "They'll hold a girl in Repentance and beat everything out of her. Break her will. They torment her, destroy her, tell her that her previous life had ruined her and nearly cost her Heaven. Only once she's broken, once that old girl has died, are they baptized *new*."

"That's why Anna thinks she's Eve?" I asked.

"Yes. Everything about their past was beaten out of her. Her real memories are repressed under the threat of more *Repentance.*"

"How do you know this?"

Louisa batted the folder towards me. "How do you think I got those charges? I *watched*. I went to the farm. I studied them. I catalogued it. I did *everything* that I could, everything the police refused to do. Everyone except you."

"You still lied to me."

"If I had told you my sister was held by a religious sex cult that brainwashes children into becoming child brides, would you have believed me?"

Nothing like all of my worst fears coming true.

I rubbed my face, but my hand traveled behind, desperately attempting to massage the pulsing pain between my shoulder blades.

I checked the forensics report once more. "And the gun?"

"I gave it to Anna," she said.

"Why?"

"Why else? To use against that pervert if he ever touched her again."

"Jacob's still alive."

"Yeah." Her voice embittered. "And he's still raping her. I wanted her to use it against him. But I had no idea how ensnared she was. She thinks she's in love with him. She probably gave the gun to Jacob the instant I left the farm. Jonah must have grabbed it from the house."

"You never reported it missing."

"That was right before the restraining order..." Louisa rubbed her eyes. "Anna testified against me. She *swore* she didn't know who I was or why I attempted to reach her."

My heart broke for her.

And for Anna.

And the other girls.

"Do you know what they do with their daughters?" She met my gaze. "Their own flesh and blood?"

I already guessed. "Only the men stay on the farm?"

"They marry the girls they kidnap. If they have sons, they stay. If they have daughters..." Louisa rubbed her fingers, as if brushing away dust. "Given away as soon as they reach puberty. Jacob's daughters, his sisters, his nieces, his granddaughters. They're married off to pre-determined men, arranged at their *birth*. They're given to men two or three times their age, and no one says a *damned thing*. God's will."

"Who are they given to?"

"This type of evil is pervasive. They have like-minded friends across the entire East Coast." She lowered her gaze. "It's profitable for them to give away the girls. Easier than kidnapping their own. Only the Goodmans are brazen enough to snatch their victims. The other families wait for their *benevolence*."

Christ.

How many families were involved?

How the hell could an entire network of underground child brides exist without anyone having an idea it was happening?

"They've taken other runaways too," Louisa said.

The resounding dread in her words twisted my stomach. I held her stare. The hollow trauma was there, hidden away, but never gone.

"Some girls never make it out of the barn," she whispered. "The ones who resist. The ones who refuse to repent. Check the family graveyard, Detective. There's too many graves for that family."

"They murder them?"

"They can't all be good little Christian wives, can they?"

My head pounded. I groaned, suppressing the urge to shake her shoulders. "Why didn't you tell me this in the first place? I could have investigated it!"

"And instead of a fire in my parents' home, they'd have murdered me in my sleep." She bit her lip until it left an indent. "You have no idea how dangerous these people are, what they'll do to keep their secret."

I had a good idea. I'd attacked their family, and now they were coming after mine.

"I'll keep you safe," I promised. "I won't let them hurt you."

"And the girls on the farm? What about them? Who will keep them safe from those men?"

The knock on the door interrupted us. I turned, ready to bitch at Falconi, but I didn't recognize the dark, nearly terrified expression twisting his features. He curled his finger for me to follow, his voice a tense warning.

"Phone call," he said. "She'll only talk to you, McKenna."

"Anna?" Louisa leapt from her chair. "It has to be!"

"Sit," I said. I followed Falconi, excusing her from the room. "You're free to go, but don't you dare visit that farm."

Louisa wasn't going anywhere. "That's my sister on the phone, isn't it? Please. I have to talk to her. I can't..."

I rushed to my desk. Louisa fought against the detective. She screamed for me, for the phone.

"*Anna*! No! Please!"

"Let her go," I said. "But keep her quiet."

I picked up the phone, anticipating the nightmare awaiting me.

Would they gloat about the teddy bear? Offer another warning?

Threaten me once more?

"London McKenna. Who is this?"

The line was silent. Crackling, but no one spoke.

"Hello?" I tried again. "It's Detective McKenna. I'm here."

A timid, innocent voice whispered over the line. "H—*hello*?"

I'd be sick.

I waved to the others. Falconi wrestled Louisa into a seat, clapping a hand over her mouth as I put the call on speakerphone.

Louisa shouted, but it wasn't Anna who'd called.

This voice was far too young. Too innocent.

It wavered, light and childish, with the breathy cadence shy little girls used when speaking to strangers.

"Hi." I softened my words. "Thanks for calling me. Are you okay?"

"I..." She was nothing if not polite. "Yes, thank you."

Falconi asked the silent question with a shrug. *Who was she?*

"Mariam, is that you?" I asked. She didn't answer. I fought the bile rising in my stomach. "Mariam, talk to me. Did something happen to you?"

"I don't want to get married."

The station silenced.

Terrified.

No.

Oh god, no.

I clutched the phone. "What's happening, Mariam? Tell me what's going on. Are you getting married?"

"…I guess so."

"To who, honey? Who are you marrying?"

A long delay.

Too long.

"I gotta go," she said.

I'd leap through the phone if it kept her on the line. "Mariam, no, sweetheart. Don't go. Can you find somewhere to talk? Stay with me."

"I gotta get dressed."

"*Dressed?*"

"I have to look pretty. It's supposed to be a special day."

"Mariam, don't hang up. When are you getting married? Soon? Tell me about it—"

The line went dead.

And my heart crushed with it.

I dropped the phone. It thudded on the desk, the only sound in the entire precinct.

Mariam was only ten years old. A child.

A *baby*.

It'd take two hours to get to the farm.

And two hours was enough time to commit countless evils.

Chapter Twenty-Two

Run.

-Him

Two hours. I could make it there in two hours.

God, I hoped the Goodman's had long traditional weddings.

I didn't let the others speak. I grabbed my gun and ran to the door. "Call the ADA. Tell her I need a warrant *now*. Falconi, can you swear it for me?"

"Go." He tossed a sobbing Louisa in a nearby chair. "Riley and I will run it to the judge. We'll call when it's signed."

I turned to Adamski. "Call the Tionesta Sherriff and the State Police. Tell them to *move*. I'll be there as soon as I can."

Adamski was already on his phone. "You don't take a *single step* on that property without a warrant. Tionesta has jurisdiction. Follow their instructions."

Screw the bureaucratic bullshit.

A little girl's life was in danger. Her innocence. Her future.

I crashed down the stairs two at a time, racing to see if I broke my neck or an ankle first. Cold sweat drenched me by the time I reached the car. I nearly hyperventilated when I pulled onto the highway.

It'd been years since I felt this sort of panic, rage…

Helplessness.

Even with my lights on, Pittsburgh traffic clustered tight and unforgiving. I veered between cars on the highway, zipped onto the shoulder when the cars slowed to stop-and-go, and I busted out of the city as quickly as I could make it without hurting any other innocent people.

I beat the steering wheel with frustrated fists. I'd *known* the wedding was coming. They'd been preparing for it, *revering* it. Anna had prattled on about the arrangements. Simon and Jacob practically salivated over the event. The damn wedding was more important than their harvest.

Probably because they sowed their own seeds this way.

And that was the disgusting truth of the family. The dirty little secret they all shared in the depths of their souls. They knew the crimes they committed—that was why they stole the runaways, the ones who'd probably never find their way home.

The Goodman's horses and cows weren't the only livestock on the farm. They treated the girls far worse than any animal. Jacob didn't see them as people.

He used them as breeding stock.

And they rationalized their beliefs with gold bands on fingers too small to wear them.

How long did I have until the horrific bastard consummated his marriage with Mariam?

Could I make it in time?

Could I live with myself if I didn't?

I crossed into Forest County after an hour and ten minutes. Adamski called, but I didn't slow the car, taking the backroad turns without regard for my own safety.

"London, you got your warrant through a Forest County judge," he said. "But you are to wait at the property line until you get back-up from the state cops, understand?"

"They aren't there yet?"

"They'll be there. Don't do anything dangerous. If it gets hot, stand down. They've got kids all over the damned place. Don't let anyone get hurt."

Only the ones who deserve it. "Nothing's gonna happen to the girls or children."

"Or yourself."

"Yeah."

"Or the Goodmans."

That was up to them. "No promises."

I pulled off the main road, spitting dirt and gravel from under my tires. Adamski kept talking, but I ended the call and parked next to the troopers, wishing they hadn't turned their lights on while they waited.

The sheriff used his car to block the path to the farm. He held an arm out as I approached. I practically threw my badge in his face.

"I'm Detective McKenna," I said. "Why aren't you inside?"

The sheriff carried an extra fifty pounds around his waist that didn't look regulation to me. His shirt buttons stretch taut, and he rubbed his belly before giving me a passive wave. What he meant as reassuring seemed pretty damn condescending.

"This is all one big mistake." He smiled. I didn't. "I'm Ron Grimber, Sherriff. I've known Jacob Goodman for years. We're all gonna go in together and just have a nice talk about this charity of theirs—"

"It's not a charity. These girls aren't here because it's a *shelter*. They're forced into marriage with the Goodmans. The women are pregnant because the Goodmans are raping them."

Grimber bristled, brushing his fingers over the thick, black mustache covering most of his lips. "That's quite a story, Detective."

"I have my search warrant."

"And that's why we're gonna go visit."

The other two troopers were even less of a help. The smallest of the three—thin enough to see through with noodle arms that couldn't have held the rifle in his car—talked on his phone to the DA. The other leaned against his car, unwilling to move.

"Did you hear me?" I seethed through clenched teeth. "They're abusing the girls. Why aren't you already inside?"

"Now, don't go twisting those panties," Grimber said. "We can't go in yet."

I let the insult slide. "Why not?"

"Because you ain't the only one who got a weird call today."

"Mariam called you too?"

"Nah." He patted a pack of cigarettes on his hand before plucking one out. He didn't light it, just set it between his lips. "One of their boys called our office. Playing a prank. I'll have a talk with Jacob. Tell him we can't have that sort of jokes around here, not these days."

"What *jokes?*"

"The boy said it was dangerous to come on the farm. Told us to stay away."

My chest tightened. "*What did he say?*"

"He said something about Armageddon." Grimber pinched the cigarette between his lips. "I don't follow that stuff. Gave me a quote too. Revelations 17:14."

I pulled my phone, checking the verse with trembling fingers. Nothing was going to settle them, not until I had a gun in my hand, poised to fire.

I read the verse aloud. "*These people will wage war against the Lamb, and the Lamb will overcome them, because He is Lord of lords and King of kings, and those who are with Him are the called and chosen and faithful.*" I stared at the sheriff. "They threatened *war* with anyone who steps on their land?"

"I told you. It's a prank. Kids must be bored. Not much farming to do in January."

I pushed past the officers, staring into the property.

They weren't bored. They had their entertainment for the day.

Mariam.

"Detective, it's just a prank, but now we got all these regulations to follow," he said. "The state says we wait for the bomb squad."

And every second we wasted was another that might be trapped Mariam with her new *husband*.

Who was it? One of Jacob's sons? Nephews?

I wasn't waiting. "I'm not under your regulations. I'll radio if I have trouble."

"Jesus Christ, lady!"

The Goodmans had committed enough atrocities in that name. I tucked my radio into my belt and ordered the sheriff and troopers to listen for my call.

"Can't come to help you if you get in trouble." He shouted after me.

"Then I better not get into trouble," I said.

Even I didn't believe myself.

I sprinted up the road to the farm, staying low with my gun drawn. My path dotted with enough shrubs and tall grass to pick a quiet and unseen trail towards the Goodman's enclave.

But the farm was empty.

I approached the houses carefully, searching over my shoulder, in the fields, around the gravel walk-ways.

No one moved. No kids yelled. No laughter.

No one chopped wood or scattered feed for the birds. A fresh layer of snow had fallen—completely undisturbed save for the cleared paths.

Forty or more people lived on the farm, but today, the land had been deserted. The homes stayed dark, the barn unopened.

Where the hell did they all go?

I aimed for Anna and Jacob's home first, though not even a footstep creaked from inside.

"*Police!*" I banged on the door with my fist. "Eve! Jacob! I have a warrant to search the property!"

I gave it five seconds before I dropped the diplomacy in favor of a solid kick against the door. The heavy wood refused to give. I crashed against the frame twice before it flung open.

Into silence.

Empty and dark.

Every curtain was drawn, and no one had flicked on a light. The home bathed in eerie stillness.

I exhaled, my breathing a shaky burst of adrenaline and confusion. Fortunately, my gun drew solid and still.

I turned the corner into the kitchen. What a difference a few days made. Anna had cleaned. The sink cleared of pots, pans, and dishes. No flour handprints dotted the stove. The room smelled sterile—bleached and thoroughly scrubbed.

"Anna!" Her real name echoed off the walls, a word unspoken for fifteen years. "Tell me where you are!"

Nothing.

The house didn't even creak. The quiet scared me more than facing a dozen cocked rifles.

Jacob's office waited at the end of the hall. I pushed the door open. Like everything else, he'd left it dark and cleaned. I'd spend more than enough time combing through his drawers and computer once I found the girls. But his space offered me nothing. The ornate bookcase and desk couldn't hide anyone.

Damn it.

I backed away, taking the steps upstairs two at a time. The emptiness didn't surprise me. Neither did the pretty guestrooms—one decorated for a little girl, the other loaded with cribs and supplies for an infant.

Where did they hide?

The curtains fluttered in the heat blown by the register. I let them move for me, peeking outside to scan the farm. The other homes remained dark and quiet—almost in mourning instead of celebrating a marriage.

What if the wedding had turned into a funeral?

My stomach clenched. I gripped the wall, forcing the thought from my mind.

How would they have punished Mariam for calling the police on their imposed wedding day?

What sort of discipline would they inflict on a ten-year-old child?

And then I knew.

I stared at the barn, proud and crimson, standing silently in the far field.

"No…" I gritted my teeth. "*No!*"

I rushed from the house, sprinting into a bright, sunshiny day entirely too cheerful for the crimes committed under that golden glow. My boots crunched in the snow, slipping as I darted up the stone walkway towards the barn.

Louisa's words beat at my brain, driving like a spike through any rational thought.

They hurt the girls in the barn. Demanded their repentance. Their blood. Their innocence.

What had they done to Mariam?

The barn had once appeared a jolly, stereotypical red. Now I feared touching the partially opened doors. The red bled through the wood, seeping crimson into the splintering frame. I peeked inside before pushing the doors open wide.

Quiet.

The haze of the morning glistened through the dust and bits of hay. The musty scent stuck in my throat, watering my eyes. Hell of a time to get allergies. Half of the stalls filled with hay, the others with machinery, tools, and extra storage for treated wood. Jonah's old furniture stock.

At the end of the barn, the Goodman's had built a storm shelter. No, a bomb shelter.

The thick metal doors were too modern and sterile to be anything but a bastion of paranoia. Though the other surfaces caked with dirt and hay dust, these doors had been cleaned. The smear of hand oils on the handle left cloudy prints over the metal. Big finger prints.

A man's prints.

Was someone down there now?

Were they holding Mariam?

Why did it have to be a cellar?

Of all the places I dreaded to go...

Of all the nightmares I'd had...

But I'd escaped my basement. Mariam was still trapped in hers.

I hauled the doors open. The metal accidentally banged against the cement floor. The echo pierced the farm's silence.

The steps faded into the darkness below.

And God only knew what waited for me.

I had no flashlight. I grabbed my cell instead, holding it against the gun as I descended. One step. Listen. Two steps. Squint into the shadows.

Water dripped from somewhere, but the basement didn't have a moldy smell. The air was fresh, circulated somehow. Whoever used this shelter used it often.

A thick, metal door waited at the bottom of the stairs.

Now or never.

"Police!" I pulled the lever and opened the gate into the Goodmans' personal hell. "Keep your hands where I can see them!"

But like everywhere else...the basement was empty.

No.

The *complex* was empty.

My cellphone flashed over the cement. This wasn't a storm shelter or a canning cellar. The structure chilled me, and not just the solid, windowless walls and earthen cold.

Nothing good happened this deep underground, where no one could see, hear, or help.

My steps echoed in the shadows. Hollow. Whatever they had built was *large*. Too big. The little light cast from my phone couldn't cover the entire space nor would it.

What sort of bomb shelter had multiple rooms?

Four rooms branched off the main hall, sealed with heavy, immovable doors. I brushed a shoulder against one. It didn't budge. A strip of metal glinted in the phone's flashlight.

A padlock.

Three of the four doors had been sealed tight. Nothing I could do without the key or bolt cutters. I wasn't desperate enough to fire a bullet at the lock, not yet, not until I knew if anyone else was down here.

But the gun rested heavy in my hand.

I had no idea what I walked into. An ambush. A rape. Hell, the wedding reception might have served poisoned Kool-Aid, and behind the locked doors were the corpses of all the women and children on the compound.

I couldn't think like that. The Goodmans hadn't showed any aggression towards their families before…

Or maybe I hadn't found the right demons.

One room was unlocked. The door slowly opened, and I peered inside.

Empty, as far as I could tell. A light switch was installed *outside* the room. I slapped my hand against the fixture.

With an electric hum, the white lights flickered on. Florescent and obscene. I stepped inside, turning just in time to catch the door before it slammed shut.

It had no handle on the inside. Whoever they kept in the room was meant to stay here.

And any child would be desperate to escape this place.

No blankets. No bathrooms. No kitchen. An undressed mattress was cast haphazardly in the corner. Stained, but with what I was afraid to guess. Let forensics have their own nightmares. I was still managing my own.

Cast around the mattress were photographs, taped to the floor. Fortunately, the young girls in the pictures were clothed. Unfortunately...

Every one of them was pregnant.

A blonde girl. Two brunettes. A redhead. Some I recognized from the farm. Others looked as if they were printed and downloaded from the internet. Girls in skirts and dresses, their hair done in braids, their tummies swollen and stretching their clothing.

The girls were all *smiling*. Bright and chipper and *beautiful*. They touched their bellies and showed off the bump for the camera. Each one prouder than the last.

Were these the last images the captive saw before sleeping at night? Excited, lovely pregnant girls no older then themselves?

Or did they fall asleep staring at the horror above?

Some sadistic artist had painted religious imagery over the room. Vivid and frightening images of hell and punishments haunted the walls and ceiling over the mattress. Flayings, beatings, demons. Fire. Every night, the poor soul strapped to the mattress via its restraints would be forced to look up and bear witness to a terrible vision of torment.

But...on the other side of the...

A bright, beautiful painting of gardens and peace, light and safety. The section of the room was small, the only object in that corner a wooden chair. Resting on the seat was a bible—apparently one of the child's only means of entertainment.

The other?

An educational plastic doll, pregnant and smiling. Part of the Goodman's brainwashing tactic. Normalizing the condition for the little girl.

This prison had no escape, and the leather riding crop resting on the high mantel over the door was not an object for the prisoner to wield. It wielded a position of power in the room.

This wasn't *Repentance*.

This was torture.

I flinched as a sharp clang reverberated in the hall. I twisted, aiming my gun, but a second passed, and I relaxed. Even beneath the ground, the ringing of the chapel's bells sang loud and ominous. The call to prayer was probably the only sound the girls ever heard beyond the preaching of the men torturing them.

The bells didn't stop, bursting over the farm in joyless melody.

Of *course* they'd be in the chapel!

The Goodmans were having their services, marrying the child off!

I burst out of the bunker, tearing through the barn and leaping the steps back to their little compound. The bells continued to chime, louder and darker now that I faced them in the light.

Maybe the ceremony had just finished.

Maybe they hadn't left the church.

Maybe Mariam hadn't lost her innocence...

I swung the chapel doors open, but this wasn't a wedding.

"*Detective, no!*" Anna's terrified cry filled the sanctuary. "*Don't!*"

The women huddled in the far corner, sobbing as they clutched their children. Anna sat in front of them all, her arms outstretched as if to protect them.

She pleaded with me, her voice rasping in fear.

"Don't move! *Please* don't take another step!"

And I wouldn't.

My left foot came down hard. I heard the click. As obvious as any of the bells or screams. A rug had covered it, but I felt the catch, knew what it meant.

Anna stared at me, her face stained with tears.

"Please..." She held her hands out as if to stabilize me. "*Please*, don't move. It's a pressure plate. If you move..."

The floor wobbled, uneven beneath my feet. "What did they do?"

"If you move, that device will explode." Anna's words struck me, shrill as shrapnel. "If you move...we'll all die."

Chapter Twenty-Three

Scream.

-Him

My life had once flashed before my eyes…but never under my feet.

My weight rested on one foot. The other paused, barely touching the ground. I wavered, but I caught my balance before my thudding heart knocked me on my ass and blew us all to the Goodmans' Kingdom come.

"Are you all okay?" I searched the faces of the terrified women. The children cried. The babies wailed. But no one appeared to be hurt. Just scared. "Everyone in one piece?"

"For now…" Anna breathed as lightly as me. "Please, *be careful.*"

"I'm not moving."

The women cowered in their Sunday best. No…their most formal wear. Little girls in pink skirts. The boys in proper jackets. Women covering their hair with lace shawls.

And three perfect angels.

Mariam and two others. All so young. All wide-eyed.

Three innocent girls in white dresses.

The gowns were silky and ruffled, laced with fancy trim and covered with a thin chiffon. They wove purple flowers into their hair and donned ivory buckled shoes.

The girls didn't fill out the dresses. Hell, they weren't even old enough to be *Christened.*

Not one, but three brides, all waiting for their husbands.

Mariam huddled in the middle of them, staring at me with pouting lips and a furrowed forehead.

She began to cry. "You ruined my wedding day!"

"Hush now." Anna touched her cheek. "Nothing is ruined. Everyone stay quiet and still."

"Where's Jacob?" I demanded.

The women didn't answer. They hyperventilated in their clustered mass, crying for their husbands.

"John left me!" A brunette no older than sixteen clutched her swollen belly. "He left us!"

"No one has left anyone." Anna shushed her. "Jacob has a plan. We must trust him. We're a family. Nothing will come between us." She didn't look at me, only the women and children. "*The Lord is my shepherd...I shall not want...*"

The other followed in chorus. "*He maketh me to lie down in green pastures. He leadeth me beside still waters.*"

Oh, Christ. I had a prayer of my own, and it wasn't nearly as peaceful as theirs.

Anna kept her eyes open, watching me as I made my motions. That was fine. As long as she could corral the women and children, I'd find a way to get out of this mess.

One that didn't involve killing us all.

I reached for my radio, slowly, letting it skim off my belt and into my hand. The movement didn't upset the pressure plate, but it wobbled me.

How long could I stand on one foot?

Well…at least until the end.

I contacted the troopers stationed on the edge of the property, attempting to keep my voice light. The strain didn't fool anyone.

"This is McKenna…" I licked my drying lips. "We have a situation."

It took a second before the return crackled in. "You got the Sheriff. Confirm your *situation?*"

I didn't know their radio call for it. "I've found a possible explosive device. What's the ETA on the removal unit?"

A longer pause. "Where is the device, Detective?"

"I'm standing on it."

"Repeat that."

"It's *under my feet.*"

Silence. The prayers faded as the girls listened more to me than Anna. I didn't wait for the sheriff's confirmation. I counted the innocents in the room with me.

"I have twenty-five civilians with me. All women and children. We're in the family chapel, second largest building on the farm." Aside from the barn, but that contained its own explosive revelation. "The device is under my feet. I need a disposal team *immediately.*"

The radio punctuated my call with a variety of shrill beeps. Grimber hailed back.

"Located any other devices?"

Good freaking question. I glanced to Anna. "I'll find out."

But she wasn't talking. She held a baby girl close to her chest and shook her head.

"Eve..." I clutched the radio. "I need your help."

Her eyes widened. "I *can't.*"

"We don't have a choice now. The state police are here. They're bringing a bomb squad. I've got police from my precinct on the way. If anyone gets hurt—"

"No one was supposed to get hurt!"

My leg wobbled. This wasn't a comfortable position, and I had no idea how long I could hold it without unconsciously shifting my weight. Hopefully the bomb wasn't too unstable.

"You gotta think of the kids, Eve. There's too many innocent people in here. I know Jacob gave you orders, but he's not here now. It's just you, me, and a whole lot of kids. You gotta tell me if there's any other unsafe places, okay?"

Anna doubled down. "Jacob *promised* the children would be okay."

"I know he did, but we've got a problem. I need your help."

She rocked the baby, holding her close, pressing her cheek against the child's blonde curls. "He said we'd be safe here. I believed him...but...don't go near the gazebo."

I radioed, issuing the order for the teams to avoid their parkette area and any other entrance to the chapel.

"Good." I sweated, but I didn't let it show. "Are the kids okay? Is anyone hurt?"

"No one has ever been hurt here, Detective."

Yeah, and the room under the barn was just a playhouse. "Good. Let's keep it that way. Make sure everyone stays calm. The team's going to come in, and they'll need it to stay quiet so they can work."

Anna cast a glance over the women and kids. It'd be hard to keep them quiet, so many were already crying. She nodded, devising a plan.

"May we pray?" she asked.

For all the good it'd do, fine. As long as the Holy Spirit didn't jostle any wires.

Or knock me down.

Or cause me to move a fraction of an inch and unsettle the homemade IED.

Ten minutes of balance was all I could handle. I wasn't in bad shape, but I was no yoga expert, despite attempting classes on three separate occasions. I held my leg out before me, wavering as it just barely grazed the ground. My back leg locked, tensed and already cramped.

This wasn't good. My heart beat too fast, and my sweat turned cold. I ignored the crushing agony in my chest. A panic attack might have given me something to do in the minutes waiting for the bomb squad, but I didn't want a forensics team boxing up the bits and pieces of my personal smithereens to return to my family.

Or James.

God...James...

The sheriff shouted from outside. "Got the bomb squad here, Detective! Just stay calm!"

A pipedream while standing on a pipe bomb. "Sure."

"Lieutenant Bryce is here from the disposal unit. He's going to oversee the dismantling of this..." Grimber didn't say the word. "He'll get you out."

"Sounds good to me."

I couldn't see the lieutenant, but he had a good, solid voice.

Something strong and baritone. Deeper than James, but not nearly as smooth.

"You're Detective McKenna?" he asked.

"We can drop the formalities now that I'm humping a bomb." I flinched as Anna's gentle scold reminded me of the Rated-G nature of this particular life-or-death situation. I apologized to the kids and called to Bryce. "Call me London."

"You're doing great, London…" He didn't sound convinced. "Are you having any difficulties?"

"I'm not exactly comfortable."

"It'll get worse."

Yeah, an explosion would feel pretty nasty. "I'm fine. Just work fast."

A plea and an order but neither seemed effective. It took them five minutes to survey the chapel. Five minutes to scan beneath the floor. Another five to check the foundation for an entry point.

And then only a minute for them to sit and confer with each other.

Hushed voices never spoke good news.

My clothes soaked with sweat, and the thumping of my heart nearly barreled me over. I gritted my teeth, but the pressure squeezed every bit of courage inside me. It left the stubbornness though, the only reason I hadn't already collapsed.

"London…" Lieutenant Bryce cleared his throat. "We scanned the chapel. The stained-glass window is clear. We're going to break it and evacuate the women and kids."

"Break it?" Anna argued. "But it's a seventy-year-old piece of art."

"And I'm standing on fifty bucks worth of nails, ball bearings, glass, and accelerants." I didn't let her speak. "Get them out of here."

The team already moved, shattering the glass window that offered the family more salvation as an escape than in worship. The artwork had been large, centered in the back of the chapel to frame the altar and, apparently, John, during their services. It offered more than enough room to start evacuating the twenty-five women and children huddled in the corner.

But they moved one at a time.

And my leg was cramped, tired, and aching with the strain of keeping me so still for so long.

Lieutenant Bryce wasn't happy. He called to me as calm as he could manage.

"London, you're standing on a dangerous bomb."

"I know," I said.

"It's got some firepower in it."

"I know."

"We're working as fast as we can."

I watched as Anna helped pass the babies and toddlers out of the window. Some cried. Some stayed silently terrified. But her attention drifted from the family to me. She could read the Lieutenant's expression from where she stood.

And I saw it mirrored in hers.

They didn't think I could get out.

That made three of us.

"Is there someone you can call?" Bryce posed the question lightly. "Someone to keep you calm?"

"You mean...to say goodbye?"

At least silent affirmation didn't lie.

My heart skipped.

My last one?

I forced a harsh breath through my lungs, the first deep one I felt confident taking since stepping on the plate. No sense killing everyone else with me. If this was it, at least we'd get the women and kids out. They'd been through enough.

So had I.

But at least I'd go down swinging.

I pointed to the phone in my pocket. "Can I use this?"

"No. Don't move. We'll use the radio." His boots scraped behind me. "Who do we call?"

What a question.

My throat tightened. I wasn't about to punish him with my last words, but I couldn't think of anyone else I needed to hear in my last moments.

"James." I pinched my eyes shut. "Agent James Novak. He's my...he's with the FBI. I'll give you his phone number."

"Good. I'll talk with him first and explain what's happening."

Not the call James ever wanted to get, but one I'd always warned him to expect.

We both worked dangerous jobs, even if his vision had saddled him behind a desk more than in the field. I got myself in more trouble than either of us liked, but we knew this was a possibility.

And after everything that had happened when I was younger...

This was just another drop in the unlucky bucket I'd ultimately kick.

Within minutes, Lieutenant Bryce had rallied James on the radio. He held it up for me to hear.

For *everyone* to hear.

Wasn't it bad enough I had to say goodbye to him? I didn't need a crowd for this. Hell, I'd be lucky if I could even speak to *him*.

I held my breath.

This wasn't happening.

This couldn't be how it ended.

My chest tightened, threatening to suffocate me in a fear I swore I'd never let overwhelm me again.

And then I heard his voice.

"London." James stayed calm, always. "Are you okay?"

I couldn't let him hear me upset. He'd already dealt with me disheveled and terrified ten years ago. After the interviews and interrogations and *memories* of what that evil man had done, James knew how dark my life had gotten. When we started dating, I'd promised him, *swore to him*, that the weak, terrified victim was gone.

I'd keep that promise.

"I'm fine," I said. "Nothing I can't handle. Might be late for dinner though."

He chuckled. "You've never been on time for dinner."

"You never have it on the table for me."

"Well, if you behave and let the bomb squad work, I'll make you a gourmet meal as soon as you get home."

"Five courses."

"Stuffing, mashed potatoes, every soy product I can find."

"I'd rather a carb coma than the other kind."

"Me too." His voice deepened, as close to worry as he'd let it rasp. He kept himself together. For me. For him. "Are you going to be okay?"

"I've been through worse." And most times, I meant it. I curled my fists. How long had my hands been trembling? "Don't worry about me."

"I always worry about you."

"I know."

The last child hopped through the window. Only Anna and the older women remained. She instructed the pregnant ones to hurry through first, but her gaze remained on me, holding my stare as if holding my hand.

Her turn came. She hesitated.

Hell no. She wasn't waiting here for me. The poor woman had been held in captivity for fifteen years. This was her escape. Her *rescue*.

"Go," I said. "I'm fine."

A tear rolled over her cheek, and she backed to the window.

"God's with you," she whispered. "Trust Him."

Yeah, I was putting my money on the trooper driving the drone under the foundation, but I nodded, if only so Anna would finally escape to safety.

"Talk to me, London." James didn't let me stay quiet for long. "What's happening?"

"I…"

Why was this so hard to say?

The last words I'd speak should have been the *first* I always said to him.

Every morning. Every night. After every call.

But revealing my feelings terrified me more than any danger beneath my aching feet.

"In case I don't get out of this…" My voice trembled.

"It's okay." He said it, and I believed him. "I know, London."

"But you *don't*. And I've never…I don't tell you enough…"

"But I *know*." His voice caressed as warm and sincere over the radio as if he whispered in my ear. At least he was far away. At least he wouldn't *see*. "We'll talk about it once you're home. Safe and sound. With me."

With him.

I stared through the window, watching as the girls were guided far from the chapel and to the waiting safety zone with flashing lights, police cars, and fire truck.

I doubted Jacob Goodman ever expected so much law enforcement to invade his home.

I'd take satisfaction in that. The children were safe. They'd find the room under the barn. Proof that they had taken those girls to be their wives.

And the three little girls still wore their pretty white wedding dresses.

They might have been kidnapped, but the Goodmans were nothing if not traditional. I doubted they'd touched them yet. Not if they truly believed in whatever sanctimonious ceremony they'd created to justify their behavior. Their quivers had to be filled with wholesomeness for their Kingdom to come.

The Goodmans had stuffed twenty-five women and children into their chapel—a symbol of their dominance. Their virility. Their *victory* over innocent flesh.

So why would they arm a bomb so near to their families?

Why would they want to hurt *them?*

"James…" I licked my lips. They cracked anyway. My heart thudded a little harder now, but a surge of confidence ripped through me. "I need your help."

"I'm not going anywhere, London. I love you. I'm right here."

The words stirred everything in me, but I forced myself to unhear it so I could think. Plan.

Put myself into the mind of a madman.

"I need a profile," I said. "And I need it quick."

"*What?*"

"You're a fifty-two-year-old white male living in a fundamentalist Christian sect. Off the grid. Separated from the world. You have your own land and property in a rural community where you're free to practice your perverted form of religion."

"London, what are you doing?"

"Despite a religious upbringing and tenants, you're attracted to young girls. Maybe for purity reasons."

"No." James couldn't resist the chance to help—or an opportunity to distract me. "It's not their purity. It's strictly dominance."

Bryce called from behind me, quiet. "London, stay still. You're wobbling."

I ignored him and the other panicking troopers. "He kidnaps young girls and brainwashes them."

James was gifted at his job. His voice quickened, intrigued. "He forces their submission."

"Not to him, but to *God*."

"No. To him. To Goodman, it's the same thing. He is the head of the family, the farm, and the church. He's assumed a Godly role." He thought for a moment. "He found the girls. Presumably he broke the girls. *How?*"

"There's a hidden bunker under the barn. He converted them there."

"Through force?"

I didn't want to imagine it. "You have no idea."

Bryce worked quickly, grabbing another radio from a trooper outside. "Get me three guys to check out a bunker underneath the barn. Take a bomb dog. Sniff it out."

"What do you make of Goodman?" I asked.

James hummed. "He thinks he's in complete control of those around him. And he likes that. He's forming his world in the image he's created. Perfect order. Perfect obedience. He's religious, but that gives him power. He takes the young girls and molds them into his ideal Christian wives because they can be trained easier. They're young enough to believe the teachings and to bend to a man's authority."

"And the women help. Tending to the children. Making the homes. Acting like a family."

"The bond between the women will be the hardest to break," he said. "They share the experience. They support each other. The pregnancies bind them to each other as much as to their husbands. They feel they are *helping* their families."

"But they're arranged marriages. They're forced into those beds. They're forced to bear children again and again."

"Another form of control," James said.

A strength surged through me. "That's also Goodman's weakness."

James and the troopers hesitated. "What?"

"If you truly believed in your teachings and the Word of God, and you believed that you were *given* these girls for your own, to make your family and grow your quiver…"

"London, don't assume *anything*."

"Would you place those women and children in danger? Would you *really* lock them in a building loaded with explosives?"

"*Don't.*" His voice hardened. "Think of Jonestown. These are people willing to die for their cause."

"Then where is Jacob Goodman to fall on his sword?" I groaned. Damn it. We'd been played. "He's gone. *Running.* This isn't a trap. He's using the chapel as a decoy. The men have escaped, and we're stuck on the farm."

"London, don't do anything stupid."

"I've already been stupid." I cursed myself. "This was a *ploy*, James. I know it."

"The disposal unit can *see* the bomb, London. Stay still!"

I raised my voice. "Lieutenant? Can you find the detonator?"

"Don't move, McKenna." Bryce didn't answer my question. "We need time to disarm it."

"No. You don't."

Because it wasn't armed.

It was *never* armed.

Jacob Goodman spent years building the perfect family. Creating submissive child wives. Offering young girls to his brothers and their children to design a utopia of his own delusions.

He'd *never* endanger the sons he'd helped to create. The bloodline he controlled.

The girls he made into his women.

"James…" I held my breath.

He yelled, the radio crackling. "Don't! London, *please!*"

I stepped off the plate.

And I waited.

The click of the pressure plate locked.

A still moment passed. Then another.

I released a breath.

"You owe me one five-course vegetarian dinner, James Novak."

James swore. "Jesus Christ, London. Do you have any idea what might have happened?"

Yeah. I might have wasted more time standing still instead of chasing after the men who deserved justice.

I grabbed the radio from Lieutenant Bryce and ignored James's lecture. My leg cramped hard as I raced through the chapel, but it didn't stop me from finding the women, surveying their shocked and relieved faces.

I pointed to them. "There's no bomb here. Jacob lied to you."

Anna clutched the baby tight to her chest and she rushed forward to me. She pulled me into a tight hug. "Detective! Thank God you're safe!"

"Jacob used you, Eve." I untangled myself from her arms. "They used *all* of you so they could run."

She smiled, tutting her tongue. "Don't be silly. They'd never abandon us."

"Where have they gone, Eve?"

She answered too quickly. "I have no idea."

My leg ached. My body shivered in an unforgiving sweat. My head pounded with stress.

The last thing I wanted to hear were any more Goodman lies.

"You do know, Eve. And you're going to remember." I stared at her, locking our gazes. "This is your chance to be free. You can go home. You can escape him."

Tears formed in her eyes. "Why would I want to *escape*? This *is* my home. I love my husband. We *all* love our husbands."

"Even them?" I pointed to the three young girls, shivering in thin white dresses. "Would they love their husbands?"

Anna didn't answer. She focused on the baby, rocking the little girl in her arms as she fought the tears.

"I just need to know where Jacob's gone," I whispered. "Then I'll take you away from here. You'll be safe with me. Everyone will be safe. And those girls over there...the *brides*...they won't be hurt tonight. I promise. The Goodmans will never touch them—"

My breath wrenched out of me.

The blast erupted from the farm's entrance—bright and ferocious, a sudden burst of fire and debris. The force of the explosion knocked us to the ground.

Then *heat*.

I tumbled, hands in the cold dirt, ears ringing.

A cough. I didn't hear it.

A baby crying pierced the shrill din first.

Every breath *hurt*, but I rose to my feet, clawing until I could stand on the aches and bruises, pain and cuts.

The women cried, shouting for their kids. The police ran, their radios crackling with a dozen calls for additional assistance.

Everyone was alive, but thick, black smoke rose from the road. Flames consumed two police cars. A flurry of uniforms dragged a bleeding body from the wreckage.

I searched the women.

Mariam sat on the ground, covered in dirt and dust, her dress ruined.

She cried, still clutching a cellphone. The call had disconnected upon the explosion.

"I'm sorry!" Mariam wailed, again and again. "They told me to do it! They said we wouldn't be safe ever again." The little girl in the stained white dress wept perfect tears. They swept over her dirty face and revealed the pink blush underneath. She handed me the cellphone, grimy and covered in dirt. "I'm sorry! I didn't want to kill anyone!"

Chapter Twenty-Four

Am I everything you expected?
Don't tell me you're disappointed.
-Him

Scrapes, bruises, and one fractured wrist.

Twenty-seven safe women and children.

Eleven missing men.

It could have been worse. A lot worse.

The station house couldn't accommodate all the victims, so we had arrangements made with the Red Cross and a local hotel. Not that the family needed much.

No one talked. No one ate the offered food. No one asked for medical attention.

No one even looked *relieved* to be free from their prisons.

And every tear that fell tore me apart.

Anna led the women as they sat in quiet and humbled submission in every corner of the precinct. Someone had to break first. Unfortunately, it seemed like it'd be the police.

"Passive resistance?"

That voice soothed me more than the ice pack to my screaming hamstring.

I faced James with an honest smile. He took my hand, bringing it to his lips. I could have done with a lot more, but the department frantically bolted from desk to desk, tossing files and making calls. The media descended on the story like a starving pack of hyenas. It'd be impossible to shield all of them from the cameras and sadistic reporters.

Officers and detectives from other departments crowded in the Missing Persons Unit to try to help, getting in everyone's way just as the thermostat broke. The temperature rose. Everyone sweated. Some of us bled. No one was terribly happy.

This wasn't time for an embrace, and I regretted every time in the past I'd ever taken his arms for granted.

"They're not giving us their names." I squeezed his hand before pulling away. He let me go, though he did tuck a lock of my hair behind my ear. The others saw, and I cursed the moment of weakness. Couldn't have my colleagues thinking I'd gone to pieces by not getting blown into bits. "What are you doing here?"

"I wanted to make sure you were okay," he said.

"I'm fine."

"…And they called me in to consult."

"Of course they did." I didn't know why I was disappointed, but he had to work too. "Take your pick of victims. We've got kids. Brides-to-be. Women who have been on the farm for years."

"Who's the one in charge?"

I pointed her out. "That's Eve."

"You mean—Anna Prescott?"

I shrugged, too tired to care. "She can be whoever she wants to be today."

James studied her—staring hard. Thinking.

How often had he looked at me like that? A victim? A source of information?

And now?

Why couldn't I just *enjoy* the way he looked at me now?

"She'll have the most answers," he said. "But she'll be the least likely to talk. Anna's fully integrated into the family. She's Jacob's wife, and that makes her important. She believes it."

"She's not conceited."

"No, but she feels like she's the only one who can protect the man she loves." He pointed to the group of teenagers huddled on a bench, warily eying the cans of Pepsi the officers offered them. "Start with the young ones. Not the girls who are most recently initiated into the family—they're living in fear of their *training*. Try to talk to the ones who are married, but not yet a fixture of the farm. The ones who haven't given birth yet."

"What makes you think they'll talk?"

"They're young." His frown darkened as he nodded towards one of the heavily pregnant fifteen-year-olds struggling to stand from her chair. "They might resent the hierarchy of the farm. They might also be confused. They've seen enough of the compound to know that this..." His golden eyes cast over the station—the computers, TV screens, women who weren't barefoot and pregnant. "This might look more appealing than working the fields and changing diapers."

Maybe. But he hadn't seen the farm.

Their home was not only lovely...it really seemed like a loving community, despite the horrors in the barn's basement.

"Do you think they'll give up the men?" I asked.

James nudged me forward. "Depends on how good Jacob trained them...and how effective an interviewer you are."

"Are you coming with me?"

"Lieutenant Clark told me to wait, and I agree. They might be more open with you."

"Because I'm a woman?"

"Yes..." James squeezed my hand once more. "And because you know how scared they must be."

That didn't make me qualified.

That made me the *worst* person to talk to them.

Nothing was worse than lying to someone with platitudes like *you'll overcome this* or *you're strong enough to beat this.*

No one was that strong.

No one ever *forgot* what happened to them.

My job was to find my missings. I did that. I brought them home to safety.

But now?

How was I supposed to manage this?

Good thing I helped with the Family Crisis/Sexual Assault Units. But I'd need a hell of a lot more help than the few people working the floor. Especially as the women refused to let any of the male detectives near their children.

I approached the women as gently as I could, wishing I had changed from my dirty, blood-stained clothes. At least I'd taken my gun off. It seemed to relieve them.

"We have doctors on site," I said. "The children and those of you in a…delicate condition…should get examined."

No one answered me. They held their children close—babies hugging babies.

Anna included.

James warned she'd be uncooperative, but we had a connection. She *had* to understand.

"There's a conference room prepared," I told her. "Doctors from Children's Hospital are on hand. They'll do the check-up here, just to make sure no one sustained any injuries from the blast. If they need to go to the hospital, we'll arrange something."

Anna rocked the fussing baby in her arms. "Everyone is frightened, Detective."

"There's no reason to be frightened."

"You've removed us from our homes. Threatened to arrest our families. The other officers keep using that vile word…"

Rape?

Fantastic.

"We're just trying to help," I said. "I promise, no one is getting arrested. And I'll talk with the detectives. I'll make sure they realize that you love your families and husbands."

"You have no idea what you've done."

And the heartbreak, the absolute *misery* and *terror* bleeding from these women, told me she was right. Just as I had no idea why the women weren't celebrating their freedom.

"Some of the kids look dazed or dehydrated," I said. "Can you agree to let a doctor see them?"

Anna held Mariam near her. The girl hadn't spoken, hadn't taken a drink, hadn't eaten.

"Okay." Anna stroked the bruise on Mariam's chin. "But they will *not* be taken from us."

"If they need any real medical attention, their mother can go with them." I glanced over the babies, toddlers, and pre-school aged kids. A dozen in all. "Who belongs to who?"

Silence.

No one answered, not even the kids.

Fantastic. Jacob must have prepared for this moment. If they were ever caught or separated, no one would reveal their children. That made it hard to separate the families and harder to pin a man for the rape.

Fine. I'd deal with it later. I allowed the other officers to approach, taking crying children from mother's arms. The babies wailed. The toddlers fought back.

Everyone screamed.

Including the women.

This was a disaster.

"The kids will be safe." I gave my promise to Anna. "They'll be back shortly. Nothing will happen. No one is taking them away from you."

Yet.

Social services was going to have a field day with this.

What the hell were we supposed to do with all of them?

Anna shushed the women with a gentle word, handing the bundle of pink in her arms to the nearest officer. The kids were escorted out.

One crisis handled.

"Okay." I faced the fifteen women remaining. Most of them were under the age of sixteen. Only Anna and one other looked older than thirty.

What had happened to the Goodmans' first wives?

And what would happen once these women aged out of their child birthing years?

The wall of dresses and shawls cloaked the women in their own code of silence. I had no idea who was who—brunettes mixed with blondes. Each of the girls was young, pale, and either rail thin or ready to pop. I'd guessed on most of their identities during my surveillance, but this wasn't a time to assume. I had to earn their trust.

Somehow.

"What are your names?" I asked.

No one acknowledged the question.

I pulled a wheeled chair over from under a desk and sat with them.

Maybe standing intimidated them? Maybe they blamed me?

Maybe they were too terrified to speak?

The other officers gave us room to work. James watched with a cautious glance from Adamski's office. It wasn't like we had a handbook for these situations. I was first response. This was triage. First I had to find out who needed what the most.

And then we'd work on healing. Trusting. *Talking.*

"Is everyone okay?" I tried again. "That was a bad explosion, and I'm worried about a lot of you. I promise, you won't get into trouble, but the doctors are going to have to know…who is pregnant?"

Not even the visibly swollen girls responded. One looked ready to pop. The other a hair past eight months. And I didn't have a clue about anything relating to pregnancy.

Were they in more danger closer to their due date?

Or was it the early stages that would have been hit harder?

They didn't speak.

Damn it. I'd have them all ultrasounded if that's what it took.

"Fine." I shredded the last of my patience. "I just need names. Which child or children belongs to you? We have babies. Toddlers. Just tell me, and we can move on."

Nothing.

Absolutely nothing.

The women stared only at the ground. This was getting us *nowhere.*

I scooted the chair closer, trying to get anyone, *someone* to engage with me. A girl. A woman. It didn't matter.

Someone had to talk.

They were *free.* They had *escaped.*

Didn't they see how precious of a gift that was? How *unlikely?* And instead of rejoicing and helping, they protected the bastards that did this to them?

I searched woman to woman. Divide and conquer. "Look around you. Look at where you are. This is a *police station.* The officers here aren't your enemies. We want to help you—protect you from people who took advantage and hurt you." I pointed to the three little brides, hiding in the tatters of their wedding dresses. "You don't have to speak for yourself, but help *them.* They're just like you were—before this all happened. They're innocent. We helped them. Saved them from becoming slaves to men who have molested and hurt all of you. Do you understand?"

No.

They didn't.

They didn't want to understand.

Every woman had tensed when I mentioned the men. How did Jacob have such a hold over them, even when separated?

"I know Jacob has scared you," I said. "Just like I know who fathered those children."

The women didn't look up. I named each of the Goodmans anyway, watching for the telltale flinch or whimper that affected each girl when I named their abuser.

"Jacob. Simon. Mark. Matthew." The oldest. And their sons. "John. Luke. Joshua. Peter. Paul. Abraham. Isaac. Amos. Levi. Micah. Thomas." It felt only right to name the last man. "Jonah."

Nothing. A few tears. But silence. Only the rustle of papers, ringing of phones, and the frustrated sighs of the other police officers.

It'd be a battle of wills then.

Fine by me.

Now that I'd gotten them out, I had all the time in the world to piss away on their denial.

"You think those men are going to help you?" I snorted. "Like how Jonah helped his own wife? I can show you the pictures. We have them over in Homicide. Hard to imagine that much blood unless you're stepping in it—"

"Please." Anna closed her eyes. "You're scaring them."

Grilling a victim wasn't procedure, but I didn't know what else to do. "Then me and you gotta talk. Do that, and I'll get your family something better than snack cakes from the vending machine for dinner."

"That won't be necessary," Anna said. "All I ask is that the youngest children are returned. If you could bring me…" Her words choked off.

"You want the baby?"

"I do."

If it got me answers, she could cradle the kid all night. I called to Adamski. "Can we get the baby girl back?"

Bruce wasn't as sly as he thought. "What's her name?"

I already knew the answer. I gestured to Anna.

She didn't speak.

No worries. I'd get what I wanted from her.

I guided her away from the group towards the interrogation room. James followed, taking my arm before I followed her inside.

"I told you," he said. "She's the leader. She won't talk."

"She has Jonah and Nina's daughter." I quieted as an officer brought in the bundled girl. She didn't stop crying until she was safe in Anna's arms. "I need her to admit to it."

"She won't. Admitting it will accuse Jonah of raping Nina."

But I had to try. "I need some leverage here, James. These women are so confused. They don't understand what I did for them."

"And what did you do?"

"I freed them."

"Possibly."

"What's that mean?"

"It's mean…to them? You've destroyed their families. Dragged them from their homes. Forced their children to endure an invasive medical examination. You've also insulted their beliefs, their pregnancies, and their husbands. They might be rapists, but these women believe their husbands are their protectors and providers. They have nothing else."

"They have their *freedom*."

"London, not everyone can escape from their kidnapper as easily as you did."

Easy?

He knew he made the mistake, but his apology came too late.

"Forget it," I said. "This isn't about me. This is about *them*. I'm saving these women."

Wasn't I?

I left James outside the interrogation room. The door closed behind me. Usually the click of the latch terrified the perps sitting in the chairs. Anna was afraid, but she didn't show it. She cradled the baby, singing to soothe the little girl.

"Detective, have you been to a doctor yet?" Anna asked. "You've been through an ordeal."

I appreciated the concern, but that didn't change the facts. "Your husband set those traps."

"You should be checked over. We all should. I thank you for the doctors. You're very kind to worry about the children."

"I'm very, very worried about the children, Anna."

"My name isn't Anna."

"Are you sure?"

She didn't hesitate. Her soft smile soothed the baby. "Of course, I'm sure."

"What do you remember about your life before the farm?"

She shrugged. "Nothing."

"You can't remember?"

"I choose not to."

"Why?"

The little coos from the baby weren't the answers I'd hoped for. Anna searched the interrogation room. Nothing would help her here. The walls were bare, the plastic chairs uncomfortable, and my voice recorder low on batteries.

A wayward chestnut hair fell over her cheek. The lock almost hid the portwine birthmark on her neck.

Almost.

"I don't expect you to understand, Detective."

"Try me," I said. "I'm listening."

"You didn't listen before…" Anna didn't accuse, only whisper it. "And you have no idea what you've done."

"I'm protecting these girls."

"So were we."

"No. The men were *bedding* those girls."

She didn't confirm it. Her silence wasn't a denial either.

"I know they got those little girls pregnant," I said.

"We *help* pregnant girls on the farm. It's charity."

"You're lying to protect them."

Anna bit her lip. "We're a family. We take care of each other."

"And the bunker under the barn?"

When was the last time Anna had been inside? The murals had been newer, the mattress relatively fresh. Fifteen years had passed since she had been taken. Did they torture her the same way? Had they beaten her and forced her to comply, or did they show her the happy, smiling pictures of pregnant girls and give her toys to play with that would reinforce their specific desires?

"What do you want from us?" Anna asked. "What can I say that will let us go back home? There must be some way to convince you that we are not in danger."

"You've been in danger, Anna."

"I'm not Anna."

"You were reported missing in July of 2002. You were on the farm by August. The dates don't lie. Jacob raped you while you were in his custody. You were pregnant by him at fifteen."

The words caught in her throat. "And my son is dead. Does that mean nothing to you?"

"You loved your son...but Jacob was wrong to touch you. He was wrong to marry such a young girl. He used you. And by all legal definitions, he raped you."

"Do not presume you understand what happens in a man's bedroom."

"It's not a presumption. There's half dozen pregnant girls out there. *Underage.* And I bet if I ask them who their husband is...Jacob won't like the answer."

"They aren't married. You'll find no marriage license."

"I'll find out." I'd do without eating, without sleeping if that's what it took. "That's my job. I help people. And those girls need help, just like you do. Just like that baby."

Anna's gaze snapped upwards. I met her gaze without flinching.

"What's the baby's name, Anna?"

A long pause. "I'm not her mother. I shouldn't answer those questions."

"Who is her mother?"

"Detective, please."

"Who is her father?"

Tears formed. I hated that I caused them.

"We've been through so much today," Anna whispered. "So much pain and suffering when it should have been a day of celebration."

"The weddings, right?" I shook my head. "Mariam is *ten years old*. She's too young for marriage. she's too young to be touched by a man in that way. Don't you realize how badly she'd be hurt?"

She shook her head, shutting down. "Our family is splintered and terrified. I have no idea where Jacob is, and neither do the others. Please, let us be."

"That's Rebecca, isn't it?"

"I can't help you."

"No. You *won't* help me." I leaned close, taking her hand. "All I need is a *nod*. You don't have to speak a word. No one will know. No one will see. I only want the truth, Anna." That didn't work. I softened my voice. "Eve. Please. Is this little girl Jonah and Nina's missing baby?"

"I'm sorry, Detective."

And then I understood.

Then I saw through the games and the silences, the fears and the craziness of the day.

Then it made *sense*.

She wasn't worried about Jonah or his reputation.

She wanted the baby.

"You're afraid we'll take her away," I said.

Anna's tears fell, choking her in a quiet sob. "She only knows her family. The farm. *Me*. It's all she has, Detective."

"You're her grandmother." A young, thirty-year-old grandmother. "You have custody rights."

Her voice hardened. "As would another set of grandparents. Enough damage has been done today. No. I won't tell you anything."

"We have DNA from both Nina and Jonah's bodies. We can compel a DNA test."

She stared straight ahead. "If you must."

"Or you can help me. Give me this closure."

"I have to do what's best for my family."

And Jacob.

She had to protect her husband.

"I'm sorry," I said. "I really am. But we'll get a court order for the DNA."

"Tonight?"

God, I wished it worked that quickly. "No. Nothing else tonight. We're arranging a hotel for you all. Your family can stay together, and we'll provide food and supplies for everyone, including the babies."

"Thank you." Anna was polite, even in obstinacy. "When will we be allowed to go home?"

Now was my turn to play coy, but I took no pride in it. "As soon as I know you'll be safe."

It wasn't the answer she wanted, but it was all I could give. I had no real time plan for her because...

We had no idea what to do.

Most of the women on the farm were underage, and until they told us their names or we found some identifiable fingerprints, we were lost.

We'd have to find their parents or call social services.

But what about *their* children? We couldn't separate mothers and children. The media would destroy us. The family would feel utterly betrayed.

And then we'd never have help finding Jacob Goodman.

I led Anna to the others, catching James's gaze on the way. Damn it. He was right. I'd pushed her too hard. I didn't get information, and I set back the investigation a few days until I could regain her trust.

But as long as I knew no one would hurt them anymore, I was happy.

And I knew what James would say about that too. Sacrificing a solid case and surveillance to rescue the victims seemed good in theory, but if we couldn't get enough evidence for the DA to convict?

The girls would go right back to the men abusing them.

I sat at my desk, staring at the piles of paperwork and notes from every one of my supervisors. The reporters buzzed outside. The Red Cross needed a headcount and ages. Homicide wanted answers about Jonah. Everyone had questions.

But I had no answers.

A tug on my sleeve turned my attention. I smiled, surprised to find one of the young girls leaning close to my desk. Ester? She'd been promised to Jacob's son, Luke.

She kept her eyes low, her hand on her tummy. Still flat, but I understood her concern. Her face had paled, and she wavered a bit.

She couldn't have been older than thirteen.

"You're pregnant?" I asked.

"I…need the restroom."

"Morning sickness?"

She nodded. I gestured to the officer at the door.

"He can take you to the women's room."

Ester wavered. "But he's a…"

A man.

Right.

"No problem. Come with me. This way."

"Thank you." She pressed her hand into mine, locking gazes for only a moment. "For everything."

I closed my fist around the curled note. My pulse raced. "Anytime."

She waved for two of the other girls to follow, and I led them into the hall, hidden from the watchful gaze of Anna and the older women.

I waited until they entered the restroom before uncurling the paper. The note was written hastily, off-center and quick.

Jacob has a bunker. He's taken the men there.

They're in the Allegheny Forest game lands.

They want to steal us back.

Please stop them!

Chapter Twenty-Five

The secret to escaping isn't finding a way out…
It's avoiding the trap in the first place.
-Him

The SWAT team suited me up with a bulletproof vest. I hoped we wouldn't need it, but my gut said to prepare for war.

"Perimeter is clear." The SWAT leader, Rick Reginald, returned to our comm center. It wasn't much, a trailer with a bank of computers and radios connected in the trees. He removed his helmet and took an offered bottle of water, sucking down the entirety before nodding to Adamski and me. "There's no sign of anyone on the property or inside the structure."

Not a chance. "They're here. Hiding."

Rick gestured over the grass, mocking the boundaries of the Goodman's bunker. "They have one entrance to this structure. No one goes in or out without us seeing. But I'll tell you…" He whistled. "If they'd gone in, they wouldn't have had to come out. Not for years."

"Years?" Adamski looked ridiculous in the bulletproof vest, especially as he kept yanking his pants up under it. "What is it?"

"A prepper bunker," I said.

Rick nodded. "It's fully loaded on the inside. We're talking guns, food, medicine, beds. They could survive *two* apocalypses in this thing. Plenty of supplies…but no people."

Then they didn't search everywhere. "These guys have nowhere else to go. This is where they'd stand their ground."

Rick tapped the camera on his helmet. "You saw everything I did. A single bed was unmade. Their generator is on. But there's no one inside."

"No girls?"

"No."

At least we had that consolation. I had no idea if all the Goodmans' children and brides were accounted for in our custody. And the girls wouldn't talk. I doubted Jacob would put any of his brood in danger while prepping for battle, but without confirmation, that sickening pit in my stomach grew.

Only one way to find out. "I'm going in. We have to find out where Jacob is hiding."

Adamski hated this idea, and he'd let me hear it the entire drive from Pittsburgh into the National Forest of the Alleghenies. The lecture had been lengthened and the trip delayed thanks to his carsickness on the backass roads. The Goodmans built their bunker far from civilization, where no one would ever think to look.

Except for us.

I wasn't letting this slime slip through the cracks.

"Leave it to the SWAT team, London," Adamski said. "Might be dangerous."

Rick wasn't as concerned. "We've completed the preliminary sweep. It's clear. Detective McKenna should see this. Maybe she can explain what the hell these people were doing."

I refused to get into the minds of the bastards I chased—once inside, that filth would remain. It took a special type of person to do that work, and I let James handle it. I didn't understand the Goodmans, but that wouldn't stop me from investigating them and exposing their every sin to the world.

"We'll find them," I said.

Adamski frowned. "*If* they were ever here."

"Ester led us here. She was brave enough to give them up. Even if they aren't here now, we might find out where they've gone."

"Yeah, and we thought the little one helped us too." Adamski pointed to the healing cut on my forehead. "But Mariam pulled the trigger and detonated that bomb. You almost died. Three state troopers are still in the hospital."

That wasn't Mariam's fault. Jacob stained his hands with their blood, not the girls. Not the ones forced to hurt others to protect their abusers.

"I'll be careful," I said.

"You said that last time…right before you stepped on an IED."

He sounded like James. Fortunately, I'd learned how to play to those fears. "And I made it out of that one alive."

"Don't get cocky."

"Don't get pessimistic." I checked my weapon and nodded to Rick. "Let's go."

Rick secured my gear twice before letting me step outside of the secured comm center. We weren't paranoid. The forest was too large, dense, and dotted with scrubs, rocks, and snow covered holes and hills to check everywhere for any other homemade weaponry and bombs.

But I doubted they'd set anything here.

This was their bastion of last resort.

The Goodman's bunker stretched deep under our feet, buried beneath the dirt and snow. It wasn't a hideout or temporary. The concrete structure was massive, excavated to protect the entire family.

"I've never seen anything like it." Rick led me to the bunker's only door. Metal and wide-set, like a tornado shelter's entrance. "Go on down. You're not going to believe this shit."

I would, because I'd seen the preview back at the barn.

But this was something different. The paranoid delusion of sociopath with limitless money and a reason to hide his prey from the world.

The steps looked almost steel, but they'd been constructed from a rigid, plastic material. White. They probably hoped to capture as much brightness as they could. The walls closed in quick, but the brushed cement polished into a light grey. Not as damp and dirty as I'd imagined.

Nothing was like what I imagined.

The Goodmans had prepared for more than an emergency. They'd built an entire estate deep under the earth.

And no one knew.

"We're talking *millions* of dollars here." Rick waited for me at the base of the stairs.

The damned hall opened into a real house. Carpets. Wallpaper. To the left—a full-sized kitchen, complete with refrigerator, dishwasher, and two massive stoves and ovens. A fully stocked pantry opened to my right. Walls of MREs, homemade canned vegetables, and a staggering variety of food supplies lined the shelves. The pantry stretched larger than the ground floor of my home, and every inch had stockpiled enough supplies for an army—or the Goodman's family.

"Jesus." I followed Rick, touching the walls. Cold. "All metal?"

"Mostly. This looks made for comfort though. Plenty of room for an entire church in here. Bedrooms are that way..." We came to an intersection. He pointed to the right where two officers searched through plain, grey and white bedding and bunk beds. "Counted twenty-five bunk beds so far. Split into rooms of five. The living quarters aren't exactly luxurious, but each has a bathroom."

"Working utilities?"

"As far as we can tell, there's septic tanks built along the entire structure. And they've dug to the aquifer below. Plenty of fresh water." Rick looked upon the bunker in awe. "They might have lived here for years without ever coming up. This is some new-age paranoia."

"No. Just an organized cult." I ducked into a separate room cordoned off from the main hallway by a thick oak door. "This room looks important."

He followed me inside. The office wasn't huge, but it fit a desk and chairs, a bookshelf, and a bank of official-looking filing cabinets. I dove at them, but each had been locked. Rick pointed to the drawer on the end.

"Already opened one." He rifled through the files. "It's paperwork for the farm. Goodman probably duplicated everything significant. Deeds and banking accounts. They stored copies here. Like I said—paranoid."

"No. Just careful." I slowly turned in the room, touching the handcrafted desk. Custom. It had to be built by Jonah. "These people planned everything. The farm. The girls. The escape. But *this* is a place they would have stayed."

"They were here. But it looks like they took supplies and left."

I hated this. So goddamned close and still they were a step ahead of me. "They didn't expect one of the girls to give them up, but they wouldn't leave this behind."

"A place like this cost some serious money and time to design." Rick rubbed his face, picking at a well-trimmed beard. "But, if I were them, Canada would be looking a lot better than some hole in the ground."

"They won't run."

"Are you that sure?"

I plunked myself in Jacob's executive chair and imagined what his ideal life looked like. The thought twisted my stomach. "They're going to come back."

"How do you know?"

Simplest answer?

"Because we have their girls. Jacob will defend his family with blood if he must. Nothing would stop him from taking what's his."

Rick wasn't listening. His radio blasted with a sudden chirp of calls and whistles.

"McKenna..." He looked up as the rumbling shudder quaked through the bunker. "Get under the desk."

Then came the explosion.

A thunderous burst of popping squealed through the bunker's metal garters. The very earth crumbled as the sudden detonation of a series of bombs ripped through the ceiling.

"Get down!"

Rick's last words heralded the collapse of hundreds of tons of dirt and steel. The ceilings ruptured with a crack of righteous thunder. The tiles gave first, clouding the room in a white dust as the steel beams un-welded from the corners.

Everything fell.

I didn't have time to scream. To think.

To hide.

I dove under the desk moments before the bunker collapsed upon itself. Dirt and stone poured through the fissure in the ceiling, mixing with the broken and burnt beams that once held the structure intact.

A metal beam punctured through the desk.

I screamed, inches from impalement. The metal gashed a chunk of my hair out, ripping through has it staked into the desk.

A second and third explosion tore through the bunker. The ground shook, tossing me side to side while trapped within the cracking frame of the desk.

The wood wasn't strong enough for the entire weight of the bunker on it. I screamed. The forest seemed to collapse over the Goodman's shelter.

They'd destroyed the bunker.

Set the bombs. Blasted it apart.

Oh, God. How many people were trapped inside?

The cracking of dirt and roots softened, and the muffled crunching slowed. The air choked with a musty, chemical smell—fibers and dust. I coughed it out as best I could, amazed my lungs still functioned.

The radios had ceased their blasting chatter. I gave it ten seconds, listening hard and shaking in my own cowardice to leave the safety of the desk.

Debris littered the floor, blocking every available path. I kicked, shaking loose a chunk of drywall that crumbled over the chair. The bunker went black. Even with a flashlight, dust and dirt filled the air. My eyes watered, but I rubbed them clear.

The ceiling above me remained intact, but there was no escaping through the hall. The walls had collapsed, and more dirt than construction materials littered the path.

Rick was gone.

Buried.

The bunker shifted, giving an ominous twist of the uneven floor beneath my feet.

I'd be killed next if I didn't find a way out of here.

I called on my radio, clicking on a flashlight from my belt. The intense beam of light surveyed the wreckage.

"McKenna." I heaved uneven breaths. "I'm okay. The bunker's collapsed."

The radio crackled. I couldn't make out the reply. I'd worry about it later. I had to get out before the rest of the structure fell in upon itself.

I knew they wanted to put me in a grave, but we were a bit deeper than six feet under. This was overkill, even for the Goodmans.

The explosion had destroyed everything in the room. Rock, debris, and construction materials blocked the path to freedom. I didn't want to aim the flashlight at the ceiling for long. The light seemed too intense for the fragile truce struck between the earth and remaining walls.

I radioed again. "Detective McKenna. I'm safe, but I'm trapped."

The fuzzy response clicked more than it formed words.

The panic tightened my chest. I ignored it, just like I fought the wave of leg-wobbling nausea that crippled me. I had no idea if the other officers received my transmission, and I couldn't hear what they'd radioed in panic. But I was *not* waiting in the cold and dark for a rescue team to strike the wrong wall and fold the rest of the bunker onto me.

I kicked a path around the desk. Three of the filing cabinets fell during the explosion. Another angled, ready to drop. I tried to move one and gave up immediately. The things weighed more than me.

Panicking wouldn't help, but it sure felt familiar.

I breathed hard and searched the room. Maybe Jacob had a satellite phone? A CB radio? *Something* that could communicate with the outside world?

Then again, what did Jacob want with the outside world? Nothing, except to escape it.

I gagged. A coppery tang layered within the haze.

Blood. Rick's and mine.

A solid stream of crimson bled from a cut on my bicep. I hadn't noticed it in the initial crash. Whatever got me had been jagged. Probably the metal. The ache pulsed deep. Not good, but at least I still stood.

I spun, checking what remained of his desk. The drawers were locked. I doubted A man like Jacob wouldn't carry his own first aid kit, not when he could make a teenager play his naughty nurse. The bookshelf was no help either. Just bibles. Annotated bibles. Theology lessons. Prepper books. I pulled them out one by one. Survivalist manuals. First-Aid manuals. Plant and tree identification. Everything people would need to survive once the rest of the world had collapsed.

A third Bible. I ripped it from the shelf with a grunt. How dare this man destroy the lives of so many and still think himself righteous? He didn't just hurt the girls.

How many police and SWAT officers did his explosion kill?

I'd have his balls in a sling for this.

I'd survived death too many times before to be at the mercy of some hackneyed, sadistic, pedophilic false prophet—

My flashlight reflected against a plastic knob tucked within the bookshelf. I leaned down, squinting through the dust.

A door.

"Oh, you slick bastard."

I gripped the knob and pulled. The entire bookcase swung only a few inches before lodging in the debris on the ground.

I kicked the drywall and flung books across the room. The shelves had cracked and fallen, and I grabbed whatever I could to shovel away the pieces of roof, wall, and dirt that blocked my path. The secret door opened another inch.

And the bunker shuddered again.

"No, no, no…" I dove under the desk just as more rubble poured through the ceiling. Three harsh cracks precipitated another stomach-twisting lurch in the ground.

The rescue crews.

The other officers must have started to dig.

Oh, God. They tried to get everyone else out…but moving the dirt and stressing the bunker trapped me deeper inside.

I had to escape now before the chance was taken from me.

Fresh air streamed from the half-opened door. I crawled along the floor, chucking pieces of wood and rocks from my feet. My fingernail caught on a piece of wood, nearly ripping away before I yanked my hand back. I ignored the pain. Had no choice. I'd rather have a piss-poor manicure than a mouthful of dirt.

Another quake. More beams dislodged. Dirt trickled from the ceiling. Closer this time. The walls began to bow under the pressure. I ripped at the bookshelf, dragging it against an unwilling floor.

But the steel beam impaling the desk blocked my escape. The bent metal had crashed at an angle into the desk, preventing the door from swinging open. I looked up.

My words shook the structure. "Cut me a break…"

The only portion of the ceiling still intact was held in place by the benevolence of the hanging beam. It supported the crumbling load well enough to let me wait as my future tomb shuttered, eager to fill with dirt.

I didn't have a choice. The wooden desk had already splintered. It couldn't take much more weight.

I grabbed a rock, took a breath, and slammed it against the desk. The frame split along the crack. I aimed the rock again, busting through the wood. The desk shuttered.

I hoped I wasn't making a terrible mistake destroying my only form of shelter.

Not that I had a choice.

The beam was too heavy to push. I sat on the ground, crouching next to the door. My feet kicked out, slamming against the metal.

Once.

Twice.

The beam fell away.

I launched for the door, escaping inside just as the ceiling roared and splintered down. Rock and mud filled the room. The debris ripped from the wall, the metal crunching in half under the force of the rock.

Then it went quiet.

And I had no idea where I was.

The flashlight lit only a part of the shaft. It wasn't large, but it fit a single person. It stretched upwards, untouched by the explosions. At least...I thought it did. The ladder fixed to the side seemed stable.

Of course, Jacob would have built an emergency exit in his own private study.

I tucked the flashlight in my belt, aiming it upwards so I could see the ladder's rungs. The cut in my bicep ached, tearing with every stretch of my arm. I gritted my teeth and climbed. It'd hurt in the morning, but at least I'd have one.

The shaft ended in a hatch. I looped the bad arm around the ladder and struggled to twist the escape. It budged at first, caught with disuse after a hopeless moment, then finally shrugged forward.

The door lifted up. Sunlight streamed in.

I grunted, breathless, and hauled myself in the snow, clawing away from the shaft with bloodied hands smeared with dirt.

I cleared the ladder, flopped onto my back, and took a breath.

A gun barrel tapped my skull.

I opened my eyes.

Simon Goodman towered over me with a sneer.

"Detective, how many times must I tell you..." The gun cocked. "Stay off of our land."

Chapter Twenty-Six

Why are you so afraid?
Don't you know it's almost over?
-Him

I'd just crawled out of a hole in the earth.

Now I'd get dropped six feet under again.

I didn't move, but my every instinct screamed to fight, punch, and kick. Unfortunately, the gun was a decent deterrent. Simon read my expression and simply shook his head.

"Be a good girl now, Detective." He reached for me. I tensed, but his hand only grazed my side, aiming for the weapon on my belt. "Relax. I'm not going to touch you."

"What's the matter? Am I too old for you?"

He cracked the gun against my head. I grunted, my vision brightening for a long moment. He hauled me onto my knees. The barrel pressed into my forehead.

"I told you once to behave," he warned.

I took some pride in that. "I'm not as malleable as your girls."

"They know their place."

And staring into the gun, I knew mine. "What are you going to do? Kill me?"

"Yes."

"You've already killed a lot of officers today, Simon. Sure you want to add another consecutive life sentence?"

"They invaded our land. Our privacy. *Our families.*"

"They're not your *family*. Those women are your *captives*." My knees dug into the dirt. Uncomfortable. A rock lodged under my leg. It wouldn't be a good weapon, but it was better than praying for the gun to jam.

Simon's jaw clenched, tensing a thick vein in his neck. It pulsed upwards, throbbing through his forehead. "We protect what is ours."

"You mean you'd kill for Jacob. Think he's gonna save you when I haul your ass to jail?"

"They shouldn't have entered our home."

"The police have a warrant."

"What a coincidence." His voice loosened, deranged. "We had a demolition permit."

The gun aimed to kill, and I believed in his intentions.

The Goodmans ran scared now—forced off their land and into the real world where not every woman cowered beneath them and not every man condoned their abuse.

"So, now what happens?" I stared at the weapon. "You kill me, stage some elaborate rescue of twenty-some women and children, and run?"

"If we have to."

"How do you plan to get them out? They're in police custody. Some are too young to move easily. Others entirely too pregnant..." I should have quieted, but I liked the twitch in his eyebrow. Had any woman ever spoken so freely to him? "Seems you're in quite the bind."

"And your predicament is no better."

"I'm not ready to die like Jonah's wife." I raised an eyebrow. "And his girlfriend. Strange. I thought you guys were monogamous?"

"I'm sure I don't know what you're talking about."

"Of course, you do. Every Goodman male gets his own pre-pubescent virgin, a little girl to transform into a perfect wife and busy little breeder. My question...does Jacob promise them to you...or do those directions come from God?"

"You talk like you don't have a gun to your head."

"What do I have to lose?" I shifted. The rock wiggled too. Good. I'd have no time to dig it out. "Tell me about Jonah."

"You've already slandered him enough."

"Then correct me. What happened to your nephew? Did he want out of the family?"

Simon frowned. "He lost his way."

"With a gun in his hand."

"It should have been a Bible."

"Harder to kill people with a book."

"He never learned what it was to be a man. To take *responsibility*."

"Like by...kidnapping a child to make her his bride?" My mouth was a magnet for the bullet, but I refused to shut up. "But he *had* a young wife. He took Nina Martin...I mean, Rachel. Even had a baby with her."

"Those are some wild accusations."

"I'll get a confession soon enough."

303

"You should be confessing your sins, Detective." He offered me a smile. "I'm giving you an opportunity."

I wasn't intimidated, just half-drugged with my own adrenaline and bad luck. "Right back at ya. Tell me what the hell your family's been doing, and I bet the DA can get you a deal. Couple years shaved off your sentence."

"You have an awful lot of confidence, Detective."

"For a woman?"

"For a woman like *you*."

"What about me?"

He just laughed.

I shifted, but I didn't reveal my would-be weapon digging into my knee, not with the gun poised at my face. The rock slid in the snow, no larger than a baseball. Not the greatest weapon, especially for a right-field reject like me. Softball wasn't my sport, and the few innings I'd played in junior high stuck me in the outfield where I wouldn't cause any trouble. I could shoot a target at fifty yards, but toss a ball? Voodoo. It didn't bode well.

Simon brushed the gun along my cheek. "We've been reading up on you, London Serenity McKenna."

"Oh, a middle name. Someone did their Googling."

Simon's grin turned cold. "I know why you became a detective."

"The pleasure of meeting assholes like you."

"So tough. So vulgar." His stare turned vile. "But I know the *real* you."

No one knew the real me. Not even James. "Who am I?"

"A scared little girl."

"Maybe you've just been around too many of them."

Simon shook his head. "No. I can smell the fear on you."

"An aphrodisiac?"

"Just a talent." He grunted. "You're scared, and that's why you became a cop. You want to feel in *control* again, don't you? You're looking for a big, bad man to punish, a way to cope with all those *terrible* things done to you in the past."

I wasn't impressed. "That's not fair. I like to punish all bad men, not just the ones who screwed with me."

"Oh, did he screw you, Detective?" Simon licked his fat lip. "They didn't print that in the papers."

"I'm surprised you read anything but the Bible."

"And I'm surprised you never turned to the scriptures after all those horrible nights spent with that creature." Simon lowered his voice. "A kinder man would have kidnapped you and provided a home, warm bed, and family where you could live your days in simple, holy matrimony."

The rock felt good digging into my knee. "Are you confessing?"

He shrugged. "A strict hypothetical."

"We're among friends here, Simon. You can tell me the truth."

"Good." He stared at me, and I hated how his gaze crawled over my skin. "It's strange, Detective."

"What?"

"That after all those things he did to you...you still recovered."

"I'm stronger than most."

He smirked. "But you've become a functional member of society. A law enforcement agent. They trusted you enough to wield a gun and chase after all those bad men that remind you of *him*."

I scoffed. "Think you're the first one to suggest it? Our DA schools idiot lawyers who think *The McKenna Defense* will get their clients off. But they keep on citing undiagnosed PTSD as the reason I unjustly collar their clients. Never works."

Simon edged closer. "So the past doesn't bother you at all? You don't have trouble sleeping? Don't see him in every shadow?"

"No." A lie.

"But you were kidnapped by the *Rustbelt Sadist*. What was his real name?"

I'd never wanted to know. "We didn't exchange formalities."

"Must have called him *something*." Simon leaned close. I pretended not to see the bulge tensing in his trousers. "Tell me. You were held in his captivity. Bound. Beaten."

"And?"

His lips twisted into a confused smile. "Did he really try to *eat* you?"

Simon got off on the details. Didn't surprise me. A sadist never hid his true fetishes. Unfortunately, I'd learned that lesson too late.

Which was why no Goodman would ever scare me.

Nothing could scare me as much as him.

"You looking for ideas?" I held his stare.

"It must still frighten you. Let it off your chest. It's obviously *eating* at you."

"Lower the gun, and I'll tell you anything you want."

"I'll keep the gun right here, and you'll tell me anyway." His voice layered thick with excitement. "What was it like sharing a bed with a cannibal?"

He'd never raped me. That almost made him a better man than Simon.

Almost.

I sneered. "What's it like sharing a bed with a *child*?"

Simon lurched. I flinched. My heart stilled, bracing for the shot. My vision darkened in the surge of panic. He didn't shoot.

His mistake.

I gripped the rock from under my knee. Dug my fingers into the soft dirt.

Pulled.

And it was free.

"You're going to die, Detective. Answer the question." Simon tapped my chin with the gun. I met his disturbing gaze again. "How long did he keep you?"

I answered honestly. "Three weeks."

"What did he do to you?"

"You're sick."

"I imagine he was worse."

That was true. "He took me captive. Tied me down. Sliced off my flesh, an inch or more at a time. Fried it in a pan. Ate it like bacon in front of me."

"Was he a breast or thigh man?"

Neither.

He aimed for my stomach.

And I still nearly retched thinking about it.

"Why didn't he kill you?" Simon demanded.

I hated going back to those memories. My hand curled over the rock, keeping me focused, grounded in the reality.

He was gone.

I was safe.

And once I got out from under Simon's gun, I'd continue to live my life free of his control.

"He kept me alive for *entertainment*," I said. "He liked talking to me. Said I was the only one who ever tried to understand him." A stupid idea. "I thought I could be a psychologist to him, help him see the err in his ways." My throat closed. "Instead he kept me alive, made me watch as he kidnapped and tortured another girl."

"He roasted her up?"

In a variety of ways. "He was a cannibal. Of course he killed her. He tortured and killed dozens of women…" I breathed through my mouth, fearing I'd still smell that sweet char of human flesh. "But he never forced any of the women to marry him. See, he might have been a sadistic freak…but even he could score his own dates."

"You little *bitch*—"

I launched the rock towards his groin, figuring at worst, I'd hit his gut, and at best…

Simon doubled over.

Bullseye.

I surged to my feet, crashing into him at full speed. He curled his fingers around the gun as we fell. A shot rocketed off. Missing me. Missing him.

Too close.

I came down on his wrist, bashing my fist into his chin to stun him. He rolled, but it opened the pressure point on his arm. A solid jab, and his grip loosened. The weapon fell.

I reached.

His hand gripped my thigh, hauling me backwards. A swift kick held him in the snow as I dove for the gun. He was faster, bigger. He batted it away and dragged me to the ground.

My chest heaved. Arm bled.

I wasn't stupid. Simon was a behemoth of a man. Overpowering him wasn't an option. I needed the gun.

But it scattered. We crawled, hand over hand for it. Kicking and punching. He attempted to headlock me. Ended when I bit hard into his arm, tearing at the flesh.

His howl of pain gave me the chance. I abandoned the gun, rolled for one of the broken tree limbs littering the clearing. The heavy wood soaked through with snow, dead from the winter and green with moss.

I didn't wait. The branch cracked against Simon's back first, flattening him to the ground.

Then I brought it onto his head.

He collapsed into the dirt.

I hit him again, just to be sure.

He stayed down, groaning. I knelt on his back and quickly cuffed his hands.

"You have no idea what you've done," he warned. "You'll never save them. They all belong to *us*."

"Not anymore." I kept my weight between his shoulders, twisting the cuffs just to make sure he knew how screwed he was. "Simon Goodman...you're under arrest."

Chapter Twenty-Seven

You can ask me why I do the things I do.

But you won't like the answer.

-Him

How many times did I have to break up this family?

I hesitated outside of Anna Prescott's motel room. The baby cried—sleepy wails easily soothed with Anna's expert rocking.

She obviously loved the baby.

And why wouldn't she? All of the mothers loved their children. That was a bond nothing could break, even kidnappings and forced marriages.

Problem was, they'd bound together. Now that the men had scattered, and the women were removed from the farm, the women had only each other for support.

They'd need help adjusting to life—real life.

And the baby…

I supposed that custody battle between Anna and Nina Martin's parents would be brutal.

I knocked—three times. The voices hushed.

"It's Detective McKenna…London. Can I speak with you?"

I expected the door to stay closed. Simon's wife, a twenty-eight-year-old woman who answered to Mary, had collapsed when told of her husband's arrest. The scars on her arms and crooked nose revealed a not-so-happy marriage, but she'd wept as if she'd lost her soulmate.

Mary was the only one who ever spoke an accusation at me. She'd tugged at her blonde hair, fell into Anna's arms, and wept.

Why are you doing this? What have we ever done to you?

The door opened. Anna rubbed the baby's back.

"Hi." I twisted the envelope in my hands. "Got a minute to talk?"

"Did you find him?" Her voice cracked with loneliness and fear. "Tell me now, in case I must inform the others."

I wished we'd found Jacob. The DA even offered Simon one hell of a deal to flip on him.

He'd refused. Stayed silent.

If they'd had let me into the pen with him, I'd had made him talk. But James was the one who refused me. He thought Simon would be *combative* with a woman interrogator.

He hadn't been a bundle of sunshine rolling in the snow either.

But Simon hadn't talked, and wherever Jacob Goodman fled was well-hidden, probably even from Anna. The way she wept?

She thought she'd never see him again.

Didn't she know how lucky she'd be if it were true?

"I'm not here about Jacob," I said. "Is it okay if I stay for a minute?"

Anna stepped aside, casting a glance over her shoulder to Mariam. She did a poor job of studying her Bible. The book fell into her lap as she looked longingly at the television—unplugged and dark.

"Do your lessons." Anna instructed her. "We'll talk about the verses once I've helped Detective McKenna."

Mariam nodded, her oversized sweat pants and sweatshirt swallowing her whole. The little girl was hardly a blonde spec on the bed. We still hadn't learned her real name, where she'd come from, and no entry in the Missing Persons database even came close to matching her.

Mariam was a complete mystery—and no one would have missed her if Jacob and his family had finished their wedding ceremony.

"Is it about that CPS again?" Anna offered me a seat at the tiny table by the window, greeting me with all the hospitality she could muster, as if the cheap motel were her own lovely kitchen once more. "Please, Detective. I understand why the police and everyone fear for these girls, but we're family. Even if they believe those horrible things about our husbands, they have to realize we have more experience with raising children than *anyone*."

That was the truth. "Anna—"

"Just let me keep Mariam and the baby near? Until this is sorted out. Until he…"

"Jacob isn't coming home."

Anna swallowed, but she remained optimistic. Or delusional. "I've kept my faith for this long. My goodness, if Moses led his people for forty years through a barren desert, the least I can do is keep my spirits up. We've a roof over our heads and food in our bellies. In time, this misunderstanding will be forgotten."

I agreed with most of it. "No one will kick you out into the cold."

"Of course not. Especially since we have a home waiting for us." Anna smoothed the baby's hair as she fussed. "I didn't build Jacob's farm, but I'll protect it the same. With or without him."

Resilient to the end.

And *kind*.

Anna hadn't blamed anyone. Hadn't fought or resisted.

That sort of submission was strange to me. She'd allow anyone to command her—husband or police. I gave it a few more days before the surrender became sweet relief, when she finally embraced her freedom and took a bite of food *she* had chosen to eat, when she took a step without asking *his* permission, when she first said *no* without a reprimand.

Soon she'd understand that we had helped her.

But first, I had to break her heart. I pushed the envelope onto the table.

"Those are the DNA results," I said. "The baby is Rebecca—Jonah and Nina's daughter."

Anna turned the baby to sit on her lap, facing me. The little cutie gave me a wide, drooly smile.

"What happens now?" she whispered.

"That's up to you. Are you ready to talk?"

The answer was no, but Anna was far too polite. "I'm not sure what I can offer you. You know our way of life. Jacob made our decisions. *All* of our decisions."

"I understand."

"You have Simon in custody. You should speak with him."

I leaned forward, playing her a bit more aggressive than I had in the past. She needed that push, that guidance. Someone to tell her that it was *okay* to help us.

Someone to replace the orders Jacob had given.

"See, that's the problem," I said. "Simon isn't talking."

It didn't seem to surprise her. "He's too proud. That's the sort of vice they warn about in the deadly sins."

"Then you have to be the one to begin this. If you talk, the others will talk too." I stayed still, my voice the only force in the room. "I know about the kidnappings. No one is in trouble except for the men who did this."

"No one should be in trouble for bringing a family together."

I could work with that. "But I don't know who the family *is*. I can't identify all the girls and women." I reached for the baby, squeezing her chubby fingers. "If someone had taken Rebecca…wouldn't you need to know what had happened to her? Where you could find her again?"

"*Nothing* will happen to her." Anna held her tighter. "I'll protect her with my life."

"So would the mothers of the other girls who have been taken. Their families must be sick with worry. *Your* family is worried."

"Jacob is my family. These girls are my family. We've been together for years." Her eyes glistened, threatening to tear. "What about *us*? We've already lost the men we love. Are we forced apart too? Because of what *they* did?"

Closer. It was the first-time Anna had ever indicated that Jacob had done something wrong.

I could use it. I could play it.

"Tell me about Rebecca." I crossed my legs and relaxed. It worked.

Anna breathed deep. The color returned to her cheeks. "What do you want to know?"

"I understand how she was born," I said. "Jonah is Jacob's youngest son. He was old enough to marry?"

"Detective."

"And Nina—Rachel—was chosen as his wife."

She was careful, each word deliberate. "They loved each other. If you believe nothing else, believe in their love."

Stranger things had happened on this case. "They were together. Rachel got pregnant. She gave birth. But...things changed, didn't they? With Jonah?"

"I suppose..."

"He lost his way?"

The conversation seemed painful. "Jonah was such a free spirit. He never deferred to his father. Questioned everything. The farm. The chores. Our ways. Even his faith."

"He denounced his faith?"

"Oh, he believed in *something*. We all do, Detective. Even you." She smiled. "I know you are hurting. I can see it. I can *feel* it in you. But you've turned from the one who could help you the most."

Unless she was talking about James, we had a vastly different worldview. "Was it a lack of faith...or a woman who drew him away?"

Anna stiffened. Struck a nerve, but it wasn't her sin to bear. "Both. It wasn't the first time Jonah ran away from home."

How ironic. Runaways escaping the farm as fresh ones were delivered. "Jacob couldn't have liked that."

"No..." Anna said. "Jonah had a gift for carpentry, but he hated working with his hands." She smiled. "He was only a few years younger than me."

"Must have been weird being his step-mother."

"A little. Jonah made it easy though. He wasn't like a son...more like a younger brother. Someone impetuous. We used to talk all the time."

Her voice turned wistful. I hadn't realized how close she was with Jonah.

"What'd you talk about?" I asked.

"He used to tell me stories about wanting to get away. To see the world." She sniffled, but she didn't let herself weep. "When he was sixteen, he was whittling in the barn, away from all the noise and kids. Had a little model train he'd carved from wood for his cousin. A birthday present. He set it down to dry, and one of our mares—a real ornery gal—grabbed it, bit it in two, and stomped on the rest. Jonah would never take a switch to a horse, but he was so mad he decided—*this is it!* That was his final straw. He packed his bags in a rage and started walking."

"Did he get far?"

"Only far enough to realize that he'd been too upset to pack a pair of comfortable shoes. He came limping back up the road five hours later, grumbling, but his feet too hurt to even throw a proper tantrum. Still mad as a yellow jacket, but he dumped his bags in the stables and stuck his feet right into the water trough. Jacob found him there, but so did the mare. Gave him a nip right on his blistered toe. Jacob thought it was enough divine retribution. Didn't punish him." Anna looked down. "Maybe he should have."

"Jonah sounded very gentle."

"The gentlest of Jacob's sons," she said. "It wasn't good for farm work and decisions though. Our way of life is hard, and it requires a firm hand. Jacob was right not to send him to college. He kept him close to home."

"Why?"

"Because..." She shook her head. "Lord forgive me for talking about those who have passed."

"Jonah would want his story to be told."

"Not this one..." Anna whispered. "Jonah liked the things our family shunned. Television. Movies. Vulgar music."

I said what she was unwilling to admit. "Women?"

Her words trembled. "We didn't realize what had happened until it was too late. He'd fallen in love with a woman outside of our community."

"But he was married to Rachel."

She was careful. "No. Rachel was too young. They were...spiritually committed."

"Is that what it's called?"

"Rachel loved him very much. They formed a bond."

"But she was forced to marry him."

"She *cared* for him." Anna held the child closer. "Can't you see what their love created?"

"But if he loved her, why have an affair with Cora Abbott?"

The question only darkened the circles shadowing her eyes. "I ask myself that every night. I suppose he met her, fell for her, just like any other man and pretty woman. Rachel was right for him, but he wanted to explore the world." She cursed herself, the first harsh word I'd ever heard her utter, and it directly only at her naivety. "I should have stopped him. Talked to him. I could have prevented…"

"Him leaving the farm?"

"He took Rachel too. He thought…he thought if he could return her to her old home, he'd be free to be with that woman. But their bond was sealed by creating Rebecca. This was God's will, Detective. Not ours. Marriage is a *gift* between a man and woman. Unbreakable."

I hated to broach his death with her so close to tears, but she had the answers. "Jonah committed suicide."

"Yes."

"Who killed Cora Abbott and Nina Martin?"

She stiffened. Probably assumed she hid it, but I saw the flash of fear, the curl of her lip, the twitch of her eyebrow. "What do you mean? *Jonah*. It was a tragedy."

"Eve, you know that isn't true."

"I thought…this was settled. The Homicide detectives—"

"They got it wrong."

"H—how—"

"He couldn't even beat a horse who had destroyed his work. Do you really think *Jonah* would kill the two women he supposedly loved?"

Anna pushed away from the table. "I *never* thought he would."

"Do you think he would murder the mother of his child?"

"No one ever considers such things—"

"Do you really think he'd leave his own daughter *orphaned* and commit a sin as great as suicide?"

"I…Detective, I don't know what you believe happened—"

"Cora and Nina were murdered by the same man who *coerced* Jonah into killing himself." I pointed to the baby. Anna no longer cradled her.

She wrapped her in her arms. *Hid* her. "Jacob threatened Rebecca, didn't he?"

"I don't know what you're talking about."

"That's why you're afraid to let her out of your sight. That's why you took her. You're protecting the baby because you thought Jacob would harm her to blackmail Jonah and Rachel into returning."

"You're wrong."

"Jacob killed those women, didn't he?"

Tears rolled over her cheeks. She shook her head, too violently.

"My husband would *never* do something like that."

"He's already kidnapped and raped you."

"Don't use that word." Her words wavered. "I think you should leave."

No way. Not now.

Not when I was this *close.*

"You saw it, didn't you?" I pressed harder. "You watched Jacob losing control over his son. Jonah would never listen. He fell in love with a woman outside of the farm, a woman Jacob hadn't *personally* selected for him. And nothing he did could return Jonah to the flock. His own *son* slipped further and further from his control. And when Jonah returned Rachel to her parents…" I stood, forcing Anna to look at me. "Jacob feared the worst. He thought Jonah would go to the police. He thought Jonah would reveal how the family had been kidnapping girls to become child brides."

"*No.*"

"He feared Jonah would ruin everything. He had to stop them before Rachel told the world that she had been raped."

"Stop!"

"Eve, I'm begging you. Just tell the truth. No harm will come to you. Jacob believed that Rachel had to die before she destroyed everything. Cora knew too much and had to be killed too. And Jonah…he was too far gone to be saved. To protect the family, Jacob killed his own son."

Anna's expression darkened, but she weakened, sputtering in breathless weeping. "You don't understand. Jacob couldn't have done this. He wouldn't hurt anyone!"

"Really?" I pulled the hand-stitched teddy bear from my bag and tossed it on the table. The evidence bag wasn't the safest container, but I'd wanted her to see. "Your *husband* sent this as a warning to my family. *After* he slashed the tires on my car, filled the inside with blood, and painted a bloody threat on my door."

Anna said nothing.

Her hands trembled. She clutched the table. The chair nearly slipped out from under her, but she didn't catch herself.

She stared only at the teddy bear.

"Jacob attempted to murder your biological sister. He set her house on fire with her inside simply because she came to me and begged for help to rescue you."

"…No."

"And this?" I tugged on the bag. "*This* was sent to my four-year-old niece. It's stuffed with *glass*."

"G—glass?"

"She spent the night in the hospital. It sliced her wrist. She's still in stitches."

Anna stumbled. I rushed forward, catching her, taking the baby before she tumbled.

"*Mariam!*" I handed the baby to the girl. "Take her. Get me a bottle of water."

Mariam stared with wide-eyes but said nothing. Never did, poor thing. Only cried.

I knelt beside Anna, offering her the water. She wouldn't drink. I forced it to her lips, tipping enough to wet her tongue.

"Do you see now?" I asked. "I *have* to stop him."

"I know this bear."

My chest tightened. I expected as much. "Did you make it?"

"Yes." Her voice faded, weak and muffled and so very far away. "*I've made these.*"

"Eve, you're not in trouble for sewing the bear. But I need your help before someone else gets hurt. Before anyone else dies."

She reached for the bear, but I took it off of her before she hugged the glass too close to her chest. Her motions slogged, as if she were drunk.

Or *remembering.*

She struggled to breathe. "*I know this bear.*"

"It's okay. You never meant to hurt anyone."

"No...I didn't...this pattern..." Tears rolled over her cheeks. "I used to make this pattern when I was a *girl.*"

"I thought you didn't talk about your past, Eve."

"*Eve?*" She stared at me, her face pale and sweaty. "That's...not my name. I'm not Eve. My name is Anna Prescott. And..." She took the bear, turning it in her hands. "I used to make these bears with my sister when we were kids. Our grandmother taught us..."

My stomach twisted. Anna gripped my arm, crushing it as a wracking sob tore through her body.

321

"Oh my God…" Her words pinched with terror. "I have a *sister*."

"Anna, did you make this bear?"

"Long ago."

"Did you sew one last week?"

She stared at the stuffed animal. "Haven't made one since I was a little girl…"

This bear wasn't a craft made years ago. The material was still taut, the stitching tight, the stuffing smelling of processed textiles. This bear had been sewn *recently*.

I sat back, kneeling on the floor. Her words washed over me.

Anna used to make the teddy bears at *home*.

She hadn't made this bear. But I knew who did.

Anna Prescott had a sister.

And now? I had a new suspect.

Chapter Twenty-Eight

If you don't love yourself, no one else will.
Does anyone care about you?
-Him

Louisa greeted me with a deceiver's smile.

The bubbly excitement bled into her voice, manic and amazed.

"Can I see Anna now?" She took my hand. I dropped it immediately. "*Please.* Where's my sister? You have *no idea* how long I've waited for this moment."

She'd waited exactly long enough for the desperation to overwhelm her rationality.

Anna wasn't at the station to meet her sister. I'd already threatened to arrest her husband and family. The last thing I wanted to do was ruin the few good memories she had of her prior life.

"Let's talk, Louisa."

I led her into the interview room. She slid right into the chair, tapping her fingers against the chipping, wooden table.

How many times did I have her in here?

How many times had she completely manipulated me?

How many times had she lied to my face?

"Is she okay?" Louisa bit her lip. Innocent? Hardly. "I'm getting my house ready for guests. I know she has a baby with her. And the little girl too. What's her name? Mary?"

"Let's not get ahead of ourselves."

"Oh, I'm sure we'll have custody battles. I read it in the newspaper."

An unfortunate leak that needed to be plugged. The phones had run off the hooks, frightened mothers pleading with me to *check again* and make sure their child wasn't one of the girls pulled from the farm. Every family missing a daughter seemed to call...except for the parents of the children Jacob had taken.

Maybe Anna was right. Maybe the girls were the unwanted ones, neglected and forgotten. That didn't help me. In fact, it only served to push them deeper into those bastards' arms.

"This isn't about Anna." I didn't bother taking the other chair. I stood, arms crossed, trying too damn hard to keep my temper in check and not choke on my own bitterness. "Let's talk about you."

"Me?"

"Got anything you'd like to say?"

Louisa pushed a hand through lively curls, careful not to touch her face or ruin the professional salon's hairstyling. The return of her sister hadn't made her a new woman—just a visit to Macy's makeup counter. With a little foundation, a lifetime of sorrows faded under a layer of creamy beige.

"I'm not sure what's happening..." Louisa grinned. "Detective, why aren't you *thrilled?* We saved everyone!"

"*We?*"

"Well, you. You put your life on the line for Anna—"

"So...*now* my safety concerns you?"

She paused. "Excuse me?"

I didn't have all the proof, but my gut wasn't wrong. I gave her only enough rope to hang herself, even if I planned to tighten that noose myself.

"Come on, Louisa." I gave her a shrug. "Drop the act."

"What *act?*"

"You played me once, and I let it go. I figured I'd do you a favor. I had to save those girls, whatever the cost. You took advantage of that."

"What are you talking about?"

"I know what *really* happened. Now I want to hear it from you."

"Hear *what?*" she asked.

"*The truth.*"

Louisa shifted. The chair creaked, and panic flashed over her face. It wasn't an interrogation room, but the closed door and lack of windows probably felt like a prison to a pathological liar caught in her own web.

"See, we've got a problem." I took my time. I thought I'd enjoy watching her squirm, tasting the guilt like a juicy, ripe strawberry. Instead, her denial irritated me like a seed caught in my teeth. "I know who's been threatening me. And I know who attacked you." I pulled the teddy bear and a manila folder from my bag. "And I know who sent this vile toy to my four-year-old niece."

Louisa's expression didn't waver. Was she that skilled a liar? "It was Jacob Goodman."

"Nope. Couldn't have been Jacob. He was too busy screwing your sister."

"Don't..." Her words clipped. "How can you say that?"

"He has a busy life on that farm. Works the fields in the day. Keeps an eye on the books every evening. Then every night, he beds your sister over and over again."

"Stop it!"

"Forces her into bed."

"*Don't, Detective!*"

"For fifteen years, he took all he wanted from her..." The words disgusted me, but Louisa kicked her chair back. Her face twisted in a dark, devious rage. "She was his *wife*, after all. And hell, after that long? She probably got used to it. Might have even started anticipating his needs."

"Enough!" Louisa covered her ears, the only reason she hadn't lunged for my throat. "I should cut your tongue out, you disgusting bitch!"

She didn't expect my grin. I softened my voice. Felt like introductions were in order once again.

"And there you are..." I said. "The *real* Louisa Prescott."

"What the hell are you talking about?"

"Don't insult me. You weren't innocent when you walked into this office, and you sure as hell aren't now." I pointed to the chair. "Sit your ass down."

"I want to see my sister!"

"You should have thought about that before pissing with me, Miss Prescott." I didn't let her look away. My stare burned just as hot as hers. "Sit. Down."

Louisa sneered, but she surrendered, plunking into the wooden seat. "You can't find Jacob Goodman, so you're taking your frustration out on me? Go ahead. What do you want to know? Nothing I say will help you find the asshole who kidnapped and raped my sister."

"Don't sell yourself short. You *did* find Jacob Goodman before. And your sister. For years, you knew exactly what's happened at Harvest Dominion Farm. You tried to get her out."

"Is that a crime?"

"No. That's being a loving sister…" I said "The crimes started when you realized you couldn't save her without *convincing* people to help."

Her lips pressed into a thin line. "What do you want me to say? I *worried* about Anna. I never stopped worrying about her. You think I was going to let that monster destroy her? I had to do *something*."

"But you couldn't save her. You couldn't even get close to the farm. No one believed you." I lowered my voice, circling the table. "So, you decided to *make* them believe."

Louisa said nothing. The panic and outrage, hysteria and timid fear blinked away. The stare that remained turned cold. Hostile.

Proud.

I hadn't seen it before—that cruel manipulation hidden so well within the panicked and flighty persona she'd adopted. The Louisa Prescott that sobbed in my office and begged for her sister's life was as fake as Eve Goodman.

"No one in Forest County could help you free your sister, so you came back to the city," I said. "You studied the Goodmans' patterns. Learned they came in every few weeks to drop off produce and furniture. How long did you stalk them before you got your break?"

"Years."

"You had to wait until Jonah Goodman was killed," I said. "That was your chance. You knew we'd find out who he was. You knew you could connect Anna's case to him, and we'd be swept into the middle of a massive investigation into the family."

"Yes."

"How did you know he was dead?"

"I didn't kill him, if that's what you're asking."

I wasn't, but it was good to know. "You still *knew*."

"I tailed them. All of them. When I realized Jacob Goodman's youngest son was having an affair, I thought it was my chance for revenge. Jacob was losing control, and I loved to watch him suffer. That pride will be the death of him."

"You never thought to kill him?"

"Believe me, I had my chances." Her voice roughened, tough and unfamiliar. "But death is too easy a punishment for them. The Goodmans deserve jail—where they'll be forced against their will just like they forced all those girls."

"So instead you pointed me at them." I opened the folder, revealing both the fire marshal's report and the forensics on the casings found at the scene. "Seems like you have a couple guns registered under your name. Coincidentally, the bullet fired through your living room window? A .45. You have a .45, don't you?"

Louisa didn't even look at the report. She stayed silent.

Fine. I'd do the talking for once.

And I'd get my answers.

"Strange thing about the fire too. Started in the basement. Couple rags. A little kerosene. Same materials you had on hand. Plus, there was no sign of forced entry on your basement door. No broken windows. No other ways for a Goodman to enter your home."

"Say it."

"*You* fired the shot through your own window. Called me. Then went downstairs and set the fire so that when I arrived the flames would just be starting and…" I shrugged. "You pretended that you were in danger so I'd think that the Goodmans were targeting you."

"I feared for my life."

I showed her the pictures of my Jeep. "And I'm still dreading what the repairs on my car will cost. It's *trashed*. Can't get the blood out of the fabric. Needed four new tires. Jeeps aren't cheap, Louisa. Did you fear for your life when you vandalized my property?"

"Detective—"

"Did you fear for your life when you sent this to my niece?" I pitched the teddy bear towards the end of the table. "You nearly took off her *finger*."

Louisa gave an irritated sigh. "Oh, don't overreact, Detective. Your family was always safe. *My sister* was the one in danger."

"And that gives you the right to file false reports? You started a fire in your parents' old home. Intimidated and threatened a police officer. You *assaulted* a child!" I couldn't hide the rage grinding my voice. "*Why?*"

She didn't apologize.

Offered no remorse. No shame.

"Because you were the only one I could make listen."

"Me?"

"You were the perfect detective for the job."

"Why?"

She scrunched her nose. "Because it's *you*. London McKenna. There's no way in hell you'd ever let a little girl get captured by a big, bad man. How could you resist a case like this? With your history, I *knew* you'd be the first officer to give a damn."

"Any cop would have helped you."

"That's not true." She leaned forward, her palms flat on the table, as if pleading with me to understand the greatest insult I'd ever heard. "Everyone knows your story. They remember the case. *The Rustbelt Sadist?* You escaped a brutal serial killer who kept you imprisoned for weeks. When I saw your name in the paper and read that you had become a *detective?* It was fate."

"My kidnapping and torture was *fate?*"

"Yes." She answered truthfully, coldly. "You were the only one who'd understand. The only one who'd help."

"I would have helped without your *provocation*." That was the sick part. "Your sister *did* need help. I would have saved them without you targeting me."

"I couldn't take the chance anymore. It's been fifteen years, Detective. It was time my sister came home."

"And for what?" I grabbed the handcuffs on my belt. Louisa offered her wrists willingly. "Do you even realize the trouble you're in? Sure, you've saved your sister. But at what cost? Now you're the one going to prison."

"Anna spent fifteen years in captivity." Louisa's voice warmed only over her sister's name. "It should have been me."

"What?"

She spoke *pain*. True pain. Soul-wrenching, without even the comfort of tears. Her eyes rose to mine.

330

"He meant to take *me*."

I froze. "What are you talking about?"

"That day. On the sidewalk. Jacob came after *me*. I'm younger than Anna. She already had become a woman. I was still waiting, and I looked it. He reached for *me*...but I bit him. Hard. Kicked and screamed. Anna was too scared to move." She trembled, hard. "And so I *pushed* her."

"Away from Jacob?"

The slow shake of her head revealed a secret Louisa kept her entire life.

"I pushed her *towards* Jacob." Her voice cracked. "And then I *ran*."

"And Jacob took her instead."

"I lived *free* for fifteen years while my sister suffered a fate that should have been mine."

"Louisa—"

"Don't you see? I had no choice. I had to do anything I could to get her back. *Anything*. I didn't care who I hurt, what I destroyed. I had to save her. It never should have been *her*."

"But your house...my car...my *niece*."

"It worked." She actually smiled. "I don't care what happens to me. Now Anna has a chance to live a real life. You have my gratitude, Detective."

In a terrible, heart-breaking way, I understood her.

I took her hand, hating her, hating myself, hating what the Goodmans did to so many innocent lives.

"And you have the right to remain silent..

Chapter Twenty-Nine

A pretty girl like you should have been loved.
You should always feel loved before you die.
-Him

James and I never had a formal dinner at home.

We'd gone out plenty of times. Ordered pizza more nights than I could count. But we didn't really eat *together*. No coming home from work to a plate of spaghetti and hunk of garlic bread.

So I boiled the water. Dumped the noodles. Cracked open a jar of sauce. I'm sure he would have preferred a couple meatballs in his meal, but he never minded going vegetarian for me.

I was beginning to think he'd do anything for me.

"Either you have something good to tell me…" James hid his smile as he sipped his wine. "Or you've poisoned the food. Though that might be an improvement from your usual cooking."

"Eat it, you jerk."

He passed me the bread. I took his hand instead.

The words came easy. It was speaking them that was hard. "Do you know that I love you?"

He hesitated, gauging my reaction. Granted, it wasn't a pleasant declaration. I spat the question as if interrogating him about my own feelings.

Not very romantic.

I'd never been *romantic* before.

"Yeah." James took a bite of his dinner. Casual. No pressure. As always. "It's nice to hear."

"I don't say it often."

"You don't have to."

"But if I had died—"

Now the fork dropped. So did his smile. "You didn't, London."

"If I had…if I had gotten blown to bits in that chapel or buried in that bunker tomb…would you have known that I love you?"

"Yes."

"How?" Suddenly, I didn't want the food. "I don't hug you or kiss you unless we're in bed. I don't say the words. I'm awkward on the phone. More awkward when we go out. We don't cuddle. We don't do *couple* things. And when I need you—"

"I'm there. I'm always there." He poured another glass of wine and took a long sip. "You want to know what I think?"

"Depends. Is this my boyfriend talking, or is it a professional opinion?"

"Both."

I'd probably never separate them. "Fine."

James pushed the plate away, but he didn't reach for me. This sort of talk was hard enough under the warmth of his stare. I couldn't take a touch too.

"Every night when we talk…you tell me about your cases. You share the details. Talk about the victims. Ask me about the perps."

"Yeah?"

"Do you know *why* you do that?"

It wasn't because I needed help with my work, and, usually, it wasn't because James was consulting for the station. I did it because…

He listened.

"Why?" I asked.

"It's because you *trust* me."

I laughed. "Of course, I trust you."

"That's not true," he said. "You don't trust *anyone*, London. Not yourself. Not your family. Not the police department. It took years for you to even consider opening yourself to me. I hate that for you, London, but I love that I'm the lucky one you let near. That's my own selfish desires talking."

"I trust people. I have to. It's my job."

That amused him. "You don't let the ones who know you get close. Your family, your colleagues, old friends. But a victim who comes to the police?" He paused. "You will *always* trust them."

I pushed my plate away, losing my appetite. "And look how good that turned out. Louisa played me."

"You wanted to help her. Any cop would have done the same."

"But she's crazy."

James always hated that word, but he tended to enjoy untangling the crossed-wires in people's heads. "She's unstable."

"I didn't see it."

"But because of her, you saved her sister."

"Did I? I handed Anna off from one lunatic to the other."

334

And that was my fault.

Louisa made bail and was already home. All she needed was a sympathetic judge who'd sentence her light after learning about her trials for her sister.

And Anna had been thrilled to be reunited with Louisa. She, Mariam, and Rebecca had gone to stay with her. Home for the first time in fifteen years.

"I should have realized something was wrong," I said. "I should have known. I should have been more careful. I just...I don't know *why* I acted how I did."

James was quiet for a long moment. He waited for me to speak, but I'd been with him for too long to fall for that trick.

"London," he said. "What's really bothering you?"

Did he want the truth or the crazy bottled up in me? Most days, they felt like the same thing.

"It's about you." I apologized with a shrug. "And me. And my job. And *everything.*"

I gripped my napkin, tearing off small chunks in my lap. It made a mess, but it distracted me from his golden eyes, the curl of his lips, the strength of his jaw.

How much he knew about me.

"I'm not sure I can do this job," I said.

James didn't buy it. "You have to."

"No, I don't. I could walk away."

"You couldn't."

"I spend day after day looking for lost kids. Rescuing children from abusive families. Saving them from assaults—sexual and physical. And *every single time*...I put myself in their place. I imagine their pain and suffering. I'm there, with them, through every single horror."

"You've always done that."

The spaghetti smelled delicious, but I couldn't stand looking at the plate. Too damn wholesome and *normal* and perfect for what shadowed me.

"This is when you tell me that it's dangerous to do my job," I said. "That it's unhealthy. That it's become an obsession. That I'll hurt myself or a victim because I'm acting too impetuous."

"So what is it?" He swirled the spaghetti on his fork and took a bite. "Are you too careless...or too dedicated?"

"Maybe both." I shook my head. "I thought this was what I was supposed to do."

"What changed your mind?"

"Anna Prescott."

James nodded. "Tell me about her."

"You know everything. You've seen her. You've seen how she acts."

"How does she act?"

"Like..." Was it wrong to be jealous of a victim? What if I simply envied her resilience? "Anna's survived what happened to her with a *smile*. She's not scarred. She's not showing any signs of torment or PTSD. She's...fine. She's healthy. She's not..."

"You?"

"Anna endured fifteen years of captivity. I spent three weeks in a basement. She's fine. I'm not."

So what was wrong with me?

"I've just…poured myself into my job," I said. "That's all I can do. And it's not healthy. It's not good. It's a shield. I'm trying to protect myself by protecting others."

"Do you want to quit?"

Yes. No.

I hated the cold uncertainty. "I can't stop now."

"Why?"

"Because this is my life. I take the work home with me. I can't sleep when I'm working a case. I can't eat. I can't see *anything* except the picture of the missing person I'm trying to find."

"And you find them," he said.

"Not always."

"Not everyone can be saved, London. But they have a hell of a good chance if you're working the case."

"What if I'm not doing it for them?" I asked.

"Are you still trying to save yourself? That college girl, grabbed off the street?"

Why lie? "Am I?"

"Of course, you are." James took my hand. I let him hold it for a few seconds longer than I usually did. "Your kidnapping will be with you forever, London. As long as he's out there and free, you will always fear that unknown. The question is…does that make you a bad cop?"

"I don't know."

"You found Anna Prescott. Saved twenty-six other women and children because you didn't give up. You *wanted* to save them and give them some justice for their suffering. Why do you fear having a unique perspective on this sort of crime?"

"James, it's not perspective. It's scars." I guzzled my wine. "Scars only you have seen."

"Because you trust me."

"Yes."

"Have you ever wondered how many people trust you?"

No.

Well, *now* I did.

And that was some hardcore guilt.

"I don't want to let anyone down," I said.

"You won't." He took another bite of the dinner. "You'll work to exhaustion before you let an innocent person get hurt."

"Is that a good thing?"

"Are you asking if you're a workaholic? Absolutely."

"Pot, kettle."

He smiled. I loved his smile. "Guilty as charged. It's why we're good together."

"You think so?"

"Don't you?"

"I think it's unfair."

"What is?"

"That you've learned everything about me, James Novak. You know more than anyone else in the world. The things I've told you, the things he made me do. I will never repeat it again to anyone as long as I live."

He listened, his expression just as patient as always. "And I'll never break that confidence."

"But I don't know the same about you. Your secrets. Your life. Those things you'd never dare tell anyone—worse than shame, worse than humiliation. Things you'd *die* before revealing. I don't know them."

"All you have to do is ask."

"It's that easy?"

He poured me another glass of wine. "We've done the hard part, London. Said the words. There's no one I'd rather share those secrets with."

"You make it sound so easy."

"I'll make it even easier." He brought my hand to his lips. "Move in with me."

Jesus.

This was one hell of a dinner.

My mouth dried. A familiar panic returned. I swallowed, but fortunately my cell rang.

I forced a quick smile and darted to answer it. "Just a second…"

"Take all the time you need." He helped himself to more of the spaghetti. "Thirty seconds or another six months. I'm not going anywhere."

And that was good.

And that was bad.

And it was all I'd come to expect.

And need.

My phone was still ringing. I cursed it, swiping to answer.

"*McKenna.*"

Adamski wasted no time, his voice low. "Patrol just got an emergency call from Louisa Prescott's neighbors. Officers are on the way."

Good thing I hadn't eaten. My stomach roiled, and the wine threatened to come back up.

"What happened?"

"Louisa's been murdered. And Anna is missing."

Chapter Thirty

You look good when you're helpless.

-Him

Two patrol cars parked in front of Louisa's house, but I'd beaten the ambulance.

Unfortunately, we needed the medical examiner.

I took the porch steps two at a time, but a patrol officer caught my arm.

"Detective…" He spat bile into the shrubs growing around her porch. "This is a bad one. Wait for homicide—they're only a couple blocks away."

I didn't need to be babysat by Homicide. "What did that animal do to her?"

"What didn't he do to her? There's not much left."

No. *No, no, no.*

"And Anna?"

He stayed quiet, offering me a pair of latex gloves. I couldn't fit them on my trembling hands.

"What about the kids? Mariam? The baby?"

Don't be dead.

He shook his head. "Not here. Not in the house at least."

Maybe Jacob let them live?

I surveyed the porch once more, my eyes on the driveway.

Empty.

Shit.

"Where's the car?" I asked. "Louisa drives a silver Honda. Where is it?"

"There wasn't a car when I arrived. You think..."

I didn't think. I *knew*.

"He's kidnapped them." I ripped off the uncooperative glove and pointed at him. "Call dispatch. Tell them we have three people kidnapped—a thirty-year-old woman, a ten-year-old girl, and an eight-month-old baby girl. Contact Sergeant Adamski—he'll get them photos."

I rushed into the dark house, grateful the lights hadn't been turned on in the kitchen. The layout wasn't so different from Louisa's parents' home, though it had been reduced to timbers and ash. The home was too small for a family of four, but for two weeks, they'd made it work. The court hadn't ruled on what to do with the kids yet, but Louisa insisted on taking in both children and Anna.

Our ADA argued with the family court to remove Rebecca and Mariam.

I'd argued against it. Despite the circumstances, the girls were comfortable with Anna. They'd been through enough without splitting the family any more. Even if it meant staying with Louisa.

I wasn't too fond of her or the pending criminal case, but she wouldn't hurt the girls.

She only wanted to protect her sister.

Was I getting everything wrong about this case?

Nothing made sense. Not the farm. Not the men. Not the murders.

And not the newest body in the string of horrific murders.

I entered the living room. My foot immediately sunk into a sopping puddle in the carpet. Blood. I stepped back, but the stain led directly to me. And why not? Everything I'd touched lately had ended up broken and bloody.

But it wasn't supposed to be Louisa.

I'd never worked homicide. Of course, I'd responded to scenes. Encountered murders. Saw bodies. But this was something else.

Even Detectives Falconi and Riley gagged as they arrived.

The monster had *shredded* Louisa, neck to legs. Blood streaked the furniture, the floors, the carpets. Jagged blotches of crimson stained the once cozy cream walls.

The body was almost unrecognizable.

"Holy shit." Falconi stepped away from the scene, pretending to analyze the blood spray patterns. "She's been *butchered*."

"Diced is more like it..." I couldn't get close to the body without stepping in more blood. I stayed still instead, staring at the once vibrant, frustratingly stubborn, absolutely infuriating Louisa Prescott. "He didn't show mercy."

"*He?*" Riley went to work, walking through the scene as if it were just another murder, just another body. "A Goodman?"

"Jacob," I said. "Had to be."

Falconi steadied himself before kneeling at Louisa's side. "Do you think he killed the girls?"

I answered with absolute certainty. "No. They're too valuable to him. A wife, child, and a baby? They're his property. He'll never hurt them."

Falconi's phone rang. He took the call, waving to me as he listened with a growing frown.

"Good news," he said as he hung up. "Maybe. A lead came in from the state's fugitive recovery team. They got a bead on a campground in Westmoreland County. Group of a dozen men camping in a remote area—little cold to be out on a nature walk."

My pulse jumped. "Is it the Goodmans?"

"Who else could it be?" Riley continued to walk the scene, piecing it together. "These guys know how to live off the land. Goodman comes to get his girls. Louisa puts up a fight. He takes her out. Gets his wife and the girl and they're gone. They go to the campground while they think they're safe."

I stared at the body, hating myself for hardly recognizing the woman who had fought so hard just to end up slashed and destroyed in her own home.

"No one does this and expects a quick escape," I said.

Riley agreed with me, a first time for everything. "He spent some time with this one. Probably kept stabbing after she was dead."

"Asshole's unstable," Falconi said. "Christ only knows what he'll do to the girls."

He wouldn't hurt them. But the scene kept a secret I couldn't breach.

Louisa didn't give me any answers, and the rest of the house was silent too. Hell, if the walls could talk, they'd probably go mute in the panic too.

Jacob killed Louisa. Grabbed Anna and the kids.

And then what?

He was a bastard and murderer, but he wasn't putting his family in any more danger.

I wished I could cover Louisa, but what was done was done. She didn't care anymore. I'd only be protecting myself.

"After doing this, there's no way Jacob would take the girls to the camp ground," I said.

Falconi didn't look up from his notes, avoiding the carnage. "Why?"

"It's too dangerous."

"He just *murdered* this lady in cold blood."

"It's not cold blood. He knew Louisa. She'd been trying to get Anna back for years. This was personal, and it was a mistake. The first one he made."

"How do you figure?" Riley asked.

"He murdered Louisa, and that puts the us on his trail. Too close to him. He's eluded the fugitive unit by staying far from Anna and the others. Now we know he was here, we know the car he's driving, we know how long he's been gone. He's outed himself."

"What's that got to do with Anna?"

"This bastard isn't getting away again. He's killed SWAT officers. Hurt me and the state troopers. That fugitive team isn't taking chances. They're shooting to kill. He knows it. Anna knows it. There's no way they'd put the children in that danger."

Riley didn't believe me. "Why not?"

The answer was obvious, and that was the reason the Goodmans were a step ahead of me, always.

"Because he *loves* them."

They weren't property.

They weren't the product of an unbridled fetish.

The Goodmans *believed* in their farm. And their wives. And their children.

They thought they were *right*.

And that's why I was failing. I could offer the women safety and promises of freedom, but no Goodman would ever take it. They thought they'd already found their paradise.

The bloody scene was too much for me. I'd search the rest of the house. Falconi took the steps behind me, scratching at his beard as I slipped through the upstairs to Anna's room.

"We've got the Amber Alerts out," Falconi said. "And I radioed dispatch the make and model of Louisa's car."

"It won't do any good," I said. "Jacob doesn't have the girls."

A bassinet rocked in the corner. Mechanical, plugged into the wall to keep the baby moving. Two slept-in beds were pushed into the corner of the room, only partially made, the quilt pulled over the mattress. Neat and tidy. Just like Anna.

My doubt disappeared.

I knew exactly what had happened here.

"Anna's not going to the campground," I said.

Falconi grumbled. "She's probably buried under it."

I tapped my temple. "Gotta think like them."

"You're in their head now?"

A flower wreath rested on the bed. I picked it up, but the ring of peonies was small. The cold chill crashed over me.

I squeezed the flowers and reached for the embroidery circle half hidden by a decorative pillow.

Oh, no.

Not again.

Falconi read the embroidered stitching over my shoulder. "*So they are no longer two, but one flesh. Therefore, what God has joined together, man must never separate. Matthew 19:6.*"

"Anna hasn't given up on her family," I whispered. "She's running. She's protecting them."

"How does sewing protect the family?"

It was just sewing—it was conditioning.

Preparing little girls for their big day.

I handed him the flowers and embroidery. "If I'm Anna...my family's been ripped apart. The men are gone. The family's bunker in the forest was destroyed. Jacob is on the run. And her sister is killed. She knows they're exposed. She's worrying about Mariam and the baby. She wants to protect them...she's trying to save the entire family."

"How?"

"By continuing with tradition. She's taken Mariam to be married."

Falconi followed close, keeping me steady as I nearly tumbled down the stairs to the door. Riley caught me before I burst outside. He gave an affirmative to the call on the radio.

"Orders from Lieutenant Clark," he said. "They're moving on the campground tonight. You gotta go. Adamski's already in route. They want you there to help with the girls."

Didn't they understand? "The girls aren't *there*. They weren't kidnapped."

"McKenna, use your head. Goodman just slaughtered this woman. He's taken Anna and the kids!"

"Jacob wouldn't put them in danger. He would have told Anna to run, and she'd go to where she feels safe. Where she has control—over herself and Mariam."

Riley swore. "Where's that?"

The same place she'd hid for the past fifteen years.

"Anna's gone back to Harvest Dominion Farm."

Chapter Thirty-One

And so you run. And you fight. And you struggle.
Was it worth it?
-Him

I hated being right.

Louisa's car was parked outside of Jacob and Anna's farm house. The engine popped in the chill, and the hood still radiated warmth. She'd driven the two hours out of Pittsburgh without a car seat, but that was the least of our worries.

At least she was alive.

At least the kids were safe.

At least Jacob wasn't with them.

Yet.

The porch steps creaked under my boots. Strange that I could hear it so clearly on the farm. No machinery buzzed. No animals brayed.

No kids played in the grass.

The police tape over the doors fluttered in the cold. No agency had patrol officers to spare to guard an abandoned property in the middle of nowhere. Anna walked back into her home with no one to stop her.

Was she the only one at the farm? I knew better than to trust the shadows.

I should have called for backup, but another officer would've terrified Anna more. She didn't need escorting home. She needed a *friend*. Someone who would protect her as much as she protected others.

The door wasn't locked. I nearly laughed. After everything she'd been through, Anna didn't secure her property? The kidnapping wasn't enough? The rapes?

She just watched her sister *die*.

And she still left her home open for the murderer to walk through.

Hell, she probably had dinner waiting for him.

I knocked before entering, gun drawn. Not that my weapon would do much against another IED or explosion. The living room was dark, but a hymn played from a stereo in the kitchen. The light over the sink cast a rosy golden glow. I followed it, picking a path through a house torn to pieces during the police's search.

Drawers emptied. Pens, pencils, paper, and office supplies were chucked into one corner. Cushions were ripped. Bookshelves tipped. Children's drawings crumpled. Wooden furniture—Jonah's dedicated work—splintered. I cursed the insensitivity. Not the Jacob deserved any respect, but Anna had put so much work and time into tending a neat and tidy house—not just for her husband, but for all the women and children on the farm.

This was still her *home*, despite the circumstances of her arrival.

Anna sat at the kitchen table, a sewing kit spread over the tablecloth. She squinted at the quilt in her hands and mended a tear in the middle. The CSI team didn't have to destroy something so lovely to find evidence of Jacob's guilt. His crimes were all around. But this space...

Was all she had.

Anna didn't deserve any of this.

She gave a sigh as the needle slipped into the material. "This belonged to Jacob's mother. She made one for each of her boys. I never had a chance to meet her, but Jacob says she was a Godly woman. Smart. Strict, but fair. Respected. *Loved.*" She sighed over the word. "I wanted to be her. I wanted to lead this family. They needed someone like her. A Titus woman. A powerful, feminine influence for the girls and the children." She chuckled. "Even the men. They'd never admit it, but every man wants a mother. It's easier for them to make the hard decisions if they know a motherly figure will be there to help them, always."

She continued to sew. I gave her a moment of quiet before approaching.

"Anna, what are you doing?"

"Oh, I'm sorry. Where are my manners?" She gestured to the empty seat across from the table. "I haven't any coffee or tea made, but we can sit together."

"Why did you come here?"

"Look at this rip. I'm not that good of a seamstress. I've tried, but I just don't have the patience. These little stitches are so tough!"

"Where are the children?"

She stared only at the needle, concentrating hard on repairing the patch. "Where they belong."

"Anna."

"They're upstairs sleeping. And I wish you would call me *Eve.*"

351

"That's not your name. That's what *he* called you."

"How is that any different from a husband calling his wife *honey* or *sweetie?*"

I didn't like the quiet in the house. Anna was usually far more chipper, talkative, even when scared. She'd drawn her hair back into a casual ponytail. The look seemed too modern for someone as timeless as her. Too *young*. I'd never recognized her youth before, especially as she had projected such a strong presence, well beyond bumbling puberty and the harsh lessons life taught to those in their twenties.

Her strength seemed to wane. When she should have flourished in freedom, she regressed. Hid with her needle and thread in a dollhouse of lies.

"Anna…we have to go back now. You can't stay here."

"We'll be fine."

I dragged one of the kitchen chairs to her side, sitting within arm's reach. She didn't move or protest. Did she ever? Did she know she had the option to refuse him, me, *anyone?*

I stared at her, my voice soft. "Did you ever oppose him? Ever fight back?"

"Why?" The needle glinted in the quilt. "He would have won."

"Are you afraid of him?"

She accidentally nipped her finger and gasped. Not so perfect after all. "No."

"Are you afraid of what he might do?"

"Detective, I know what Jacob has done in his life." She sucked on her finger, nursing the pinprick. "I know what he's capable of doing."

"And you still came here."

"This is my home."

Denial? Fear? I couldn't tell anymore. "This is your *prison*."

The quilt lowered. She folded it tight and placed it on the table, crossing to the cabinets without asking if I wanted to join her in a mug of tea. I let her work in silence, boiling the water and pouring two mugs. She added sugar to hers but brought the bowl over to me. I took the mug with a quiet *thank-you*, and together we let the cups warm our hands.

"May I ask you a personal question, London?"

It was the first time she'd used my name. "Of course."

"What happened in your past to make you so distrustful of the world?"

"Aside from working in law enforcement?"

"Is that it? Working for the police has jaded you?"

"I've seen a lot of brutality. Crimes against woman and children. Kidnappings. Murders."

"Is that what happened to you?"

The tea was an excuse to delay speaking, but I'd always hated Earl Grey. Too floral for me. I forced it down, wishing it hadn't tasted so much like perfume.

"We're alike, Anna," I said.

"I refuse to believe that."

"Why?"

"Because I'm *happy*."

That stung. "I'm not a ray of sunshine, but does this life really make you *happy*?"

She admired her kitchen, touched the table cloth, swirled the tea in her mug.

And smiled.

"When you first found this place…" She asked. "When you found the women here, realized we had children, what did you see when you looked at us?"

I answered honestly. "I saw people who needed help."

"And I see a family."

"Families don't hurt each other."

"Jacob hasn't hurt *any* of us."

"What about Jonah? Rachel? *Louisa?*"

Her eyes lowered. "They weren't family anymore."

"They're blood."

"They tried to destroy us."

"Anna, there was nothing to destroy. This family is built on lies and abuse."

Anna shushed me, a finger to her lips. "London. I know you worry. But I am *not* a victim. What Jacob has done to me…I wanted. I wanted to be his wife. I wanted to live this life. I wanted to give him *children.*" The tears welled in her eyes. "It is my greatest, most shameful regret that I can't give him any more children."

She was just lucky he hadn't killed her for it. "What does Jacob say? How does he explain this to you?"

"What is there to explain? Look at this beautiful land. These homes. The way the children smile. How can you look at this farm and see anything but a warm, loving family?"

"Because the *ten-year-old girl* upstairs is responsible for creating that family."

"You think they're too young to understand the miracle of life?"

"Yes. So does the law."

"It's *holy.*"

"It's *abuse*. These are little girls who are promised to grown men. Young, underdeveloped *children* forced to have sex with adults and bear their children. Doesn't it frighten you?"

"You know what truly frightens me?" She stared into her tea. "A world where those same girls are lost, abandoned, and cast out onto the streets, scrounging and begging for a simple meal."

"You'd rather them suffer on the farm?"

"We don't suffer!" It was the first time she raised her voice, and even that sharpness was defensive. "I'd rather they live happily on this farm. Warm and loved. The girls we've taken in are the ones who ran away from real abuse. They've never heard a kind word. They didn't know the Lord. We gave them a home and hope and an opportunity to be a part of something wonderful. We offered them this life."

"Jacob didn't offer them anything. He forced them."

"No."

"Think about the day he 'found' you. Did he ask you to join a family before he knocked Louisa unconscious, hauled you from the sidewalk across from your home, and stashed you in a van?"

Anna tucked a straying lock of her ponytail behind her ear. "You wouldn't understand."

"I'm listening now."

"Then you won't believe me."

"Try me."

Her words calmed. "God chose him for me."

"Did God tell you that…or Jacob?"

"Neither. It was my own divine revelation. I realized the truth as soon as I woke in Jacob's care."

"You woke in his custody."

Anna held my stare. "Would you prefer if I said I woke in his arms?"

The thought made me sick. "Did he make you—"

"He didn't make me do *anything* I didn't want to do. I was young, but the Lord brought us together for a reason. When he told me what he hoped to achieve, the vision for his perfect life...I was overwhelmed with joy."

"His plan was to kidnap children."

"He saved them. From themselves. From others. He saved their *souls*." Anna stood. She checked the hall before closing the door to the kitchen. "Do you know how we found Mariam?"

Christ, we'd been trying to figure that out for weeks.

Who she was. Where she came from. How to find her parents.

"How?"

"She was living on the streets. Her mother was a crack whore." She covered her lips, scouring the curse with a quick apology. "She never knew her father. Her mother sold her for a dime...and not the currency. That poor girl lived in a heroine den for two weeks before she could escape. She'd been beaten. Starved." The words trembled. "And those animals *raped* her. Over and over. You would use that word to describe the love between a husband and wife, but I know what it *really* means. *I* treated her wounds. *I* healed what those barbarians did to her. She was half-starved and feverish, sick and begging for death. But we showed her what kindness was, and she chose this life."

"You took her in, healed her, and then..." My heart broke for the little girl who never had the opportunity for a childhood. "You would marry her to a grown man?"

"You think it's cruel."

"Yes."

"We live in different worlds, Detective."

"But we follow the same laws."

"Those laws are *wrong*. They apply to perverts and pedophiles. What we do here is *good*. Yes, we're matched at young ages. But our souls are connected to our husbands. We love each other. It's always, *always* for love."

Christ, I hoped the others were as delusional as her, if only to spare them the terror of a life lived for another's desires. "Tell me what happens here. How are they married?"

"So you can arrest the men I love?"

"So I can *understand* what this family is." I took her hand. "So I know that it's possible to survive something like this."

I sweated, but I was so close to the truth. How could anyone live through the trauma that she'd endured and be *unaffected*? It wasn't Stockholm Syndrome. It was as if…

As if she never lost control of her life.

Was she strong or weak? Self-assured or ignorant?

I had no idea, but every minute Anna spoke dizzied me with my own terror.

Would I ever be half as confident as she?

Anna spoke quietly, reluctantly. "We celebrate when we're able to welcome someone new into the family. Yes…they're taken. But once they're here, they understand why we made the decision to save them. They forgive us. They thank us."

"How do you make them understand?"

"Scripture."

"Anna."

"Prayer and counseling."

"Anna, I found the room under the barn."

This gave her pause. She drank her tea. "It's a special place."

"Did Jacob take you there?"

"We've all been there, London. It's not what you think."

"It looked terrifying. A bare mattress on the floor?"

She dismissed the concern with a wave. "It's dressed when we're hosting a girl."

"No food or water."

She smiled. "I prepare their meals myself. More food than they can eat. Free-ranged chicken or beef from our own calves. Fresh water from our springs or milk from our cows. Believe me, they eat better here than they ever have before, especially since they'd come from situations with no food or malnourishment. We give them a healthy diet—in moderation, so they don't get sick by stuffing themselves."

"Do you ever withhold it?"

"If we do, it's *fasting*. It's for a purpose."

"What purpose?"

"To show them that we are their caretakers, not captors. We can give them food. Shelter. Clothing. *Love*. And all they need to do is accept it."

"But accepting it comes at a price?" I nodded to the gold band on her finger. "Marriage."

"That is a *reward*."

"Getting married?"

She winked at me, playful. "You should try it, London. A lovely woman like you deserves her happiness—any happiness."

"I'd like it to be my choice."

358

"And it's their choice too," she said. "Mariam might be young, but she understands what we ask of her. She knows the responsibilities and the benefits of a marriage."

"Which are?"

"Serving our husbands. Leading good lives. Bringing children into the world."

"And you think a ten-year-old can do this?"

"Of course. She's ready to be wed."

"She's still a *child*."

"Girls are becoming women at younger and younger ages, London. Surely you must see that in your work. It's not unusual for ten, eleven-year-old girls to be ready for that blessing."

"Just because her body is ready doesn't mean she's mentally or emotionally prepared."

Anna didn't believe me. "Our world is simpler than yours. She has nothing to fear from starting young. She's been educated, and she'll stay educated. Math, English, homemaking. But instead of suffering in public schools rotten with debauchery and sin, bullying and useless classes, she'll learn what's important. Scripture and family."

"But no high school. No college."

"She won't miss that hellish experience."

"Some people like it."

"And Mariam likes what we can offer her." Anna refilled her teacup, offering me a second mug as well. I reluctantly finished the overwhelmingly perfumed tea just to be polite. "Believe me. This life is a demanding one. The farm nourishes us, but working the fields is hard and exhausting. Our husbands love us, but their attention is sometimes overwhelming. And the children...oh, God love them, but sometimes…if I think I'll see *one* more diaper…" Her laugh quieted too quickly. "But they're the reason we do this. We are to be fruitful and multiply."

"Even the young girls?"

It didn't seem to matter to her. "As soon as the body is mature, we begin. God created us for a purpose. If he deems her ready to partake in this miracle, who are we to judge what is too young or too old?"

"How can she even have a healthy pregnancy?"

"It's more dangerous the older you get, Detective. Tick-tock."

"I'll take my chances."

"Teenage pregnancy scares those with more modern sensibilities, but it's normal for us. In your world, the girls have no help. They need to work outside the home to pay the bills, they must finish school, and they're pressured into societal values that diminish a woman's role in the home. And what does it give them? Just headaches and stress."

"That's life."

"Not here. You worry, but Mariam will be closer to twelve when she gives birth—"

"*Anna!*"

"But she'll have *support*. That's what a family is—a structure of comfort and support. The women watch the kids. The men teach the kids. The family protects the kids. We start early because we *can*, not to punish the mothers or inflict some sort of pain on them, but because in this community, we are able to focus on what's important. We stay on the farm, grow our own food, raise our children. It's the way life is supposed to be. *And let us consider how we may spur one another on toward love and good deeds, not giving up meeting together, as some are in the habit of doing, but encouraging one another—and all the more as you see the Day approaching. Hebrews 10:24-25."*

She *believed* it.

Anna believed everything her husband preached.

How could I save this woman when she so eagerly abandoned truth and reason to sympathize with a monster?

The tea swirled in my mug. The smell turned my stomach. But Anna drank hers. I did the same so she wouldn't stop talking.

I'd need to drink a gallon of black coffee to get the taste out of my mouth.

"You still think we're wicked," she said.

I didn't want to say it. "The children...are they ever hurt here?"

"They're disciplined, but they aren't beaten."

"And in bed?"

Anna raised her eyebrows, shocked, but not shy. She chose her words carefully. "They are never harmed. We all have our wifely duties, but even the youngest wife understands that moment with our husbands is a sacred event. Our husbands do not hurt us, and we understand what is to happen if we are to grow with child."

"You don't consider that abuse?"

"How can creating a child ever be considered *abuse*?" She turned away. "I feel so sorry for you, London."

"Why?"

"I don't think you'll ever see how blessed we are. Every day, we live the way the Lord intended. The fortunate few here swell a little more each day with a life inside of them. The rest count the days until they may be wedded to their soulmate, so they may experience the joy that is creating a child with their husband." Her voice weakened. "I can't have that for myself."

"I'm sorry."

"I wondered if I was being punished," she whispered. "Jacob insisted it was meant to be this way. It took years before I realized he was right. I have no children, but this farm is like my child. I tend the land. I counsel the marriages if there are problems. I teach the girls how to raise their children. I help Jacob with the finances. I would die for this farm, for my family."

My heart hurt for her. "If you don't escape from Jacob, you just might. If you really want to be a mother to these women and children..." I blinked. The room swirled. "Anna, you have to do the right thing."

"And betray my husband?"

My vision blurred. What the hell was wrong with me?

Anna leaned in, her brows furrowing. "Are you all right, London?"

I forced a sharp breath and nodded. Better than she'd be. Better than Mariam.

I pulled the flower headdress from my pocket, resting it on the table.

Did my words slur?

"So Mariam is getting married?"

"Yes."

"To who?"

Anna paced again. I didn't expect that. She nervously tangled her palms in her dress, murmuring a prayer.

"*Please* understand, London. I have no children of my own."

"I know."

"And everything I do is for the benefit of the farm. My every decision is made out of love for my husband. And I love Mariam so very much. I care for her."

"Who is she marrying, Anna?"

"It's not that simple."

"I thought the farm was all about simple?"

Anna apologized with a hand over her heart. "She's not a virgin."

My eyebrow rose. "And?"

"And no matter how heinous her past, even if it wasn't her fault...she can't marry one of our boys as she is."

"*What?*"

"It isn't fair to her husband. A man expects his wife to know only his touch."

"What are you saying? She was *raped.*"

The words tumbled from her mouth—a declaration and excuse blended into a horrifying reality.

"She can never be pure, but she can have *children.*"

"What does that have to do with it?"

"This farm is meant to be fruitful. Jacob is meant to have more sons."

I turned, but Anna was quicker.

The tea kettle crashed against my temple.

I fell to the floor. The hit was hard, but I couldn't feel it.

Couldn't feel anything.

The room swirled, floated, and crashed in on me. I tasted floral.

Perfume.

Poison.

"Mariam was brought to us by God, just like Hagar was given to Abraham by Sarah. Mariam will bear Jacob's children."

I couldn't speak. Couldn't move.

Couldn't save Mariam.

Anna whispered in pure honesty.

"I won't let you stop their blessed union."

Chapter Thirty-Two

No more fighting. No more begging.
Sleep now, and it will soon be over.
-Him

My body fell limp.

Anna approached, reaching for my hand. I swung a weak fist instead. She easily dodged it.

"*Stop...*" The words couldn't form. "What..."

Anna had very little physical strength, but even she could haul me around like I was a child. She looped her arms around my waist and pulled.

I kicked. It did nothing.

"Drugged?" Even my breath slurred.

"It's harmless," she said. "We give it to the girls if they're nervous on the wedding nights. It goes...easier for them if they aren't scared."

Sick.

All of them.

I fought, but every motion slowed, like fighting through the slurry that jumbled my mind. Anna pulled away from the table and dragged me to the cellar door. I twisted, but the door opened.

She wouldn't.

She *couldn't*.

"I'm sorry, London." Her foot pressed hard into my thigh. The cement cellar stairs prevented my escape. "I have to protect my family."

"Anna...*no*..."

"Please. Call me Eve."

She kicked.

I slammed into the top step, the cement edge cracking my head.

I didn't have the breath to groan. My momentum surged, and I spiraled down three, four, *five* stairs, slamming my shoulders and hips, knee.

Every scrape and bump shattered through me. I couldn't feel the pain, but I knew it'd be serious. My fingers didn't bend the right way, and I crashed to the cement basement floor end-over-end, landing on an ankle that bent, popped, and settled under my weight.

It didn't ache. Just went numb.

Oh no.

The drugs seized me. My mouth dried, and the weight of my own body crushed me against the dusty basement floor, lying in a heap between the shelves of jarred jams and canned vegetables.

This wasn't how it was supposed to end.

Not now. Not after I'd survived so much.

I struggled to breathe against my own weight. The floor was no help, and neither were the useless limbs weighing me down. I rolled only a few inches, kicking myself over to stare into the light streaming from the kitchen upstairs.

How much of the drug did she give me?

My heart beat a little slower.

I couldn't move.

And that was safer. We weren't alone anymore.

The front door crashed against the wall.

Jacob Goodman's booming voice surged through the house.

"*Eve!*" He shouted, the word spat more as a curse rather a call of affection. "*What did you do?*"

Anna's voice was too muffled to hear, but she quieted Jacob as best she could. Their steps creaked overhead, and his boots stomped against the kitchen's hardwood.

"Hush. You'll wake the baby." Anna's words warmed, a touch of sun in the middle of a raging storm. "Oh, Jacob…I missed you—"

He didn't let her finish. "What are you doing here?"

"I know I shouldn't have come back."

Her words choked off, almost as if he grabbed her. Their shadows darkened the kitchen, blocking the light for a brief moment.

"Do you have any idea what you've done?" Not a question—a demand. This wasn't a man who ever gentled his speech, even for a wife demented by her own love for him. "You were supposed to stay *away*. We weren't ready to meet again. What have you done?"

A pout. "I had to see you."

"And now this might be the last time you see me alive."

"Don't say such things…"

"What the hell happened at that woman's house?"

The air struck through my lungs, unmovable and aching.

I tensed, trying to listen, trying to *survive*. Shock helped.

Why didn't Jacob know what had happened tonight?

Unless…

Unless he hadn't been there.

"Louisa?" Anna's confidence sickened me. "Don't worry. She won't try to separate us anymore."

"What did you do?"

"What had to be done."

"*Eve.*"

"She was trying to keep us apart!"

A crash.

Jacob's fist went through the china cabinet. Anna yelped, but she stayed resolute. Her shadow chased him around the kitchen.

"Jacob, you're bleeding."

"Let it go. I'm fine."

"Don't be silly. This is an important night. You need to be whole and healthy."

"Leave it! Tell me what you did! No lies. No smiles, Eve, so help me…" His breath rattled, and he hesitated in speaking the words, as if he himself didn't believe them. "Did you murder your sister?"

"She's not my family anymore."

I had to get out of here.

Had to get to my feet. Had to radio for help.

Had to tell *someone* what insanity had drenched us all in blood tonight.

Anna had murdered Louisa.

She killed her own sister—a woman who would have done anything, even given her *life*, for the one person she loved most in the world.

What a worthless sacrifice.

Louisa's sister had died a long time ago. And neither Louisa, Jacob, or I could recognize the villain who had taken her place.

A scrape. Chair against wood. The cabinets opened, and a plastic box popped. I stared through swirling vision and caught a glimpse of Anna passing the cellar door with a first-aid kit.

"Why did you do this?" Jacob asked again, less patient than before. "Tell me now, before your husband and God——"

"I killed her."

He grunted pure pain. Heartbroken. "*Why?* Why? We were coming for you. I told you. Again and again. If this happened, I would *always* come for you. But trying to get passage into Canada, especially with all the kids would take *time*."

"I couldn't do it. I can't be without you, Jacob."

He paced again, his steps heavy. "You didn't listen."

"Neither did you. It was *time*."

"I decide when it is time."

"If we waited any longer…if something had happened to you and your sons…"

"We were safe."

"How did I know? You couldn't call. You couldn't find me. I had to make sure you had another child before you were all taken away."

"Nothing was going to happen to us! Stop thinking the worst, Eve, and have trust in your husband——"

He stopped talking and interrupted Anna with a harsh shush. A still moment passed.

The basement door creaked open a little wider.

If I wasn't dead yet, I'd be soon.

"Eve." Jacob's whisper was as frightening as his roar. "Is that McKenna?"

Her voice went baby-soft. "She tripped."

"Is she dead?"

"Maybe."

I laid still. Easy to do. The drugs had stolen every ounce of my strength.

Jacob swung the door wide, flashing the light on. He didn't swear when angry.

He prayed.

"Our Father in heaven…did she follow you?"

"They think you killed Louisa," Anna said. "We have to do this now, Jacob. Before they take you away."

"Take me…" He turned. His shadow darkened the basement. "No one is taking me away. Not from my family. Not from *you*." He steadied himself with a deciding breath. "And that includes the girl. I won't do it."

"You won't do what?"

"I won't have her bear my child. And that's the last I'll speak of it."

Anna didn't have to drug me. That revelation would have knocked me out.

I lifted my head as best I could, but specs of dust and cobweb bound me to the cold floor.

The drugs were getting worse.

So was their fight.

Anna didn't yell, but the submissive whimper in her voice was far shrewder and more calculating than I first recognized.

"We decided this long ago, Jacob," she said. "You deserve children. More sons. Mariam can give you that."

"*No!* No. *You* decided that. You were the one desperate for children. You were the one who wanted Mariam so badly!"

"For you! She was always for you!"

"I don't want her!" His shadow moved quick, and I feared he'd hurt Anna. Instead he pulled her close, his forehead on hers. "I want my *wife*."

"I can't be a wife to you. Not fully."

"Neither can that girl. She doesn't complete me. *You* do." The shadows parted. "You did. Once."

"What does that mean?" Anna didn't yell, but she grew exasperated. "Jacob, we've talked about Jonah. You said you understood. You said it needed to be done."

"He was still my son!"

"He was going to destroy us!" Anna began to sob, her words broken in ugly sorrow. "I did what I had to. What no one else had the courage to do!"

"You killed them."

Pure shock kept me awake. I clawed toward the stairs. My fingers failed me first. Their voices faded and shifted, loud then soft, nonsensical then clear and frightening.

"I didn't touch him," Anna said. "The others...Rachel would have gone to the police. Jonah's dirty little mistress? She threatened us all. I did what I had to do."

"But my *son*..."

"He *left* you, Jacob. He left all of us. He wasn't your son anymore." Her voice regained a bit of confidence, soothing her husband. "But I didn't pull that trigger. Jonah did. Jonah couldn't live with the guilt of disobeying his father, of jeopardizing the safety of everyone here. He took his own life. He did it to ensure you would forgive him."

"At your insistence."

"Jonah lost his faith."

"And you lost your mind."

"I've done what was necessary to protect us. I made a promise to you, Jacob Goodman. I promised that I would protect this family. That I would do everything I could to ensure our survival and serve you like the wife you deserve." Her voice evened. "I've sacrificed so much for you, my husband. Everything. My life. My body. And now my marriage bed."

"Don't."

"This isn't about me, Jacob. This is about *you*. Your bloodline. The good you're doing in this world. I've found women for your sons and nephews. I trained those girls to become the perfect wives and mothers for men worthy of that *gift*. Don't turn away now. God is testing our family. We will overcome."

"And what would you have me do?" he asked.

"Take Mariam to your bed. Lie with her. She is ready to bear a child, Jacob. She will swell for you. I promise."

"It's too soon. She's not yet broken."

"As soon as she is impregnated, she'll submit. She'll understand the gift of your seed. The instant she feels your son growing inside of her—"

"I'm a man of God, Eve. I won't betray my vows."

"This isn't a betrayal." She soothed him, whispering her words between gentle kisses. "This must be done. I cannot give you the children you deserve. *And Sarai said to Abram, 'See now, the LORD has restrained me from bearing. Please go in to my servant. It may be that I will obtain children by her.'* Sarah gave her handmaid to her husband. She gave him a second wife. A second *chance*."

"And this is what you want?"

"It doesn't mean I love you less, Jacob. It means I will do *anything* for you, even wish another woman into your bed so that, by her, you bear more sons. And she's is *young*. So young. She can be bred for years, Jacob. Decades. It is a boon to find one so...prime. A blessing. God has willed this."

"It's the only solace I can take."

Anna sighed. "You are not betraying me, Jacob."

He didn't answer. Not immediately. The air rasped through his lungs first. Harsh and unforgiving.

"I won't betray you, Eve. I am not an unfaithful man. Like you, I'll protect my family. Just as I will do anything to save my blood line."

"And that's why I love you, Jacob." She spoke through tears. "We are meant for each other, my love. Years from now, when we are old and grey, we will look upon this family in joy. Together, we can live as God wills. Together—"

I sensed the shift in his words. The coldness.

The vile *hatred*.

Anna didn't.

And that's why she died.

"Eve, there is no together," Jacob said. "I must be faithful to my wife."

"Jacob?"

"My new wife."

The gunshot crashed, deafening in the cement cellar.

Anna's body stiffened, paused at the top of the stairs, then fell backward.

She died before she struck the last step. She collapsed on the floor next to me, bent and broken. Bleeding.

But her lifeless eyes still stared at her husband in lovelorn wonder.

Chapter Thirty-Three

You let this happen, London.
This is your fault.
-Me

Plink. Plink. Plink

Cold.

Musty.

Wet.

I didn't jerk awake, but the slow pound of my heart rattled me into consciousness. It rumbled in my chest. My head. My aching lungs.

Plink. Plink.

My fingers finally responded. They curled up tight, gripping the grainy, squishing softness beneath me. Soft, but cold. I sank.

I'd never stop shivering.

Mud?

I laid in mud.

It covered everything. My skin. My clothes. I coughed, spitting what had collected in my mouth. It tasted like iron.

Maybe the Goodman's farm had mineral rich soil?

Or maybe everything they owned was stained with blood.

I opened my eyes. The darkness suffocated me. I lashed out with a hand and struck a solid wall.

Not made of wood or plaster. It gave as I poked into it. A rough tendril grazed my finger.

A root?

"Oh God."

The words didn't form right, couldn't rasp into the cold, but the realization hit me hard.

I woke outside, in the darkness, huddled in a grave.

The dirt hadn't piled over me just yet. Chunks of half-frozen debris had crumbled from the walls during the pouring rain.

I squinted and looked up.

Plink. Plink. Plink.

The rain struck something plastic. A tarp.

My eyes never adjusted. The night had stolen every last bit of light.

And my strength faded with it.

My teeth chattered. The drugs wore off only once the mud stole the last of my body's heat.

How long had I been in the hole?

Was I too late?

What happened to Anna?

I forced myself up and groped my surroundings. I flinched as I struck something hard.

And stiff.

The grave offered no help. Six feet of terror imprisoned me. I had to lean close before I realized what I touched.

A scrap of material. A cold firmness. Fine strings of silk.

"Jesus!"

I leapt away from the body, wiping the sticky mess from my arms, legs. Mud? Blood? Did it matter?

Anna was dead.

And I shared what would become of her grave.

I fought the urge to yell. No one would come looking for me—no one that would be willing to save me.

The drugs must have knocked me out, and Jacob tossed me in the grave with his wife. But the rain interrupted his funeral services. He'd covered us with a tarp. Maybe waiting until the night dried out before he could bury the worst of his bad decisions.

Or maybe he had a reason to leave us.

Something important waited for him back inside.

Mariam.

I had to get out.

No matter how insane Anna's plan was, Jacob understood the reality of his situation. He wasn't making it out of the country alive. He'd be caught. His family imprisoned.

In his last night of freedom, he had only one chance to save his bloodline.

He needed more children—and Mariam would bear them for him.

My legs didn't want to move. The cold stole the strength the drugs had missed, but I'd escaped a grave enough times this past month that the literal walls and dirt couldn't scare me.

I had to climb out, had to escape. No one else would save Mariam.

If I wasn't already too late.

If he hadn't already—

I launched at the walls, clawing at the fresh dirt, soaked through with rain and Anna's trail of blood. No use. My fingers sunk uselessly into pure softness. My feet stuck in the sloppy, swallowing mud.

This wasn't going to be how my life ended.

Not stuck in a grave.

Not failing to save a child.

Not *hating* myself for not seeing the goddamned truth when it was in my face.

I'd been the victim before. Now I was the fool.

I'd fix this. Anna's mistake was underestimating me. She'd tricked me. Used me. Manipulated me. Just like her sister. Just like the entire Goodman family. So what if I was naïve?

My fingers practically froze, my lungs ached, and my heart thudded through whatever sludge Anna used to poison me, but I refused to surrender. Nothing could stop justice from imprisoning every last Goodman.

Or…

I could kill the bastard myself.

He deserved it. The pain. The failure.

I could kill him, claim self-defense, and only this grave would know the truth.

Vengeance was buried easier than a body.

Mud slipped through my fingers, slimy and wet. The tarp leaked, and frigid rainwater poured into the hole. I jumped for it. The tarp crinkled in my hands, but I crashed down, tripping over Anna's unmoving leg. I landed in a puddle. The world swirled.

Too soon to jump.

Damn it. I didn't have any other options. Not like Anna would help me out of this.

Poor thing.

Delusional victim.

Villain.

I leapt up again and successfully grabbed the tarp. It pulled down. The night wasn't any brighter without it, but the faint outline of trees helped to keep me centered. Less panicky.

Less terrified.

And even more enraged.

I hopped, my hands scraping for one of the bare roots Jacob had hacked in digging the grave. It slipped once, but I leapt again, holding tight to the thick tendril coiling just over my head. It was enough. My arms ached, heavy and slow, but I wasn't letting go.

I pulled. The root tore my hands. My palms probably bled. At least they still could, unlike the corpse lying behind me.

Just tossed into the dirt.

Fifteen years of adoration, love, and submission—left in a bloody heap.

Or was it the opposite? Did I read the relationship wrong?

Anna was forcing Jacob into bed with a child. *She* murdered his son. Killed Rachel and Cora in cold blood.

She groomed the girls on the farm for molestation and abuse.

And *smiled* as she told me the truth.

I broke over the edge of the grave, but the rain made the grass too slippery to grab. My fingers twisted within the blades. I sunk again. A fierce kick into the mud did little but crumble it further. I lurched with a groan.

One leg over the side. The other didn't want to move. Not as numb now. I wished it was. My ankle screamed in agony, but it swung over the edge.

The darkness tried to push me back down. I yelled, swearing, forcing my body over the edge.

Then I was free.

And panting.

And shivering.

Dying?

Maybe not.

I stared into the sky. The clouds swirled overhead. Rain pelted down, silencing everything except the sleety droplets that washed away all evidence of evil, blood, and depravity.

But I still knew where to find it. It'd take more than rain to hide the disgusting truth.

It hurt to breathe deeply. I did it anyway. Savored it. The drugs surged with one last dizzying wave. I threw up. The purge choked me, but it felt good. Freed of whatever heavy pit ate my stomach from the inside out.

Clearer.

Focused.

Now where was Jacob Goodman?

My cellphone and gun were gone. I'd expected that. I'd have to find something else to defend me. God only knew what Jacob had planned.

The gravesite hid in the darkened tree line. He hadn't buried Anna on the farm. That seemed a worse insult than killing her. I searched the grasses. Ours wasn't the only grave, but this wasn't a family plot. Too barren for a place of honor with no headstones or markers. Smoothed dirt and grass grew in sparse patches. Even in the darkness, the land bumped and roiled.

Who was buried here?

I knew the answer, but I didn't want to confirm that dread. The girls buried in this lost patch of land had been lost a long time ago.

Cast out by the Goodmans. Untrainable. Unwilling to *protect* the family.

I counted six impressions in the dirt before I turned away.

I couldn't do this now. Not while there was still a little girl to save.

I picked a cautious path over the fields, untrusting of my heavy feet over the uneven earth. The rain chilled everything, but I sweated with chattering teeth by the time I reached the farm house.

Every light was off.

Jacob knew better than to bring his new bride home. Anna hadn't even changed the sheets in their bed yet. He'd killed his wife, but it wasn't his first plan. He honored his women in his own perverted way.

He wouldn't take Mariam in their bed.

He'd go somewhere else. Somewhere hidden. Somewhere they wouldn't be interrupted.

I stilled on the path—surrounded by barren homes, darkened windows, and all the evil that had ever swirled within the commune. The barn stood ominous and terrifying on the horizon.

He'd search for his own repentance before claiming his new child bride.

But the barn was silent. No one had ever heard the screams from beneath it. I circled the side, peering in a secondary window to check for movement. Nothing. Jacob and Mariam must have already gone beneath.

I edged to the door, keeping my back close to the wall as I snuck inside.

The stalls were empty, and the scent of damp hay poured from every shadow. I stepped lightly, regaining strength with each movement. Adrenaline was a hell of a lot more powerful than whatever Anna used to drug me. It didn't make me smart, but it kept me focused.

I searched for a weapon—*anything* to defend myself. A pitchfork wasn't effective, but it'd have to do. I didn't have much time. Jacob left the bunker's doors wide open.

Such a hurry to get within.

Why the rush?

The answer was as obvious as it was revolting.

I ripped the pitchfork out of the hay and held it to my chest. With a held breath, I peeked down the stairs to the bunker.

Clear.

This was it.

I clenched my teeth against the writhing pain in my ankle and began my descent into Jacob Goodman's personal hell.

The heavy door tried to squeal as I opened it. I took it slow, one millimeter at a time, achingly patient as it ground against the cement. I let only enough space for my body to pass inside before guiding the door shut once more. Only the light exposed me.

And I didn't think Jacob had his eye on much else beyond his young bride.

Mariam's voice carried from the Repentance room. Prayers?

No.

Vows.

"*...in sickness and in health...*" Her words trembled, soft and confused.

Jacob spoke for her, his voice rasping and quick. "Till death do us part."

"*Till...*" Mariam began to weep. "I don't want to die."

"Say it."

"But—"

"God is listening, Mariam. He must hear your vows. Promise your husband. Do it now."

My stomach turned. Mariam's sniffles echoed in the hall.

"*Till death do us part.*"

"Good girl."

I crossed to the room, back to the wall as I peered inside. The sick bastard had Mariam dressed in a gown again, only this one was too big. The silk didn't fit her.

Because it wasn't a dress.

It was a slip. Anna's.

How convenient for the animal. A wedding gown and lingerie in one. Not that it mattered to him. He'd rip it off of her soon enough.

Jacob wasted no time on bouquets or rice tosses. He led Mariam to the bare mattress in the corner of the room, guiding the little blonde angel to her knees beside their makeshift marriage bed.

"Say your prayers, Mariam." Jacob's instructions clipped as he reached for his belt. The metal tinkling of the buckle screamed louder than her muffled words. "We are married now. You are my wife. Do you know what this means?"

Obviously, she did.

Mariam flinched as his hand grazed her shoulders.

The bastard let his fingers wander to her front. She stopped praying. He pinched, and the words began anew.

"Good girl," he whispered. He unbuttoned his shirt pulling each apart one-by-one with an agonizing slowness. "You will serve me as my wife now, Mariam. Submit to me. You have a duty to both me and the Lord. Do you know what it is?"

Her head bobbed. The curls fell before her face—freckled and still so rosy with a touch of baby fat. She couldn't fill out the slip. No curves. No breasts. No hips. Anna claimed she had reached puberty, but it must have happened only recently. Mariam couldn't have weighed more than sixty pounds—a third of what her husband weighed.

This was still a *child*.

And Jacob reached for the button of his pants like a panther circling a wounded animal.

"God says we are to be fruitful and multiply." Jacob's hand stroked her hair. Mariam wept. "And we will begin tonight. You will lie on the bed, Mariam."

Her terror sliced through me. Agonized. Pleading.

"I...I don't...*I want Eve*. Where's Eve?"

Jacob had no patience for her. "Lie on the bed. Now."

Sobs wracked her shoulders. The little doll crumpled. "Please. I don't—"

The crack came suddenly, his hand against her cheek. She fell forward in shock.

And went still.

Just what he wanted. His pants unzipped. The bastard turned from the door as he began to stroke the rod that would not spare this child.

Now was my chance.

His commands sickened me. He pushed her onto the mattress, kicking open her legs.

"Pull the dress up, Mariam." His words rasped with lust. So much for his vows to Anna. "Say your prayers and be thankful for this."

She did as she was told. "For...for what?"

Jacob's preaching convinced no one but the devil hardening in his pants. "For the chance to please your Lord in your submission to your husband."

He made his move, kneeling over the bed.

And the only prayer I ever meant was intended to send his soul to Hell.

I launched towards him, cracking the handle of the pitchfork over his head. It stunned him, but only for a moment. Jacob roared, ripping off the mattress and bursting to his feet.

The handle poked hard into his gut. He gasped, almost falling to his knees.

I blamed the drugs for my bad aim.

"You little bitch..."

Mariam screamed. He ignored her, reaching for the gun in the jacket tossed into the corner.

I didn't give him the chance.

Didn't wait for an opening.

Didn't stop to assess if I was in mortal danger.

I flipped the pitchfork, shoved him into the wall, and rushed forward. The pointed metal flashed once in the low light before imbedding in the soft flesh of his chest. His head struck the painted mural of hell pinning him on the edge of the pitchfork.

A fitting end.

A howl of pain echoed off the barren walls, but he didn't crumble.

He strengthened.

The prongs dug into his shoulder. I threw my weight into the jab, slamming him against the cement with the bloodied prongs.

I should have aimed for his throat.

"You're on the rebound pretty quick, Jacob." I held the pitchfork steady, grinding the pressure into his wound.

Jacob thrashed, reaching for the tines. His prayers grunted out between ragged breaths. His eyes burned, wide and wild. He didn't beg God for forgiveness.

He cursed me. Insulted me. Prayed for deliverance against me.

I grinned. "Harder to fuck with someone your own size…and age?"

"She is my *wife!*"

"No. Your wife is lying in at the bottom of the grave you dug for her." I narrowed my eyes. "That was your plan all along, wasn't it?"

"God was guiding me."

"Did he guide you to the gun? Hold your hand as you *shot* your wife?"

Jacob's voice dropped. Blood pulsed from the wound, staining his skin and the hardened muscles with crimson.

"You couldn't understand."

"Eve lost the ability to have children, so she set this up. The marriage. Finding Mariam. She was more obsessed with your balls than you were, ain't that right, Jake? She wanted to spread your seed any way she could, even if it was outside of her own womb."

Jacob struggled. He didn't respond to the pain, only to my own taunting words.

"The woman I killed wasn't the woman I found so many years ago," he said.

"She wasn't a woman then...she was a *girl*. And you didn't *find* her. You kidnapped her. Like you did all the other girls on this farm." I grinned. "What happened? Little Eve got to be too much for you?"

"*Yes!*"

No cause to lie with his blood pooling on the floor. "Don't tell me she didn't fit into God's plan?"

"No..." Jacob sneered. "She made a mockery of it. Eve was corrupted. Obsessed with this farm, our life, protecting it. I loved her, but she hated herself for what she could no longer give me."

"You're blaming her? After so many years and brides and girls impregnated? You told her bearing children was her *wifely duty*—her promise to God and husband. And you're surprised when fifteen years of brainwashing backfires?"

"She killed my son!"

"And how many other women have you killed?" I dug the prongs in deeper. "How many girls have you raped? How many children are buried in the far fields because they didn't believe as Eve did?"

Jacob's body flexed. The inhuman rasp of his voice chilled me to my core.

"I'll put you back in that grave, and you can count every last child I gutted."

Pure fury fueled his movements. He roared, clawing at the pitchfork. He jerked—once, twice, then reached for the handle.

The wood cracked like a toothpick in his blood soaked hands.

I fell backwards as he ripped the metal head from his shoulder. The blood poured off of his pale flesh. The wound hadn't weakened him.

He flipped the tines.

Sneered.

And lunged.

The sharp pop of the gun froze his expression in a morbid shock.

He didn't have time to turn. To think. To ask.

Jacob fell forward, crashing to the floor. The shot ripped through his back, shattering his spine.

He was dead before his head cracked off the cement.

The gun shook in Mariam's tiny hands. Her eyes widened with tears as her husband's blood stained her wedding dress.

"I told you I didn't want to get married."

Epilogue

Don't ever think that you're weak.
You're the strongest woman I've ever met.
-James

It was the first time I left the station at five o'clock sharp.

And I had good reason.

I met James outside of my house. The keys felt heavy in my hand. I set them in his palm.

"You do it," I said. "Your first night in our house. *You* should open the door."

"I've opened the door before..." His eyebrows rose. "London, don't treat this as something strange or new."

"It is."

"It shouldn't be."

He pulled me close, offering a kiss I hadn't asked for but wanted nonetheless. "The only thing changing is how often I'll get to hold you now."

"I don't mind that."

"And how many nights we'll spend together after work."

A desperately needed stress reliever. "You make it sound so good."

"And how often I'll get to say that I love you."

"You're a sweet-talker, James Novak."

"One of my many talents."

He opened the door and waited for me to enter first. His boxes lined the walls, the stairs, most of the available space on the floor of my living room. He'd brought a damn library, for all the good it'd do him to try and read the tiny fonts. Still, the books smelled nice. Warm and smart. Kind of like him.

My phone chirped as we crossed to the kitchen. James pulled the frozen vegetarian lasagna from the fridge, but he hesitated as I read the message.

"Gotta go in?" he asked.

Adamski's text made me smile.

Bail denied at arraignment. Gotta make some room in the jail for these sons of bitches.

"Looks like I'm done with my overtime," I said.

"Arraignment went well then?"

I sat at my table. *Our* table. "It's still going to be hell on those girls during the trial."

"They'll cooperate."

"I don't think they will. They looked to Eve for guidance. When I told them Jacob had murdered her...they shut down. They're terrified. All they have now are their husbands, and I think that scares them more than anything."

James set the oven to preheat and leaned against the counter. I liked having him there. It felt...

Right.

"They'll get the help they need," he said.

"What if it isn't enough?"

"For them...or for you?"

I exhaled. For the first time in weeks, the breath cleared my head, my chest, my soul. "I got my help. And it worked."

"Did it?" James took a bit too much pride in my recovery. "Who in particular helped the most?"

He wouldn't like my answer. "Eve Goodman."

"You mean, Anna Prescott?"

"No." I tapped my phone on the table, letting it *clink clink clink* as I tried to understand my own thoughts. "Eve was who Anna wanted to be. She idolized a woman who didn't exist."

"And you?"

"I was jealous of her, of how easily she'd *recovered* from her kidnapping and captivity. I couldn't understand why she was so self-assured. I thought something was wrong with me." I shushed him before James gave a smart-ass retort. "I thought she was stronger than me because she'd survived for so long. I didn't see who she really was because when I looked at her...I saw myself. Someone who needed help. A victim who didn't even understand the horrible things that had happened to her."

"But now?"

"Anna was no victim. Maybe at one time she was, but she groomed those little girls for the men. She worked with Jacob every step of the way. Maybe to survive. Maybe because she honestly believed it. But she wasn't a victim anymore. She became the root of the evil."

"It's not your fault," James said. "You wanted to help her."

"But I didn't *see* the truth. I should have, but I let my emotions blind me." I held his gaze. "It won't happen again."

"I know."

"I've been naïve, but it won't interfere anymore."

James snitched a piece of frozen cheese from the lasagna. "Why not?"

"What do you mean?"

"Why shouldn't it interfere?"

"You think I should let myself get swayed by emotion?"

"Someone needs to be," he said. "Someone's gotta be on that force trying to help the victims regardless of how insane or wild a theory might be. You did your job, London. Not because you were a victim, but because you'll stop at nothing to save someone from danger. And I think that's a very admirable quality in a detective and the woman I love."

He deserved the salt shaker thrown at his head. Instead I slipped to the counter and leaned into him. "I owe it to you."

"You owe it to no one." He leaned close. "I'll take *some* of the credit. Only one last thing to do."

"And what's that?"

"Gotta let the world know."

"Know what?"

"How much I love you." He winked. "I learned something from the Goodmans too."

"What's that?"

"That I better start planning our wedding now."

Silly man. "Don't get ahead of yourself."

"You can run, but you can't hide."

That's what *he* had said too.

But coming from James?

I liked the chase.

The End

Made in the USA
Lexington, KY
15 April 2017